HEAVY

A STEEL BONES MOTORCYCLE CLUB ROMANCE

CATE C. WELLS

D1514009

This book is a work of fiction. Names, characters, places, and incidents are the product of the author's imagination or are used fictitiously. Any resemblance to actual events, locales, or persons, living or dead, is coincidental.

Copyright 2021 by Cate C. Wells. All rights reserved.

Cover art and design by Clarise Tan of CT Cover Creations
Cover photograph by Golden Czermak or FuriousFotog
Cover model Nick Pulos
Edited by Nevada Martinez
Proofread by Kayla Davenport

Special thanks to Lily Luchesi of Partners in Crime Book Services, Kara M., Elisabeth J., Sara F., Katee R., Layne K., Erin D., An C., and Nina V.

The uploading, scanning, and distribution of this book in any form or by any means—including but not limited to electronic, mechanical, photocopying, recording, or otherwise—without the permission of the copyright holder is illegal and punishable by law. Please purchase only authorized editions of this work, and do not participate in or encourage electronic piracy of copyrighted materials. Your support of authors' ability to earn a livelihood is appreciated.

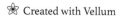 Created with Vellum

1

DINA

I wish everyone had a name like Heavy Ruth. It'd make life so much simpler.

He's heavy. He's ruthless. He's labeled.

No guessing or trying to pick up cues—no wondering if a twitch is a facial cue or the beginnings of a sneeze. How straightforward everything would be if you learned a guy's name, and you knew the important things right away.

I like straightforward. I like simple. I like predictable, quiet, and in my control.

And I hate every single agonizingly awful second of this present moment.

I'm perched on the end of Heavy Ruth's bed, my stomach knotted and queasy, my brain numb from the buzzing. I snuck into his room at 4:26 a.m. Now it's 7:37 a.m., and he's still sleeping. He's on his back, splayed like Da Vinci's perfect man—the circle pose, not the square.

Da Vinci would not have used Heavy Ruth as a model. His proportions are all wrong. His head's too big, for one. It's hard to tell whether he has a prodigiously large cranium or if it's all that hair—the bushy black beard and the wild black mess on top of his head—but it throws off the symmetry.

His chest is big, too, but it's on scale with his legs. If his thighs are thick tree branches, then his chest is a massive trunk, and his head is the leaves. The dimensions are correct for a sequoia, but not for a man.

He snuffles, hacks a cough, and scratches his crotch. My breath hitches, but he doesn't wake up.

Realistically, he could sleep for several more hours. I cannot sit cross-legged and cramping by his enormous feet much longer. I'll have to pee. I don't have to now, but I will, and worrying about it prompts my wonky brain to produce cortisol, and cortisol surges always make me have to pee.

I pick at my nails—I don't even try to stop myself. Desperate times and all.

I could poke Heavy very lightly. Or make a low humming sound. He'd wake naturally, and he might not immediately lunge for the pistol on his night table.

The gun—it's a 9 mm Sig Sauer with a thumb safety—is three inches from his right hand. If he startled awake and went for it, I might be able to drop off the bed and onto the floor before he could squeeze off a round. But, I can't do a rough estimate of my odds since I have no idea how fast he can aim and fire.

Pretty fast, I'd bet.

The gun is a complication. I didn't notice it until I'd already eased onto the end of the bed. I'd tried to creep back off the bed and hide it away from him, but the motion almost woke him, and he's much closer to the gun than I am.

It was an obvious complication to overlook, but when I'm overstimulated, I only register the broad strokes in my surroundings.

It's like opening your eyes underwater. You can see, but it's disorienting, and you're more focused on not drowning than the scenery.

Motorcycle clubhouses are overstimulation central. Loud, smelly, and lousy with simultaneous visual stimuli. Even though I was staring at the floor, and I only stole glimpses to navigate up here to the bunks, I saw multiple pairs of bare tits and one flaccid penis.

At least Heavy Ruth's room is dim and quiet. It smells earthy—like wood and old books. It's not a bad smell, per se, but it's strong. There are too many visual stimuli here, too. I mostly stare at his feet poking at the sheet, but I slide a glance around the space every so often.

An entire wall is dedicated to a murder board. Like in a detective show. Photos and newspaper clippings and index cards are connected by red string and thumb tacks. I don't look in that direction again. If I tried to make sense of it, my battered brain would crack.

There are full bookshelves. More books stacked on the floor. A table with a chess set.

Above his bed, there's a poster of a pin-up girl from the sixties. I can't stop checking it out. She's naked, on her knees and leaning back, propped on her hands, her huge, perky breasts thrust up, smiling from ear to ear.

I can't tell if it's a Duchenne smile or not. She's contracting her zygomatic major muscle, but she's wearing too much eyeliner to tell if her orbicularis oculi are engaged.

Duchenne smiles are genuine. All other smiles are warnings. I learned that from social skills group back in middle school.

I hate smiles. I wish they came with labels. Clear ones like "real" or "sleazy." Not "Duchenne."

Heavy sniffs again, and I straighten my spine, but then

he lets out a whistly, grumbly snore. Ugh. This part of my plan is subpar. I hate waiting, and I really hate waiting in one position. It twists my innards, and I get bloated.

I could tickle the bottom of one of his big feet. His instinct would be to reach down, not toward the gun at his side. Or I could touch his dick. It's tenting the thin sheet as much as his long feet. He has an erection. It started twitching about a half hour ago, and it's been rising steadily since like a ghost in a sheet.

I'm no expert, but it seems disproportionately large in terms of length and girth. And bulbosity of head. It's as if a stout prairie dog wearing a stormtrooper helmet is alerting. Or a fat man's fist is slowly thrusting upwards.

And it's twitchy. What kind of tensile strength does a dick that size have? Prodigious, I bet. I could nudge it and find out. Kill two birds with one stone.

But it would be wrong to touch Heavy's dick without his consent. By that logic, it would also be wrong to tickle his feet. But my lower stomach aches. I'm wearing leggings. I can't pop a button and ease the pressure. I need to move. What can I hum?

What song would wake a man like Heavy Ruth in a good mood?

"Are you just gonna look at my cock, or are you gonna touch it?" A bombastic bass voice, gruff with sleep, rolls like thunder from the head of the bed.

I jump in my skin, choking on a breath.

He's awake. His eyes are wide open. They're pitch black and glittering, which is strange since the shades are drawn, and the room's cast in gray shadow.

Eye contact is too much, so I dart my gaze back to his dick.

"It would be wrong to touch it without your consent," I mumble.

It seems even bigger now, but I think it's a matter of angle, not an actual increase in size. It's pointing more towards his head than the ceiling.

"I consent," he rumbles, drawing himself up, sniffing and hacking, until he's settled upright against the head of the bed. The sheet falls down, baring his chest. Yikes.

He's very muscular. A man his size should be more barrel-chested, but he has definition. Slabs for pecs. His abs aren't a pack; they're chiseled from the rock-hard mountain of his torso.

And he's hairy. I wouldn't call it a pelt, per se, but it's no smattering. It trails in a downward direction, laying flat, not wiry. Is it soft or scratchy like a horse's mane?

His dick is still covered by the sheet, but black curls and a hint of purplish-red peek out. I've never seen an erect penis in real life. Growing up with four brothers, I've seen plenty of flaccid ones. And a lot of bare ass. Especially Cash's. He's an idiot.

I flash a glance at Heavy's face. His eyes crinkle at the corners. He licks his lips and dips his gaze down to his lap.

He wraps a massive hand around the base, over the sheet, and slowly strokes toward the head. The motion pulls the sheet lower. I can see a little more. It looks like the skin's pulled taut. Would it be hot to the touch?

Logically, it'd be hot. It's blood flow, right? Increased blood flow causes a rise in temperature.

But how hot? Warm like a blush? Or burning like when you bake in the sun in the middle of summer?

"It's okay," he urges. "Come closer, little girl."

He strokes it again, root to tip. A damp spot shows up on the fabric.

I raise up on my knees. I need to take the pressure off my belly, and I'm antsy. Squirmy.

"You can do whatever you want. Come on," he urges.

I like those words. I can never do whatever I want. I can't now, either, of course, but I rerun what he said through my memory so it'll stick. *You can do whatever you want.*

I *am* curious, but I don't actually know what I'd *do* with a dick. I'm on the internet all day long. I've seen porn. I understand the possible permutations, but I haven't thought through what I'd *try*, if the opportunity arose.

It's definitely "arisen."

"Well?" he prompts.

I dart another glance at his face.

Oh. Ugh. He's smirking under his thick beard. Smirks are the opposite of Duchenne. It means he's mocking me. I don't like being teased. I'm an easy target, and people who make fun of an easy target are assholes.

I scooch backward and slide off the foot of the bed.

"Pass."

He lets out an exaggerated sigh and arches a thick black eyebrow. "Then, what can I do for you, Miss...?"

I blink a few times, try to sift out the extraneous stimuli and find my way back to my train of thought. I wander over toward his murder board, but I'm careful to keep my back to the wall. If I look, I'll get lost again.

It's time to execute my plan. I designed it so that I don't need to think clearly to put it in action. I knew I'd be over-stimulated. I just need to follow the script. I draw in a deep breath.

"It's not what you can do for me; it's what *I* can do for you," I begin. I stole that line from a movie.

"You still have my consent, baby." He licks his generous

red lips. Then he stretches his arms over his head, biceps bulging, as he yawns like a sea lion and cracks his neck.

He isn't taking me seriously. I clench my teeth. It doesn't matter. He will.

I plunge ahead and recite my next lines.

"I have proof that in 2001, Des Wade and Anderson Watts planted five crates of black-market Kalashnikovs in a box truck driven by Stones and Knocker Johnson with the intention of framing the Steel Bones Motorcycle Club."

I sink back against his murder board. A push pin digs into my shoulder blade. I force myself to watch his face. I hate it. It hurts. But I need the information.

His expression had been relaxed, lips curving up, but as I speak, it transforms. He bares his teeth, narrows his eyes, his jaw jutting. His entire body tenses, and somehow, he seems bulkier.

My heart kicks up its pace.

He rises from the bed, allowing the sheet to fall—and he's naked and hairy and bulging with muscle. He crosses the room in one giant step to loom over me, vibrating with menace, almost seven feet tall, snarled hair falling over his shoulders, fisted hands the size of hams.

My heart goes even crazier, thumping against my ribs. I need to run, but he's between me and the door.

No. Stop. No running. This is a panic response. I just need to breathe through it and wait for him to reply. Then I say my next line. All I need to do in this moment is be still.

But my body thinks he's a predator, and I'm prey. I'm itching to bolt. I could duck him. Big is slow, right?

But I'm not in real danger. Come on brain. You know this. I have what he wants more than anything else in the world. I'm in control. I force myself to suck down a breath.

"You don't know what you're talking about, little girl," he finally says.

His voice has lowered, impossibly deeper. Shivers zip down my spine, and I break into a cold sweat.

I cough to clear my throat and visualize my script.

"On August 7, 2001, Steven Wayne Johnson and his son, Brian Lee Johnson, were pulled over by the state police on Route 29. By no coincidence, there was a photographer there from the county paper."

I bet the photo from the front page is on the wall somewhere behind me.

"What's your scam?" Heavy widens his stance, broadening his shoulders. He was already a giant before. The move is gratuitous, but my body recognizes it as aggression.

My heart bangs. It's going to explode and bust out of my rib cage like an alien in the movies. The contents of my chest cavity are going to leak all over his expensive wool carpet.

I dig my nails into the skin on the back of my hand, letting the pain center me. My heart is fine. It's reacting normally to stress. I just have to keep going.

I swallow and plunge ahead.

"It was a setup. Watts used his clout—and the local hand wringing about rising crime—to push through a stalled development deal for the Petty's Mill waterfront. Des Wade, the developer, made millions. Anderson Watts used the publicity to tip a close race for state senator."

Heavy looms closer and closer. He still has an erection. His flushed dick bobs every time he breathes.

"What's your name?" he bites out.

I assume he's glowering down at me threateningly, but my gaze is glued to his dick. It's pointing up at me. The vein pulses.

"It doesn't matter," I say to it. "Do you want the evidence you've been looking for or not?"

He bristles, his chest vibrating with vicious, animalistic reverberation as he spits out, "If you're gonna proposition me, little girl, look me in the eye."

I can't. Not now. "Pass."

I can force myself to maintain eye contact with my mom or my best friend Rory, but in this moment? No way. I wouldn't be able to speak.

He lurches forward, bracing a thick arm on the wall, caging me in. His forearm is larger in diameter than my calf. Veins pop from the muscle. He's not even flexing.

"You don't get to pass," he says, grabbing my chin.

I screw my eyes shut.

He digs in, bruising my jaw. "What's your name?"

"Boris Stasevich."

"Your name is Boris Stasevich?" He forces my chin higher 'til my neck stretches as far back as it'll go. I keep my eyes closed.

He's so close. Heat radiates off him. He smells like the outdoors. Wood and leaves and tilled soil. Also beer.

He could snap my neck. He could bash my head against the wall. Blood pounds in my ears.

I have a script. I have what he wants. I'm in control.

"Boris Stasevich sold Watts the guns," I manage, my voice quavering. "Stasevich was extradited five years ago. As part of his appeal to stay in the U.S., he gave testimony against Watts and implicated Wade."

"Bullshit. Never happened. That would have been national news."

"The feds buried it. Stasevich lost his appeal. They put him on a plane to Moscow. He was dead within weeks."

He's silent for a moment. I can hear him breathing.

"Very entertaining," he finally says. "You read a lot of spy novels?"

"I don't like fiction."

"You sure like telling stories."

"I have the affidavit."

"Show me."

"I want something in exchange."

He laughs, bitter and booming. It blasts over me, and now I tremble. If he weren't holding me up, I don't know if I could stand.

I grab his wrist. His fingers don't loosen their unforgiving grip on my jaw. I'm in control, but he's stronger. A fear response is natural. He's killed before. Many times. That's why I'm here.

I can't help it. I peek up from under my eyelashes. His lips twist, his eyes blaze. With the hair, he looks entirely uncivilized, a prehistoric man, a creature of violence and rage and appetite.

He doesn't seem like a reasonable person, but I've done my research. Heavy Ruth is a genius. I run through the evidence. Perfect SAT. Summa cum laude as an undergrad. Perfect GRE. Named author on a half-dozen frequently cited papers on sustainable design. He could have gone to Silicon Valley and made a billion dollars.

He's a murderer, but he's rational. He's motivated by protecting those close to him.

Instead of bailing to make his name in big tech, he came back here—to his small town, decimated by opioids and the collapse of domestic steel. He took over his dad's motorcycle club, and turned it into a construction company with billings that match the largest developers on the coasts. And that's what he's declaring on his taxes. He could be worth two or three times as much, and he did it in less than a decade.

He employs hundreds. He has politicians in his pocket, and not a soul will shit-talk him in public. I've spent months online, researching him and the MC. People keep his name out of their mouths.

That's power.

He's worth millions, and he bunks in the clubhouse and dresses like a lumberjack mixed with a fugitive from a punk rock apocalypse.

He's terrifying, but predictable. He'll act in the interest of his club.

Predictable is good. I have what he wants. I'm in control.

"Well?" he snarls.

I blink. Sweet lord. I lost focus. His hand is a vise around my jaw, and I'm wandering off into la la land. I can't afford to glitch out. I have to follow the script. What's my next line? Oh, yeah.

"Do you know the movie *Strangers on a Train*?"

"Who do you want me to kill for you?"

Oh. Yeah. Of course, he has.

"I'll kill him myself. I need help with the—logistics. And cover up."

Heavy's hand darts forward, it doesn't register until I feel him squeeze my left boob. It hurts.

"What are you doing? Stop."

I jam myself back into the wall as if that'll help. He ignores me, running his hands over my other breast and belly, rough and brisk. Then he rips my button-down tunic off and drops it to the floor, his gaze raking down my front. My entire chest flushes pink.

I bring my arms up to cover myself, but he flips me, and

now my boobs are smooshed against the murder board. He rips my bra off—doesn't even bother to unclasp the hooks—and then he drags down my leggings and panties to my ankles, holding me in place with a forearm against my shoulder blades. It feels like a steel bar. A whimper escapes my throat.

He yanks the leggings off my feet. My ballet flats go flying.

He whirls me to face him again. My back is to the wall, and I'm naked except for black liner socks. It's cold. I huddle, wrapping my arms around my breasts, jamming my thighs together to try and hide my pussy.

We're both naked.

I'm gasping. I have goosebumps everywhere.

What's happening?

I can't process. There's static in my brain. I cower, but there's nowhere to hide. I'm stuck. Pinned in place.

And he's too big. I can't stare over him. Can't stare around him.

"Stay put," he barks, collecting my clothes. He stalks to the door and pitches them out into the hall.

He doesn't come back to where I'm plastered against the wall. Instead, he lowers his bulk to the edge of his bed, facing me, knees wide. The mattress sags, and the springs creak. Dear lord. He still has an erection.

I lower my eyes to the beige carpet. It's freezing in this room. My nipples have hardened to points, and I'm shivering.

He's looking at me.

What's he doing?

Thinking.

That's what I'd be doing.

He's thinking, and he's gawking at my naked body.

Is he thinking *about* my naked body?

No. There's no way. I've dropped a bomb on him. He's considering the angles. Even if it's kind of a no-brainer. I'm giving him everything he wants, and I'm not asking him to add a body to his count. All I need is back up, and uh, disposal services.

I have no qualms about pulling the trigger myself, but I'm not stupid. I'm on the spectrum. I struggle with certain things, and I don't want to implicate myself in a homicide because I glitched out in the moment.

Should I ad lib? Repeat the offer? It usually doesn't go well when I speak off the cuff.

Besides, I feel weird. There's a strange tension collecting low in my belly. Like during hide-and-seek when you're trying to stay still and silent, and the other person is close and inching closer. It feels like I have to pee, but I don't.

What does he see when he stares at me?

My parents call me a tomboy. I've explained a hundred times that the term is problematic, but that doesn't stop them. They mean I have short hair and small boobs. And I work with computers. I pick my cuticles, and sometimes I go a few days without a shower. I'll wear the same hoodie for weeks. I sleep in boxers. I like gaming and guns and military history.

Still, the term is problematic.

I glance up from the carpet. Heavy's back is ramrod straight, massive shoulders squared, hands resting on his muscular, hairy thighs. His dick is level with his abs. And he's looking at my chest.

I flush hot all over like I'm a struck match. I drop my gaze, and my arms fall to my sides.

Why did I do that?

Now he can see everything. The thrum in my belly swirls and pools between my legs. I tingle. My breasts plump and ache. The air's chilly, my skin's burning, and everything's sixes and nines. It's an overload of weird, new sensation.

I press my palms to the wall and study the vacuum cleaner lines crisscrossing the carpet.

This feels dangerous.

And backwards. My brain glitches, not my body. My body's predictable. It doesn't function perfectly—I'm the queen of upset stomachs and headaches—but it never does *this*.

The longer he stares, the more I'm filling up with something.

It's too much, but—

I like it. I like his eyes on me.

It's quiet and dim in the room. No movement. Nothing is touching my skin. No chafing or itching or constriction. The only stimulus is his gaze and the riot it's stoking inside me.

I change my mind. It's not too much. It's not enough. This is a good feeling. This is a candy rush or a hit off some dank kush.

Maybe I would like to touch him. I bite my lower lip, inch forward, and somehow, I break the spell.

He snarls, grabs the sheet, wads it up, and hurls it at me.

"Cover yourself."

My face bursts into flame.

I snatch the sheet from the floor, wind it around me like a toga, and tuck it tight above my breasts.

I misread the situation. If I wasn't clutching the sheet in a death grip, I'd whack myself in the head like I did when I was a kid.

This isn't sexual. I'm extorting him. He's not lusting after me. He's plotting.

This is very embarrassing.

No man has seen me naked before. I'm not shy or repressed, but I am an introvert, and at this point, pretty much a recluse. When I was in high school, my brother Cash bullied any guy who dared talk to me. I have internet friends, and plenty have asked me to strip during video chats, but I'm not ending up on a free porn site.

Can he tell what he's done to me? That would suck.

Maybe he has no idea. I do have the "flat affect."

He jerks his head toward the door. "When my people comb through those clothes, are they gonna find a bug?"

"No." It would be really dumb to record myself pre-meditating murder.

Of course, if there was a bug, "his people" wouldn't find it. You'd think a guy from M.I.T. would hire better tech people. I broke into his systems in a matter of hours, and I've been reading his emails for months now. He can't spell worth shit.

He reaches for the night table, and my heart leaps into my throat. He grabs his phone. I wipe my palms on the sheet. If he noticed where my head was, he's not acknowledging it. That's good.

He scrolls and taps. "Mikey? There are some clothes in the hallway in front of my room." He pauses. Grunts. "Yeah. Take 'em out back and burn 'em."

He drops his phone onto the mattress and falls silent. I get the sense he's staring at me again, but I learned my lesson. I study his feet. They're like shovels.

He's probably trying to make me nervous, but I'm already nervous. I've been on edge since I got in the rideshare. I stole a handful of my mom's chill pills. That's the only way I lasted for four hours in the back of a compact car with damp upholstery and the lingering odor of weed and French fries.

Then, I had to crouch behind a truck in the clubhouse parking lot until it got late enough that I figured everyone would be drunk and unsuspecting. Sneak in. Dodge the folks still partying. Find the stairs. Open several doors before I found Heavy's bedroom.

I can't get more nervous. I'm already one hundred percent nerves, and I have been since noon yesterday.

Longer, truth be told. Since I decided Uncle Van has to die, and I can't trust anyone else to do it.

I don't want to stand here and be stared at anymore.

I shuffle over to a wingback chair and sink into the soft leather.

"You have a lot of fuckin' nerve." His voice booms in the silence.

"A hundred percent," I agree.

He makes a grumbling, snorting sound. "What's wrong with you?"

"I'm neurodivergent."

"Not that. I mean the blackmail and the conspiracy to commit murder. And trespassing. And breaking and entering."

"Oh." I knead the sheet. It's high thread count. Very nice. "I have good reasons."

"Yeah?" He's incredulous. "And what are those?"

I didn't script an answer to that question. I thought offering Heavy Ruth the heads of Anderson Watts and Des Wade on a silver platter would be sufficient. I figured he'd want to know as little as possible.

I'm not good at reading people, though. Or anticipating reactions, or correctly identifying motivations.

I also suck at lying.

"Revenge."

"You want revenge?"

I nod. I also want to stop my uncle from hurting anyone else, ever again, but I want it to hurt. So that's revenge, I think. Not vigilante justice.

"Against who?"

"My uncle."

"What did he do to you?" There's an odd note in his voice. I can't quite name it.

"He hurt my friend. He broke up my family. He's evil."

"'He who is without sin among you, let him throw the first stone.'"

Is he quoting the Bible at me?

"'It is joy to the righteous to do justice; but it is a destruction to the workers of iniquity,'" I answer. My parents dragged me to church every Sunday until I was eighteen, and I have an excellent memory.

"'Cease from anger, and forsake wrath. Don't fret, it leads only to evildoing—'" His voice booms louder. Sonorous. Pretentious.

I interject and finish the verse for him. "'—For evildoers shall be cut off, but those who wait for Yahweh shall inherit the land.'"

His lip twitches. "I'm not a hired gun, little girl. You're playing a dangerous game."

"This isn't a game."

"What did he do to your friend?"

It's not my story to tell. I ignore him and pluck an ivory chess piece from the board. The queen. It's smooth and cool. I roll it in my trembling fingers.

"Put that back," he says. "I'm in the middle of a game."

I cast a glance at the board. "Don't worry. I'll put it back. C7."

There's a pause. "You play chess?"

"4D, baby," I say. It's a joke. My plan is as straightforward and obvious as they come. I'm blackmailing the president of a motorcycle gang to help me kill my uncle and dispose of his body.

He growls and rises to his feet. I draw myself flush against the back of the chair. Why is he standing? What changed?

Oh, crap. I didn't answer him. He asked a question. I made a smart remark. He's angry.

I can always see where I go wrong in retrospect, and I can never, ever see it coming.

He swoops down, grabs me by my upper arms, and hikes me into the air. By some miracle, the sheet holds. He lifts me like I weigh nothing until I'm eye level, pressing my elbows so hard they compress my sides and steal my breath.

I'm trapped.

His *head* is twice the size of mine. It's like looking into the face of a statue. I glance down. I'm dangling a foot and a half off the floor, and I still have the queen clutched in my fist.

"Look me in the eye," he demands.

I bite my lower lip and jerk my head no.

He gives me a shake. My teeth rattle.

"You're hurting me."

"I'm a murderer, aren't I?" he sneers.

"Yes. You are. There are at least seven bodies buried on Half Stack Mountain."

His grip tightens, fingers biting into my flesh. If he had nails, he'd draw blood.

"How do you know that?" he asks.

I didn't. Not for sure. Not until he just confirmed it.

It was deductive reasoning. I started with the premise that a formerly one percent motorcycle gang had killed before. I searched local news for reports of missing men and cross-referenced them with known associates of Steel Bones or their rival club, the Rebel Raiders. Then, I hacked into the club members' credit card accounts and looked for patterns.

In the days right before or after each of the men were reported missing, Steel Bones bought gas or cigarettes at locations along eastbound Route 11. Eastbound Route 11 leads to Half Stack Mountain, nothing else. I wrote a program that compared satellite images of the area. I found beavers building a dam on the north face, the emerald ash borer decimating acres of forest, and someone planting trees in one very random place near the south summit.

Or digging graves and then planting trees.

I'm inferring a whole heck of a lot, but by his reaction, I'd say I'm not too far off base.

Still, a magician doesn't reveal her tricks.

"I'm not going to tell you."

He drops me. I land on my feet—barely—and stagger, but before I can bolt, he has me again. His huge, calloused hand wraps around my throat. His grip is so tight I can feel my pulse throbbing. I clutch his wrists on instinct. He's not squeezing.

Much.

Yet.

My heart gallops faster, my entire body rigid. I want to fight. Scream. Claw at his bare, hairy chest. It's so hard to remain still.

But he's not going to kill me. I have what he wants. He's posturing.

If he was going to kill me, he would have already done it. It would be so easy for him to break my neck. I can feel his strength. He'd snap my spine like a twig.

This is intimidation. I have the information he needs, so

I have the upper hand. He's trying to regain dominance. He can't kill me.

He could torture me, though. I'd fold in no time. I freak out at gross textures and bad smells and loud sounds. I force myself to meet his eyes. It hurts, but I hold for the count of ten.

"I'm not going to tell anyone else, either," I promise. "If you help me."

"You're blackmailing me."

"You're strangling me." My gaze drops, and I exhale. "Two wrongs don't make a right."

He sighs and eases his hand down my shoulder. His touch is rough. Abrasive. But it's not irritating. It makes me shiver.

"How did you get in here?" he asks.

"Your bedroom?"

"The clubhouse."

I shrug. "The front door."

"You walked right in?"

I nod.

"Did anyone see you?"

"No." I don't think so. I kept it moving.

"How did you find my room? Do you have the floorplans?"

"I opened doors until I found you." I grimace, remembering a pimply ass pumping between a woman's spread thighs. She was propped on the edge of a dresser, an arm slung around the guy's neck, scrolling on her phone. It was sad and also very slurpy.

"No one called you out?"

I shake my head. His security is pretty lax, especially for a quasi-criminal enterprise. I imagine they don't commit felonies on site, but still, it's sloppy.

"What's your name?" he asks again.

"I think we should keep things anonymous. You know, because of the co-conspirator thing."

"Why aren't you scared?"

"I am." On impulse, I grab his hand and hold it to my chest. My heart's pounding.

"Why don't you *seem* scared?"

I lift a shoulder. "Alexithymia."

He snorts. "You seem to know what you're feeling."

I blink. He knows what alexithymia means? I'm surprised, but I guess he *is* a genius. Perfect verbal score on the SAT means he knows a lot of random words.

Alexithymia is the inability to identify or describe your own feelings. It's why I had a chart of facial expressions hanging above my desk until I graduated high school. And why I had a shelf of "social stories" as a kid, the kind where a little girl lost her kitty and felt sad. Then, she found the cat, and she felt happy.

I hated those stories with a passion. The little girl was way too irresponsible to care for a pet.

"Racing heart. Cold sweat. Gun on night table. Threat of strangulation," I tick off on my fingers. "Fear."

It's not rocket science. I have trouble with subtle or new emotions, but the big ones—fear, sadness, shame, happiness, anger. I've got those down.

"So, you want me to help you kill your uncle. And then you'll give me the evidence against Watts and Wade?"

"Yes."

"And you won't say anything about what you think you know? About Half Stack Mountain?"

"No. I promise."

"Oh, you promise, do you?" He's saying what I want to hear, but his tone—it doesn't match. "And then you disappear to wherever you came from, and we never speak again? Strangers on a train?"

"Yes. Strangers on a train."

"Sit." He presses my shoulder, gentle but insistent, and I sink to the chair. My system is wrecked from being flooded with wave after wave of adrenaline. I'm getting shaky. I need water. And a break.

He crosses the room. I'm so overstimulated that I close my eyes. Just for a second. Just to regroup.

A safety clicks.

My eyes fly open. He's aiming the Sig Sauer at my head. A cry flies from my lips.

"I'm a good shot," he says, calm and even. "It won't hurt."

I shrink against the high back of the chair, my gaze darting to the lowest shelf on the bookcase by the window. Plato's *Symposium*. Dostoyevsky's *Crime and Punishment*. The *Bhagavad Gita*. Perfectly lined up with each other and the books to either side.

He's not supposed to hurt me. That's not how the plan goes.

"If you kill me, you won't get your evidence."

"I know it exists now. I have a name. I'll find it."

His arm is straight, unwavering. The barrel doesn't move. He's going to do it. He's going to shoot me. I whimper. I misjudged. Again. So badly.

"It's not personal," he says. "You're a threat to my club. My family."

"I'll walk away. I won't tell anyone about the bodies on the mountain. I swear." My voice sounds wrong. I don't sound like me.

Blood pounds in my ears. There's too much. The gun, the man, the hair, the nakedness, the leather creaking when I shift, the sweat behind my knees. The *Symposium*,

Crime and Punishment, the *Bhagavad Gita*. I want to close my eyes, but I don't want darkness to be the last thing I see.

"What's your name?" he asks again.

"Dina." My voice cracks.

"I'm sorry, Dina." He draws in a breath. Hot tears burn my eyes.

I brace. The clock on the wall ticks. And ticks again. I count my breaths. My last breaths. One. Two. Three. I can't look at him. All I can look at is the barrel of the gun.

"Please don't," I whimper.

And then, by some miracle, there's a loud, rapid banging at the door.

"Heavy! You awake?"

It's a man. It sounds like—I don't dare hope. I leap to my feet, make to dash for the shelf by the window, but Heavy already has me scooped in one arm and dangling.

The knocking continues. "Heavy! Wake up! It's an emergency, man!"

Oh, I do know this voice! Tears trickle down my cheeks. He'll save me. I gulp down a breath to scream, but before I can, I'm slammed against the wall next to the door, a meaty hand clamped over my mouth.

"Don't make a sound," Heavy snarls. Then he opens the door. I'm wedged between it and the wall. He positions himself so that he can point the gun at me, and the person in the hall can't see.

"What?" he barks.

"I need some men. My mom just called. My sister's disappeared. Mom thinks she might have gone for a hike in the woods. Maybe gotten lost or hurt." John's panting and speaking fast.

I want to call out, but the gun is so close. Inches from my

chest. Oh, my god. If I scream, he could fire. And then shoot John.

Heavy wouldn't shoot a member of his own club, would he?

If my big brother knew Heavy was holding a gun on me, John would kill him. Without hesitation. If John attacked, Heavy would defend himself. Heavy's armed, and John might not be. I swallow down my panic, muffle the whimpers I can hardly control. John can't know I'm here.

"How many men do you need?" Heavy asks.

"As many as you can spare."

"Take everyone. Call in Smoke and Steel, too. How long has she been gone?"

"Since lunchtime yesterday."

"Jesus. And your mom just called?"

"Dina keeps odd hours. No one realized she was missing until breakfast."

"Dina?" Heavy's hand tenses on the pistol.

"Yeah. I'll call Forty. Have him muster the men. I need to be on the road."

"How old is Dina?"

"Twenty-four."

"Twenty-four?" Heavy repeats in his low, gravelly bass.

"Yeah. She's, uh, got issues. She doesn't leave home. She doesn't drive. No friends. We don't know where she went. The hike's a guess. This isn't good, man. She's on the internet all the time—"

Oh, my god. He's making it sound like I met a perv in a chat room. I mean, I've run into my share, but I'm not stupid.

He's also making me sound mentally incapacitated. I mean, he's not lying. I don't leave home. Or drive. But I do have a friend. Rory Evans. She lives in the city now, but even when we were neighbors, we talked online most of the time.

I have a job. I do freelance coding. Some cybersecurity. And I can read a damn compass. I'd never get lost in the woods.

"I'm sure she's fine," Heavy says. "Go. Call me with an update."

"Thanks, man." John slaps the doorframe and jogs off.

Relief floods my chest, followed by a cascading rush of fear. John's taking everyone with him. No one will hear a gunshot. No witnesses. And Heavy knows there's already a story. I went for a hike, and I never came back.

My breath comes in short pants. I fist the sheet somehow still wrapped around my cold, shivering body. I screw my eyes shut, and I can't stop the high-pitched moan from coming out of my mouth. It's too much.

"Be quiet." Heavy closes the door with a snick.

I can't. I mash my lips together but I can't stop the sound.

"You're Dina Wall?" he demands.

I slide to my butt, wrapping my arms around my shins, burrowing my head between my knees. He can shoot me down here. I've had enough.

"You're John Wall's sister?" he prods, nudging me with his foot. He's angry. Loud. I press my palms to my ears.

"What are you doing?" he booms. You can't muffle a voice like his very much. It's too deep. "What the hell are you doing?" he repeats even louder.

I'm trying to block him out. I'm trying to mute his over-sized, homicidal, too-damn-loud self. I made so many mistakes.

He isn't interesting—an object of curiosity. He's danger-ous. A cold-blooded criminal. I'm aware of the irony. That's why I'm here, after all.

He's not being reasonable. The logical call is to take the deal. Maximum reward, minimum risk. How is killing me safer than helping me dispose of a body?

He's irrational.

And unpredictable.

And I don't like those two things at all.

I rock, knocking against the wall. The impact hits me like a swig of whiskey. My mom and school had mostly "redirected" stimming out of me by the time I graduated high school, but the neural pathways are still there.

I wish he'd just do what he's gonna do, instead of looming there, too close, smelling like Black Jack gum.

Finally, he grunts. And then I'm tucked to his chest, and he's hauling me across the room. Another door opens. He lowers me, carefully placing me on a cold, hardwood floor, and leaves. It smells like fabric softener and boots. I peek. It's a small room. A closet. Pitch black.

There's no window. No way out. I jump to my feet and try the door. There's no lock on the smooth knob, but it doesn't budge.

And then there's a hammering around the frame.

"Are you nailing me in?" I shriek.

"There's a chair under the doorknob, too. Don't bother trying to escape." He drives in a few more nails. "Steel Bones might have been easy to get into, little girl, but it's gonna be a bitch to get out."

He chuckles, bombastic and evil. Another door slams, and then there's silence.

I grossly miscalculated.

I roll the queen in my fingers and scoot into the far corner.

Then again, so did he.

He didn't shoot me. He didn't snap my neck. He didn't shove me at John and tell him to handle me.

I'm not dead. I'm locked in a closet. That means I have what he wants.

I'm in control.

I lay on my side, curl up like a shrimp, and let the dark and quiet turn the volume down in my brain.

2

HEAVY

S ince I turned thirteen, I've always been the biggest man in any given room.

I duck through doorways. Everything on my bike is extended—brake level, shifter, footboards. A hundred years ago, folks at fairs would pay to gawk at my freakish ass. In these modern times, people make way. Whisper. Scamper out of my path.

I'm a big motherfucker. Everyone is smaller than me.

The woman I just nailed into my closet—Dina—is a slight little thing. She comes up to my chest. Neat, compact, finely wrought.

And I'm shakin' like a goddamn cold, wet dog.

I pause in the hallway, drag on a pair of jeans, and drop the hammer to the floor. Then I lean against the door and listen.

The rooms up here ain't soundproof. If I'd have shot her with no silencer, a half-dozen men would've come runnin'. John Wall would've seen his sister slumped dead on my chessboard. Game over. It would've been a hell of a scene.

But I wasn't gonna shoot, was I?

When I stared down the barrel of that gun and she blinked those round, blue eyes, my shitty knees got weak. They ache when it rains and click when I go up the stairs, but they've never almost given out on me before.

But those big eyes. Blink. Blink. I felt it. Not just in my dick. In my gut. Never happened to me before.

Dina.

Short name. Short woman. Big damn eyes.

There's no sound from the closet. No muffled sobs. I didn't figure. Little Machiavelli's probably in there plotting her next move.

She should be on her knees, praying. I had the pistol leveled. Safety off. Despite whatever the fuck's gone wrong with my insides, I was drawing in the deep breath, ready to exhale and gently squeeze. I didn't lie. My aim is always true.

But her ears were peeking out of her black hair. I couldn't center my shot 'cause I was distracted by her tiny little ears.

And, damn, those eyes—what color blue is that? Cobalt? Azure?

It's probably good she hides those eyes. They're unnatural. Distracting.

She's distracting. And she's a problem. Doesn't matter that she's small, she's dangerous as hell. She's a drunk idiot capering around with lit explosives, blind-folded. If she were a man, I'd have no compunction about putting her down. Relation to Wall or no.

I bang my forehead on the door once and head off to the common room. I need to shake this off, whatever it is. Think the problem through, then come back and do what needs to be done.

I dial Harper as I clomp downstairs. "Where are you?"

"At the bar."

"The clubhouse bar?"

"What other bar's open this early?"

My sister's drinkin' way too damn much lately. It's not even nine in the morning.

'Course, I already got propositioned and blackmailed, and I held a gun on a woman, so maybe I need a drink, too.

Dina was shakin' so bad when I carried her to the closet. Trembling like a rabbit. When she put my hand on her skin, I could feel her heart thudding through her breastbone.

I grit my teeth.

She should be scared. She should be quaking in her weird socks that don't cover nothin' but the tops of her toes.

I scrub my chest. I got indigestion, and my antacids are upstairs. It's some shit—I'm hardly thirty, but 'cause I grew so fast and I carry so much bulk, I got every old man complaint. My joints tell the weather, my arches are fucked, and since I gotta constantly cut so the weight stays muscle— and greens make me bloat—my belly ain't never right.

Can't figure why my guts are knotted now, though. I didn't eat yet.

When I get to the hall, I scan the floor. Harper is perched on a stool, glass of red poured and the bottle standing ready. Creech is passed out on a sofa with a woman on top of him. I don't recognize her. There's a pissed off clanging coming from the kitchen. Ernestine must be up.

The front doors are open. They're not original to the garage, but I had them custom made to run along the existing tracks. They're reclaimed oak, polished to a shine, and solid. It's easier to leave 'em cracked than shut 'em behind you.

A woman as slender as Dina could slip right through.

I tug them shut as I pass to the bar and gingerly lower my ass next to Harper. The metal still creaks.

I slap the counter, and she swivels her head to face me, wobbly as a bobblehead.

"We need better security."

Harper rolls her red-veined eyes. "We've talked about this. 'When we are able to attack, we must seem unable.'"

"You really gonna quote Sun Tzu at me at the ass crack of dawn?"

"Hey, it's five o'clock somewhere," she smirks, raising her glass.

I lean over the bar, rustle up a bottle of bourbon, and clink it against her merlot. Ain't gonna help the indigestion, but it can't hurt the nerves. I'm still jangly.

My closet door ain't gonna give. Dina's goin' nowhere. Still. I'm unsettled. I got the kind of shakes you get after a near miss on the highway.

I treat the feeling with a long swig of Kentucky's finest. "We need to go for a walk."

"Fuck, Heavy. I'm in heels." She's wearing her court clothes. Black skirt, shiny white blouse, fuck-me pumps with red soles.

"Your policy," I remind her.

We don't talk business anywhere but outside or in church with countersurveillance measures fully employed. No documents on site except legit company records. The clubhouse is wide open to party crashers, hangers on, and randos.

Our goal is to seem really fuckin' *unable*. Nothing to see here. Just a bunch of drunk rednecks. We'll beat your ass if we don't want you around, but we ain't gonna bother locking a door.

"My policy sucks," Harper mutters, lowering herself unsteadily to the floor.

"Agreed."

Harper snorts and clutches her bottle. She's stumbling as we head down the back hall, past the kitchen.

"You still drunk from last night, or startin' early?"

She hiccups. "To be honest, little brother, it all kind of blurs together."

She flashes a grin. Her teeth are stained red.

I hold open the door to the yard, and she sails through, chin high. A drunken queen.

I love my big sister. She's vicious, nasty, and loyal to the bone. She practically raised our brother Hobs after our mom passed, and she went into the law so she could protect the club.

She's a royal cunt, but what blade isn't sharp?

She stumbles in the grass, and I barely grab her upper arm before she faceplants.

"You're falling apart," I point out, grinning fondly to take the sting out of it. We both know she's losing it. This isn't a new development.

She sighs, tightening her grip on the neck of the bottle and tucking her free hand through my elbow.

"I'll be fine once it's all over."

I lead her past the bonfire pit and stage to where the trees begin. There's a dirt bike trail that we stroll down when we talk business.

We're silent for a while. It's spring. The ground is wet with dew, and the sunlight has a dingy gray cast, but the birds are chirping, and the woods smell rich with thawed soil and new green shoots. The world is at peace.

What's Dina doin' right now? Is she freaking out?

She's fine. She's been in the dark fifteen minutes max.

She wants to kill a man. If she's up for that, she can handle cooling her heels in solitary for a few hours.

Maybe.

She clearly has issues. Her manner—I wouldn't call it robotic. More impassive. Almost as if she's reciting lines. She stared blank-faced at the floor while soliciting murder.

She should leave a man cold.

But the way she holds her body—a shiver zips down my spine. Most women strut or shrink around me. I'm rich, but I'm also intimidating. Ugly. Brutish. Dina was curious. Gawking at my cock. Showing me her tight little body while she snuck peeks with those big blue eyes.

My dick jerks in my jeans. I was hard until I picked up the gun, harder than I've ever been. Right now, my balls are aching. I have to shake it off. At the moment, I need the blood flow to my brain.

"What's got you out of sorts?" Harper says, breaking the silence.

I raise my eyebrows. I didn't say anything. I'm stompin' along in the mud, thinkin' my own thoughts. "Who says I'm out of sorts?"

"Your face does. It looks weird. We got a big problem? Bigger than usual?"

"My face looks 'weird'?" I scowl at her in all seriousness and wiggle my ears.

She snort-squeals.

I still got it.

She shoves my shoulder. "Yes, your face is always weird, but right now, it's weirder than usual."

"How so?"

"I don't know, Heavy. Like you're thinking."

"I'm always thinking." It's true. I can't turn it off. Never could.

"Yeah, well, maybe you should think less." She pokes my chest with a long red nail. "Do you ever think that?" When she's drunk, she gets handsy.

"All the fuckin' time."

"'Cause you're *always* thinking." She tries to dig her bony elbow in my ribs, cackling and chugging her wine. Then she hits a slick patch, slides, and nearly does a split in the mud. I've got her, though. Again. I hoist her right back to her feet.

She tugs down her blouse. It's come loose from her waistband. "I love you, too, little brother."

I didn't say it out loud, but she knows where we stand. I got her. Always.

I quit dickin' around and get to the point. "We have a problem. Bigger than usual."

"So I gathered."

"I had a visitor this morning. She propositioned me."

"Heavy, that's not a problem. That's a solution. Seize the day. When's the last time you got your dick wet?"

I ignore her. "She asked me if I'd seen *Strangers on a Train*."

"That TV show with the eighties kids playing dice games in a basement? With the upside down?"

"No. That's—" I shake my head. "She wants me to help her kill a man."

"As your lawyer, I advise you to decline." She swallows a hiccup, and it comes out a belch. "Well, how hot is she?"

She's not hot. She's boyish. Short black hair, not much meat on her bones. Little apple-sized titties with puffy pink nipples.

Well, not boyish, exactly. She's got hips and an ass, but they're—proportionally small.

"So, pretty hot," Harper muses.

It's immaterial.

"She knows about Half Stack Mountain. And she claims she has evidence proving Watts and Wade were behind the blown job."

"Get the fuck out of town." Harper shoves my shoulder again, misses, and stumbles. Her eyes flicker. She's considering the angles.

The blown job has so many goddamn angles.

"The blown job" is what we call the debacle that tore the club in two back in the day. It should have been a simple run across state lines. A few crates of black-market cigarettes. Low risk, low reward. I was a kid at the time. My father was supposed to be behind the wheel, but at the last minute, he had to bail. Dad's VP, Stones Johnson, and one of his sons, Knocker, took the job.

That was the end of the club I was born into.

The cops pulled the truck over at the county line. There were guns under the cigarettes. Stones and Knocker went to jail. Stones died there. His other sons—Inch and Dutchy—founded the Rebel Raiders. And in time, they went hunting for revenge.

When Stones passed, Dutchy worked out his grief by taking a baseball bat to my brother Hobs' head. We buried Dutchy under a maple tree. Inch retaliated, attacked Pig Iron's daughter. Scrap beat Inch to an unrecognizable pulp and spent a decade upstate for it.

So much horror and death, loss and pain. And all the while, Des Wade's star rose. He's businessman of the year, and last election cycle, Anderson Watts' name got floated for Vice President of the United States.

It's not to be borne.

"Now your face looks normal," Harper says.

"Pissed?"

"Homicidal." She smirks and picks her way toward a felled tree on the side of the path. "Let's sit."

I lower myself beside her on the mossy log. It's a good height for me. Harper's legs dangle a half foot above the ground.

She drains her bottle and chucks it behind her. I'm gonna have to remember to get that before we leave. If she threw it in poison ivy, I'm rubbing her face in it.

"What's the evidence?" All of a sudden, she's miraculously sober.

"An affidavit from the dealer who sold Wade and Watts the guns."

"Why haven't we heard about it?"

"The story is that the guy was extradited to Russia. From what my visitor says, I'm thinking the feds could have made a deal. A prisoner exchange with the Kremlin. Something like that. Maybe they buried the allegations to preserve the deal. Or they were protecting Watts. Or using the info for leverage. Lots of possibilities."

"Did she show you the affidavit?"

"Nope."

"So, it could also be bullshit?"

"Lots of possibilities," I repeat.

"She knows where the bodies are buried?"

"Yeah."

"Who does she want you to kill?"

"An uncle. Sounds like a personal vendetta." I snort, remembering. "She says she'll kill him. She only wants logistical support."

"Well, isn't that special." Harper examines her nails. They're fake, long, and sharp. Dina's nails were bitten to the quick. No polish.

"The law doesn't distinguish between murder and

conspiracy to commit murder. Did she give you the name of the arms dealer?"

"Boris Stasevich."

"Did you kill her?"

My gut cramps. "No."

"Where is she?"

"My closet."

Harper raises a sculpted brow, but then she shrugs. "We have to kill her."

I tense, and all my little aches and pains make themselves known. I'm tired. I'm tired in my bones.

I crack my neck and roll my shoulders. I'll pop an aspirin when we get back to the clubhouse. Drink some coffee. I don't have time for rest. Never have.

"Heavy, she's a liability."

No one's touching her. The thought is immediate. Loud.

I don't look at it too closely. It's not logical. It's not even true—I'll do what needs doing. I always have. But I don't say any of that out loud.

"Her name is Dina Wall," I say instead.

Harper lets out a long whistle. "Wall's missing sister. I thought she was a kid?"

"I did, too, but she's twenty-four. She's some kind of shut in. Lives with her parents."

Harper's silent for a few beats. "We still have to kill her."

"She's Wall's family."

"She could put every last one of us behind bars for life. She could put a needle in your arm."

"We don't touch family."

"We put a bullet in Ike Kobald."

"If we hadn't, Nickel would have. It's not equivalent."

"It's precedence," she argues.

"This isn't a court of law."

"Wall doesn't have to know." Harper shifts to face me. Her gray eyes are cold as ice. She was never soft, but these days, her hardness has petrified. It's sharp enough to cut. "I can do her if you don't have the stomach."

My throat constricts. She's deadly serious. She would, and I don't think she'd lose a second of sleep.

This isn't how it's supposed to be. I make the sacrifices. I carry the weight so the club can be whole. That's the deal that makes it bearable.

"I should have never let you go after Des Wade."

Fucking him is what's done this to her. I never should have condoned it.

Her lips curve in a bitter smile. "It was our only move."

We both know that's not true. Harper has always advocated the direct approach. Snatch Wade one night in a parking lot. Beat the truth out of him. Record it and show Knocker Johnson. Bury Wade under a nice dogwood. Or an elm.

I'm the one who argued that Knocker wouldn't believe a confession made under duress. That kidnapping a son of one of the state's most highly regarded families would be too much exposure for the club.

I didn't suggest that Harper seduce him. It was her choice, but I didn't give her another one. I was working on it, but she's impetuous. One night, she video calls me from his apartment. He's asleep in his bed. She's in her bra and panties, a kitchen knife in her hand, an eyebrow cocked.

If I had blinked, she would have done him, then and there. I convinced her that searching his place was the smarter move.

I should have let her slit his throat. She's been Mata Hari for a long time now, and she's breaking under the strain.

I made the wrong choice. One of dozens. That's what a leader does.

You make the hard calls and then carry the guilt and regret when shit crashes and burns. If your shoulders aren't strong enough to bear it, you don't deserve the mantle.

"You can stop whenever you want." I've said the words a dozen times.

"No, I can't," she says. She offers me a sad smile. "Not until we finish it."

In one way or another, we've been trying to put this behind us for twelve years. Ever since Twitch passed.

Twitch, the old head with no kids who was a second father to all us little shits. The guy who had time for us—who taught us engines and how to throw a punch and that Page and Clapton ain't shit next to Hendrix. He'd seen it all, and he showed us—or tried to—that there's nothing better in life than the open road, cold beer, and banging your wife.

Harper and I had come home for the funeral. The wake was at the clubhouse. I hadn't been to Petty's Mill in four years. The rot was in the air. The men who'd raised us, who'd fought for their country and worked themselves to the bone—they were wasting away. Jobless. Leaning hard on the bottle and all but given up.

Harper and I made a pact. Rebuild. Restore. Revenge.

Steel Bones would rise from the ashes. The prodigal sons would return to the fold. And the fat cats who'd built their names on our broken backs would pay.

Everything had been taken from us, even our pride, but the fight was still there. In our blood.

That was so many long years ago.

"If Dina Wall really has the evidence, this could be over." I lean back to take in the steel gray sky.

Harper sniffs. "We have a name. We can run the lead down ourselves."

"She says she has access to the documents now."

"Let's get them from her and then kill her."

"She's not going to just hand it over. I—tipped my hand."

Harper quirks an eyebrow.

"I held a gun on her, safety off."

"Why didn't you shoot?"

"Got interrupted." I don't mention the minute that ticked by before Wall banged on the door. Or her delicate ears. The bone deep reluctance that came out of nowhere. "There's no guarantee we'll be able to run down the affidavit on our own. It's been a decade, and we haven't yet."

We fall silent. Somewhere in the thicket behind us, a stream babbles, swollen with melted snow from the mountain. It'll be a dry gulch by summer.

It's a beautiful day out here.

What's Dina doing in the closet? I should have thrown in a water bottle before I nailed the door shut. What if she needs to piss? What if she hurts herself somehow? Panics in the dark or trips and breaks an arm?

It's a closet. It hasn't even been an hour. She's fine.

She's got grit, even if she's naïve as hell. She's the frog in the fable who gives the scorpion a ride across the river and wonders why when she gets stung.

She's brave, though. In a reckless, oblivious way. Outside of the people in this club, it's hard to find brave folks these days.

"Well, as the club's lawyer, I advise you to end the bitch. She's a walking RICO charge."

She widens her eyes, expecting me to argue. Or concede.

She's not wrong. But how do I fucking argue that her eyes are blue and her ears are small? And I want to watch her. Like she watched me in bed. I want to see how she moves; I want to hear what she has to say when she's not reading from a script in her head.

What is wrong with me? I'm not soft. Not any part of me.

RICO is a federal charge. And I'm not the only one who stands to lose. The stakes are as high as they come. It's the future and freedom of every brother in Steel Bones. It's their families. Their kids.

The weight bears down on me, compressing my lungs.

Dina Wall could destroy all the people I care about and everything I've built in one fell swoop.

I *know* this. But still—

I keep my mouth shut.

Harper raises an eyebrow. I look away, stare down at the moss on the log. She's silent for a long moment, and then she says, "Well, if you prefer to roll the dice, I do have another idea."

I twist my neck. Harper's booze-bleary eyes are narrowed. Calculating.

"What's your idea?"

Her lip quirks. "Spousal privilege."

"Like when a mafia wife doesn't have to testify against her husband if she doesn't want to?"

"Like when a mafia don can bar his wife from testifying against him if *he* doesn't want *her* to. In this state, the witness-spouse *or* the party-spouse can invoke privilege. Communication *and* testimony. In cases both civil *and* criminal."

"No shit?"

"We take marital harmony very seriously in Pennsylvania." She emits a dry laugh. "Of course, nothing would stop her from blabbing to the cops if she were so inclined. She could help them build a case and then disappear."

"Right now, she has no motive. She wants our help."

"Unless you pissed her off enough by holding that gun on her."

She didn't seem pissed. She seemed terrified. Her pupils ate up that shocking blue until her eyes matched her hair. She'd balled her fists and tightened her muscles, and she was shaking like a leaf on a tree.

I don't mind scaring people. It's useful, and I'm good at it. But I liked her better curious and sneaking peeks at my dick. I liked that a lot. Too much.

"You're saying marry her?" I ask.

"Yeah. And then do what she wants. Help her to kill the uncle, but make sure she pulls the trigger. Get it on video. Then you'll have leverage against her. Mutually assured destruction."

"It's risky."

"Too risky," Harper agrees.

"There has to be a simpler way."

"Beat the information out of her. Then put a bullet in her brain."

"I'm not doing that." It's out of my mouth before I realize it.

"Getting soft in your old age?" Harper smirks, toeing a shoe from her foot. She tries to scrape the mud off on the mossy log. "You owe me six hundred bucks."

"For the shoes?"

"For the billable hour. The shoes are a thousand."

"You could have pulled some rubber boots on before we left."

"Regrets, I've had a few." She gives up on the shoe with a huff. All she's done is smear moss on it. "We done here?"

"We are."

"So you gonna get hitched, little brother?" She's enjoying this way too much.

"John Wall's gonna fucking kill me."

"He doesn't have the heart."

"Seems I don't either."

"I don't know, Heavy. Your back's not really to the wall, is it?" She pats my thigh. "I know you. If it really came down to the club or this woman, you wouldn't hesitate."

"Harper." I wouldn't admit it to anyone else, but this is my partner in crime. Ever since she lured Dutchy Johnson out of Sawdust on the Floor and distracted him while I slashed his throat. My first kill. So long ago now. "I hesitated."

"You don't when it counts."

She's so certain; it has to be true. She's the smartest woman I've ever met. Smarter than me.

This plan is insane.

But as we walk back to the clubhouse, there's an easing in my chest.

I'm closer to my revenge than I've ever been before. And just in time. Knocker was released a few months back, and he's been stirring the Raiders against us, baiting us into all-out war.

If Dina has what she says, Steel Bones has a real chance at brokering a lasting peace with Knocker and the Raiders. And destroying Des Wade and Anderson Watts. Making it right.

And I get to play with a cute little murder pixie while I do it. I almost have a spring in my step.

"You might want to wipe that shit-eating grin off your face before you propose to the blackmailer," Harper says.

I laugh, and it echoes through the woods.

3

DINA

This closet is a mixed bag.

As a rule, I like small, dark spaces. I'm a hider. I have been ever since I was a kid. If I get freaked out, I find the most confined space I can and wedge myself in. I like the closeness and the quiet.

I don't like not having the choice to leave. And I have to pee, the floor is cold, and it smells like motor oil, man, and rubber boots.

I'm also scared for my life. The fact that Heavy left without killing me bodes well, but what's he doing now?

I didn't give him anything to go on. The name Boris Stasevich alone isn't going to get him anywhere, not with the caliber of tech guy he has on payroll. I entered the Steel Bones system with a drive-by download. I lured their IT "specialist" with a website offering free orc porn. That dude is no cyber-ninja.

Heavy could be getting his people to check me out. He'll find even less on me than Boris the Russian. I did college online, and I've been consulting for the same company since

I graduated. I have no social media. I stick to message boards on the dark web.

Of course, he might be arranging a way to kill me that won't leave a hole in his favorite chair and blood all over his stuff. He could be looking for a plastic sheet.

My belly hurts. I'm not bloated anymore, but I'm nauseous. I haven't eaten since before I left home. When my stomach's empty and I'm stressed, I feel like I'm gonna hurl. I never do, but it's still miserable.

I've always had a messed up digestive system. It goes with the ASD. Mom did all the things you're supposed to when I was growing up. No gluten. No casein. No sugar.

I don't know if it helped, but I eat donuts and drink soda pop all the time now, and I'm no worse off than I was when I was younger. No better, either.

Why am I hyper-focusing on my stomach?

Because I'm close to losing it and falling into a full-blown nuclear meltdown.

I don't want to die.

Back home, it seemed so logical. My uncle did something unforgivable. He hurt Rory, my only friend in the world. He harassed and threatened my brother Kellum's daughter and her mother. Tried to run them off. He has to be stopped.

My eyes burn, and I rock. Just a little. I hate thinking about it.

I like structure. I need routine. Mom, Dad, and I have Sunday dinner and Friday movie night and Taco Tuesday. No one bothers me in my turret, but they're always around —Kellum in his house down the hill and Jesse in his trailer by the apple orchard. I don't give a crap where Cash stays; he's an asshole.

Uncle Van took all that safety and predictability and

smashed it. Tainted it. Kellum almost lost his child for a
second time. Dad sits at the table late at night now, nursing
beer after beer, eaten by guilt. Mom forgets to put dinner on
and stares out the living room window, up at Uncle Van's
vacant house at the top of the hill.

Everything is different. Rory's not down the hill; she's
across the state. She's hurting, and she's scared. Meanwhile,
Van swans around the city, posing for pictures at black tie
affairs, convinced he can do whatever he wants because he's
rich and totally without a conscience.

I figure I can do what I want, too. I don't have normal
people feelings either. Someone has to stop him, and if I
don't, no one will. Kellum's tried to talk Rory into testifying
against him, but she won't, and I get it. She wants it to have
never happened. Me, too.

I can't erase the past, but I can erase him. And once I
decided to kill him, the plan popped into my head fully
formed.

I knew about Steel Bones. My brother John's been a
member since before I can remember. I got bored and
searched them up years ago. They used to be hard core. I
found the photo of the sheriff arresting the bikers on the
side of the road, cartons of cigarettes scattered on the
ground around a crate of rifles.

They've supposedly gone legit, but I figured the club was
a place to start. I don't know any other criminals. It didn't
take much digging to find the offshore accounts. The shady
overseas associates.

One fake orc porn site later, I had full access. They're
careful with communication. There's no evidence of blatant
wrongdoing, but there are so many clues. Calendar events
without locations or subject lines. Credit card charges from
Medellin and Odessa.

I don't read fiction, but I like spy movies, and I love a puzzle. I haven't quite figured out their entire game, but Steel Bones is far from clean. They're in deep with mobsters from all over the world.

I figured helping me bury a body would be nothing.

I miscalculated.

And now I'm trapped, sitting in the back corner of a closet on a pile of flannel shirts. The floor's so cold that my butt's still freezing despite the heap.

I really have to pee.

I tuck my knees tight to my chest. I put on one of Heavy's shirts when I made my nest. It's ridiculous. As big as a sheet.

How much longer will he be?

I'm uncomfortable, and my brain's hanging on now—barely—but what happens when it's forced to be idle for hours on end?

On the other hand, I don't want to die, so maybe Heavy can take his good, sweet time.

I should be planning what to say to him. How do I convince him that I would never go to the cops?

I wouldn't. Obviously, that would be stupid. I'd implicate my brother and myself.

I really thought I was dealing with a smart man, but if he can't see that, I don't know what to do.

I'm stewing, picking at my cuticles, when there's a scraping at the door.

He's back.

I clamber to my feet. I've come up with nothing. I've sat here for hours, and all I have is a numb butt and a painfully full bladder.

There are a few bangs and a muffled curse, and then the door swings open, bright daylight flooding inside. Pain shoots into my brain. I squeeze my eyes shut.

There's a grunt.

"What did you do to my shirts?" Heavy growls.

"Sat on them," I say in the direction of his voice.

"Why are your eyes closed?"

"It's too bright."

"You were in there an hour and a half, tops." He sounds grumpy.

"I have a light sensitivity."

"You're really fucking delicate, aren't you?"

In some ways, yes. In some ways, no. I shrug a shoulder, and his huge shirt slips down. He sighs and stomps into the room, his footsteps echoing. All that's missing is the *bum, bum, bum.*

Then he tromps back, coming straight for me.

"Why are you smiling?" he grumbles.

Plastic carefully slides behind my ears. Sunglasses. I blink and open my eyes, my fingers flying to the frames. They're comically huge.

"*Bum, bum, bum.*" I can't help it. My lip twitches. "You stomp around like a cartoon giant."

"You need me to nail you back in a little longer to learn some respect?" He swings the hammer at his side.

"Respect is earned, Popeye."

"I look nothing like Popeye."

"Whatever you say, Shrek."

"You've got quite a mouth on you for someone who's been cooling her heels in a closet."

I shrug. "I don't have a filter."

"You should get one."

"You should get a thicker skin, Gaston."

He chuffs, kind of like a horse, and then he places an enormous palm flat on my chest and slowly pushes me backward.

I duck to the side, away from his hand. He lets me. "No. I don't want to go back in the closet. I have to pee."

He raises his eyebrows. I shut my mouth. Point taken.

"Well, then. Come along, Princess and the Pea."

He grabs my elbow and hustles me out into his room. There's a door I hadn't noticed on the wall with the murder board. He opens it, revealing an en suite. Thank goodness. I wrench my arm out of his grasp and sink onto the toilet, sighing with release.

It feels so good. I wouldn't have lasted much longer.

A throat clears from the doorway. "You don't want privacy?"

"You can shut the door if you want."

He doesn't move. He's watching me. I don't care. There's not much to see. His shirt comes to my knees.

I wipe quickly, stand, and flush. I've rolled the shirt sleeves past my elbows, but there's so much fabric, the folds come loose. I get a cuff drenched when I wash my hands, and it sticks to my skin like a warm, wet tongue.

I shake my arm, but all that does is knock the soaked cotton momentarily loose before it slaps back against my forearm and stays plastered there.

This sucks. I hold my arm at a distance, but it doesn't help. Obviously.

"What's wrong with your arm?" he asks.

"Nothing." It's the wet, slappy, gross sleeve.

Suddenly, he steps into the room and grabs my hand in his huge, rough mitt, holding it up as if he's reading my palm. He rotates my wrist. I stare at the red plastic buttons on his shirt. He's so big, even his chest rises and falls more than a normal man's as he breathes.

He's so much. Too much. Busting his balls hasn't made him any more manageable in my mind. My insides are going crazy, like Pop Rocks and soda pop, but not just in my stomach. Everywhere.

Maybe it's the fact he held a gun on me. That he could have killed me. That he still might. That's enough to mess with anyone's equilibrium.

I can't even look at his buttons anymore, so I focus on the clean white towel. The entire bathroom is immaculate, and everything is oversized. Huge double sink. Jacuzzi tub. It's really nice for an MC clubhouse. Not that I have anything to compare it to.

Since I'm not looking at him when he speaks, I startle. I jerk my hand, and he lets go.

"Get some clothes from a sweetbutt," he says. A sweetbutt? Oh. He's on the phone. "Size small. Bring them to my room." There's a pause. "Now would be good. You think I'm callin' now 'cause I need a dress tomorrow?"

I catch my reflection in the mirror. I look like a child in a grown up's clothes. My hair's a tousled mess. I lower my nose to my armpit and wrinkle my nose. I stink.

"Do you want a shower?" Heavy asks. I check. He's talking to me this time.

From this angle, I can see him in the mirror. For me, a reflection isn't as intense as direct eye contact, even though he sees me looking at him. And he watches me back.

He's retreated to the doorway. He's broader than the frame, so he kind of hunches, peering through, his arms braced on either side, massive biceps bulging. Under his threadbare red flannel, he's wearing a faded black T-shirt tucked into worn jeans. The flannel is identical to the one I borrowed.

Except for the wet part, I like this shirt. It's soft from washing. He cut the tag out, and it's so loose, the seams don't chafe. Once it dries, it'll be fine. I don't want to wear a sweetbutt's clothes. Girly clothes have the worst fabric. And, like, rhinestones and embroidery and shit. I shudder. That's not gonna happen.

Heavy strokes his beard, eyeing me as I lean against the sink. It's like he's waiting for me to say something. Oh. Yeah. He asked about a shower.

That's a bad idea, right? It would be freaking amazing to wash all the smells off—the air freshener from the rideshare and the driver's awful cologne and the vape smoke from downstairs—but I shouldn't. I don't see a gun, but he could have it tucked in his waistband in the back. Maybe he wants me to get in the tub so that when he shoots me, it's an easy clean up.

My panic makes a valiant attempt to kick into gear, but my nervous system's pretty much on the fritz at this point. Too much adrenaline for too long. And not enough sleep or food. My fight-or-flight response is tapped out.

I twist the faucet back and forth without turning on the water.

"Are you going to kill me?" I direct the question to the mirror.

He shifts his weight. "Maybe not."

"Are you going to help me?"

"Yes."

A thick sensation fills my chest. It's not exactly a good feeling. This is a good *thing*, though. It's what I wanted.

"So that's it? You help me, I help you, and I go home?"

"That's not it, little girl." He sets his jaw. "You've put me in a difficult position."

"I told you that I'm not going to tell anyone where you bury the bodies. It wouldn't make sense. I'd be implicating myself."

"Or entrapping me."

"I'm not."

"I can't know that."

"So we're at an impasse?" My throat tightens. This isn't an impasse. He's bigger, stronger, armed. I can lie to myself all I want, but he holds all the cards.

"I have an idea," he says. "A proposal."

"Yeah?" I force myself to face him, but my gaze falls immediately to his well-worn boots.

I'm examining the scuffs on his toes when he says, "Will you marry me, Dina Wall?"

What?

My gaze flies to his face. His black eyes twinkle, and his lips are curved. He's not serious. Obviously. He's making fun of me.

My cheeks burn. "This isn't a joke."

"No, it's not. You want to conspire to commit murder? I want assurances that you can't turn state's evidence."

The heat seeps away. He's not mocking me. This is a tactic. "Oh," I exhale. "It's a legal maneuver."

"You could call it that."

I don't know much about spousal privilege, but I watched enough lawyer shows with my Gram before she passed. I understand the gist. Wives can't be compelled to testify against husbands and vice versa. It's actually fairly clever.

"We'd get an annulment afterwards?" I muse.

"A divorce," he concurs.

Why a divorce—?

"We'd only need a divorce if we had sex."

"We're going to have sex."

I blink, and a prickly heat blossoms between my legs. I gaze at his beard while his eyes rake my face. He's scrutinizing my expressions as he drops his bombs. He's going to get frustrated. It drives my family nuts that I don't react. They think I don't care. I do, it's just all my processing happens way deep in my brain—nowhere near the synapses that connect to my facial muscles.

He won't stop staring. He probably expects a response.

"I don't think you can say that with any degree of confidence," I offer.

"Why not?"

I shrug. "I am curious, but I've never done it before. It wouldn't be prudent to start with a prodigiously large penis. That would probably be very uncomfortable."

He lets out a strange, garbled sound. Like a turkey got strangled.

I shift. I'm achy under the soft flannel. My breasts are almost itchy. Hot. I really do want a shower. Cool water would feel good on my skin.

"You're a virgin?" he asks. His voice has dropped an octave lower, the deepest bass I've ever heard in real life.

"The concept of virginity is problematic."

"I can solve it for you."

I check his face quickly. The corners of his eyes are creased, and his lips turn up.

"You're teasing me." As I duck my gaze back down to the floor, I see the tent in his jeans. Very, very prodigious.

"I am," he confirms. "But I'd make it good for you, baby. I promise."

I'm already shaking my head. "I don't think intent matters. It's about logistics."

"You came to me for logistics," he points out.

A chill settles my chest, sobering me. I did. I'm not here to explore new things or trade ripostes with a boss biker. I'm here so he can help me kill my uncle. I need to get this back on track.

"If I marry you, you'll help me?"

He exhales noisily. "Are you sure you want to do this? No offense, but you don't seem the type."

"What type?"

"Vengeful."

"It's not just revenge. It's justice."

He laughs. It has a bitter ring. Even I can make that out. "And you're the judge? You're confident you can tell revenge and justice apart?"

I'm not. Except for the big ones—anger, pleasure, fear—I'm not sure I know the difference between any emotions. It doesn't matter, though. If I do nothing, the wrongs stand, and Van is free to keep hurting people. My family has turned their backs on him now, but what about in a few years?

Every Sunday at church, we're admonished to forgive. Mom and Dad pride themselves on their virtues. Love of God and neighbor is the core of who they are. They'll let him back in if he comes around with his hat in hand. And then he'll tear us apart again.

I can't read people, so I go by what they have done as a predictor of what they will do in the future. Van will hurt the people I love again. There's no doubt in my mind. Kellum had his chance, but he got nowhere. It's my turn.

"I'm confident," I say.

He clicks his cheek. "Then, it's a deal."

God, I hope he doesn't want to shake on it. I don't want to touch his hand again. It was much too... enveloping.

Lucky for me, there's a loud knock from the bedroom.

"Stay here," he orders and strolls off.

I flip the faucet and fill my cupped palms with cool water, suddenly aware of how thirsty I am.

There are murmurs from the other room and then a

door shuts. Heavy reappears in the doorway as I lap up one last handful of water.

He groans. Not sure why. "What are you doing?"

I slide him a glance. He has sparkly fabric wadded in his hands.

"Drinking." I'd have thought it was obvious.

"Jesus," he says. He disappears again and returns with a bottled water. "Here." He sets it on the vanity. "And here." He thrusts out what appears to be a gold dress.

"Oh, hell no." I trip a step backwards.

It's a *tube*. And it's made of *sequins*. My skin tries to crawl off my bones.

"I'm not wearing that."

He holds it up. It looks like a miniature pillow case for disco enthusiasts. "What's wrong with it?"

"Turn it inside out."

He pauses a second, and then he does. Oh, god. It doesn't even have a liner. It's sequins inside and out. Tiny scales with jagged plastic edges. That's horrible. Who would make something like that? Who would wear it? By choice?

"Nope. No way."

"You can't wear my shirt to the airport."

What airport?

I sink to the side of the tub and squeeze my eyes closed. The sunglasses aren't enough. It's too bright in here with those ugly ass sequins. And I've never been to an airport. Or flown in an airplane. What do they even *smell* like with all those people and windows that don't open?

Ass. I bet that's what it smells like. Or worse. Air freshener.

I flick my thumbs and gnaw on my lower lip until it hurts. My nail beds will be raw and bleeding by tomorrow.

Heavy releases a long, grumbly sigh, and then he firms his tone. "Get up. Put on the dress."

"Pass."

"You don't call the shots."

"I'm not letting that thing touch my skin."

"You're being a child." His words are clipped and fast. He's losing his patience with me. Everyone does eventually.

"You wouldn't make a child wear that monstrosity."

"This is ridiculous."

"It'll take less time if you find me different clothes."

I'm not trying to be a brat; it's just a fact. People don't get it, but they should. Tall people gotta bend through doorways. Short people need ladders. I need natural fibers. You can dress me in synthetic blends—lord knows my mother tried—but it'll be the equivalent of watching a dude Heavy's height bang his head on a doorframe until either the head or the wood gives. Not a fun way to spend your time, my mother can attest.

"You're not in charge here, little girl," Heavy booms, deciding brute force is the way to go.

I don't dignify that with a response. Of course I'm not in charge—he's gargantuan and he has a gun. And yes, in the grand scheme of things, I know it's objectively ridiculous to be this stubborn about a dress. If I could deal, I would deal.

And you know what? That's an excellent point.

"Why are you being so stubborn about a dress?" I ask.

He blows his cheeks into rosy, round puffs and tramps forward.

"Get *up*." He grabs my upper arm and tries to draw me to my feet. I go limp. He snarls and drops me. I slump back to the edge of the tub, leaning against the tile wall.

"Goddamn it," he bites and rips my shirt open. Buttons

go pinging off the tiles. Cold caresses my breasts, and my nipples pucker to hard points.

Heavy's breathing quickens. He has the shirt I was wearing fisted in his huge hands. I peek up.

He's staring at my tits. His gaze flits down to the juncture of my thighs.

For some reason, it's not too much to watch his face since he's not making eye contact. I crane my neck and look my fill.

He's not an ugly man, he just has so much hair. This close, I can make out the bone structure underneath the thick beard. He has high cheekbones, a strong jaw, and full lips. He might be conventionally attractive if he shaved. Beautiful even.

His ragged pants echo in the stillness.

Why is he so interested in my lap? My legs are closed tight. All he can see are dark curls. I don't wax or anything. I'm very sensitive to pain.

His gaze slides back to my face. I glance over at the sink. I liked it better when he was looking down.

Hmm. I have an idea.

I scooch until I'm sitting on the ledge at the foot of the tub. Then I lift my left leg, propping my foot on the side of the bath. I let my knees fall apart. He makes a strangled sound.

The cold hits my exposed pussy and goosebumps break out all over my white thighs.

"You showing me, baby?" he says, his voice low as a whisper. He's not frustrated with me anymore.

I wriggle until my hips are canted slightly up. I guess I am showing him. Warmth spreads in my belly like I've thrown back a shot, and the tile is chilly on the bottom of my foot. I curl my toes to keep from slipping.

This is crazy. I like it.

He drops to his knees. The floor doesn't shake, but it seems like it should. It's like an oak was felled in the forest.

He's close now, only an inch or so away from the side of the tub, only a foot and a half from my exposed pussy. His eyes are glued between my legs, so I can handle looking at his face again. It's amazing. If he'd been in the social skills book my mother made me read with her when I was a kid, I would've paid attention.

What's the man feeling, Dina? Is he feeling happy?

The man is not unhappy.

His tongue darts out to lick his slightly parted lips, and his thick brows knit as he squints. Squinting means interest. Or bad vision.

"That your pretty cherry?" he growls.

I do a crunch and peer down, but I can't see what caught his eye. I've checked myself out plenty with a hand mirror, though. "It's probably my hymen."

His jaw twitches. "It's so pretty."

"So you said."

"Why don't you spread those pussy lips? Show me that sweet little clit. Has it popped from its hood?"

I have no idea. I'm definitely wet. There's a strange fizzing in my veins and a warm swishing low in my belly like a washing machine as it agitates a load.

I slip my fingers between my folds and find the stiff bud. It aches when I brush it. My breath catches. Heavy leans forward a degree or two. I can see him even better now. There's color along his sharp cheekbones—not red, he's too tanned for that. But a shading that lightens as it disappears into his beard.

I love his beard. It isn't waxed and styled like a lot of the guys I chat with online. It's bushy and coarse, and reminds me of a thicket. It makes it hard to see the exact shape his lips are making. Lips are so much easier to read than eyes.

His face is a Picasso painting—curves and angles that form shapes I can't recognize. Is he turned on? I'm turned on.

"Are you gonna let me touch it?" He's breathing hard. He wants to touch me.

Do I want him to? It seems like a really bad idea. Not that long ago he was holding a gun on me.

"You were going to shoot me."

"I would never have gone through with it."

His gaze darts to my face so mine slides to his chest.

"I don't know if you're telling the truth."

"I'm not a liar." His voice drops even lower.

"I couldn't tell if you were." It's a sad fact. I suck at lie detection.

He's quiet for a minute. "Murder is a risk. I don't take unnecessary risks. You said you'd marry me, so we have an alternate plan now. Less risky."

Until you consider that we're getting married so that he can help me commit murder, the logic holds. "That is a weird argument to get into my pants."

"You aren't wearing pants."

My lips twitch. "Touché."

"I'm not used to gettin' down on my knees for a woman, let alone stayin' down this long." He rests a hand on the edge of the tub right next to where my foot is braced.

"You can get up anytime. You're in charge here, Atlas." I smirk, and I curl my toes into the meaty side of his huge hand.

He flashes his white teeth. "Oh, I don't think I am," he says.

He captures my foot and envelops it in a warm grasp,

then he pushes my knee back toward my shoulder, gently, slowly, opening me up even more. The air is chilly on my wet folds, and the tiles are smooth on my ass and my back. His palm is rough on the sole of my bare foot. It's a lot of sensation, but they're all okay. Good. Nice.

He drops a bristly kiss on the knee he's pushing back. "Can I taste that cherry, baby?"

I want—something. I'm throbbing. Swollen. Everything's collecting between my legs, gathering, pulsing. If I were alone, I'd rub my clit until I came.

He groans. "Yes, show me how you like it."

I glance down and blink. My fingers found my clit of their own accord, and I'm playing, tracing lazy circles around my hood, and it feels good. It's taking some of the pressure off so I can think.

Women like oral. It's in all the smut I read—usually around thirty percent. The couple bangs at fifty, and I usually DNF at that point. I don't need to watch people communicate badly and screw up their relationships. That's my life.

Anyway, other women like getting eaten out. Would I? His beard is intense. Probably scratchy. Which might feel good. Or it might be awful. And then there's the tongue to consider—I'm already shaking my head no.

"If this is all you want to do right now, this is all we do." He gently sets my foot back down on the edge of the tub, and he shuffles closer before sitting back on his heels. His lips are curved. He's smiling.

It's so strange. He's enormous, kneeling at my side, smiling, patient, watching me. His jeans are tented, I swear, three-quarters of a foot in the air.

I want more.

I want him to touch me. Just to see. I reach out and grab

his wrist, pull his hand between my legs and rest it on my lower belly. The corners of his lips draw back so far that I can see his back molars.

"Okay, then. We can do a little more." He skims my dark curls with his thumb, lightly. I squirm. It tickles. His laugh resonates in the back of his throat.

I'm still idly playing with my clit, my hand ridiculously small next to his. He brushes my fingers aside and takes over. His touch is firm and certain but light. The pad of his index finger has a fine grain. Even slicked with my wetness, his touch has an abrasion that mine doesn't. It's not a bad sensation. It's nice.

My nipples strain into the space between us. I want him to touch my breasts, too. But that might be too much, so I cup myself, and he moans.

"That's so fucking hot. Your sweet titties are aching, aren't they? You want my mouth on them, don't you, dirty girl?"

That might feel good. I still have scratchy beard concerns, but his full lips look soft, and I bet his mouth is hot, and his tongue would feel amazing rasping across my hard nipples.

"Yes," I exhale, and it's like I shot a starter pistol. His head dips, and he's palming me, tasting me, laving me with his wet tongue and sucking, drawing me into his hot mouth. His beard does scratch, but it's a good scratch. The kind that makes me arch my back.

Between my legs, his touch firms and quickens, and that shouldn't feel good either, but it does. I don't want light and unalarming anymore. I want firm, sure, demanding. I want him to do something I don't expect. He must know a thousand things that I don't, and I want him to show me.

"More," I pant, and I dig my fingers into his wild hair,

and it's thick and coarse. I pull. He snarls, his head rising, his blazing black eyes finding mine for a split second before my gaze flies to the ceiling.

"You want more?"

"Yes." That's what I said.

He's quiet for a moment. "It's gonna hurt before it feels good."

"I don't like pain."

"You have to trust me."

"I don't."

He lets out a strangled laugh. "This is a strange position for two people who don't trust each other."

"You don't trust me?"

"I don't know you."

Oh. Yeah. He doesn't. Theory of mind is my Achilles heel. I assume other people feel what I feel and know what I know. It never fails to throw me when I realize for the bazillionth time that they don't.

Heavy gently untangles his hair from my fingers and eases back. "Did I lose you?"

His breath is warm on my forehead. He's giving me space, but he hasn't backed off totally.

"What do you mean?" I ask.

He taps on my temple. "You get lost in there?"

"Always."

He laughs. "Come on." He scoops me up like it's nothing, and in five strides, we're at his bed. He flops onto his back, and I bounce, settling a little above his belt like a cowgirl. I'm split open, and my knees don't quite reach the mattress.

This is all new sensation. Cotton on my pussy. Denim brushing my ass. His hands are at my waist, securing me. He's grinning. I'm on top, but it's like being on top of a bull. Top doesn't mean in control. Not at all.

I usually need control. I need to know what's going to happen and when and for how long. But it's like when I decided to do this—to leave home and make things right—I muted that need, and I guess this is what happens when I let go. I end up stuck on top of a man mountain, buck naked.

"You have your clothes on." I rest my palms on his chest.

His hands are traveling all over me now, stroking my back, massaging my breasts, my thighs. "It's better if I keep 'em on."

"Why?"

"Because you're nowhere near ready to take me."

When I wriggle back, my ass presses onto his hard cock. The zipper's got to be killing him.

He sucks in a hiss. "Stop that." He doesn't wait for me to comply; he scoots me forward until I'm propped mid-sixpack.

I rock my hips forward. The friction feels good. My pussy is making a wet spot on his shirt, making the fabric even smoother against my swollen pussy.

I flash a glance to his face. His lips are curved, his mouth slightly parted. He's propped his head up on some pillows.

"That feels good?"

"Yes," I pant. Something's building. Twirling. Spiraling.

His fingers find my clit again, and I squeeze my eyes shut. "Baby, I'm going to slip a finger into this wet slit, okay? It's gonna be tight. It might twinge a little. If it hurts, you just slap my hand away, all right?"

What's he going on about? I can't sort through it all—the sensations, the words. They're all garbled up together.

And then he stops. My eyes fly open, and I claw my nails into his hard pecs. "Why'd you stop?"

"I'm gonna put a finger inside you. Okay?"

Okay? I don't know. "Will it hurt?"

"Yeah. Probably a little. I don't know. You're pretty— intact." He's shifting under me, resettling me a little lower on his belly, unbuttoning his shirt.

"Why then?"

"It'll feel good."

"How do you know?"

His torso vibrates with a rumbly sound. "Experience."

I bet he's done this tons of times. I know he's a big deal around here, and women flock to that kind of energy. And even though he's big and scary, he has the muscles and the height and the hair. Honestly, I can't think of a man more suited to appeal to the cave woman brain.

I don't like pain, not even needles, but I don't like this feeling either—like I'm a balloon being blown fuller and fuller, and I want to pop. I *need* to pop, but I can't.

"You promise it'll feel good?"

"I swear."

I screw my eyes closed again. I don't want to watch.

There's a rummaging. The rip of a zipper. His left arm is reaching around my side, his forearm brushing up and down against my ribs. He must have taken his dick out. He's stroking himself. My heart trips into a faster beat.

With his free hand, he's teasing my clit again, petting my folds. I bite my lower lip. It's good, but not enough. I arch my back, open up as far as I can, and then he dips his thick finger inside me, coating it in my cream, and then he pushes in.

I freeze. It pinched. And now his finger is inside me.

Does it hurt?

It did. For a second. But he did it quickly, in one smooth motion. I wriggle a little. His thumb is gently circling my clit, and that feels good. I don't know about the finger. It kind of hits the spot, but it's also weird. I'm perched on top of his massiveness, and he's touching my insides.

"How's my curious kitten?" he pants.

I wish he'd shut up. I need to focus. I rock my hips experimentally. Yeah. It doesn't hurt.

And then he moves. Slides out and in, and I can feel my channel flutter. The whole thing cranks from a maybe to a definite yes. I like this. My hands rise to pluck my straining nipples, and that makes it even better, spurs everything onwards.

"Oh, yeah. You gonna play with those titties? Does that feel good?"

"Yeah." I wouldn't be doing it if it didn't.

"Yeah," he repeats, and then I'm even fuller. He's slipped two fingers in me, and again, there's a twinge, but I don't care at all. I'm hurtling toward an orgasm, but it's different than lying alone in my bed or in the shower. It's *more*—better—because I'm not in control of it, he is, but that's okay since he knows exactly what to do, exactly how fast and how hard. I don't have to concentrate. The good feelings just keep coming in waves, bigger and bigger, until bam, a huge one crests through my entire body.

"I'm coming!" My abs clench and my thighs shake. I buck, and he snags my hip so I don't go flying off while he strokes the last drops of pleasure from me with those crazy fingers.

I flop down on top of him like a rag doll. His chest hair is crinkly, and his skin is hot and damp. That should be a gross combination, but somehow his scent makes it tolerable. He smells like the outdoors. Dirty but in an okay way.

He's rising and falling below me, breathing quicker, jiggling where he's jacking his dick. A smacking sound grows louder and faster, and then he grunts, and there's a hot splatter on the back of my upper thigh. He exhales, and then his rough hand begins to roam, smoothing my back, stroking down my spine, cupping my ass. He avoids the wet spot on my leg.

I push up on my elbows and try to peer over my shoulder. "Is that cum?"

"Ayup."

I freeze. "Stop." He does. On a dime.

Smart man.

I'm teetering. My brain's reconnected from the temporary short an orgasm always causes, and it's barfing up all the information in one spew of mixed signals.

It's bright as hell in here. I lost the sunglasses. Where are they? Why didn't I notice when they knocked off? Did I take them off? Are they broken? I shouldn't move in case there are shards of glass, but I'm on top of a man.

He's hairy, but that's okay. And he has a strong smell, but it's natural, and natural is fine. Animal smells are fine.

But his cum is on my leg, and it's wet and warm and kind of trickling down my thigh, and that is not okay, and it has a smell, too, kind of yeasty, and that might be natural—I don't know. I've never had cum on my leg before, and now my heart's pounding, and my hands are balling into fists, and I don't dare open my eyes to see just how bad it is because it's so damn bright in this room—

Smooth plastic slides behind my ears. "You lost these."

I blink. And breathe. "There's cum on my leg," I bite out.

He swipes my thigh with his forearm. The flannel seems to mop most of it up, enough so that I can flop off Heavy in a graceless dismount and stumble a few feet away. He pushes up to sitting.

"I need a shower." Nothing is dripping anymore, but the

cum *was* on my skin, and there's no way I'm checking, but I bet it's tacky to the touch.

"I feel so cheap," he says. I hesitate in the door to the bathroom. He's joking.

That dress is bunched in a glittery heap on the tile floor. I kick it out the door with my toe.

"I'm not wearing that," I announce in the direction of the giant lounging on the bed before I firmly shut the door.

4

HEAVY

By the time my murder pixie comes out of the bathroom in a billow of steam, scrubbed bright red without a stitch on, I've cleaned up down the hall, changed my shirt, bought two first-class tickets to Vegas, and got Wash, one of our skinnier prospects, to fetch one of Crista's hoodies that she leaves behind the bar. I took his drawstring sweatpants, too.

I threw some shit in an overnight bag, leaving most of it empty. This trip ain't gonna take long, but I'm gonna need to buy her some clothes when we get there. I don't like her in the prospect's pants, and she is very particular about what she wears.

She's obviously on the spectrum, but I don't think that's the whole story. I went to school with a lot of autistic folks at M.I.T. Given, it was mostly men. All men, now that I think back. The eye contact avoidance, the monotone voice just a little louder than you'd expect, the flat affect. She's got all that. But she is more than the stereotype.

She's got balls. A twisty, curvy brain. Some kind of white

knight complex. And the abandoned, greedy libido of my fuckin' dreams.

I had no idea I'd get off on being used for sex, but holy shit —she was a kid in a candy store, riding my hand like a cowgirl. Is she discovering her wild side or is this inexperience? And how did she get to twenty-four and not pop that cherry?

There were streaks of blood on my fingers when I washed my hands. It's popped now.

It makes me feel oddly—possessive.

I don't do possessive. That kind of shit is contrary to the whole lifestyle. We live this way for the freedom. Freedom doesn't include getting my mind twisted over a homicidal virgin with no sense of self-preservation.

I'm no misogynist, but my world ain't gentle. The women in this club have thick skins. They hold their own because if they didn't, they'd be dead or under a man's boot. Princess and the Pea would be eaten alive if I left her with them.

As soon as I walk back into my room, she proves my point, and I gotta listen to her bitch about how the hoodie's too big and the sweatpants smell like Takis—both fair criticisms—before she'll follow me out the back.

The clubhouse is still quiet. It's a weekday and everyone has business they need to be doing. I get a prospect to drive us to the airport in the Range Rover. I ain't leaving my ride in satellite parking overnight.

Dina settles in the back seat and takes out her phone. I sit up front and make calls. Charge is up at the Patonquin site, and he's got things under control. The electrical is almost done in the main building, and we've dug the foundation of the annex. We were set back a few months when the Raiders went Vandal on the site. In retrospect, we were lucky we'd only gotten as far as erecting the frame.

Forty is coordinating the manhunt for Rab Daugherty, the Rebel Raiders' VP. We're gonna use Rab as leverage to get Knocker to the table. With Dina's evidence, the plan has a much better chance of working. It had relied on my honeyed tongue, and while I do have a certain eloquence, I don't think Knocker gives a shit about anything Steel Bones has to say. Two decades upstate, a good deal of it in solitary —cold, hard proof might not sway the man, either.

Forty keeps it short. There's nothing new to report on the Raiders' front. I call Harper, but it goes to voicemail. She's probably still in court. At least she ain't drinkin' there.

This has all gone on too long. When Knocker got out, I'd hoped he'd have no interest in a feud, that he'd satisfy himself with hot fucks, cold drinks, and long rides. At minimum, I thought there'd be time for rapprochement, but he came at us hard and quick. He wants revenge. I suppose I get it.

"Boss?"

I shake myself. While I was lost in thought, the prospect had pulled up in front of departures.

"Thanks, kid." I grab the carry-on out of the trunk and open Dina's door. Her nose is in her phone. She hasn't noticed we've arrived, either.

"Dina?"

Her fingers are flying over the screen.

I clear my throat. "Dina?"

No response.

Honk.

She startles, arms flinging wide. I barely hop back in time. Wash grins and taps the horn again.

I tip my head to him. "Obliged."

He gives me a smartass salute. Dina tumbles out of the car, tucking her phone into the hoodie pocket and tripping over her own feet. I grab her upper arms and hold her steady. Her eyes are all whites, and her gaze darts wildly from the curbside check-in to the automated doors to the vehicles haphazardly pulling over to unload people.

It's hectic. I bet she doesn't deal well with hectic.

It'd be a hell of a thing if she's cool when I hold a gun on her or lock her in a closet, but then freaks out in the middle of a crowded airport terminal surrounded by security.

"Where are your sunglasses?" I ask.

She's already sliding them on.

"We're at the a-airport," she says. Her voice wavers. Not good.

What do you do in this situation? I don't generally deal with women when they lose their shit. I ain't a gentle man, and I don't have any edibles on me.

"Go on." I nod at the door.

She stays put.

I clear my throat.

She pays me no mind.

I glance behind me, thinking maybe Wash can honk again, but the Rover's gone.

"Walk," I finally say and give Dina a helpful push toward the entrance. She stumbles forward a few steps, and then she digs in her heels. In my mind, I hear the screech and smell the burnt rubber.

Ah, shit.

"We got to catch the flight. So we can get to Vegas. And get married. To do the exchange. That's the plan."

It's feelin' a little more *Snakes on a Plane* than *Strangers on a Train* at the moment, but change is a constant.

"Right." She's tracking the people coming and going through the automatic doors. I fold my arms and try to look like a law-abiding citizen having a casual conversation. With my size, I can't help drawing notice, and I don't need TSA to get curious. Shit is already complicated.

If I'd been thinking ahead, I'd have snagged a jay from Deb's desk drawer and had Dina blaze up during the ride. Probably best I didn't, though. Crista's doing better, but Deb still needs her medicine.

I'm about to try prodding her again when Dina seems to come to some kind of conclusion. She squares her shoulders and draws up her hood until her face is almost hidden.

"Okay." Her jaw clenches, accentuating her little pointy chin. She exhales in a huff. "What do we do?"

All right. Atta girl. She's pulling it together.

"We get on the plane."

"No, what do we do *first*?"

She needs an itinerary? We don't have all damn day. I hate waiting at airports. I didn't leave a lot of time.

I glare down. Her hands have disappeared in the long sleeves, and she's swaying like a drunk sailor at sea. Okay. She needs an itinerary.

"We get in line. Get our ticket from the counter. We get in another line. Go through security. Then we sit until they call boarding. Get in a line. Get on the plane."

"I don't have a ticket."

"I got that covered."

"I don't have ID."

I bend over and fish her purse out from my carry-on bag.

She snatches it from my hand. "You had this all along?"

"I found it under my bed."

She nods. "I stashed it under there while I was waiting for you to wake up."

"It, uh, doesn't have what it used to have in it."

She was packing a butterfly knife with her chewing

gum, lip gloss, and hand sanitizer. I had Wash put it in my office when he brought the hoodie.

"I'm gonna need that back," she says.

"No problem."

I guess I'm expecting her to need a little more coaxing, so when she takes off, I actually have to catch up. Doesn't take more than two steps. My stride is at least double the length of most people's, and she has short legs. Shapely. Hot. But, short.

She makes a beeline for the gates. I steer her toward the self-serve counter. When it's our turn, she stomps right up to the machine, hits a few buttons seemingly at random, and then squints up at me. "How does this work?"

"You could let me do it." I hit cancel and take it from the top.

She huffs and stares into the middle distance, biting that sweet, pouty lower lip. A picture flashes in my mind—her back arched, eyes scrunched tight, hips bucking in tight jerks as she comes.

Now I've got a stiffy and a girl actin' weird as we queue up for security. I always get "randomly" selected for special screening. The line's pretty long. We might very well miss the flight.

The closer we get, the more Dina's craning her neck and bouncing on her toes.

"You put your bag on the conveyor belt?" she asks.

"Yeah."

"I don't have a bag."

"No, you don't."

This is a weird fuckin' conversation.

"Then I walk through the metal detector."

"Yup."

"I empty my pockets in that basket."

"There's pockets in those sweatpants?"

"No." She pats herself down. "I put my purse on the belt, though. Or do I put it in the basket?"

"I don't think it matters."

"It won't fit in the basket."

"Then put it on the belt."

"You're going to put your bag on the conveyor belt."

I can't tell whether she's troubleshooting a possible problem or if we're starting at the beginning of the conversation again, so I say, "Yeah."

She tilts her head up at me. With the hood up and sunglasses on, she looks suspicious as fuck.

"Can you put the hood down? Maybe take the glasses off until we're through security?"

"I look like an FBI wanted poster, don't I?" She flashes a wry smile.

"Yeah, but cute."

She frowns. "Cute is for kittens and babies."

"I like kittens and babies."

"You look like you eat kittens and babies," she says as she reluctantly lowers her hood and tucks her sunglasses into her purse. Her face is white as a sheet. This is really getting to her.

"You're right about the eating pussy part."

That gets me a soft snort. Her eyes aren't really focused, though, and she's flicking her fingers so much it's drawing notice.

"I know I'm being weird," she says, shuffling forward as the line moves.

"Hadn't noticed."

"I've never been in an airport before."

"So you said."

"I have to rehearse new things."

"Like earlier? When you recited that script at me?"

"Yeah." She slides me the quickest glance. Her eyes are so damn blue, you should be able to see clear to the bottom. "I had a lot of time to work on that."

"How long?"

"Almost a year."

"You been planning this for a year?"

She stares at her feet. "It's not a joke to me. It's not a whim. If you think I'm going to change my mind—if you're humoring me so I give you what you want—I'm not."

She sounds dead serious, but she's also struggling to navigate an airport. There's no way she's gonna be able to take a man's life in cold blood. It ain't like in the movies. The action isn't on screen; it's in your head. In the chasm between being a person, a sinner who can be forgiven his sins, and a killer, a man who's decided to play God.

I remember that step into nothingness. I thought it'd be a crossing over, but it was a weight. A crushing weight. And afterwards, you're left like Atlas, out in the dark, holding onto the world you don't belong to anymore.

Luckily, I don't have to answer her. It's our turn to walk through security.

I go first, figuring she'll take it easier that way. Miraculously, we don't get tagged for enhanced screening, but she gets looks. If she weren't so pretty, her quirks probably wouldn't draw notice, but you just expect an attractive woman to carry herself a certain way and that ain't Dina. Best I can describe it is that she moves like a marionette getting jerked on strings.

Maybe that unsteadiness is why I'm hovering. I walk close by her side, sit next to her on the seats while we wait for our flight to be called. I'm crowding her, and she shifts and leans and huffs, and I'm finding that very amusing.

Women in my world don't inch away. They don't hump my leg like they do Charge, either. I'm a scary man. Even eager pussy treads warily. Eventually, though, if enough liquor's flowing and it's late, I'll find a female crawling on my lap, high on the danger of playing with a man of my reputation.

I take what's on offer if I'm in the mood and the woman knows the score. I'm not in the market for an old lady or a hassle. I'm too busy, and I've never been interested in the domestic life.

And yet, here I am, signing on for a wife and one hell of a hassle. At least Dina has no interest in anything other than her phone. She's glued to the screen again, an intent frown scrunching her face. She's got wireless earbuds in her little ears.

I stretch out my legs in preparation for being folded up like an accordion. I always buy myself two seats, but leg room can't be bought for love or money. I should get myself a private jet. There's enough cash in the coffers. A jet reeks of laying up treasures on earth, though. I'm a fallen man, but I try to be a righteous one all the same. On the day of judgment, I want to look my Maker in the eye and claim only those sins I've chosen.

Next to me, Dina tucks herself into the far corner of her seat. God forbid her body brush mine. I extend my arm across the back of her chair, let my hand dangle against her upper arm. She casts me a cantankerous look. I grin.

She shrugs and knocks my hand away. "You're manspreading."

"That's a bad thing?"

"Yes."

She hasn't taken her eyes off that phone. I go ahead and

squeeze her shoulder, scooting her into my side. She stiffens immediately.

"What are you doing?" she hisses.

"Getting cozy with my fiancée."

"I'm not your real fiancée."

"We're about to get really married. What are you, then?"

"Hot and uncomfortable."

A laugh busts from my belly, drawing the attention of all the folks in front of gate thirteen. Her delicate fingers fly to my lips, pressing on them. My dick leaps to attention. I nip a tip, and she hisses, dropping her hand.

"Be quiet. People are staring."

"People always stare. I'm a walkin' Guinness Book of World Records entry."

"Well, people don't stare at me." She's back to texting a mile a minute.

They do though. She might not notice, but she catches the eye. I don't know if it's her off manner or her uncanny pixie face, but she gets her fair share of second glances, even next to me.

"Doesn't hurt to look." I fiddle with a lock of her black hair. She ducks her head. "You're really jumpy for a woman who was ridin' my fingers a couple hours ago."

Her fingers still on her phone. Finally.

"I don't see why you need to make this harder." She glares at a patch of carpet by my boots.

"How am I making this harder?"

For a long moment, I don't think she's gonna answer me. Then she exhales a deep, exasperated breath and says, "You know the Mariana Trench?"

"Sure. Deepest part of the ocean." I'm above average at *Jeopardy*.

"Ever heard of the barreleye fish?"

"Can't say I have."

"It has a transparent head, and it's eyes point upward."

"Bitchin'."

She huffs, but she's not as tense as she was a minute ago. Her shoulder feels less like a wooden hanger.

"Yeah. It is. Anyway, it's perfectly designed for life in the ocean right below the limit of light penetration. It's got all these extra rods in its retinae that let it pick out the silhouette of its prey swimming above. It's a wonder of nature."

"And you're a barreleye fish?" I'm above average at metaphors, too.

"Yeah. Do you know what happens when you haul it out of its habitat?"

I can guess, but I let her tell it.

"First it gets blinded, and then its body is crushed from the pressure change."

"Flying to Vegas ain't gonna kill you, baby." I know I'm being insensitive, but what do you say to that?

"No, it won't. I just get to hang out for hours at whatever depth it is when the barreleye fish's eyes are burning and its bones are slowly splintering. It's awesome. So, maybe you could give me some personal space to really revel in the sensation."

Well, now I feel like a dick. I ain't backing off, though. That's not a thing I do. Instead, I grab her purse, find her sunglasses, and prop them back on her small, upturned nose.

"What about security?" she says.

"We're through security."

"Your arm's still on my chair."

"You're gonna have to get used to that."

"You're an extremely difficult person."

"Yeah," I acknowledge. It's only the truth. "In the sea of life, I'm a nuclear submarine."

"Now you're manspreading into my analogy."

I lean over until my beard tickles her cheek. "After we get hitched, I'm gonna manspread your thighs and plunge all the way into your Mariana Trench."

She snorts, but there's a real smile playing at her lips.

I dart out my tongue, lick her ear lobe real quick, and she jerks like she's been zapped by a jolt of electricity, her arm flying out to whack me across the face.

It smarts—she nailed me good—but I'm laughing when they make the announcement for first class to board. She walks ahead of me through the jetway onto the plane like it's the green mile. The flight attendant guides her into the first row. Hope she likes the window seat. I need the aisle.

I stow my bag overhead, and cram myself into the seat so other folks can pass, knees nearly to my chin. I hate air travel.

Dina perches on the edge of the leather seat, visibly quivering, gaze flicking wildly from the window to the passengers filing past to the air nozzle and light buttons above. Is she gonna freak out? Would liquor help or hurt?

"How you holdin' up, barreleye?"

"Air travel is the safest mode of transportation," she mutters.

"Yup."

"The odds are extremely good that the plane will not fall out of the sky."

"That is statistically true."

"Studies show that takeoff and landing are the most dangerous parts of air travel."

"I've heard something like that."

She's flicking her fingers like crazy, rubbing the skin raw.

I grab a hand. It's like holding onto a mannequin. She flicks her free thumb even harder. She's gonna draw blood.

I rest the hand I've got on my thigh, and I don't know what else to do, so I stroke it like a cat. She leaves it there, and slowly, she tapers off with the flicking.

"Sounds like you've done your research," I add.

She jerks a nod.

"When did you do that?" She didn't know in time to prepare.

"On the car ride here."

"That's what you were doing on your phone?"

"Yeah." She has her eyes glued ahead where the flight attendant is shutting the door. "And I texted my parents. Told them to check their email. Where I told them I'd gone camping with Rory." She finishes with a nauseous moan.

"Are you gonna lose your shit?"

"Odds are extremely good." She's kind of rocking now. I shift so no one can see her past my bulk. I don't think she'd want to draw attention.

"What exactly is freaking you out?"

"It smells weird in here. Canned. It sounds weird, too." Her voice is loud, but the acoustics in the cabin muffle her.

"I cannot disagree." A commercial airline is the exact opposite of a bike. "You want me to get you a whiskey?"

I've already got my hand up, waving over the flight attendant who's been tracking me since we boarded. From the way she's got her shoulders back so her top strains across her tits, its 'cause she's interested, not scared that I'm trouble —which is always the preferred response from a woman.

"No. I'll be fine." Dina buckles herself in.

"You don't look fine." I shake my head "never mind" at the flight attendant.

"Crawl out of my ass, Ginormo."

"I'll let that one slide since you're freakin' out."

"Don't hold back, Hoss. I'm tougher than I look."

She don't look tough in the slightest. Her hood is down, and her hair's mussed, jet black tufts sticking out at all angles. Like most men, I dig long hair on a woman. I like a nice handful to jerk her by and to twist in my fist while I fuck 'em from behind.

I like makeup, too, and big tits, thick thighs, and a juicy ass. I'm a typical man. It's easier if they're tall—I don't get that crick in my neck—but height doesn't matter when they're on all fours. I like tattoos. Pierced nipples, a pierced clit. That's all good.

Dina doesn't even have pierced ears. She looks like a skinny teenage boy in her getup. Makes sense since she got the pants from a teenage boy. There's nothing about her that should turn me on, but my dick is at half-mast and has been since a few minutes after I busted my load on her leg.

I don't like that she's unsettled, and there's nothing I can do about it. I scrub at my chest. I left my damn antacids at the clubhouse.

"What do you normally do when you're losing it?"

"I don't lose it." She's crossed her legs, and her knee's going a mile a minute. The TV flashes on, and the safety recording starts playing. Her eyes are hooked, her pupils growing larger and larger.

"No?"

"Not since I was a kid."

"What did you do as a kid?"

"Hid."

"Where?"

She tosses a shoulder. "Wherever I'd fit. Where no one could see me."

"Well, you'll be all right then." The flight attendants

buckle themselves in for takeoff, and I stretch my legs into the aisle, almost groaning with relief. "No one can see past me. You're in your own little hidey hole over there."

It's a toss away line. I don't expect it to work. But somehow, it does the trick. She leans forward, peeks over, checking to see if what I say is true. It is. I'm pretty much a human wall.

She stops jiggling her knee, and then, as we accelerate down the runway, she stops flicking. She keeps her eyes screwed shut and her body braced for impact as we ascend to cruising altitude, but then she relaxes, cracks her neck, tugs the hand I've been holding all this time, and takes out her phone.

She taps and smiles. "Oh, yeah. There's Wi-Fi."

"It's free in first class."

"Yeah, you paid, what? A couple hundred bucks to get free wi-fi. Deal of the century."

I ignore her smart remark and take my phone out, as well. I check my messages. John reports that his parents heard from their missing daughter, and apparently, she's camping with her good friend Rory. Harper reports that Forty is now dragging his ex along with him on the search. That's gonna be a problem. Nevaeh Ellis is trouble.

Harper's not gonna tolerate having her around. She's protective as hell, and Nevaeh did Forty dirty. Maybe it's good Forty's taking her along for the ride. If Harper catches her on her own, she's not above delivering a beatdown.

What's Harper gonna make of Dina? Dina's a real threat. Harper's not gonna be satisfied by mutually assured destruction for very long. Once the dust settles and we've dealt with Wade and Anderson, she'll want Dina dead. It's the logical move.

A growl sounds in my chest. Dina's gaze flies over to where the seat belt extender cuts into my abs.

"You hungry?" she asks.

"I could eat." That's true one hundred percent of the time.

She blinks and goes back to her phone.

I don't want to think about this shit anymore. Later, there'll be time enough for trouble.

"What are you doin' on that phone?" It looks like some kind of game.

"*Elfin Odyssey.*"

"What's that?"

She rolls her eyes. "It's a game."

"What kind of game?"

She huffs, real irritated to be interrupted. "The kind where an *elf* goes on an *odyssey.*"

"I like games." I take her phone. She squeaks and snatches it back.

"Don't touch my stuff."

"I wanna play."

"You want to play *Elfin Odyssey*?"

"Ain't doin' anything else at the moment." And my thoughts are making me uneasy.

She holds out her hand. I unlock my phone and slap it in her palm, keepin' an eye out as she downloads an app. I open it, and it asks me if I want to join a quest.

"Do I want to join a quest?"

"Yeah. Hold on. Don't click anything yet." On her phone, she's texting someone. "Okay. Enter this code." She shows me a number.

"This is a multiplayer game?"

"Yeah."

"So we're gonna shoot people together?"

"This isn't a battle royale." Her distaste for the concept is clear.

"I like a good battle royale."

"You're going to be disappointed."

I'm about to reply, but I get the avatar screen. There's a bunch of knights, ninjas, centaurs, pirates—all kinds of critters. I select myself an elf. I'm hot. Long blonde hair, flowy pink dress that shows off my tits.

I appear in a green field. The graphics are cool. Realistic but with a warm, hazy filter.

"What now?"

There's a popping sound and two huge motherfuckers show up beside me. "Shit. How do I kill these guys?"

"You don't. That's me and Rory."

"Who's Rory?"

"She's the Frost Giant."

She's blue, hooved, furry, and she's got massive horns. I type *what's up Rory* into the chat, and I check out Dina's avatar. She towers over my elf, smooth clay with black holes for a mouth and eyes.

"You're a golem?"

"Yup," she says, texting her friend. I steal a peek. She writes *he's okay*. I'm oddly flattered.

There's something fitting about my little murder pixie picking an animated statue, ruled by forces outside her control, as her avatar. It's as good an analogy as the barreleye fish, I suppose.

"What do we do now?" I ask. "Rescue the princess?"

"This isn't the 80s."

Dina and Rory take off down an incline, and I follow.

"Besides," she adds. "That's a tired trope. Princesses can rescue themselves."

"No doubt." The frost giant snags a glowing box, and we

get coins. Sure feels like the 80s up in this game. "So what's the objective?"

"Rescue a princess."

I glance at Dina. She shrugs. "Rory likes it."

"And who's Rory to you?"

Before she can answer, the music changes, the light dims, and a three-headed dog charges onto the screen. It leaps for the frost giant. I tap buttons like crazy, but all my guy does is jump and flutter her glittery wings. The golem throws itself in front of the dog. There's a splash of red on the screen. Then—poof—all three of us are back in the grassy glen with zero coins and sixty percent life force left.

"Shit. Cerberus doesn't usually attack until you're on the path to Mount Alysia."

"I thought you said this was an odyssey."

"Odysseys are treacherous," she says as the three of us head out again. This time I snag the glowing box.

"Cyclops," I grunt, angling for the lead. We're not gonna get eaten by a dog again.

"Sirens," Dina answers, falling in behind my elf. I see she's read her classics.

"Lotus eaters." I keep it going.

"Scylla," she replies.

"Charybdis."

"Circe." She smirks. "The first woman to posit that all men are pigs."

I chuckle. "You know your Homer."

"Both ancient Greek poet and Simpson." She winks.

Who *is* this woman?

You can't shut Wall up about Mona and the kids, but he doesn't say much about his folks. They own a horse farm in Stonecut County. He's got brothers—Cash meets up with us to go hunting before the rally in Anvil every year. Cash is a loud mouth, but he knows the mountain, and he's brilliant with a recurve bow. If Wall's ever talked about a sister, I never paid any mind.

An uneasiness rises in my guts. Lotus eaters is a good reminder. I can't afford to lose sight of the big picture. Dina might seem harmless with her video games and her quirks, but it doesn't change the fact she's the greatest threat this club has ever faced. She's a living, breathing RICO charge. And she wants me to help her kill a man.

I can't afford to be lulled into a false sense of security by her size and her inexperience.

This isn't a game. This is real life. If you shoot a man, he doesn't reanimate when you start over.

I know she's chosen to play a heartless monster, but I don't believe that's her. Not for a minute.

So what do I do when she wants her quid pro quo?

5

DINA

I t's dark when we land in Las Vegas. The city lights are a neon motherboard edged by a pitch-black horizon. It's late, so the airport is less crowded, and I'm adjusting. I *am* capable of handling change. I hate it, but I can do anything I have to do. My therapist was on me all the time about my "rigid thinking" when I was a kid, and maybe my thinking is rigid, but *I'm* not.

Mom's convinced I'm agoraphobic—or I will be if she doesn't make me go to church and the grocery store with her —but I'm not afraid of leaving the property. I *choose* not to. Why is it that when everyone else lives life how they want it's the American way, but when I do, it's a disorder? People don't make sense, and they don't like differences.

Kind of makes places like Las Vegas truly weird. The vibe is so different from Pennsylvania. There are ads everywhere for casinos, magicians, circus acts, acrobats, singers— it's exactly how I imagined, but more faux class, less retro kitsch.

How come folks can't handle differences in people, but

when they're on vacation, they're like "I want to pay a hundred dollars to see dudes painted blue playing drums?" Weird.

Heavy herds me through arrivals, not touching me but matching his pace to mine and grunting when I head the wrong direction. People stare and whisper.

Do they think he's famous? He could be a professional wrestler, I guess. Cash and I watched a lot of WWE when we were kids. He always wanted to practice his moves on me. It was easy enough. He leaped at me from a windowsill, and I pretended to fall.

I don't think Heavy looks like a wrestler. There's nothing flashy or smooth about him. I know for a fact he's clean, but to look at him, you'd figure he smells like wood smoke and dirt.

When we get outside, it's scorching. At least ninety-five degrees. We wait at the curb for the car Heavy ordered. There's a muddy flyer on the concrete. A stripper dangles from the neck of a buff cartoon beaver smoking a cigar. It reads "smoking hot beaver." I guess there's plenty of kitsch in this town, too.

"Are we getting married right now?"

Heavy's checking his phone. "We're going to the hotel. I have to take care of some shit, and there's paperwork. We can get married tomorrow." He casts me a look. "We need to buy you a dress."

"No lace." I shudder. Lace is worse than sequins.

I wouldn't mind getting hitched in sweats, but not in this heat. A night in a hotel will be okay. Heavy and I can mess around again. Right after he jizzed on my leg, I wasn't sure if I liked it, but the memories kept coming back to me on the plane.

I liked the way his bulk felt under me. Between my thighs. Like I was riding a giant beast. At any second, he could have thrown me on my back, taken charge. But he didn't. He behaved for me.

I kept picturing his expression. Heavy-lidded eyes. Lazily curved lips.

And his taut muscles. The crisp black chest hair.

I was squirming in my seat, worried I'd make a damp spot on my sweatpants. I'm not wearing underwear.

I wouldn't mind doing it again.

It felt good, and I came way harder than when I play with myself, but that's not all. I loved being on top. Heavy held a gun on me, stripped me, and locked me in a closet, but he ended up on the bottom, asking me what I wanted. I love irony. I don't always get it, but when I do, it's delicious.

Except for hogging the arm rest, he hasn't touched me since we got on the plane. He was fun in *Elfin Odyssey*—we got all the way to the Bonsai Forest, and he destroyed all kinds of things I thought were indestructible—but he's clammed up since we disembarked.

I put it out of my head. I have no idea why people react the way they do. The logical response to that kind of limitation is to give zero shits. Mom is the only one who still bothers trying to get me to understand people.

You insulted her when you said the pie was salty. He was waiting for you to stand so he could pass you to get out of the pew.

But isn't there less of me in his way if I'm sitting than if I'm standing? That one still makes no sense to me.

Anyway, Heavy's absorbed in his phone, so I ignore him and examine the beaver brochure. It's a coupon for twenty dollars off at the door. Clearly, I don't understand strip clubs. There's a cover? Don't you just tip the dancers and overpay for beers. Cash is always bitching about having to drive two hours to Shady Gap to pay seven bucks a bottle for domestic at the gentleman's club. My twin is a class act—very discerning tastes when it comes to light beer.

Eventually, a limo pulls over. Heavy has a word with the driver, and then he opens the door and jerks his chin for me to climb in. The upholstery is black leather, the paneling is wood, and the smell is air freshener layered over women's perfume with notes of stale sex and weed. I take the seat furthest from the mini bar and roll the window all the way down.

Heavy sort of crams himself into the seat across from me. Even with his shoulders hunched, his head brushes the ceiling and his knees are bent at what has to be an uncomfortable angle.

Maybe that's why he rides motorcycles. So he's not hemmed in. I understand the feeling. I was raised riding horses. Horses are hella easier than people. Stamping, chuffing, rearing, butting. Compared to a smile or a conversation, it's like horses hold up signs. *I like you. Stop doing that. I'm ready.*

And then there's the dude across from me. I'm going to marry him tomorrow. I get why. He's trying to limit his exposure the best he can. It's a business relationship.

But he seems—seemed—into my body. He fingered me.

So we have a personal relationship, too.

And in the airport and on the plane, he was cool. More or less. So this is becoming a friendly relationship?

But now he's ignoring me, and being all stompy and scowly, and I keep forgetting that I don't care.

This is why I don't people.

Besides my immediate family, I've had two friends in my whole life. Glenna Dobbs, who was my best friend through seventh grade until she dropped me like a hot potato. Apparently, I was a social liability, which is ironic since she's now the town pariah. It's a long story, but basically, Glenna Dobbs played Nancy Drew, and forgot that everyone in River Heights couldn't stand snoopy Nancy Drew.

And then there's Rory.

Rory is my person.

I need to call her. I missed our regular calls this week because I was preoccupied with putting my plan into action.

I hope Heavy booked two rooms. I need privacy. I open my mouth to ask, but he's actually talking on his phone now, grunting every so often as a muffled voice drones on.

I make the mistake of looking past him out the rear window. Lights *everywhere*, flashing, neon, super bright. There are crowds of people, palm trees, towers, and a Ferris Wheel and a hot-air balloon and tons of digital billboards.

It scrambles my brains, but I can't look away. I slide into the numbness of overstimulation. I'm not Dina anymore; I've sunk two or three levels below the surface, looking up.

The limo drops us in front of a casino on the strip. Somehow, I crawl out and follow Heavy through sliding glass doors into a gust of arctic air conditioning.

There is a fountain in the lobby. No, three fountains, and the entrance to a mall to the left, and more signs, restaurants and a walk-through safari, and a comedian who was big in the 90s. A bazillion things go bing, bing, bing, and even though everything is marble and glass and larger than life— and smoking has been banned inside for a decade at this point—there's still a faint whiff of cigarette in the air.

This is hell on Earth.

My skin crawls.

How many eyeballs do they figure we have? It's like if nails on a chalkboard, a pokey bra wire, and squeaky shoes were a place, and then that place slapped you in the face. In desperation, I dig in my purse for my earbuds, pop them in, and crank noise-cancellation to the max. If I just look at Heavy's boots, it's tolerable. Just.

After we stop by a boutique and buy me some clothes, we trek a quarter mile to reception. Heavy checks us in, then leads the way to a bank of elevators. He doesn't give me a key card. I should have asked for two. Too late now. I'm not crossing that lobby again until I have to. The fountains cause people to swerve left or right, and they're all heading to different wings, and so visually, the impact feels like watching a hockey game with ten pucks in play.

Sometimes I think of myself in terms of *Elfin Odyssey*. I am at ten percent life force. Red bar. I need a break.

We get on an elevator, and another couple follows us on. They're holding hands, but they're not talking or looking at each other. The man hangs his sunglasses from his collar. The woman shakes out her sweaty shirt.

"It's a hot one," she says.

Shit. Small talk. One of my goals on my I.E.P. when I was in school. I had to sustain a back-and-forth conversation of at least three turns with seventy-five percent consistency. I glance at Heavy. His nose is back in his phone.

"The locals don't think anything of it, but—" She makes a yowling sound. What does that mean?

Ugh. Weather. I can do this.

"Yeah. I hear it's calling for rain later in the week." Forecasting rain—or snow in the winter—is conversational gold. Doesn't matter if you're right or not. It lobs the ball right back over the net.

"It is?" the woman replies. "Can't come too soon. We're from Minnesota. We can't handle all this dry heat!"

The elevator dings, the door opens, the man draws the woman out, and I don't even have to take my conversational turn. Score.

It's silent as the elevator ascends. It takes me a little while to realize Heavy's not on his phone anymore. He's staring down at me.

"What?" I ask.

"You have no idea whether it's calling for rain later this week in Las Vegas," he says.

I don't see how he can know that for sure, but he's right. "Nope," I concede.

"Who taught you to lie like that?" His voice is pitched slightly lower than usual. It's raspier. There's a tension in his frame. I can't identify the emotion. I'm exhausted. Seven percent life force.

"The public school system."

The elevator dings. He exits, and I follow. I'm expecting him to head down the crazy long hallway, but he stays in the lobby area with a decorative table and mirror.

"Explain," he demands.

I watch our reflection. His black eyes glitter in the harsh artificial light, tiny creases at the corners. I like his eyes. They're like a silverback gorilla's. Even if I could read eyes, I don't think I could read his. They aren't like other people's. I wouldn't have a frame of reference, no handy poster.

He sniffs. "I'm waiting."

I don't know why he cares, but it's no secret. "I was in a special program in elementary and middle school. I had social skills every day."

"And they taught you to lie?"

I lift a shoulder. Pretty much.

Honesty is a ridiculous concept. You must always tell the truth, except when the truth is hurtful. But sometimes you have to tell hard truths. That's called tough love. And sometimes you have to lie to protect people's feelings. Those are white lies. Fibs are okay, and everyone tells them—but lies are wrong even though everyone tells those, too.

My family says I'm a bad liar, but somehow, that's not a compliment. My grandma used to say tell the truth and shame the devil, but in social skills group, we practiced saying things like, "I'm doing well, thank you" regardless of how we actually felt.

So, yeah. I figure honesty is like nudity—something other people care about that doesn't mean much to me at all.

"Conversational turn-taking was one of my individualized educational goals. It's hard to get to three turns with the truth. Lying is more efficient."

"Bullshit." A sharp line appears between Heavy's eyebrows and his full lips turn down. He doesn't agree, or maybe he doesn't like the fact. But I've done the math. I'm right.

This is what's wrong with neurotypicals. Their rules don't make sense, and they get their panties in a bunch when you point it out. Or worse, they drone on and on about why they're right despite clear evidence to the contrary because of some philosophical principle that doesn't hold in real life.

I seriously thought Heavy was smarter than this.

"How was your day?" I throw at him.

He glares.

"How was your day?" I ask again.

"Fine," he bites out.

I make an obnoxious buzzer sound. "Lie. You got blackmailed. You've been wedged in one undersized seat after another. Your phone has rung, like, one thousand times, and it always sounds like a problem. Your day sucked. How was your day?" I ask again.

A strange rumbling sound is coming from his chest now.

"It sucked," he says slowly, enunciating each word.

"Looking forward to your stay in Las Vegas?" I'm smirking. I've run the numbers so many times. Lying is just more efficient.

"Yes."

I make a buzzer sound. "Lie—"

"—Not a lie." He steps toward me, one pace, then another, forcing me backward. I can't see us in the mirror anymore. My shoulders hit the wallpaper. He's between me and the bank of elevators and the long hall and everything. My hands fly up to his chest. Not to push him away. But to rest there. Lightly.

His ribs rise and fall against my fingertips.

"I'm looking forward to riding your sweet pussy like you rode my fingers. I'm looking forward to prying open that brain of yours and fucking it just as hard." He bares his teeth, flashing his pointy incisors. "I look forward to ruining you, little girl."

I swallow hard. "I don't think I'd be into skull fucking. I'd probably puke."

He makes a choking sound. His face—it's hard to describe. It's kind of like what happens when a cartoon character gets slapped?

"What the hell do you know about skull fucking?"

"I've seen it in porn." Not on purpose. I don't search it up or anything. It just shows up randomly on the home page sometimes before I can click on "female orgasm."

I like watching men make women come for real. It's hard

to find, and honestly, I'm not sure if I'd know if the women are faking it or not, but I like what I like, you know?

Heavy rocks back on his heels and runs a hand through his hair. "That's not what I meant."

"That's what it sounded like."

A gaggle of young women come stumbling down the hall, laughing and boisterous. Heavy grabs my hand and tugs me in the opposite direction.

He mutters something indecipherable.

"I don't know if I'd be into sucking cock, but I'm curious. I wouldn't mind trying it out if I knew I wouldn't choke. I have a pretty sensitive gag reflex."

His grip on my hand tightens, and he picks up the pace.

"I don't want to swallow cum, though." It was warm and thick when it hit my leg. Like bisque. I only like bisque when it's freezing cold outside. Otherwise, that consistency is gross.

Two guys in khaki come around the corner and blink. They heard me. One snickers, and the other smirks. Not a Duchenne smile. Heavy puffs his chest, and they hurry past. Heavy lengthens his stride, dragging me along.

"This is a really long corridor." It makes sense. The hotel and casino take up the entire block, and a block here is at least ten times longer than a block in Stonecut. Still, with the dark red carpet and gold walls, it feels like a horror movie.

Finally, when we're almost to the emergency exit stairs, Heavy slides his key card in a door and kind of flings me inside. I was expecting—something else.

We're in a corner room, so there are two walls of floor-to-ceiling windows with a view of the city lights and the pitch-black desert beyond. It's a suite with a sunken living area, white leather sofas, and glass coffee table that just screams "snort cocaine off me." There's a kitchenette, a garish chandelier hanging over a round table, and three doors opening off the main area. The closest is a powder room. That means two bedrooms.

"Sweet. I get my own room." I make for the nearest door, but I don't get two steps before I'm in the air. I shriek, scrabbling for purchase, but Heavy has hoisted me under his arm, and my shoulder's wedged in his armpit, my legs dangling.

"What the fuck are you doing?" I kick air and grab at him, but it's like clutching a rock face.

He shoves a door wide with his shoulder, and then he dumps me on a huge bed. I bounce and land on all fours.

"Stay." He points his finger at me and kicks the door shut so hard it slams. He's being very aggressive. Even when he held the gun on me, he wasn't this physical.

I pop up to sit on my heels. The edges of my shoe soles are touching the comforter. Shoes don't belong where you sleep. It's almost as gross as socks in bed.

Heavy's chest is rising and falling more quickly than our speed walk to the room would cause. He's widened his stance, and his fingers are twitching at his sides. I'm guessing he's pissed.

I sigh and sink to my butt. It's time for my least favorite game. Figure out what I did to piss off the neurotypical.

"I'm sorry," I venture, reaching back to take off my flats.

"For what?" His head tilts the slightest bit to the left.

"For doing it wrong and making you feel uncomfortable."

Usually, those two things cover about everything. My mom's the only one who actually cares that I understand what I've done anymore. Everyone else who knows me has pretty much accepted the way I am. They know I either don't mean it, or I can't help it. Even Cash lets it go when I inevitably do or say something a little too blunt.

Heavy's still looming there.

I toss my shoes, one by one, off the side of the bed.

"Are you stripping?" he asks, his voice like rocks in a tumbler.

"No." I tilt my head until it's at the same degree as his. "Do you want me to strip?"

He's silent for a second, and then he bursts into motion, pacing toward the window, yanking the cord to raise the blinds. It's crazy dark past the blaze of the city lights. No stars. Velvet blackness.

The room is lit by lamps on the night tables. It's a mellow light, easy on my eyes. The comforter is cool, fluffy cotton. I want to stay in here awhile. Even with Heavy being weird, it's relatively peaceful. I feel my life force charging up.

He turns an armchair to face the bed, and then he lowers himself down, extending his legs to their full length. He steeples his fingers. It's a very villainous pose.

"Okay. Strip."

I rotate to face him. I don't understand what's happening —which is not a novel experience for me at all.

"Aren't you mad?"

"I was. But I can put it aside for the moment if you want to show me those sweet little titties again."

"Why were you mad?"

He exhales slowly. "Maybe mad's not quite the right word."

I try really hard not to roll my eyes. "Is mad close enough? 'Cause I don't do nuance."

A smile plays at his lips. "No. I guess you don't."

"Are you gonna tell me or what?"

"Are you going to take off your top?" He arches an eyebrow.

I shrug, yank the hoodie over my head, and chuck it next to my shoes. My nipples harden instantly in the air conditioning. Heavy makes a rough humming sound.

"Touch 'em," he orders.

"Why did you get pissy?"

He sinks back in his chair, and again, there's a long pause before he speaks. "I don't like you lying. I don't like other people hearing you talk dirty. I don't like dropping ten g's on women's clothing when the woman doesn't give a shit."

That's a lot to unpack. He did buy me a crap ton of clothes. Did I say thank you?

I stretch out my legs and prop myself back on my hands, so I'm comfortable. I'm mulling it over when he adds, "I don't like that for some reason, I feel compelled to tell you the straight truth."

See? He doesn't like me lying, but he doesn't like telling me the truth. The concept of honesty is bonkers. More ambiguous than smiles. Or words like "fuck" and "yeah, right" and "bi-weekly."

"If you lied to me, I probably wouldn't know." Not unless it was super obvious.

He draws a knee up. "You shouldn't tell people that."

"It becomes apparent pretty quickly when you get to know me."

He sucks his tooth. He does that a lot when he's thinking. He runs his tongue over a pointy incisor. I'd call it a tell, but Heavy is the kind of guy who looks like he's always thinking, so it's not really a tip-off that the wheels are turning.

"You need to go back where you came from. A farm, isn't it? Out near Stonecut?"

I nod. His eyes drop to my breasts. They're kind of thrust up since I'm leaning back.

"You don't seem like a country girl."

"What kind of girl do I seem like?"

"Trouble."

I snort. "I never get into trouble. On purpose."

"You say you're gonna kill a man."

I don't want to think about that. Not in this moment. He brought it up, though, and he still doesn't seem to understand. "I *am* going to kill a man."

"You have no idea what it takes."

"That's why I came to you."

"I'm not killing him for you."

"I don't need you to. I need you to help me cover it up."

"You can't possibly understand what you're talking about doing."

"I'm a country girl. I can shoot a gun."

"I'm not talking about that." He's staring at me, intent. Deadly serious. I'm gazing past his left ear at the sparkling city lights. "You don't want to live with blood on your hands. Do you know what that's like to carry? Every moment of every day. It's not an albatross; it's a rotting corpse. Your shadow. You'll never breathe easy again. You'll never sleep deep. You won't have a choice anymore about the person you want to be. You'll be a murderer. At the end of the day, that trumps all."

I'm not so dense that I can't tell he's talking about himself.

"I'm not like you."

He laughs, and it's a sour sound. "No. You can hardly walk through an airport without losing your shit."

The cold is puckering my skin. I wrap my arms around my bare breasts. Guess the stripping plan is out.

"John's mentioned you," he goes on. "You're a shut in, right? You work on computers, never the leave the house. And you're gonna kill a man? Your uncle? So not even a stranger—family. And then you're gonna go back to your tower or whatever and you're gonna live with that? Alone?" He scoffs. "There's no fuckin' way."

He doesn't understand. He doesn't need to. And besides, I'd never betray Rory by explaining it to him.

"You don't have to worry about that. All you need to do is bury the body."

He shakes his head. "You're living in a fantasy land."

"You're making false assumptions."

"No, little girl. You are."

I raise my eyes to the ceiling. "Why do you care? You help me, you get your evidence. The state of my conscience is not your concern."

"Why do you want him dead?"

"He committed a crime. He has to pay."

"With his life?"

"Yes."

"He hurt you?" he bites out.

"I already said he didn't."

"So this is some kind of vigilante justice?"

"There's no such thing as justice. He did what he did, and time only moves in one direction. But he's not going to do it again."

His voice has changed again. "And you have to be the one to stop him?"

"No one else has."

For a moment, he seems at a loss for words. Finally, he

coughs to clear his throat and says, "You don't know what you're doing."

Then he stands, all business, and strides from the room.

"We'll get married tomorrow," he throws over his shoulder as he goes. "I have shit I need to take care of."

He shuts the door firmly behind him, and I flop back on the bed like a starfish. The pressure in the room seems to drop. I half expect my ears to pop.

HEAVY IS EVEN HARDER to figure out than most people. When he carried me in here, I thought we were gonna mess around again, but it turned out he wanted to talk. I'd rather have made out.

I still don't get what pissed him off.

He didn't like that I lied about the weather? Is he that fastidious about his principles? There's no way. Dude's a criminal. He didn't get his knickers in a twist because some randoms overhead me talking about skull fucking. He's the president of a biker gang.

I guess it would suck to spend a bunch of money on someone and not get a thank you. Oh, shit. Did I say thank you? Probably not. Despite Mom's efforts, my manners are garbage. It's 'cause I don't really care about clothes. But I do know you're supposed to be appreciative even when you don't like a present. I just don't ever remember.

What was his other beef? He didn't like it that he feels compelled to be honest with me?

That's definitely his problem. Nothing I can do about that.

There's the thump of a door shutting from the other room. He must have left the suite. I let myself sink into the fluffy comforter. There's a knot tightening in my stomach. I will definitely kill my uncle, but I'm far from at peace with murder. My face lacks expression; I don't lack feeling.

Heavy's completely wrong. I understand what I'm doing. I've been plotting it out for months, and the whole time, I've been hoping with all my heart that my brother Kellum—the acting sheriff—would make it right. He hasn't. He can't. So I don't have a choice. I carry this either way. Once I kill Van, at least I know the burden won't get heavier.

My phone rings in the pocket of my hoodie. I roll over and reach for it. There's only one contact who I'm not currently sending straight to voicemail.

I wriggle back onto the heap of pillows at the head-board. "Can't sleep?"

Rory's voice, as always, is gentle and small. "Your family keeps calling."

"Don't answer. We're camping, and we don't have cell service."

"They sound really worried in the messages."

"They didn't open my email, so they freaked out."

As always, Rory is understanding. "Well, you've never left home before."

"By the time I called, they'd formed a search party."

"You should have told them before you left."

"Mom never would've believed me if I told her we were going camping to her face."

"I don't think anyone believes you now. Kellum called. He left a message. He said to tell you not to do anything stupid."

"I'm not doing anything stupid."

"Just a solo road trip, right? To clear your head?" Rory's changed since she moved to the city. She never questioned me before. I was her hero.

I press my eyes closed. I'm not going to lie to her, but I'm not going to let any more ugliness touch her either. "Actually, I'm in Las Vegas. With a man."

"What?" Rory the mouse actually shrieks.

I pull the phone away from my ear.

"What man?" she demands.

"Just a man."

"Did you meet him on the internet?" Rory's worried. I can read her feelings better than almost anyone's. I've known her since she was five years old and I was eleven, so I've learned them as she grew.

"Yes."

"The fairy in *Elfin Odyssey*?"

"Yeah."

"What's he look like?"

"Kind of like a mountain man. Kind of like one of those Scottish athletes who throws telephone poles."

She's quiet for a moment. "So he's hot?"

No. Not conventionally. His face is too rough hewn. He's definitely an endomorph who lifts, not a natural athlete. You can tell if he started spending time on the sofa, he'd be sporting a beer belly in no time. He also has a lot of hair.

But damned if he doesn't turn me on.

"I like the way he looks."

Rory sighs like I've said something really romantic. It's so hard to believe that despite everything—the junkie mom, the struggle with school, what happened with my uncle—Rory still lives with her head in the clouds. I don't want to change her, but she needs to see things a little more cynically.

"It's just a fling. I'm scratching an itch."

"So it's not serious?" She sounds disappointed.

"Not at all."

"You've never left home before."

"I never had a reason to."

She sighs again. "I'm so happy for you."

And she is. There's no doubt in my mind. Rory's like my brother Jesse—one of the rare, truly good, truly pure people in the world.

I met Rory on her first day of school. She was five. I was eleven. We were both in the special program at the school in Anvil, so with all the stops, we were on the bus for almost an hour both ways. Rory had been born premature and addicted to opioids. She wasn't stupid, but where an average kid would need five iterations to master a new concept, she'd need twenty. At home, no one had the inclination or sobriety to work with her, but the ride was long, and helping Rory passed the time.

My most peaceful moments as a kid were hunched down in a vinyl seat over a wheel well, bumping along the country roads up Stonecut Mountain, heads together as we worked on Rory's math facts or her spelling list.

When I graduated, Rory and I started playing online RPGs so I could still keep her company on the bus. For all intents and purposes, I'm her big sister. When Pandy Bullard asked her if she wanted to take over the job cleaning my Uncle Van's house, of course she said yes. When he did what he did, of course she didn't tell a soul.

I'd never have known if she hadn't left town without warning. But she can't lie. She's worse at it than I am. There's no way Rory Evans wanted to "try to make it in the big city." She craves routine more than I do. When she wouldn't talk, I went snooping, and I saw the CCTV footage from the camera mounted on Van's garage.

Rory would do anything to protect me. And I'd do anything to protect her.

This is what Heavy doesn't understand, and why would he? I haven't explained. I won't. It's no one's business.

I didn't use to be able to navigate the world this well. I was perpetually lost in static. And people? People were like the crowd in the episode of *Star Trek* when Kirk is kidnapped to infect an overpopulated planet—unknowable and omnipresent and menacing.

And then there was Rory. She was hungry, so she asked to share my lunch. And then she smiled. Or she was cold, so she wriggled under my jacket and fell asleep. So I brought her an old coat, and she wore it every day, even when the weather turned warm. If I wanted to do times tables for an hour, she was down with it. If I felt like rehashing the plot of my favorite *Buffy* episode for the one hundredth time, she listened. Rapt. Happy.

My uncle hurt her. I know about the NDA he made her sign. The money he's holding over her head to keep her quiet until the statute of limitations on a civil case runs out. I can imagine the pressures he's applied, but Rory loves me. She'd keep her silence just to spare me.

She's a very convenient victim, and Van knows it. How long before he decides to go after her again?

The thing about me is that I'm naïve and oblivious until I'm not anymore. I don't willfully deceive myself. Theory of mind doesn't come naturally, but once I understand what a person is, I don't lie to myself about them.

My uncle targeted a vulnerable eighteen-year-old, hurt her, and used his money and influence to make her go away. Then, out of greed, he tried to run off the mother of Kellum's child, again. Just like he did years ago. It's a pattern of behavior. He'll do it again. And why not to Rory? She's alone now, and he must think since she hasn't told anyone, he's home free.

To my parents, an ugly scene and an estrangement is somehow a conclusion, a fitting end. Life can go on, safe and pleasant in bucolic Stonecut County. Of course, they don't know about Rory. But even if they did, I bet they'd be content with cutting Van out of their lives. Out of sight, out of mind.

My brain doesn't work that way. I think about it all the time. Rory's face on the video. Scared. Crying. Helpless.

I wanted to reach back across time, through the video, rip her out of that moment that went on and on. Tuck her into our seat on the bus. Let her cuddle into my side.

I took care of her when I couldn't manage myself. Mom likes to talk about the specialists and the program in Anvil like they're the miracle workers, the reason why I'm verbal and somewhat competent at life. But it was Rory. It was loving someone that gave me a path out of my head and into the world.

"You know I love you." It slips out of my mouth.

Rory laughs gently. "I wasn't sure you were still on the phone. I thought you got distracted."

I do that a lot. Rory leaves me on speaker and watches her shows when we talk. She's used to my ways.

"I was remembering the bus to Anvil."

She makes a soft hum. "Those were the days."

"When I'm done here, I'm going to come out and visit you."

"Whoa, Dina Wall," she teases. "You're really bustin' loose."

"I'm not a shut in."

"No," Rory happily agrees. "You're a homebody."

"I go camping with Dad and Cash all the time."

"You used to."

She's right. I haven't gone on a hunting weekend for a few years now.

"It's not totally insane that you and I would go on a trip together," I argue.

"No more insane than you going on a solo road trip to meet up with a man in Las Vegas."

"It's just I've never wanted to leave Stonecut before. Now I do. So I did."

"I never thought I'd leave Stonecut either." There's a weight in her words, but I can't place it. Regret? Relief?

"We're not tied to Stonecut. We can go wherever we want."

"We can be whatever we want, right Dina?" There's a hollowness in her voice. We both know that's not true. We are how we were made.

There's that saying from Aristotle—give me a child until he is seven, and I'll show you the man. Not true for Rory and me. My destiny was written in my genes, Rory's in the chemical bath she somehow survived, asleep in her mother's belly. Some paths have never existed for us, and wishing won't make it so. For Rory and me, what we are is we what we can overcome.

"If you want it, I'll do anything to make it happen," I swear to her.

"I want you to fall in love and find a place that's full of people like you so you don't have to be alone all the time."

She's getting lost in her pink clouds. She hasn't done this in a while. Not since she left Stonecut. I usually yank her right back down to Earth, but maybe this once—

"People like me?"

"Fairy godsisters."

That's what she used to call me when she was little.

"And I'll marry a prince?"

She laughs. "Oh, no. Not you. You'd be so bored with a prince."

"The evil villain then?"

"You wouldn't tolerate the evil."

"So who would I marry then?"

There's a second's pause. "The dragon. High in his mountain cave, guarding his treasure, breathing fire on everyone. You'll flit into his lair and drive him nuts, rummaging around in his booty."

"Wouldn't he just eat me?"

"No. He'll see your true self, and he'll know you're a treasure worth more than all his gold and jewels." Rory's voice is breathy. I bet her eyes are hazy like when I'd read her Hans Christian Andersen and Charles Perrault on the bus.

"What if I don't want a dragon?"

"Then you can steal a sword and suit of armor and ride him off into the sunset to rescue damsels yourself."

"I like this story better."

She's quiet again. This time longer. "You know you don't need to rescue me, right Dina? I'm okay."

"I know."

"I'm tougher than you think. I've got a job. Things are coming together."

There's a lump in my throat, and I don't know what to say.

"I'm happy you left Stonecut, too. We're finally living our lives. No one knows us out here. We can be whoever we want. Right?"

"Yeah." My eyes are scratchy. "I have to go now."

"Are you going out with your new man?"

I stare at the high stucco ceiling and listen to the rush of the air conditioning in the silence. "Yeah. We're going to go out dancing."

"Until your soles wear out?"

"Of course."

"I love you, fairy godsister."

"I love you, Rory Evans. I might be busy tomorrow. Don't worry if I don't log on to *Elfin Odyssey* until late."

"I won't. Night," she whispers.

"Night," I whisper back.

6

HEAVY

Dina will be fine on her own for a while. She ain't goin' anywhere. She's committed to her little revenge fantasy, and judging from her expression in the lobby, she's not gonna be keen on exploring.

I head back downstairs. I'll check in with Forty, play a few spins of roulette. Can't say I'm feeling lucky, but I needed to get out of that room. It was getting too close in there. The air was gettin' to me.

Dina does not have the scent of a woman. Women smell like hairspray and perfume and fancy coffee, and if they've gotten a little ripe, they smell like pussy and sweat. I love how women smell. But Dina—

Best I can describe is she smells like outside. Wind. Sunshine. Musk. Like an early morning ride in spring, the dew and the chill and the bracing scent that gives you that rising, expansive feeling in your belly, the one you get when you're all alone and the world is new. That illusion.

She's not much to look at. Tiny titties. No meat. Her hair's a pretty enough color, but it's too short. Her lips don't pout. Her legs are slender. Nice. But they don't draw the eye.

I like tits and ass and swagger. I like a woman to toss her hair like a stripper. Long fingernails, tight skirts, everything hanging out. I like the shit that got the girls in trouble back in high school. Bellies, boobs, and butts. I'm a simple man. I appreciate simple things.

Dina ain't simple. She's not sexy. There's no logical explanation for why it takes the entire elevator ride for my dick to deflate.

I don't think about women. Unless, like Nevaeh Ellis, they're a problem. And I sure as shit don't ponder how Nevaeh smells. Probably like Jager bombs and bad decisions. Which reminds me. I dial Forty as I make my way across the vast lobby to the casino.

"Any news?" I ask when he answers. He's panting hard.

"None."

"You running a marathon?" He's really out of breath.

"Naw. Choppin' down a fence."

I do a little math. "At one o'clock in the morning?"

"I wasn't doin' nothin' else."

Fair enough. "Maybe we need to go back to the drawing board. Come at Knocker from a different angle."

There's the crack of splitting wood. "I don't know. Since we've been beating the bushes for the Raiders, they've been quiet. It's a decent stop gap until we have a next move."

"How's Patonquin?"

"Fine. Charge ran up there earlier to check on things. No problems except the usual."

"Cost overruns, lazy sons of bitches, and shoddy materials?"

"Check, check, and check."

"I love construction."

"Ain't got nothin' on demo work." There's another crack. "So you're in Vegas?"

"Yeah. Harper caught you up to speed?"

"She did. Me and Pig Iron. You're fuckin' insane, man."

"You think I should have called chaos?" That's our code for an execution, a double tap to the back of the head. Chaos was a dude we caught spying for the Raiders way back in the day. As I recall, we buried him under a blue spruce.

"Hell, no!" His voice raises, incredulous. "What's wrong with you? Give her back to Wall. Have him handle his damn sister. Chaos? *Jesus Christ.*"

I agree with him, but I argue—as a thought experiment. "She's a liability."

"The *lifestyle* is a liability. We don't do that kind of shit."

"She knows everything."

"You think she's gonna put a needle in her own brother's arm? And that she'd come to us beforehand? Give us a heads up? It don't make no sense, man. She's got some kind of issues, right?"

"Autistic." Probably Aspergers if that were still a diagnosis.

"Okay, autistic. And she's what? Early twenties? Some kind of hacker genius who lives in her parent's basement? And calling chaos is your first inclination? You've got to see how that's all kinds of fucked up."

"She's a time bomb. If she's nuts enough to come to us with this revenge scheme, she's nuts enough to turn state's evidence."

"She's Wall's *sister*. She *is* us. And what's her motivation for destroying her big brother's MC? She sounds like she's in trouble, and she doesn't know where else to turn."

There's a rawness in his voice. A rasp. Pain. I know Forty Nowicki like I know my shadow. His dad was my dad's VP, just like he's mine. My mama let him suck at her tit when his mom got too wasted. We learned everything together—crashing bikes, flaming out with older chicks, puking our guts out before we learned to put liquor before beer.

I know Forty Nowicki, and he might be talking about Dina, but he's thinking about Nevaeh Ellis. That bitch is poison. She acts all flighty. Vulnerable. But the instant she doesn't get her way, she burns everything down and strolls away. We watched her do it when Forty left for basic training. If he lets her in, she'll do it again. A twist is a twist.

I can hear the thwack of ax on wood through the phone, and Forty's ragged breath. "What did Nevaeh do now, brother?"

"Nothing. She's fine." There's a loud crack, a sharp grunt, and then Forty mutters, "Fuck. Splinter."

"I can always have Harper and Annie run her off again."

"You do that, I'll kill you." His voice is a snarl—as serious as I've ever heard him. He's a goner. She's got her claws in him again but good. Last time, there almost weren't pieces to pick up. How can he be so blind?

"It's your call, brother."

"Yeah. It is."

"And Dina Wall is mine."

There's a pregnant pause. That didn't come out how I meant it.

"I mean I will handle this situation as I see fit. Harper thinks getting hitched will give us enough cover until we can get some leverage on the girl."

Forty snorts. "It's like that game, ain't it? Kiss, kill, or marry."

"It's not a game."

There's another long silence. "No. It ain't. You hurt John Wall's baby sister, you'll destroy this club. You can't take the easy way out anymore." He lets out a wry laugh. "You're in deep shit, my brother."

"I can handle Dina Wall, and she's gonna deliver Wade and Anderson to us trussed up like Christmas turkeys."

"No doubt." He doesn't sound convinced.

"How much trouble can one woman be?"

He laughs. "You just might find out." There's a thunk.

"I'll let you get back to your home improvements."

"I'll call if there's news. Congrats on the shotgun wedding. Give my regards to the old lady."

I pity him for a minute, outside his own house in the middle of the night, taking his frustrations out on a fence, run ragged by a woman.

Until I sit down at the roulette table and yawn.

AFTER A FEW SPINS, I check my messages—the Ukrainians want a meet and our guy in the Renelli organization is picking up a disturbance in the force. We're good with our Italian neighbors, but instability in Pyle would bring federal attention to our neck of the woods, and that we do not need. I'll call him back tomorrow. After the wedding.

Never thought I'd live to think those words.

I'm heading toward the slot machines when a gruff and boozy holler rings out.

"Mr. President!"

Oh, hell no. It's not possible.

And then a cigarette-ravaged voice begins to bellow the wedding march. "Duh duh duh-duh duh duh duh duh duh duh duh." Somewhere along the line it turns into "Pomp and Circumstance."

I turn.

Rolling towards me is a motley crew of old timers in varying degrees of drunkenness, whooping loud enough to echo off the gilded vault ceiling.

Grinder's the singer. Boots is the one calling my name. They've recruited a prospect—Bush—to push his wheelchair. Gus follows along, bashful, the most dignified of this merry band of idiots.

Excepting the prospect, they've got more gray hair, gin blossoms, and paunch between them than a pack of mall Santas, and to a man, they're righteously drunk. How the hell did TSA let them on a flight?

I stroll to meet them before security gets called. They're wearing their cuts, and even pushing seventy, they got the look of men who never did learn to act right.

There's a general back clapping and hooting before they simmer down enough to let me get a word in edgewise.

"What are doin' here, my brothers?" I direct the question to Boots. Oddly enough, he's most likely the brains of this particular operation.

"You think we'd let you get hitched without a proper bachelor party? Never let it be said that the president and CEO of the Steel Bones Motorcycle Club bought the cow, and he didn't go down smellin' of pussy and tequila!"

"Pus-sy!" the prospect echoes, cupping his hands around his mouth. Guess he's the hype man.

"How did you, uh, know I was here?"

"Deb."

Deb was not looped in, but I should have known. Two men can keep a secret if one is dead, and I don't think even that holds true for an MC. The airline charges probably triggered a credit card alert. Deb would've gone to Pig Iron. As an officer, he knows the basics. He would've told her to keep it on the down low, but Deb does what she wants.

That means it's a matter of time before Wall knows that I have his sister. Hopefully, he'll hesitate before trying to kill his brother-in-law.

In the meantime, I ain't got nothing to do until the ceremony booked for tomorrow afternoon. And someone did say pussy and tequila.

"So, bachelor party, eh?"

The cacophony that four old men can make in a space the size of the Cow Palace is quite remarkable. Grinder passes me a flask as we roll Boots toward the exit. They've got a white stretch limo waiting.

"We didn't have time to pick up women," Grinder apologizes.

Boots waves him off. "We'll get 'em where we're going."

"Where're we goin'?" Bush's eyes are shining. I don't know if the kid's left Pennsylvania before. My guess would be no. He's related to Big George somehow, and his people are townies from way back.

"I don't know, man. Wherever the president wants. What do you say, Heavy?" Boots swings his stumps into a seat, swatting as Bush tries to help. "What's that famous place called?"

Boots looks to Gus. Gus shrugs.

"The Peppermint Pig? The Happy Hippopotamus?" Boots screws up his wrinkled moon face, thinkin' hard. "You know, it's a name for when a chick's face is too busted to bang?"

"Double-bagger?" Gus suggests.

"Cleveland Brown?" Bush tosses over his shoulder as he scavenges in the bar and then flips us all a miniature.

"Ain't no chick with a face too busted to bang," Grinder opines. Bush scoffs at that as he fusses with his shiny boy band hair, and Grinder takes umbrage.

"You ain't gonna be a hot shot forever, young blood. The time will come that you look like Gus here. He was pretty, too, back in the day. Bitches lined up for miles."

Guy flashes a wan smile. He's always been a melancholy dude, as long as I can remember. His skin's sallow, and he's got a gut and rubbery arms, but you can tell that back in the day, he would have pulled the pussy. He's got the cut jaw and the imposing frame. Life broke him back before I was born.

"What happened, Gus?" the prospect asks.

Gus sniffs and snags the cigarette from behind his ear. "Heroin," he says. "And then the hepatitis."

"Shit." Bush drags out the word.

"You've been sober, what, twenty years now?" Grinder says.

"Almost." Gus nods. He flicks his Bic and the limo fills with the scent of Marlboro Reds, the smell of my childhood. I relax against the plush upholstery and down my tiny vodka.

"Prospect." I snap. He tosses me another nip.

Gus recently reconnected with the kid he had back when he was using. The guy's my age. Adam Wade. Des Wade's cousin. By adoption, not blood. Still, quite the coincidence. It's a small world.

You'd think having his son back in his life would give Gus a reason to smile, but he's even more down in the mouth. Maybe it's easier to live without than with the reminder of all you lost.

No matter that the guy was raised with a silver spoon, blood tells. No sooner than Adam Wade came around, he was brawling in the parking lot of The White Van and banging a sweetbutt, my girl Jo-Beth. They're shacked up now. I wish them well.

When I've got the itch, I ain't particular about which

club whore rides my dick, but somehow Jo-Beth and I always ended up playing cards instead of fucking. She's got an uncommonly sharp mind for a woman who's paid the bills on her knees. Adam Wade better watch himself. Jo-Beth's a survivor. No matter what position she's in, she'll come out on top.

What would Jo-Beth think of Dina Wall? On the surface, they're nothing alike, but there's a practicality to the both of them. A defensive stance that suggests the world's been against them since day one. I suppose, in a way, it has.

What's Dina doing now, all by herself in the suite? She'll be fine. She has her phone. She probably needs some peace and quiet.

Is she in bed with her top off still? Maybe she's playing with those little titties with the sweet berry nipples, sliding her fingers under the waistband of those sweatpants to rub her stiff, pouty clit. Maybe when I get back, the room will reek like a woman's cum.

I cough to clear my throat and shift in the seat, yanking at my britches. I'm hard enough to pound nails. It doesn't make sense. She's skinny. And kind of cantankerous. She don't scream "sex." More like "feed me a damn sandwich."

I'd like to feed her. Stuff her with steak and potatoes until she's got a food baby in that smooth tummy, pop that belly button, and then lay her on the bed, kneel beside her, and jack my seed into her pretty bow mouth, watching her lick every last drop with her pointy pink tongue.

She'd be into it. Like back at the clubhouse. Totally lost in her own experience. Using me for my body.

For having such a distinctive physicality, that's not what people use me for. Protection. A livelihood. Power. Status. Making the hard calls, doing the hard shit. The rush of sidling up next to a killer. I'm everything to everyone.

There's something to be said for being Dina Wall's cheap thrill.

I snort and sigh, and then I roll down the window. Gus flashes me a guilty look and exhales in the direction of the cracked moonroof.

Bush refreshes our drinks, and I polish off a whiskey as Boots and Grinder argue about where we're going. Boots is stuck on remembering the names of The Spearmint Rhino and Coyote Ugly. I'm not gonna help. It's too damn funny listening to him.

"Dude," Boots calls up to the driver. "What's the strip joint named after an animal?"

"The Bald Beaver?"

"No. Bigger critter. Like you'd see on one of them safaris."

"The Pink Elephant?"

"No. Smaller. I think." Boots' wrinkled face squishes as he ponders the relative size of an elephant and a rhinoceros.

"Is it a land animal or a water animal?" The driver's holding his cell to his mouth like he's about to ask Siri.

"If I knew that, man, I wouldn't be asking."

I've got to remember to tip the man well.

All of a sudden, Grinder is struck by inspiration. "Oh! I know the place. Driver, you heard of the Velvet Box?"

"Sure, man, sure. That's a classic." He turns his blinker on and pulls into the turn lane.

"Oh, that joint was the best," Grinder crows. "The choicest pussy. High class. We found it when we came though in '75? '76?"

"The place we saw Mitch Ryder passed out in a corner booth?" Boots' voice rises in excitement. "That was '76. On the way to Sturgis."

"Who's Mitch Ryder?" Bush asks.

"Boy, you don't even know," Boots cackles.

Sorry to say, I don't either.

I shoot another miniature. Scotch. I'm finally feeling the warmth in my gut. It's been a hot minute since I tied one on. I stretch my legs down the center aisle, relaxing. How long has it been since I relaxed? Longer than a hot minute.

"How is Nevada on the way to South Dakota?" I ask.

Boots' forehead creases. "Could have been on the way *back* from Sturgis. I don't know. It was the seventies."

I don't bother pointing out that neither makes any geographical sense. With Boots, reality has a more impressionistic quality.

"Was that where we found Charge's mom?" Grinder muses.

"No, we picked her up by the side of Route 66. Outside Barstow." Boots is certain about this. "And that was in '93. Or '95?"

"Fine woman." Grinder raises his miniature.

"The best." Boots clinks his bottle.

"Where did she end up?" I ask more out of habit than expectation that I'll get a straight answer. I've been after this story for years.

Charge has never cared, but there's something in me that abhors a mystery. The old timers will spin tales for as long as someone's listening, but they're always vague as hell about the woman who gave birth to Charge and left him with a one-legged vet who made his money selling weed and tackle.

I'm expecting the run around I always get, but Boots and Grinder must be more wasted than they appear because they exchange a glance. Grinder drops his empty miniature to the ground and takes out a fifth of SoCo he had stashed somewhere under his cut. He takes a long swig and exhales long and gustily.

"Berkeley, wasn't it?" He looks to Boots.

"I don't know, man. She was all over for a while, but she did eventually go back to where she came from."

"What did she say she does?" Grinder asks.

"Professor." Boots almost looks proud.

"Charge's mom is a professor at Berkeley?" I'd think they were bullshitting me, but there's no way Grinder or Boots would've heard of Berkeley otherwise.

"Yeah. She's done well for herself." Boots grins. "She got a husband, and kids, and grandkids and all that."

"You talk to her?" I had no idea. No one did. Except, I guess, the other old timers.

"She disappeared for a while, but for some time now, she's been calling every so often. Around Christmas. Charge's birthday."

"You never said." Charge would have mentioned it. As far as he knew, she was in the wind.

"She didn't want me to say nothin'. I think she's comin' around, though. She's been talkin' about flying out for a weekend."

"Yeah?" Grinder grins. "Tell her to leave the husband at home."

Both men cackle, and then they grow quiet, dopy smiles lingering on their wrinkled faces.

"Most beautiful woman I ever seen," Grinder sighs. "Before or since."

"Amen." Boots nods.

"Why did she leave?" I ask.

The smiles fade. "Well, she didn't want to see him every day, right?" Boots says as if this makes sense.

"Who? Charge?"

"Yeah. She didn't want him. But you know, she was Catholic, and she was only, what, sixteen?" Boots looks to Grinder. He nods.

"You knocked up a sixteen-year-old?" Times were different, and the club was all about the free love, but my dad wouldn't have countenanced that shit. Not for a minute.

"Nah. She came knocked up. That's why she was on the road." Boots' mouth turns down at the corners. "They did a number on her."

"Who did?"

"You tell it, Grinder." The wrinkles on Boots' forehead deepen, a rare look of sadness blanking the sparkle in his rheumy eyes.

Grinder hacks, clearing his throat. Bush leans forward. "She came from money, right? She wasn't a hippie or nothin'. She came from Yorba Linda."

"Nixon was from Yorba Linda," Gus pipes up. He'd been quiet, but he's riveted, too.

"She went to some prep school with a bunch of other rich kids. At some party, she drank too much. Passed out. She woke up with an asshole holding her down." Grinder's grizzled jaw is clenched.

The truth settles on my chest. Another weight to carry. "Charge doesn't need to know that."

"I didn't think he did," Boots says. "It's why I never told him. But now—I don't know. Jimmy came about in much the same way."

Jimmy is his old lady's son. Charge is set to adopt him. Harper's handling the paperwork, and it's almost a done deal. On occasion, Charge brings up hiring an investigator. Find the degenerates who hurt Kayla. I put him off. Convince him there's no way to track down the perps so many years after the fact. I ask him if this is what Kayla wants, or if it's him—his pride talking.

He drops it. But to be honest, I have a decent shot of finding the men. This happened in Gracy's Corner, seven or eight years ago. People don't move around in our neck of the woods. And people talk. The kind of bastards who'd hurt a girl her age? They end up with records. They're probably in the system by now. A good PI could run 'em down.

But then I'd have to let Charge kill Jimmy's father.

It's so easy to justify. The man's a rapist, not a father. And that's the truth. Maybe that's how Jimmy would see it if he ever found out. Maybe Charge's conscience would never feel the slightest twinge, and Kayla would finally get closure.

Or maybe that's the kind of poison that eats away the edges of people, rots relationships from the inside.

Of course, I could find the man and kill him. Never let Charge know. Add the bastard to my burden. No vengeance for Charge. No closure for Kayla. Just another tree on a mountain top. The air in the world would be a little clearer.

And if every time I look at Jimmy, in the back of my mind, a voice whispers, "I killed your father," it'll just be another voice in the chorus.

I don't regret a single life I've taken. I don't feel guilt. I have always done what has to be done, no more, no less.

But more and more these days, I am tired. So I put Charge off. I let one of the hard things remain undone.

I focus back on the conversation. "I thought she was a wild child. Banged her way through the whole club." When the old timers get to waxing reminiscent, that's the story they tell.

"She did." Grinder nods. "I think she was tryin' to wash the taste of that asshole out of her mouth. Or forget. Women don't ever act the way you expect they would. They got their own reasons. If you're gettin' married, best remember that."

"Ernestine never fails to put your ass out when you wander away from the ranch."

Grinder puts up his hands and smirks. "My mistake, Mr. President. You're the expert on old ladies."

They all bust out laughing. Even the prospect. I lift a shoulder, happy I can amuse them.

Soon enough, the atmosphere goes somber again. There's a silence filled with the thick scent of cigarettes and spirits, and then Boots speaks up.

"She was gonna take care of it. I drove her to the clinic up in Pyle. We sat in the truck a long time, her fiddlin' with that crucifix she wore. I told her if she didn't want to do it, she could leave the baby with me. Kids runnin' everywhere back in those days. What's one more, you know?"

"So she just left the baby with you?"

"Ayup." Boots smiles, remembering. "He was easy. And when I had the inclination to go for a ride, there was always a sweetbutt who'd watch him for some bud."

"It's a miracle he survived to adulthood." I remember my mom—before she got sick—always chasing Charge into the shower or feeding him. She called him the feral child.

"He had his brothers. He was fine." Boots slaps my knee, gently, and leaves his gnarled hand there a moment. "You know you can set the weight down, boy. You got brothers, too. You ain't alone. You never been."

His smile is crooked and gap-toothed, and there's that odd light in his eyes again. "You got all these plots and machinations. All these high falutin' ideas about vengeance and justice. That ain't it, boy."

"Then what is?"

"Pussy, beer, and the open road."

There's a murmuring of assent like in church.

"Don't make shit complicated." The limo rolls to a stop, and Boots gives my leg a final squeeze. "Seize the day."

"Carpe diem?" I open the door before the driver alights and unfold my legs. They're killing me.

"Gesundheit." Boots winks and tips back a bottle.

"Gentlemen," the driver announces. "The Velvet Box!"

FIFTEEN MINUTES LATER, after wrestling the wheelchair out of the trunk, searching the seat cracks for Gus' lighter, and listening to Grinder have a conversation with Ernestine at top volume about where he left the registration to the Buick, we stride into the hottest night spot in Vegas—in 1976.

First impression is that it smells like boiled eggs.

Bush breaks the silence. "Where's the pussy?"

It's obvious that at one time, the flocked wallpaper was crimson, as were the leather booths. Now, everything's a faded liver brown. There's a parquet dance floor—empty and sagging toward the middle—and the mirror behind the bar is smoky with age.

There are a few dudes scattered around drinking alone and an older couple at a table, ignoring each other, noses in their phones. Elvis is playing on the grainy sound system. "Love Me Tender."

No one looked up when we entered. Not even the bartender. He's slowly wiping down the counter with shaky hands, hunched over, vacant eyes downcast.

"Is that Mitch Ryder?" I jerk my chin at the portly man slumped on his side, passed out in the corner booth.

No one bothers to tell me to fuck off. The dejection, the faded splendor, the crestfallen expressions of my brothers—

it shouldn't make my lips twitch, but I'm swallowing down the chuckle.

This is probably the farthest afield Boots has gone since he lost his second leg to the diabetes. And lord knows Ernestine keeps Grinder on a tight leash when she lets him come home. Bush finally crosses the state line, and this is where he ends up. Poor bastard.

I clap the prospect on the back. He doesn't have time to brace himself, so he staggers a step before he catches himself.

"I'll call the limo," I say. "We'll go to the Spearmint Rhino."

"The what? No." Boots shakes his head. "I don't want to drive around all night."

"I ain't standin' around with my dick in my hand for another hour while y'all try to figure out that wheelchair," Grinder declares.

If they'd let me do it, it wouldn't take a second, but they'd rather make the prospect do it.

Gus just grunts and shuffles off for the bar. I guess we're hanging out at the Velvet Box.

Four rounds of shots later, we cram ourselves into a round corner booth opposite the big fella passed out and slowly but inexorably sliding under the table. There's a bottle of tequila between us, and the bartender has instructions to bring whiskey once we've gotten to the bottom. At the rate we're goin', he may as well be heading over now.

"Twenty bucks he hits the ground in twenty minutes." Grinder gestures at our unconscious compatriot.

"I'll take that action." Boots casts up his eyes in concentration. "I say fifteen."

"I say 'til closing," Gus says. When there's a general scoffing, he adds, "Lot of mass on that dude. Object at rest tends to stay at rest."

"Two hours." I split the difference. Gus has a point, but the slow slippage suggests gravity's working against the man.

We're all silent for a while, contemplating our bets. I let the ease sink into my bones. The old timers make good company. They ain't tryin' to impress me like the young bloods, and we ain't got business like I do with Forty and the others in the inner circle. Nothing to talk about but glory days, football, and bullshit.

A rare peacefulness settles in my chest along with the burn of the liquor.

"So why you gettin' married?" Grinder finally asks as if the question has only just occurred to him. "You knock her up?"

"Who you marryin' anyway?" Boots adds. The floodgates open. "And where'd you meet a woman?"

"There're women everywhere," I point out. "Half the population."

"You ain't never even had an old lady." Grinder shakes his head. "And you gettin' married? That's a step not to be taken lightly."

"Are you and Ernestine married?" I'm realizing I have no idea. I don't remember a wedding, but it could've been before I was born. Neither wear a ring, but with the number of times she's put him out, that might be out of convenience. There are tons of pictures hanging in Ernestine's house. None that I recall with her in a white dress, but that doesn't mean anything. Biker weddings don't tend to be traditional.

Grinder's mouth turns down. "Common law. Yeah."

"You mean you and Ernestine ain't married?" This seems to be news to Boots, too.

"I said common law, didn't I? We file our taxes as married." Grinder goes to pour himself another shot, but he fumbles, and tequila sloshes onto the table. "And we're gettin' off topic. This is about Heavy."

"So who is she? Danielle finally wear you down?" Boots asks.

Danielle's been trying her hand since high school. I indulge her when I've got the urge, but I never let her think it's anything it's not.

"No. You don't know her."

"She knocked up then?" Grinder grimaces in sympathy.

"No. It's, uh—" How do I explain this? We're brothers, but I didn't bust my ass for the past decade making us legitimate to implicate the old timers in murder and conspiracy. "It's a marriage of convenience."

"Oh, son." Grinder shakes his head. "Marriage ain't convenient."

"What's that mean? Sweetbutts ain't cleanin' your place like you want? Get a house mouse." Boots elbows the prospect—who's all ears—to pour him another shot.

"Like you got Shirlene?" Grinder snorts.

Boots' face blazes red. "If Twitch was alive, he'd crack your skull with that bottle and piss in the hole."

Grinder raises his hands. "If Twitch was alive, he'd crack your skull for letting his old lady do your washing."

"You cain't tell that woman what she can and cannot do." Boots' fingers are shaking.

It's known he has a thing for Shirlene, but he'd never disrespect a brother like that, especially since despite the years, the loss of Twitch still lingers over every ride, every picnic, every church meeting. Twitch was truly a great man. Served his country. Worked his fingers to the bone. Rode until the cancer broke him. They don't make his kind no more.

Since he passed, Shirlene watches out for the older brothers. Boots ain't got a chance in hell. That woman's heart was buried with her old man. She's passing time, waiting for him.

I can see it with my eyes—you'd have to be blind and incapable of feeling not to—but I cannot fathom that devotion. Not sure there's any other word for it.

I'm devoted to this club. My brothers. Family. The people who rely on me to make it right.

But a woman?

My mother was a fine old lady. She had dinner on the table by six every night—and for some reason, two o'clock on Sundays—and she kept us kids clean and clothed. She turned a blind eye to my dad's indiscretions, and when we were real young, she cut loose at the clubhouse on occasion.

She was the daughter of a deacon, and she kept a foot in both worlds. Ignored Dad's ranting and snuck all three of us to St. Alban's to be baptized and had "Slip" tattooed over her heart.

She was a good woman, but I've never wanted what they had. Muffled tears behind a locked bathroom door. Sharp words when Dad stumbled in late at night. Bacon and fresh squeezed orange juice in the morning. Dad, red-eyed and reeking of beer and piss, puking in the upstairs bathroom from the smell. And then the hell when she got sick, and he gave up, and then they were both gone.

"So why you marrying this mystery woman?" Grinder asks, breaking the broody silence we'd lapsed into.

"Her name's Dina. She's Wall's little sister."

"The one that just got lost?"

"She wasn't lost."

"She ends up with you in Vegas, she got lost." Grinder snickers. "Wall know you're marrying his sister?"

"Not yet."

"So's this your way of saving yourself a beating for fuckin' his little sister?" Boots lifts a bushy gray eyebrow. "Plan's doomed to fail. You're in for an ass kickin'."

"Heavy could take Wall any day," Gus says. "No doubt."

"Now I don't know about that." Grinder leans back and surveys me like I'm cattle stock. "Wall's got more muscle mass."

Gus scoffs. "Definition ain't mass. Heavy has the weight and height advantage."

Grinder rolls his eyes. "Two inches. Not enough to matter."

"That what Ernestine says?" Boot quips and Bush chokes on his drink. Grinder slaps the side of the prospect's head.

"All I'm sayin' is that motivation counts. And our illustrious president has apparently lured Wall's innocent little sister into the lifestyle. Got her to run away from home. Done dirty things to her." Grinder folds his arms decisively and rests them on his gut. "He's gettin' his ass kicked, and in my opinion, so be it."

"She's of legal age," I point out.

"She was still livin' at home. If you did my Jennifer like that, I'd kill you," Grinder declares.

I don't point out that his granddaughter's been begging rides off the younger brothers since she was in junior high. Both kinds. No one would take her up on the offer, but that doesn't stop her from putting it out there.

"Dina is twenty-four." I catch the bartender's eye and raise a brow. We've polished off the bottle. Bush's squinting in the hole, looking for the worm. "No worm in tequila," I tell him. "That's cheap Mezcal."

Dude's face falls.

"If she's twenty-four, why you marrying her?" Grinder's like a dog with a bone now.

"He knocked her up," Gus says.

"I didn't knock her up."

Grinder ignores me completely. "She probably made him swear to keep it secret 'til they was hitched. Wall's people are church folk."

There are so many holes in the theory, but it'll do. I blank my face. "No comment."

"That's it! He knocked her up!" My brothers hoot and holler and bang the table. "Barkeep! A round on the house! To the next generation!" Howls echo off the stained ceiling.

Across the way, the portly gentleman startles awake and crashes to the floor, knocking the table sideways.

"Forty-two minutes. I'm closest. Pay up." Grinder holds out his palm.

Boots left his wallet in Petty's Mill, Bush has no cash, and Gus has a five with a rip down the middle. I pass Grinder a hundred. He snaps it and holds it up to the light. It's worth the extra not to hear him bitch for the rest of the night.

"We're high rollin' now, ain't we?" he crows.

"We are." The bartender shuffles over with another bottle, and I settle in, resting my arms along the back of the booth.

For the next few hours until close, my brothers reminisce about the old times, way back when they were boys and the steel mill was still open, the blast furnace coating the town with red dust. They talk about the war—which means Vietnam for

Boots and Grinder, Desert Storm for Gus—and the club before the blown job, running cigarettes into New York, breaking kneecaps for the Renellis when they needed extra men.

Funny tales of fuck ups and near misses that have Bush wheezing, tears streaking down his cheeks. And then, as they always do, the stories turn dark, the losses tallied, the opposite of counting coup. The mill closing. The men done in by drink and bad luck. Crashes, cancer, incarceration, mesothelioma.

And then we get to the blown job. Our original sin.

Heads hang. Shake. Through all of it that came before, brotherhood was inviolable. Until the night the cops pulled a truck over on the shoulder of Route 29.

And then comes the heroic song. The old king's son returns from afar, bringing light back to the kingdom. A knight sacrifices everything for his princess. Lost loves are found. The enemy is rendered toothless. Prosperity reigns.

We are in the happy ever after.

I am victorious. I've saved my brothers. The arduous journey is at an end. I should exhale and enjoy the spoils.

But instead I scour the internet and pin clippings to my wall, tied together with the web of red yarn.

I should be at peace, but I am weary. And alone.

And drunk as fuck.

When the lights come up, I stagger to my feet, grateful to see the driver making his way over. I don't know if I can make it to the limo under my own steam, and if I fall on an old timer, I'll kill him.

I sling an arm over Bush on one side and the driver on the other and force my legs to take my weight.

I puke before I get in the back while Boots hollers, "What's open after hours? I wanna see some titties!"

"I wanna go home," I slur. "Dina—" Then my head hits the minibar, and I black out.

When I wake up, it's daylight and Bush is tripping over my prone form as he piles into the backseat reeking of women's perfume and weed. I'm half on a seat, half in the limo's narrow aisle. My face is plastered to cold white leather.

"What time is it?" I rasp. My mouth tastes like a dirty sponge.

"Time to get hitched!" Boots caws from the front. "Drive on, my dude!" He slaps the dashboard, and I belch pure tequila and stomach acid.

When she gets a gander at us, Dina's gonna run for the hills.

That'd be for the best.

This whole thing is insane.

Bright sunlight streams through the moonroof. I screw my eyes shut and pass out again as the limo pulls onto the Strip.

7

DINA

I'm not a morning person, and it doesn't matter what time I actually wake up. Until I have my coffee and stare into the middle distance for a while, I'm no good. And my "good" is not great. Especially with strangers.

So when the door flies open and I'm jerked awake, I scream and leap onto the back of the sofa. I press my back to the wall and tuck tight. Fight and flight aren't an option, so my body goes for armadillo.

Five men spill into the room and then freeze mid-motion. They're the world's burliest, grizzliest, shaggiest superhero squad. Heavy's front and center, red-eyed, hair more tangled and wilder than I've seen it yet. There's a young guy. An old man in a wheelchair. Two other grandpas in leather vests, faded jeans, and shitkickers. They're all kind of listing to one side or the other as if their ships are sinking.

They're drunk.

And I'm not wearing pants. My T-shirt is bunched at my waist, and I'm showing my bare ass. If I unfold myself, I'm gonna show them all my bare front.

I need coffee.

"Why you up on the back of the sofa, girl?" the man in the wheelchair asks. He's the first to move, rolling forward. He's smiling. Duchenne. Very Duchenne.

"I got startled."

"Fell asleep on the sofa?" He stops by the coffee table.

"Yeah." It felt weird in the bed. I didn't know when Heavy was coming back or where he was going to sleep or what he expected to happen. I don't like uncertainty, so I got the spare blanket from the closet and slept in the living area.

"You're John's sister," he says, still smiling. He looks happy. The other men fall out. The older guys slump into chairs. The young guy staggers to the kitchenette and opens the fridge. Heavy stays where he is. I can't look at his face, but for some reason, I'm okay making eye contact with the guy in the wheelchair.

"I'm Boots," he says.

"Dina."

"I don't mean no disrespect, Dina, but I can see your ass."

"I know."

From behind, Heavy growls and stomps forward. He grabs the blanket and tosses it over me before lowering himself to the sofa. My gaze slides to him. It's easier to look at him in profile.

"So what you doin' up there?" Boots asks.

"I was startled."

He nods. "You're a little slip of a thing, ain't you?"

I hop down to sit on a cushion. I drape the blanket over my lap and sit cross-legged. "I need coffee."

"Right. Prospect!" he hollers over his shoulder. "Coffee!"

"Ahead of you, boss," the young guy says. He's rummaging in the cabinets now.

"You should know, before you get mad, we kept him out," the guy with the big gut says. "He didn't even go into the titty bar. He was passed out by that point."

"Why would I be mad?"

The older guys exchange a look I can't read.

"All right, girl," Boots says. "All right."

I don't get it. "Why would I be mad if Heavy went to a titty bar?"

"You shouldn't," the guy with the gut says with emphasis. "Ain't no reason to be difficult if he's comin' home to you."

Now I'm really confused. "I'm not difficult. I just need some coffee. I'll make it myself." I don't know what the guy in the kitchen is doing, but I don't hear anything percolating. I stand, and the blanket falls, I guess a few seconds quicker than my shirt.

Boots sucks in a breath, and the two other guys make strange noises.

"Did she just flash her pussy?" Heavy grumbles. His head is in his hand, propped on the sofa arm.

"Ayup," Boots says. "I like her."

There's a general hum of agreement.

"Don't look at my old lady's pussy," Heavy says, and the others rush to assure him they didn't, they didn't mean to, they hardly saw anything.

I can't even. I need coffee, and I need no one to say anything for a good half hour.

I elbow past the dude still pawing through the kitchen cabinets and make myself a cup using the single serve machine. The others can fend for themselves.

When my mug is filled, I take it into the bedroom. It's almost noon. Neither Rory nor I ended up able to fall asleep, so we met up in *Elfin Quest* with this centaur we hook up with sometimes. We finally got to the Silver City before the centaur had to go to work. He lives in the Philippines.

I plop on the side of the bed, sip my weak brew, and stare out the window at the city. The sky is bright, bright blue, not a single cloud. Between where I sit and the low, brown mountains in the distance are a cacophony of build-ings—gold windows, black pyramids, red and blue turrets, fountains spraying plumes from the middle of sapphire blue fountains.

It's busy and bold, but the room is cool and quiet, so I can let it all slowly sift in.

I'm not in Stonecut County anymore. I left all on my own. I got myself to Petty's Mill, and I snuck into an MC clubhouse and blackmailed the president. I got locked in a closet, and afterward, I let a man finger me, and I came for the first time from someone else's touch. I liked it. More than liked it. Now I'm in Las Vegas, and I'm okay.

Not great. My tummy is tender from whatever the stress is doing to my guts, and my mind's not the clearest. But I'm fine.

I've always known that if I *have* to, I can do anything. But there's a difference between knowing you can and actually doing it.

I'm doing it.

The door creaks open. I hope it's Heavy. I want to ask him if we can ride the roller coaster I can see a few blocks away before we get married. Or after. Whichever. I love rides. I made my parents take me to the carnival every year even though I'd inevitably have a meltdown from the crowds.

Heavy sits beside me and the mattress dips. He has two steaming white cups in his hands. It smells hella better than mine, but I still drain my paper cup before I take what he's offering.

"You got real coffee?"

"We sent the prospect downstairs for it."

"Is that the young guy?"

"Yeah, Bush."

"Who are the other ones? Besides Boots?"

"Grinder is the talker. Gus is the silent one."

"I didn't know they were coming."

"Me neither."

"They don't know about the plan, do they?" I'm sure they don't. Heavy's not foolish.

"No. They think we're getting married for real."

"They really believe that?"

"They figure you're knocked up."

"I'm on the pill."

There's a beat before Heavy replies. "And why's that?"

"To regulate my period. It used to come whenever. I hate inconsistency."

He makes a chuffing sound. "I can see how that'd be bothersome."

"If we were to have sex, we should also use a condom." I don't think I'd like latex inside me. I hate plastic cleaning gloves, the powdery sweaty feel and then the grossness when you peel them off. But condoms are smart. I can deal. I could pretend his dick is a dildo. Which is weird, but—

"Baby, you're gonna love my cum in your pussy." He makes an effort to give me a look, but with his bleary red eyes, it's less than convincing.

But it's an interesting question. Would I like the feel of cum inside me? Can you really even feel it? Is it warm? I guess it drips out. Maybe you feel it then.

"TBD." A thought occurs to me. "Do you have an STI?"

"Pardon?"

"You know. HPV, chlamydia, etcetera—"

"—Nope."

"How do you know?"

"No symptoms. Clean bill of health the last time I got tested."

"When was that?"

He sighs and shifts. "I've got the hangover from hell, baby. If we don't get rollin', we're gonna miss our appointment at the Office of Civil Marriages. Maybe we talk about this after?"

"So we don't have time to ride that roller coaster before we get married?" I point to the red single track that makes a full loop-de-loop.

He exhales, and then, out of nowhere, he laughs. It's deep and booming, and I can't help but peek at his face out of the corner of my eye. He looks a little pale under his beard, but he's smiling, and it has the look of a surprise about it.

"We can go after."

"Sweet." I hop up. "Dibs on the first shower."

I'm mid-step when he grabs my wrist. I glance down. His huge hand goes nearly halfway up my forearm.

"You weren't mad I stayed out all night?" he asks.

"No." Grinder said something about that, too. "Am I supposed to be?"

He slowly shakes his head. "No. I guess my ego's strong enough to recover from the blow."

That doesn't make any sense at all. I tug my arm. He doesn't let go.

"When we fuck, I ain't gonna hurt you. You can trust me on that."

"I think pain is unavoidable. I'm a virgin, and you're really big."

He chuckles. "See? Just like that, my ego's fine again." He tugs me back between his thick thighs and runs a rough palm over my bare hips. Shivers race through me, zinging up my spine and down to my toes. "You need to be sure."

"I'm sure." I want to know what it feels like, how good it can get. I've never been curious before, but he's—different. Here is different. I'm different.

He doesn't like my answer. His grip firms on my hips. "You need to think about it."

"I know what I want."

"You *think* you do."

He makes no sense. I gently but firmly peel his fingers away. "Heavy, you can't possibly know another person's mind better than they do."

He seizes my waist again. "I know the real world a far sight better than you do, little girl."

I pat his knee and tug myself loose again. "There's only one world. And we both live in it."

I leave him on the bed, staring at the city skyline I was just admiring. Bigger than life. All alone. A shadow in his eyes.

A feeling rises in my chest. I don't recognize it. It's warm, but barbed. Achy and a touch wild, but also full and sinking. I can't describe it, but when I turn my back to Heavy and close the bathroom door, it's still there, and it's still connected to him, a kind of emotional echolocation.

Strange.

This whole adventure is so very strange.

And I'm about to get married.

A LIMO DROPS us all off in front of a liver brown and glass windowed municipal building. I'm the first out.

The ride was only fifteen minutes, but the reek—sweet Lord. The guys are sweating last night's liquor out of their pores, and they've all got their distinctive scents as well. Gus has an eau de wet ashtray. Boots reeks of weed. Bush has doused himself in body spray, the kind that has no corollary in nature and has a name like "Epic Chill."

What does epic chill smell like? Sure as hell not the back of this limo. Cash used to wear that shit in high school. I wouldn't get in the car with him.

Grinder smells like hotel hand soap. But *a lot*.

Heavy smells fine. He had three breakfast burritos before we left, so there's a hint of bacon and jalapeno about his beard, but the leather of his SBMC vest overpowers it. All the men are wearing their cuts. I've seen John in his cut plenty of times, but it's different when there's a group, and it's a uniform. People gawk. They make way.

Heavy holds the door for me, and as we head for the elevator—the civil marriage office is on the sixth floor—the men surround me. Bush rolls Boots along by my side. Heavy leads. Grinder and Gus follow behind me. I feel short, but also almost like I'm floating in a lazy river. All I need to do is follow the current. The bombardment doesn't bother me so much—the fluorescent lights, the echoey hallway, the muffled voices behind doors, glimpses of cubicles behind glass, people brushing past, trailing perfume and coffee, corridors leading left and right—because I can let it wash through me. I don't have to *do* anything else, so it's tolerable.

We don't have to wait long when we get to the office. We stand in a cordoned line for maybe five minutes before they escort us into a room with a low tiled ceiling and beige carpet. There's a white picket arch and a mirror along one wall. The officiant, a woman in a navy pantsuit, asks the spouses to take their places.

I don't know what to do.

Grinder kind of pushes me forward, and Heavy takes my hand. We stand toe-to-toe in front of the arch.

I've got my arms crossed tight. They have the air conditioning blasting, and I've got goosebumps all over. I threw on an outfit we bought yesterday without a lot of thought. It's a red jersey wrap dress with short sleeves and a sash belt. It's soft, no tag, and no annoying seams. It's also really thin. My stiff nipples are totally visible through the fabric.

I shiver. Heavy grunts. Then he's shrugging off his cut.

"Here. Arms up."

I raise them, and he slides his soft leather biker vest onto my shoulders. In terms of size, it's ridiculous. It's like when I was a kid in scouts, and we had to make ponchos out of black trash bags. My arms are still bare and freezing, but my torso's warming up.

Heavy keeps a grip onto the lapels and sort of holds me to him. He leans over and says low so only I can hear, "We don't have to do this."

I tilt my head back and stand on tiptoes. He bends his shaggy head.

"We're already here," I whisper back. "And we paid the seventy bucks."

I figure that'll be it, but he tightens his grip on the vest, tugging me even closer. "We can walk out now," he says.

I don't get it. This was his idea. Spousal privilege and everything.

He's staring down at me intently. My eyes are glued on the collar of his faded black T-shirt. It says *Spank the Devil 'II*, and there's a graphic of a blonde pinup with a skeleton over her knee.

"It's no big deal," I say to the skeleton.

"It isn't," he answers, and I can't tell if it's a statement or a question. There's too much going on. Everything was fine, but now there's zipping and zooming inside me. Freezing air gusts from an overhead vent. Gus coughs.

On instinct, I rest my fingertips on Heavy's solid pecs. I'm not steadying myself. I'm not pushing him away. This isn't a big deal. We're not getting married for real. I've never even *thought* about getting married for real. That's for the far distant future. Or never.

I wish the officiant would just get on with it, but she's backed off a few steps, giving us space. I bet people chicken out all the time at the Office of Civil Marriage in Las Vegas.

Almost by accident, I look up and meet Heavy's eyes. They're dark and deep—like staring into a starless night in summer when the air's dense with humidity, thick and impenetrable.

His eyes don't bother me anymore. It doesn't scramble my signal. I can look my fill the same way I do with Rory and Cash and the rest of my family. But it's not at all the same. It's not comfortable. The contact is giving me a thrill, nimble fingers tripping up the keys on a piano, playing the scales up my spine. My breath shallows.

Why aren't we getting on with it? Is he having second thoughts?

"We don't have to do this if you don't want to," I tell him.

His lip quirks. "I know."

"It was your idea," I remind him.

"I suppose it was." His mouth curves into a bemused smile.

"We don't have to do this," I repeat.

I have no intention of going to the cops. Why would I? I'd implicate myself and set my brother up for a conspiracy charge. Maybe he thinks my conscience would bother me, or the guilt would drive me to confess a la "Tell-Tale Heart," but that's not how I'm made. My frequency is sensation, not emotion. I don't operate on feelings.

"We did pay that seventy bucks, didn't we?" he says.

"Yeah."

His eyes crinkle at the corners. And he leans closer and kisses me.

It's not quick. Not long. Firm. Prickly from his beard. It feels like a drop of dye in a glass of water, a burst of bright color and then a slow, mellow diffusion down my limbs to the tips of my toes and my fingers, still bracing against his chest.

He doesn't back up right away. He lingers, nose brushing my cheek to nestle behind my ear. Like he's smelling me.

"Why are you sniffing me?"

His laugh vibrates against my neck, and then he stands. "You smell good."

I do? I crane my neck, try to catch a whiff, but I don't smell anything. I guess in comparison to the other guys, "recently bathed" smells pretty damn good.

"Are we ready?" the officiant asks, taking her place.

"As ready as we'll ever be," Heavy answers.

She smiles and clears her throat. Grinder—who'd been rambling about something—pipes down.

"Robert, do you take Dina as your lawfully wedded wife, to have and to hold from this day forward, as long as you both shall live?"

His real name is Robert?

"I do."

My hands are still on his chest, so I feel the words rumble through his shirt.

"Dina, do you take Robert as your lawfully wedded

husband, to have and to hold from this day forward, as long as you both shall live?"

"I do."

When I say it, he smiles. Duchenne.

"Then by the power vested in me by the State of Nevada, I now pronounce you man and wife. You may kiss the bride."

Whooping and hollering fill the room.

And then Heavy seizes my waist and lifts me up. My legs wrap around his waist of their own volition. A hand cradles one of my ass cheeks. A forearm against my back presses me to his chest, and he takes my mouth. This kiss is different than the last one. So different.

There's tongue. His tongue. In my mouth. Slicking against mine. Plunging and twining. And it's not gross. Well, it's objectively gross, but I don't mind it. He tastes like mellow spices and late nights and the salty German licorice I love.

I suck his tongue the next time he plunges it deep, swallowing his ragged groan. He likes it, too. My dress has ridden up, and I can feel his hard belly through my panties. He's panting, and I'm doing it to him. He's so big, and I'm so small in comparison, and his body is dancing my tune. I don't even know the song, and he's winded.

And then—plink—a radio dial twists off, my incessantly noisy brain goes silent, and there's only him.

Heavy.

Warm in my arms and between my thighs. The rise and fall of his chest are gentle waves lapping against a lake shore, and he's rich and steady as the forest, mossy green and vivid blue, the deep goodness of dark soil and the antic-ipation of wind rustling leaves high in the treetops.

He's synesthesia. He rewires touch to memory, taste to color, sound and smell.

This isn't too much. It's a wonderment. I want to hold on tight, so I do. I squeeze my thighs, winding my arms tight around his strong neck. Now I'm lost in him.

I don't know how much later, the officiant coughs, and Heavy chuckles, brushing a kiss close to the corner of my eye.

"All right, then, wife," he murmurs and sets me down gently.

The sensation fades, the office building rushes back into my awareness—discordant and unwelcome—but Heavy's holding my hand. I squeeze, just a little, and he squeezes back.

The men swarm closer, and there's a lot of back slapping. I stiffen, but no one touches me. Heavy keeps me tucked at his side, so they just grin my way. I stare at the carpet.

Eventually, Grinder barks, "Can we eat now?"

The gang moves out, stomping raucously back through the building and piling into the limo, and a disagreement breaks out about where to have dinner.

Grinder is a big fan of the casino buffet. Boots wants steak. Gus wants sushi. Boots is of the opinion that if God meant Man to eat fish raw, he'd have 'em grow on trees. Gus is of the opinion that Boots needs to get out more.

The driver suggests a compromise—the Grecian has a buffet known for its steak and sushi.

Everyone's happy, and when we pull up out front, the prospect let's out a whoop of full-on delight. "It's a titty bar!" he crows.

"Well-played, driver." Grinder gives him a nod.

The man grins back at us. "This all right by you, hoss?" he asks Heavy.

Heavy glances down at me. I meet his gaze, and that chilly delicious feeling prickles across my skin. I love looking into Heavy's eyes. It kicks like a shot of moonshine. I love just being able to do it.

"I guess you don't want to go to a strip club for dinner, eh?" he asks.

"It's fine by me." I've never been to one before, but I'm curious. "Are there going to be other women there?"

"This is the Grecian," the driver answers, twisting in his seat. "Ladies dance downstairs, men upstairs. Plenty of VIP rooms, too, if y'all want a private party. Very classy. There's a grotto on the main floor. Working waterfall and everything."

The prospect is already out and hauling Boots' wheelchair from the trunk.

"We don't have to eat here if you don't want to," Heavy says again. He fiddles with the lapel of his cut, his fingertips grazing my collarbone. He never took it back after the vows. It hangs off me like saddlebags on a horse. I don't really mind. It smells like the barn back home. "We could go back and eat somewhere at the casino," he offers.

"I thought bikers did what they want," I tease.

"We do." He leans close so he's speaking just to me. Behind us, Grinder and Gus are struggling to help Boots out of the limo.

"So what do you want?" I try to murmur back, but I don't quite nail it. Voice modulation is a crapshoot with me. It was worse before Rory. When we talk, she does this thing where she repeats part of what I say back, but with the right prosody and volume. Initially, she did it because I was older and therefore cooler, and it was a case of imitation is the sincerest form of flattery. Now she does it because I told her it helps me.

"Steak. Maybe surf and turf," Heavy says.

It takes me a second to remember what we were talking about. "So here's good then, right?"

"Not if it p—, uh, if it makes you uncomfortable."

"See? You're really, um—sensitive—for a biker." It's not a criticism. Men should be sensitive, right?

One second his face is in neutral, and then he flashes a grin, baring those pointy incisors that I'm obsessed with. His eyes sparkle as they narrow the slightest bit. The smile is not Duchenne. It's something else. What?

He grabs me by the scruff of my neck. My lungs catch. I couldn't look away if I wanted to. And I don't. He's wolfish. He's a fairy tale monster, glowing eyes blinking in a dark wood. I squirm, the flood of wetness between my legs tickling my folds.

"I am very sensitive to whether you're comfortable or not. When we get back to the hotel room, I'm gonna lay you flat on your back, and you're gonna spread your thighs and hold your knees while I take that virgin pussy. I don't want to have to calm you down first 'cause you got mad that I was lookin' at other women's titties while I ate my lobster."

I choke on an inhale.

That's a lot to process.

And I'm taut now. And achy. In all kinds of places. My nipples. My plump pussy lips.

I gulp and try to sort out a response. "Wouldn't I be looking at other women's boobs, too?"

His head cocks slightly. "Yeah," he says slow. "I guess so."

"I don't eat seafood, though. Or meat. Do you think they have pasta?"

"Absolutely."

"Then can we go?"

His brow furrows for a second, but then he inclines his head, lets go of my neck, and gestures like a gentleman for me to precede him out of the vehicle.

A thrum of excitement pitter pats in my belly. I've never been to a strip club before. And then there's what he said we're gonna do later—

I can't really think about that right now. I can imagine it, though. He painted a clear picture. Me, on my back. Legs bent back to my ears. Bared to him. Him rising above me, blocking out everything else. His cock lining up with my slit. Wanting in.

Me letting him in.

Shit. That's too much for right now. I'm hungry, and this is all too surreal, and I'm really curious about whether the strippers wear pasties or not. I've always wondered how they stick on, especially if you're sweating.

I head toward the white canopy emblazoned with "The Grecian" in a gold geometric font. There are naked marble statues of a man and a woman on either side of the entrance. The woman is hiding her face behind a fan. The man is wearing a fig leaf. Doesn't that say something about the patriarchy.

There's a line cordoned off with a velvet rope, but no one's in it. It's a little early in the day for the dinner rush, I guess. Heavy has reached my side by the time the doorman sweeps open the tinted glass doors and waves us inside.

"Enjoy yourselves," he says with a great deal of gusto.

I realize my mistake the instant we cross the threshold. I got cocky. I let curiosity overwhelm caution.

Sensory overload crashes into me.

Dark. Strobe lights. Pounding bass. Food smells, liquor smells, perfume smells, body smells. Air conditioning blasting. Fake marble columns and a water feature, a trickling fountain covered in ivy. Curved stairs and topless women in high heels gingerly teetering down one step at a time.

Bare boobs everywhere.

There's a main stage with a pole—no three poles—and a wall of mirrors behind the dais and a mirrored ceiling, so if you look at a certain angle, the mirrors reflect each other and a woman's bare legs crisscrossing like a hundred synchronized swimmers getting smaller and smaller to infinity.

I smell turkey and stuffing. And vanilla. And citrus-scented cleaner.

I dig into my purse for my sunglasses, but somehow Heavy has them, and he's carefully propping them on my nose. I go back into my purse for my earbuds. Once they're in, it's a little better. I venture closer to the stage.

There actually aren't a lot of people here. It's mostly men at the tables, but there are a few couples. Topless women in very short white skirts and gladiator sandals deliver drinks and work the room. For some reason, all the women's boobs are glittery. Gold.

Despite the thumping music, no one's dancing, and everyone seems very chill. Lots of smiling and low conversation.

And then I see the dancer on the stage.

"Ho-ly shit." It slips out of my mouth.

She's writhing in front of the pole in a sparkly pink G-string and matching garter. She undulates and pops her ass, and then she reaches up, grabs the pole, and lifts both her legs straight up until they're horizontal—no strain on her face, not a quiver in her taut muscles. She slowly and grace-fully spreads her legs into a V, and then she flips herself upside down and vertical in a perfectly straight line before lowering her legs into another V with the pole pressed to her crotch.

Like. It's. Nothing. No wobble. No red face. No grunt.

I slap Heavy's chest. "Did you *see* that?"

He lets out a small cough. "Uh, what's the right answer here, baby?"

Now she's spinning down, but in slow motion. "I want to try that."

Who am I kidding? I'd slip right down the pole and bonk my head on the floor. I go riding and hiking a lot, so my thighs and calves are pretty strong, and my core's okay, but I have no biceps. After all, I spend most of my waking hours coding or gaming.

Now the dancer's taking a moment to bend over, jiggle her ass, and toss her hair. I bet she's playing for time to recover her strength.

Then she's back on the pole, climbing upside down, holding herself steady by an ankle as she rises and arches her back, opening her arms with a flourish, almost horizontal in midair.

"She's so strong," I murmur.

I could watch her all day, but Heavy's leading me across the main floor through some fake Greek columns to an annex. There's another bar here, ladies strutting and dancing the length of it, squatting every so often to let men tuck cash in their garters. There's a huge buffet along the far wall. Dessert table, salad bar, a carving station with a man in a tall white hat and everything.

Grinder, Boots, and Gus are already bellied up, helping themselves.

Heavy gestures for me to go ahead. The mingled scents hit me, and my stomach clenches. I've only had coffee so far today, but with all the weirdness, I'm not exactly hungry. I serve myself some plain noodles and grab a few foil packets of butter. There's steamed broccoli, the least offensive green vegetable. My hand hovers over the spoon.

At home, I mostly eat on my own at a natural break in my work, but Mom expects all of us to come to Sunday dinner—Jesse, Cash, Kell and his family. Mom always makes broccoli, and whatever she cooks for an entrée, if there's a sauce, she puts mine on the side. How I like it.

I like routine. The known. Choices that aren't really choices because I've made them a hundred times before.

I should hate this buffet. This club. This loud town.

But this isn't terrible. Not entirely.

So far, it's—like Heavy. Booming. Vibrant. Omnipresent. With him, there's no way to be above it all. He's too colossal. He makes you aware of yourself because you can't help but compare your size in relation to his.

He wants to have sex.

But he's really big.

It might be awful.

But it might not.

I get horny like anyone else. Usually at a certain time in the month, right before my period, I get restless, and my bullet gets a workout. Sometimes I toy with the idea of getting Cash to take me with him to the bars in Shady Gap. Pick up a guy. See if that would be more satisfying than my vibrator.

It's a nonstarter. Cash would never be cool with me hooking up with a rando. And besides, I know myself well enough that if I wait a few days, the urge will fade, and I'll be way more into chocolate cake than dick.

I'm not at the horny point in my cycle right now, but my body's doing some of the same things. My breasts are tender. There's just more general sensation in my body than usual.

And somehow it's connected to Heavy. And being out here in the great unknown. There's a connection between those, too, like I'm an astronaut on a spacewalk, and Heavy is Skylab.

Even now he's pulling out my seat, tucking me beside him at the far end of the table. I have to crane my neck past all the guys to see the action.

I scrape the butter into my noodles and stir. It's not quite melting, but it's viscous enough to spread around.

A waitress comes over and takes our drink order. Grinder asks for a bottle of their oldest whiskey. Bush orders an orange crush.

"What about you, honey?" she purrs, craning her neck to see me past Heavy.

"Whiskey's fine." I prefer bourbon, but I'm not particular.

When the butter's spread as even as I can get it, I dig in. It takes a while for me to notice that the guys are staring at me. Well, Grinder and Boots. The others are watching a woman twerk on the bar. Or the basketball or tennis games on the widescreen TVs hanging above it.

"You got a whole buffet, and you get noodles, no sauce?" Boots asks.

"There was steak up there, girlie," Grinder says around a mouthful. "And roast beef. Turkey."

"Bar-b-que. Pit beef. Pit ham," Boots adds.

"Chicken." Grinder wrinkles his nose.

"I don't eat meat."

Gus and Bush pivot to face me. Grinder's fork pauses midair. Heavy keeps shoveling food in his mouth, head down.

"What do you mean, you don't eat meat?" Grinder says.

"I don't eat meat." I'm not unfamiliar with this reaction. I get the same thing from Cash's hunter friends.

"'Cause you don't like it?" Boots ventures.

"For environmental reasons."

"En-vi-ro-men-tal reasons," Grinder repeats. "Heavy, you hearin' this?"

Heavy doesn't stop chewing.

"You married a tree hugger?" Grinder pushes.

Heavy takes a minute to swallow. "Seems so," he says as he chugs half a glass of water.

"You eat fish?" Bush calls from the far end of the table.

"Some." Atlantic mackerel, Alaskan salmon. A few others. I also eat game that I kill myself, but it's always a pain in the ass to explain the nuance to folks hostile to the idea of sustainability, so I usually don't mention it.

"If God didn't want us to eat meat, why is animals made of it, then? Huh?" Grinder's poking his fork into the air.

I have nothing to say to that.

"Heavy, what's the Good Book say?"

Heavy takes a second to swallow, and then he says, "'Every moving thing that lives will be food for you. As the green herb, I have given everything to you.'" He grins down at me and winks.

I sigh. I guess we're doing this again. "'But food will not commend us to God. For neither, if we don't eat, are we the worse; nor, if we eat, are we the better.'"

Heavy's smile widens. "'One man has faith to eat all things, but he who is weak eats only vegetables—'"

"'—Don't let him who eats despise him who doesn't eat. Don't let him who doesn't eat judge him who eats, for God has accepted him.'" I finish the quote for him. It's Romans, and before my grandparents passed, it came in handy at a lot of family dinners.

While Heavy and I are going back and forth, the waitress returns and passes out snifters, leaving a bottle by Gus who fills the glasses. He slides two toward Heavy who nudges one against the side of my hand.

"'Whether therefore you eat, or drink, or whatever you do, do all to the glory of God,'" Heavy says with a note of finality and raises his glass.

I take the drink, clink it against his, and sip. It's good stuff. Burns real nice going down.

"Grinder, what the hell did they just say to each other?" Boots asks.

"Couldn't say. They seemed to come to an accord there at the end, though."

"Well, then, amen!" Boots declares and toasts us, tossing back two fingers of Glenfiddich with a gusty exhalation. He plunks his empty glass down. "Another round!"

The subject is dropped in favor of reminiscences of strippers the old guys have known—a woman named Plum who ended up with Gus's son, a rich guy who got his ass beat in a parking lot by a dude named Nickel, another woman named Story who stripped to "Danny Boy" one night and had the whole club singing along in tears, her mother Sunny who'd pop ping pong balls from her coochie, and if a customer caught one in his mouth, he'd get a shot on the house.

"Fine woman," Grinder sighs, resting back in his chair and folding his arms over his gut. The men have each made at least three trips back to the buffet, and the table is on its fourth bottle of whiskey. We've switched to bottom shelf.

"The dentist is a lucky man," Boots says. I'm fairly sure that makes no sense, but I'm on my second drink, and everything is warm and fuzzy. There are more people now than when we arrived. It must be close to actual dinner time. I'm not terribly bothered, stuck in my corner with Heavy and a table between me and the rest of the room.

And then a bachelor party rolls in. They're late-twenties, sales bro types. There's always a guy like them in development meetings, a dude named R.J. or Bryan who says things like "it'll be a lay-up" and "we need to swing for the fences on this one."

The ladies have been dropping by and chatting at our table, but when these guys sit down, there seems to be more dancers both up on the bar and circulating. It gets loud with laughter and shrieks, and the scent of conflicting colognes almost overpowers the buffet. I never knew I preferred leather and stale smoke.

Heavy throws his napkin on his plate and pushes back. "Brothers, shall we adjourn to the other room?"

There are grunts of assent, and Grinder re-buttons his pants. We file back to the main room, and it seems like the bros by the buffet were an advance party. There's a sea of blue button ups and khakis. The guys don't seem to notice, but to my ears, they add a braying and smarm to the joint that pushes the overstimulation dial closer to the red.

We take a round table in a far corner with a view of the entire floor. Again, Heavy guides me to the seat on the end and sits between me and the rest of the guys and the room. We're close to the side of the stage, and from this angle, I can watch the dancer from the back. Her trapezius muscles ripple and bunch as she climbs and lowers herself on the pole.

I don't think I've ever seen a woman in real life with such defined back muscles. Does she lift? Dumb question. She lifts herself hand-over-hand and then holds herself still while she defies gravity. That's her entire body weight plus whatever those crazy light-'em-up high heels weigh.

I want to just watch her and marvel, but my brain is struggling to sort the stimuli. The bass beat, Boots' gleeful, drunken commentary. The sticky table.

And Heavy keeps looking at me and looking away. And touching me. He pushes my sunglasses back up when they slip a little down my nose. Wipes a drop of whiskey from my lower lip with his rough thumb.

It's a lot of touching. It makes my nerves raw, and that's bad, but also, only in this weird place and time, and only because it's him—it's also good?

Even when I'm still shivering inside, I kind of want him to do it again. Like a tickle.

A dancer brings another bottle of whiskey and a round of beers, and she stays to sit in Bush's lap. She's doing a thing where she lies flat across Grinder's lap, nestles a shot glass between her boobs, and encourages him to grab it with his lips.

Do the dancers like their jobs? They're really good at it.

Who has the power here, the men with the money or the women laying across their laps, letting them touch, but only so much?

What does it feel like to be as physically strong as the woman climbing the pole? What does it feel like to have everyone's eyes on you, and you don't mind, it doesn't shut you down, it doesn't even seem to register except for a few seconds here and there between acrobatic feats of impossible strength?

And then the dance is over. I clap. Apparently, that's not what you do. There are some wolf whistles, but mostly the crowd doesn't react. Then the dancer struts along the edge of the stage, and the mood changes.

She kneels and tosses her hair, and men wave dollars. She crawls to them, making a show of offering herself so they can tuck them in her G-string. It's playful and vamp-ish, but the men in khaki pants are dumb and vulgar—having a friend take a pic while they mime licking her ass while she's not watching, taking the dollar away at the last minute and making her crawl closer. They make it gross.

I squirm and stare at the table.

Heavy nudges me. I guess he said something. I pop out an earbud.

"Too much?" Heavy repeats.

"Those guys are assholes."

"Want me to kick their asses?"

I glance up, and he's smirking, a thick eyebrow raised. He's joking. "You could do that, couldn't you?"

He lifts a shoulder. "Do you mean physically? Or ethically?"

I had been picturing him plowing through them like a one-man stampede, but I'm intrigued. "Ethically?"

"They do have an ass kicking coming to them, but ethi-cally, I do not believe I'm obliged to deal it out in this partic-ular case."

"But in other cases you would be?"

"Sure. If the place had no bouncers. If it was my club. But—" He nods at two beefy guys in black T-shirts, standing along the wall, hands clasped in front of their barrel chests. "House rules haven't been broken."

"Those guys are being douches."

"So you want me to kick their asses?"

"Would you?"

He smiles. "Now that's a more interesting question than *could I*, isn't it?"

"I don't see the difference."

"*Could* expresses ability. *Would* expresses willingness. Would I be willing to beat down some jackass in a strip club because his behavior toward a stripper offended my wife's sensibilities?" His lips soften and his eyes crinkle at the corners.

My wife. A shiver zips down my back. I cock my head and wait for his answer.

"Abso-fuckin'-lutely," he finally says. He seems delighted by his own answer.

I can tell that he's delighted. I don't have to parse the clues—eyes, mouth, posture. I can read it in a glance. Delight.

My chest prickles with warmth. "You don't have to do it. I think the bouncer's going to do something."

One of the guys has stepped forward, and the other is talking into the radio clipped to his shoulder.

"You know, I have an idea," Heavy says. "You want to go somewhere quieter?"

"Yes." Always.

He bends closer to my ear. "You see any girls you like?"

"What?"

"Which girl do you like the best?"

It's a weird question. "They're all pretty." Every one of them is built like a Barbie. "Which one do *you* like the best?"

He kind of blinks at me. He does that a lot when I say things. Like he's streaming video, and he's buffering.

"You wanna know my type?"

"Sure."

He seems to consider a moment, and then he scans the room.

"There," he says, and nods to a woman chatting up a table of bros. She's tall, with wavy blonde hair down to her butt and a full sleeve tattoo on her left arm. It's gorgeous work—hibiscus blossoms and crosses in bright colors. Her boobs are huge, and she's stunning, but for some reason, the bros don't seem to be testing her.

"She's really pretty." I bet she laughs a lot. She has that generous mouth and ready smile that makes you think she does.

Heavy hums low and leans even closer. His beard rasps my cheek. I inhale, and the vivid green and rich brown, birdsong and dew, warm baking sunshine on a day when it's bright but breezy, fills my lungs.

Synesthesia.

Why does it happen with him? It usually only happens with numbers, letters, days of the weeks, things like that, and it's never this intense. Mostly colors, only occasionally a smell.

I'm so distracted, I don't register what he says. "Come again?"

He kind of frowns at me. "I said yes, she is, but turns out, I got a thing for little short-haired girls in big sunglasses."

I wiggle in my seat, and my cheeks heat.

I'm nothing like the tattooed woman. For one, I have no ink. No piercings either. I love the look, but my pain threshold is ridiculously low. I don't have her physical presence. I hunch. Shuffle. Sexy is not my thing. Or I didn't think it was.

"Why?" I ask.

"Why what?"

"Why do you have a thing for me?"

He licks his full lips. "I have no idea what's gonna come out of your mouth."

"And that makes you want to bang me?"

He chuckles. Just once. "Yeah. Actually. It does."

"I don't get it."

"Neither do I." I want to hear more, but he's raising his

hand, gesturing to the tattooed woman to come over. I thought she was focused on the bro table, but she notices Heavy immediately, excusing herself with an easy assurance, sauntering right over. Sashaying. Whatever it's called when there is a lot of hips and swaying boobs.

"Hello, gentlemen," she says with a wide smile, and the guys reply in a babble of welcome and admiration.

"Hello, ma'am," Bush says with a whistle, and she tussles his hair. Then she poses, long-nailed hand on a gold-glittery cocked hip, one knee bent so her hip pops. She stares directly at Heavy—no hesitation—and she slides her pink tongue slowly along her bottom lip.

"And what can I do for you, sir?"

My stomach tightens. I don't like how she's looking at him. Like it's easy to do.

Without thinking, I put my hand on his forearm. The flannel is soft. I knead it with my fingertips. Heavy leans back and rests an arm along the back of my chair. My stomach muscles unclench.

"My wife and I would like a private dance. Do you think you could arrange that?"

Her smile broadens, and she cranes her neck to check me out. "Hello, there, beautiful. I almost didn't see you behind that big ol' man of yours." She takes a few steps closer and offers me her hand. "Let's go have some fun, sugar."

I don't like touching strangers, but I also don't like not knowing what to do, so I let her grab my hand and guide me away from the table. Heavy follows close in our footsteps. Behind us, the table erupts in hoots and hollers almost loud enough to drown out the bros.

"I'm Anise," she says.

"Dina," I reply.

"Who's the big guy?"

"Heavy."

"Yes, he is," she laughs, warm and husky.

As we move through the floor, clumps of bros shuffle back and divert their paths to give us a wide berth. I noticed this in the airport and at the casino, too. Heavy's like one of those emergency signs on the back of a truck—he moves and people yield.

When we've gotten a few yards, Heavy reaches out, touches Anise's shoulder, and whispers a good while in her ear. I can't make out what he's saying because he's on the side with the earbud still in.

"Cash up front and the house doesn't need to know?" she says.

Heavy nods.

"She's okay with it?" Anise nods at me.

"She will be."

What are they talking about?

"I think we can make that happen for you," she says and winds her fingers between mine. I don't know what's going on, but for once, the anticipation is stronger than the anxiety.

I have no reason to trust Heavy, but for some reason, I do. I let Anise lead me up the curving stairs into the dark. Heavy's at my back. I'm not the least bit scared.

WITH HER HEELS, Anise is easily eight inches taller than me. She smells like patchouli and sandalwood, but it's a faint scent, as if it's coming from her hair and not her skin.

At the top of the stairs, the music changes. Downstairs was rock and hip hop. Up here it's R & B, mellow with a thick, drowsy beat. The ceiling isn't so high, and the space is more intimate with smaller tables and votive candles.

There are a lot of men.

The dancer on stage is a man, and both men and women in gold thongs are hanging out at tables, some with groups of women, some with couples. Everyone's drinking wine. There is chardonnay in the air.

Anise lowers her head and asks me, "Which one do you like?"

I glance back at Heavy. His face is impassive. This has to be his idea, but his beefy arms are folded, and he's not saying anything. Am I supposed to pick another woman? A man?

My pulse picks up. I can feel it throb in my neck. I've never done anything like this before. Never even thought about it. My fantasies aren't complicated. A hot guy, oral, hands all over me that feel good and aren't annoying. That and the bullet on my clit are usually enough to get me there.

I mean, I've watched about everything that exists on the internet. I'm curious. But most porn does nothing for me, or it makes me worried for the future of humanity.

I never, never, never thought about watching real naked people dance up close. I don't like getting close to people with their clothes *on*.

But this—I really want to know what might happen.

"He's cute. Do you like him?" Anise jerks her chin at a guy who's flirting with a table of women who look like my middle school teachers. He has dark brown hair styled in an artfully disheveled quiff, a deep tan, sleepy, hooded eyes, and a bright white smile. From here, it looks Duchenne.

I look up at Heavy. He's still not giving anything away.

"Yeah, okay," I say. "He's good."

Anise gives my hand a squeeze and then drops it to

saunter over to the man. She seems to apologize to the women, draws him away to a chorus of protests, and whispers in his ear. His smile grows, one hundred percent Duchenne, and he bumps his forehead lightly to hers. They're the exact same height.

Anise takes his hand and brings him over.

"This is Gio." She introduces him to me. "You're gonna love him."

It's weird. Both of the dancers pretty much ignore Heavy even though he's close to my side. They lead the way down a hall, past a bouncer in a "STAFF" T-shirt, to a room at the end. It's small. The ceiling is mirrored, and so is a wall. There's a pole on a square platform in the middle and a sturdy wood chair. The unmirrored walls are lined with tan leather couches. There's also a small round table for drinks.

"Champagne?" Anise asks, and when Heavy grunts in the affirmative, she uses an intercom on the wall to place an order.

Heavy settles himself in the middle of the couch and slaps his thigh. "Come here."

For a second, I don't know if he's talking to me or her.

"I think your man wants you," Anise says as she grabs the pole and circles it with a few idle steps.

It's clear now that Heavy's looking in my direction. I don't know what to do with myself, so I shuffle over and perch on his knee. He immediately wraps a thick arm around my middle and pulls me flush to his chest. My legs dangle on the outsides of his meaty thighs.

I'm spread open. And that's an unsettling sensation. But he surrounds me, and that feels—nice. Enveloping, but in a good way. Like a comforter. I let my head rest on a hard pec.

"How do you want this to go, boss?" Anise asks Heavy.

"He does what you want," Heavy tells her. "He" means

Gio, the male dancer. "My wife says stop, everything stops. Otherwise, everything is a go."

Anise smiles and licks her cherry red lips. "I like that idea."

Gio chuckles. "Works for me."

Anise prods the wood chair with the glittery toe of a high heel. "Sit there, honey."

Gio obeys, casual, knees spread, grinning. He has an erection. It's poking through his sparkly gold thong. My face heats. His boner causes a gap, and I can totally see shaved skin. And ball sack.

Gio's not looking at us, though. He's intent on Anise as she swings lazily around the pole. They're making steady eye contact, breaking only for the second when her back is to him. It doesn't seem to bother either of them in the slightest that we're watching. I think they might enjoy it. Both of their mouths are softly curved upwards, and their bodies are relaxed.

I'm not. Heavy's hold on me has loosened, and now his forearm is a bar across my lap, and as the seconds pass, I feel less safe and more—held. My feet don't reach the floor. I'm not touching the couch. There's nothing but man under me. Behind me. Around me.

At least it's more peaceful in this room. The R & B is piped in through a speaker on the wall, but other than that, it's quiet. The lights are low, and nothing flashes or changes color.

This close to Heavy, all I can smell is him. I close my eyes and inhale. In the best possible way, he smells like the barn back home. Machinery, straw, sunbaked horsehair. Some of the tension leaks from my muscles, and on its own, my body conforms to his, my shoulders to his chest, my bottom to his lap and the pokey hardness popping his zipper.

"There we go," he murmurs in my ear, gravelly and languid. His beard is bunched against my shoulder and the side of my neck. Raspy and coarse. But I don't mind. It doesn't tickle, and if he stays still, it doesn't abrade.

"What are they going to do?" I whisper. Anise has temporarily abandoned the pole to get a tray from a waitress in the hall.

"Whatever she wants," he says. "She's calling the shots."

Anise sets the tray down on the small table, pops the cork, and pours four glasses. She hands one each to Heavy and I.

I can't navigate this situation and drinking, so I down mine in three gulps and pass my empty glass to Heavy who sets it back on the table.

I'm definitely a little tipsy. Not enough that anything is spinning, but my insides are swooshy, and the part of my brain that doesn't overanalyze everything is floating like a balloon.

Anise struts over to Gio with the two remaining glasses. He smiles up at her from the chair, and she slowly lowers herself into his lap, facing him. Her ass flexes, and she arches her back. Then she looks at us over her shoulder and frowns.

"Hold on." She stands again, backing up. "Turn the chair," she tells Gio.

He rotates it so that when she sits on him again, Heavy and I have a side view. We can see her breasts brush his sculpted pecs and her pelvis grind against his erection. She hands him champagne.

"Cheers," she says, and they clink glasses, smiling at each other. Gio sips, sets his glass on the floor, and then rests his hands on her lower back. His touch is so tentative it almost hovers over her sparkly skin.

"Uh, uh," she tuts, gently slapping his shoulder. "Did I say you could touch?"

He grins and drops his arms to his sides.

"The big man says *I'm* in charge." She winks and boops him on the nose.

Underneath me, Heavy shifts. His breath is quickening. I tilt my head back so I can see his face from the corner of my eye.

"Can you tell if they really like each other?" I ask him as quietly as I can. I'm not sure I nailed a whisper, but neither Anise nor Gio glance over at us.

Anise is grinding on Gio's lap now, tossing her long hair. His eyes are glued on her breasts, and every so often, he licks his lips and swallows.

"I think they do," Heavy says.

"How can you tell?"

"She pointed him out to you. He's got a hard on."

"*Why* do you think she likes him?"

Heavy shoots a dark, inscrutable glance at me before he goes back to watching the show. "She probably knows he'll make her feel good."

"How does she know that?"

Heavy's hold around my waist tightens the slightest bit. "Maybe they've done this before. Maybe she's got a sense about him. Seen him with other dancers. Maybe they've worked together a while."

I don't have a sense about people. Not unless they're grade A, prime assholes like Cash. He might as well have "dickhead" embroidered on his shirts. But most people? I'm flying blind.

I have no idea how Heavy is with other women. And I've known him for less than forty-eight hours. He could be the world's most devious manipulator, and I'd never see it coming.

But here I am. Considering.

What would it be like to have sex with him? I've already done some stuff with him, and it was all right. He touched me. I came. It felt good until the sticky wet part at the end. More than good. Amazing.

Would it feel like that with anyone?

Cash has a friend named Darren. He gawks at me when I'm in my bikini beside the pool in the backyard. I always figured if I decided I wanted to have sex, Darren would be up for it. He's dumb enough not to worry about pissing off Cash.

Darren's objectively hot. He's clean. His opinions about virtually everything including desserts are about fifty years out of date—dude loves my mom's Jell-O molds—but he means no harm, and he's about the best you can do in Stonecut County.

I don't think it would feel amazing with Darren. But with Heavy?

I squirm in his lap, and he nuzzles the crook of my neck. Shivers zing across my skin from nerve ending to nerve ending. Across the room, Anise tugs Gio's head down, guiding him to her breast. He licks her nipple, and then he pops the whole thing into his mouth and sucks. She grinds harder, losing the rhythm of the song. It's less of a dance now, although she's playing with the other boob in kind of a choreographed way. There's a sheen of sweat on her face.

"He seems to know what she likes," Heavy murmurs.

I make a noncommittal hum. My body's demanding a lot of my attention. There's sorting through how Heavy's body makes me feel, and then there's the visual of the couple in the chair. It's a lot. My gaze slides away, and then it's drawn back, and I'm overloaded all over again.

Usually this is the point when I meltdown, but it's like my circuit breaker has already been tripped, so I can let the experience keep flowing over me, tucked against Heavy's broad chest.

Gio strokes Anise's back, tracing the notches of her spine. Gentle. Reverent. Anise seems oblivious to him. Her eyes are screwed tight, and she's biting down hard on her lower lip, panting.

"What do *you* like?" Heavy asks. There's a rawness to his voice, a fracture.

"I don't know yet."

He makes a weird sound. "Do you like how he's touching her? Gentle?"

I shrug a shoulder. "*She* likes that."

"I'm not gentle. I don't go slow."

I know that should be terrifying, but heat blossoms in my lower belly.

"But I'll be gentle tonight," he goes on. "I'll go as slow as you need."

"Tonight?"

"Oh, yeah. When we get back to the hotel, I'm poppin' that cherry. It'll be all about you. Just like this. But once I break you in, baby, it's gonna be about me. Understand?"

Not at all, but I am turned on. My nipples chafe against my bra. I rock my hips experimentally, and the friction of my pussy against his jeans feels good. Heavy groans.

"I guess you do," he chuckles.

In the chair, Gio grabs Anise's ass, and she drops backwards, back curved, so her boobs thrust high in the air and her hair dusts the floor. She's beautiful, and Gio's expression is pure appreciation. They don't seem to notice us at all.

Anise straightens, and she takes one of Gio's hands, guiding it between her legs. My thighs clench, and my breath shallows.

"What's she doing?" I know the answer. I don't know why I'm asking Heavy.

"She wants to be touched."

I do, too. I squirm, but Heavy doesn't move.

Gio grins as he slips his fingers in her G-string, but Anise seems to get another idea. She bats his hand away, stands, and then nudges his chair until he rotates it to face us. Then she straddles his lap and looks at Heavy.

Do I like that?

Instinctively, I reach back and clutch his hair. I don't yank his head down so he can't see, but I could. If I wanted to. Heavy rumbles. It's a pleased sound.

"You don't want me to look?"

I want to look. It wouldn't be reasonable if I didn't want *him* to watch.

He gently disentangles my fingers from his hair. "Or don't you want her to look at me?"

That's not reasonable either.

But no.

I don't like her looking at him.

Now she's reaching for Gio's hands, placing them on her round hips. Gio tugs her G-string down and she steps out of it. She's buck naked except for those high heels. Gio trails his fingertips back up the inside of her leg, and she widens her stance. She's completely shaved. Her pussy lips are a rosy pink, and her clit peeks out like the tip of a tongue.

She leans over a little, tilting her hips, and Gio cups her between the legs and shakes. She moans.

She's still looking straight at Heavy.

My stomach clenches.

No, I really don't like that.

I glance over my shoulder at him. He's watching Gio touch her. Of course. I was watching that, too. I tense. My hands had been resting on Heavy's forearms, but I fold them high on my chest. My spine stiffens.

"I don't want anyone lookin' at you either," he breathes in my ear. "You know how many fuckers I almost punched today? Every one of those frat boys who checked you out. The doorman. The dude carving the turkey. The limo driver. The dude behind us in line at the courthouse."

"He was checking me out?" That marriage isn't off to an auspicious beginning.

"I don't want anyone's eyes on you but mine."

"That's nuts."

He lets out a wry chuckle. "You think I don't know that?"

We're silent a moment, and I let myself soften back into his chest. "I don't want anyone looking at you, either, but you're so big, there's no chance of that."

He tightens his arm and laughs softly.

Anise's glance drops to my face, and for a second, she frowns. Then she slaps Gio's hand. He drops it immediately. She struts over to the couch, arms extended, palms open. What does she want?

"Gimme these, honey," she says, grabbing for my hands. I let her take them and draw me to my feet. She lifts my arms to my side. "You're such a pretty thing under that big ol' leather vest," she says. "So shy."

Behind me, Heavy snorts.

Then she urges me back to straddle Heavy like she was doing with Gio, but Heavy's a much bulkier man, so there's no way.

Heavy widens his legs and Anise guides me to stand between them. Then she drops my hands and grabs his, placing them on the sides of my bare knees. His palms are rough, but his touch is light. He skims upward, under my dress, over my hips. Anise strides gracefully away, returning to Gio.

When she turns, she's looking at me. We're mirror images. She's tall and assured and feminine and muscular. She knows what she's doing. She can read the room, and somehow, she knows how to orchestrate it all. It's a feat as mind-blowing as the acrobatics with the pole.

Heavy's hands cup my hips, and Gio's rise to massage hers. Gio smiles at me. My dress falls over Heavy's forearm, so I'm not on display, not really. But they obviously know he's touching me. I lean back a little, resting my back against Heavy's chest.

Gio winks. "Now you're getting' comfortable," he says.

"Don't talk to my wife, friend," Heavy says, even and calm, his voice vibrating against my shoulder blades.

I tense, but Gio chuckles, no offense apparently taken. "Sure thing, my man."

He turns his gaze back to Anise who's dancing, slow and languorous, grazing her fingers over her own taut curves and firm breasts.

Why is it okay for Anise to talk to me but not Gio? Why did a thrill shoot through me when Heavy warned him off?

I don't understand these dynamics, but they weave a spell, muffling the extraneous stimuli and focusing my mind. It's a puzzle I don't have to solve. A maze I can just wander.

Heavy's touch, his smell, my body's new reactions, the rising, greedy wanting that makes me press against all the points of contact between us. That's all I need.

Anise props herself on Gio's lap, and he plays with her

nipples, plucking the buds until they're stiff peaks. She circles her hips, and it's a dance, but it's also not.

Heavy slips his fingers under the elastic of my panties, and with his other hand, he cups my breast. His touch is light. Idle.

The overwhelming sensation is being wrapped in his trunk-like arms. It's not too much. It's not enough, either.

I know this is chemicals and hormones, not magic, but there is no meaningful difference, not when my insides are turning into liquid gold. Not when all of this is happening, and I'm not splintering.

I'm sailing. Soaring.

The song changes, and Gio's mood shifts. He stops lounging and grinning. His muscles tighten, and his eyes glint like diamonds. Anise was in charge, but without warning, the script is flipped. Gio maneuvers her so she's closer to him and—holy shit—his dick is out of his thong. His balls, too. He definitely shaves.

Instinctively, I back into Heavy. His beard bristles across my bare arm.

"Are they gonna have sex?" I hiss.

"I believe so."

"Did you ask them to?"

"I didn't suggest they go this far specifically, no, but I asked for a show. And, I did say anything goes."

"Anything is definitely going," I mutter. I've never seen people have sex in real life. "Should we be watching this?"

His laugh shakes me. "I don't think they mind."

Gio guides Anise up and back until she's poised on top of him. He fists himself, angles toward her rosy pussy. She's glistening. Her sparkly body lotion glitters gold in the creases of her slick folds. Her eyes are closed, and there's a fine vertical line between her perfectly sculpted eyebrows.

Gio whispers to her—I can't make out the words—and she lowers herself onto his cock. It's not nearly so long and thick as Heavy's, but she moans, and she sounds pleased. She rises up, and now he's shiny with her juices.

I'm panting. "She likes it," I manage between shallow breaths.

Heavy hums in agreement. "She's controlling the pace. She's focusing on what makes her feel good."

"That's why he's not moving?"

"He's giving her time to get settled."

"His face is all scrunched up." Gio's brow is knit and under the straight edge of his chin strap, his jaw is clenched so tight it's blanched white.

"It's hard for him not to thrust into that sweet pussy."

"But he's giving her time," I say.

"Yeah." Heavy's voice becomes impossibly deeper and grittier. "Tonight, I'm gonna give you all the time you need. We'll get you dripping wet, and I'll ease inside, inch by inch, and I won't move at all until you tell me you want more."

My muscles tense, head to toe. "It's gonna hurt."

"Probably. A little. But then it'll feel real good. I swear."

Anise's head tilts back. She's found a rhythm. Gio's rocking into her now, watching himself slide in and out of her stretched core. Anise's nails are digging into his tan thighs, leaving pale half moons.

They both have their eyes closed, and their movements don't seem at all like performance now, more like they're working together toward something, wordless and intent, oblivious to the world. It's not as smooth or rehearsed as before—it's kind of awkward, actually, and there are squelches—but it's captivating.

"Why do you want to do this? With me?"

I know why *I'm* game. Curiosity. Carpe diem. And this

feeling I don't understand, a sensation I can't untangle from his thick beard and booming voice and how he kind of looks scared when I catch him staring at me from the corner of my eye.

He's way larger than I'd like to start with, but I'm not going to get this kind of opportunity again once I go back to Stonecut County. No strings sex isn't really possible in a small town.

Heavy doesn't answer me right away. I almost forget I asked, distracted by the increasing pace of Gio's thrusts and the way Anise's breasts jiggle.

"Maybe I want something for myself," he finally says.

I don't understand.

I guess I was expecting him to say I turn him on, or I'm hot, or something like that. I'm not. I'm cute, but I'm built like Gumby, and I know it. I don't mind. I don't have to wear a sports bra when I go horseback riding.

I want something for myself.

Yeah, I don't get it. He's the president of the club, right? The CEO of the company. Everything is his. Does he mean like in his personal life?

I have everything to myself. Most of the time I might as well be in one of those antique diving suits with the big round heads, floating through the deep, murky sea, trying to make out what's right in front of my face. Having it all to yourself is overrated.

"What do you mean?" I ask.

Again, he takes his sweet time before he speaks. The whole time, he strokes my sides, gently cupping my breasts or smoothing and squeezing my bottom. It keeps my body at a low boil, the line between stimulated and overstimulated. I rest my cheek on his chest so his beard will tickle my ear lobe when he speaks.

Gio pounds into Anise faster and faster. She's moaning pretty constantly now. I don't think they care about us at all anymore.

Heavy coughs to clear his throat. "Well, it's like—I got a Bobcat. I got a Fat Boy. Got a Road King. At some point, lots of folks have ridden bitch on all three. But I also got a Pacer I restored from parts. It's too small for my size. I lay her down half the time I take her out. But nobody's ridden her but me."

I understand even less now.

"That Pacer is my favorite ride," he says as if that explains it all.

"Because no one else has ridden it?" I am not down with the idea of virginity being tied to a woman's worth. Also, is he saying he's too big for me? I want to get laid, but not "laid down."

"Yeah, and because I made her. She responds to me."

"If we go with your analogy, you're a shit rider, and this is some kind of exclusive ownership thing?" I grimace.

"I guarantee you won't complain about the ride, but yeah—" He grabs between my legs. "I'm gonna own this pussy."

"What does that even mean?"

"That means it's gonna beg me, just like it's doin' now, grinding against my hand like a greedy little thing."

Oh. I am. I'm doing that.

He laughs, and it isn't mocking. It's rich like espresso or polished mahogany. The sound seeps into me, and now the liquid gold inside me is bubbling. I think this conversation is turning me on more than his touch, more than the show in the chair across the room.

It's like he's whispering secrets to me. People don't do

that. No one's like "let's confide in the girl who's no good at subtlety and can't control her volume."

He's saying things only for my ears. I don't want him to stop. Any of it.

"So you want to have sex with me because I'm a virgin. That's disappointing."

He chuckles and nips at my earlobe. Shivers scramble down my neck. "Oh, yeah. I love expanding your world, blowing your mind. That airplane ride gave me a taste for it."

I twist my neck to try and see him better. He drops a kiss where my eyebrows knit together. "I love the look on your face when you see something new. Your lips part." He cradles my jaw for a moment, holding me still, his gaze searching mine. "You tremble like a wet rabbit."

He lowers his voice. "I can't wait to see your pussy take my cock for the first time. I want you to freak out until I calm you down. I want you to trust me and get confident, and realize you love it, and lose yourself like you did back at the clubhouse." As he goes on, his touch firms, his arms flex, holding me tight. So tight.

"Why?"

"Do you need to know?"

"Yes."

He sighs. "Dina, I don't have all the answers."

And then he's quiet. He holds me as Anise's moans turn to whimpers, and Gio starts really pumping into her, hard, as she rubs her clit.

"She's going to come," I say. Heavy murmurs agreement. I didn't realize I said it out loud.

Anise lets out a long groan, her thighs shake, and Gio grabs her hips, driving into her. Then he lets out a small shout and a huge smile breaks across his face.

She sinks to his lap, her legs as limp as noodles. She drops her head back to Gio's shoulder. He nuzzles her neck and murmurs something inaudible in her ear. She smiles drowsily.

After a moment, she draws in a deep breath and moves to straighten herself up.

"No," Heavy interrupts. "Not yet. I want my wife to see after."

Anise's lips curve, and she snuggles back against Gio. He wraps an arm around her waist, and with his other hand, he carefully smooths strands of hair behind her ear. He murmurs more, his nose to her cheek, and she giggles.

"They like each other," I say. Anise has let herself sag into him until her belly folds. She's not trying to be sexy. Gio can't stop touching her, flicking her nails with his fingertips, kissing her shoulder.

"Yeah," Heavy says. "She let him make her feel good, and now she's letting him enjoy the moment."

"I thought women want to cuddle, and men want to fall asleep or eat a sandwich or something."

"That's a bunch of bullshit, Dina." Heavy arches a bushy eyebrow. I think he's teasing. "A man wants to know he's robbed his woman of the ability to walk or speak. He doesn't want her hopping up to make a BLT."

"What does a woman want?"

"That's the eternal question, ain't it?" He shrugs. "Probably a sandwich. Or a nap."

I like both of those things.

Somewhere along the line, Heavy stopped petting me. My skin is now hypersensitive, and my panties are damp, but the swishing, swirling, bubbling feeling has quieted. It's still there like glitter at the bottom of a snow globe, and I bet he could stoke it back to life at any second, but for now, we're just calm and close. In each other's space. Basking.

I inhale his outdoorsy scent, and we're all silent for a while. Eventually, there are footsteps in the hall. They don't stop at our door, but still, it rouses us.

I sling my purse across my chest while Heavy slaps Gio's back and slips something in his palm. Anise rises on her tip toes and kisses Heavy's cheek. Then she crosses the room and gives me a hug. Now there's gold glitter on Heavy's cut.

"Y'all have a wonderful rest of the evening, now," she says, tugging her panties back on.

Heavy leads the way out, and I follow, my brain somehow numb and reeling at the same time.

"You wanted me to see that," I say as we make our way down the stairs.

He grunts.

"Why?"

"Because I wanted to know."

"Know what?"

"The questions that are in your mind. How you see it."

He's talking about sex. "How do I see it?"

"Best I can tell, like a movie in a foreign language without subtitles."

I laugh. He's right. That's how I see most everything.

"Can we go ride that roller coaster now?" It's late, but this is Vegas. It might still be running.

He busts out laughing, and I have no idea why.

8

HEAVY

The first time I bumped into someone and knocked them on their ass was in seventh grade. I shoulder-checked a teacher, a young guy with a slight build. Mr. Anscomb. It was completely unintentional. I was walking down the hall, and my growth spurts had outpaced my spatial awareness. I got put out for three days even though my mom went toe-to-toe with the principal.

In retrospect, I probably got three days *because* Mom went toe-to-toe with that asshole.

No one believed the long-haired son of the local MC president was innocent. And in a sense, I wasn't. We young'uns weren't raised on sex, drugs, and rock-and-roll, but we sure as shit were raised *with* 'em. Brawlin', huntin', and ridin'. Flashed titties and polishing off beers left unsupervised. It was the life. Charge, Nickel, Scrap, Forty, and I were all doin' time at Petty's Mill Junior High, and everyone knew it.

Ever since that incident with Mr. Anscomb, I've known my size. There was a time I reveled in it, flexing on the football team, walkin' towards a gang of wannabes at the carnival, gettin' my jollies by watchin' as they parted to flow around me, a rock in their stream. Or taking a sudden step toward a dumbass with a big mouth just to watch him jerk back and duck.

If you want my origin story, that's it—shoulder checking a history teacher. Not the legendary father, gone too soon. Not the mother, gone even sooner.

Not the Blown Job or when the baseball bat cracked my little brother's skull or when the guidance counselor sat across her desk from me junior year, flipping through my file, forehead furrowing as she realized the sixteen-year-old greaser with the full beard had a 4.5 GPA and a perfect SAT score, and she said, "Well, you could go to a pretty good school with these grades. What are you into?"

The beginning was an accident. An unintentional swing of the arm, and from the consequences, I came to understand that I am a force whether or not I want to be. From October until June, I watched Mr. Anscomb flinch every time I raised my hand in class.

I am stronger than other men. Bigger. I see further. I'm the guy my brothers look to—at first only because my voice boomed the loudest, and I stood two heads taller—but later, because I was the one who knew his own strength.

Because my brothers followed me, I lead. I've stumbled. Made mistakes the club is still paying for. But I don't knock into folks by accident anymore. Haven't for a long, long time. But people have never stopped making way.

I am a legend. They see me coming, and they clear out of my path. *Everyone.*

Except Dina Wall.

This fun-sized woman has careened into me at least a dozen times since I had the limo let us out at the intersection of Tropicana Avenue and Las Vegas Boulevard. She has the spatial awareness of a bumper car. Every time she collides with my side, she goes "oof" and grumbles. Cracks me up.

I inhale cooling desert night air, and my lips twitch.

I needed a walk to get myself under control.

Back in that VIP room with Dina shivering in my hands, stage whispering in my ear, paying me hardly any mind although I was caressing her titties like a fuckin' potter at his wheel, there's nothing I wanted more than to unzip my jeans and coax her to ride my cock, too.

But that's the rub, as Shakespeare said. There is no coaxing Dina. My *wife*.

My tipsy, clumsy, oblivious *wife*.

She's still wearing my cut. Never thought I'd take it off, but now I'm not sure I want it back. I like it on her.

She's still wearing her sunglasses, too, as she gapes at the fountains and palm trees and electronic billboards. It's late enough that the crowds have thinned, and the other tourists give us a wide berth, flashing me the usual wary glances.

Back at the clubhouse, when I woke up with her on my bed, Dina avoided eye contact. Then she started sneaking peeks. Now she meets my eyes, and it's like looking into a glass-bottom boat all the way to the floor of the deep, blue sea.

What goes on in this woman's head? She never reacts how I predict. I never know what's going to come out her mouth, but there's always an unassailable logic to what she says.

I know people. I play the tune. I'm the puppet master. The mastermind.

Dina doesn't give a shit.

I'm a fisher of men, and she's a brown trout. Too canny to catch.

There's a weightlessness to being powerless. A mellow high. I like it.

So even though my dick's half hard, and my heart has not stopped ka-thunking at the idea of unboxing her, I slow my stride. The roller coasters aren't running. The only thing she's ridin' tonight is me.

A few blocks from our hotel, Dina stops to stare at the side of a casino. It's a three-story high LED billboard advertising one of those acrobat circuses. The performers are naked except for thongs and painted in make-up to look like fantasy creatures—unicorns, griffins, centaurs, and dragons.

I loom beside her. Her jaw is clenched, and her body's vibrating. Or squirming. I slide her sunglasses on top of her head 'cause I'm curious. Her hand reaches to snatch them back, but it gets twisted in mine, so I grab her fingers and hold on.

She frowns, squinting, but now I can see her gaze track the acrobats and then drop to the concrete sidewalk, as if she needs to rest between ganders. The blue feathers and green sequins and red scarves reflect in her black pupils. She's taken. Utterly taken.

Lightly and carefully, I nudge her with my elbow. "What?" I ask. She'll know what I mean.

"I wish I could see this."

"We can." I'd planned on flying home tomorrow, but no reason we can't take in a show before the flight. We aren't gettin' an early start. Not with what I'm gonna do to her once we get to our room.

"No, I can't." She bops her sunglasses down with her free hand and tugs me to get a move on.

We're still holding hands.

Ain't never done this before with a woman. It's an

awkward height differential, but—I'm not letting go. I can guide her so she's doesn't bang into shit so often.

"Why not?"

"Too much stimuli."

"Even with the sunglasses and earbuds?" I saw her struggle at the airport, but I figured it was like jumping into a cold pool, and she would grow accustomed. At the strip club, she seemed fine, and that was a lot of stimulation.

"Yeah."

"But you were okay back at the club."

"I wasn't okay."

"Could have fooled me." She was entranced. I've never been more turned on in my life than watching her lick her lips as another dude's cock slid in and out of a messy, pink pussy. Ain't a kink I thought I had, but I like to watch my wife get excited watching another chick get dicked.

Wife.

Should have a false ring to it, but it doesn't.

"I was Little Mermaid-ing," she says, like that's a whole explanation.

"Come again?"

"Yeah. You know the original? The Hans Christian Andersen story?"

"Where she dies at the end?"

"Yeah, that one."

"That story is morbid as shit."

"I know, right? It's awesome." She tilts her head back and grins at me. "In that version, when she grows human legs, she says it's like walking on knives and sharpened needles."

"And that's what it was like? Back at the club?"

"That's what it's always like in public—at the grocery store, restaurants, the mall."

"You didn't say. We could have left."

"I didn't want to leave." She wriggles her hand loose, and trip-dances a few steps ahead, turning to face me and walking backward. Jesus. She's gonna fall and crack her head open on the sidewalk. "I wanted to see the world. Enchant a prince. Earn my immortal soul."

I scrub my chest. An unpleasant burn rises in my throat. Indigestion. "What prince?"

She snickers. "I don't know. I'm not particular. Doesn't have to be a prince."

I see we're talking about me now. About her, and me, and what I'm about to do to her. "So anyone who can bury a body would do?"

"Not *anyone*. I have standards. I want a good time."

"So I'm a good time? A walk on the wild side?" That's good. That's fine. That's what this is.

"I don't know. So far, all you've done is put a ring on it and bought me stuff." She grins. Imp. "And now we're taking a leisurely after-dinner stroll. Not really *wild*."

Bullshit. "I held you at gunpoint and made you come so hard you quivered like a kitten in a bathtub."

She tosses a slender shoulder. "Yesterday's news." Then she wrinkles her nose. "And don't put kittens in bathtubs."

And then it happens—like I knew it would. Her heel lands wrong, and her arms windmill. Before the shriek escapes her lips, I've plucked her up. Without hesitation, she wraps her legs as tight and as far around my waist as she can get them. I hoist her higher, and now she's smiling down at me, arms circling my neck. I keep on strolling.

She slides her sunglasses on top of her head and gazes down, so I stare up into her wide blue eyes. Beyond her upturned face, the hazy night glows orange from the light pollution. I squeeze her ass so her pubic bone grinds against my linea alba. Her knees dig into my obliques.

It feels like when my boot heel clicks into place against my bike peg.

"You're going to carry me all the way?" she asks, short of breath.

"Don't want you walking on knives."

Her fingers find my hair, combing, fisting. She studies me, and I'm reminded of the quote attributed to Nietzsche, the warning that when you stare into the abyss, the abyss stares back.

The abyss is beautiful. Delicate. Mysterious. Ballsy and neurotic. Not like any woman I've ever known before, but also somehow as familiar as the crisscrossing on my own palm. I carry her, and I feel light. My knees don't click. My back doesn't ache.

"You're a prince among men, eh?" she teases, her soft fingers moving to my face, my wind-red cheeks, the lines at the corner of my eyes that I've had forever.

"I'm gonna carry you over the threshold, wife." We're a block away, and my pulse is kicking up. I've picked up the pace. I want her touch everywhere. I want her softness all over my rough, work-worn skin.

"We're not really married," she says.

"You signed the papers. You said, 'I do.'"

She rolls her eyes. "There's more to marriage than that."

She brushes the tip of her nose across the tip of mine and then nestles it beside, inhaling. It's so strange on the one hand, but on the other, I want to nuzzle her pieces, too, breathe her in, see how far I can push this moment before it deflates back into everyday proportions. Right now, it feels huge. Huge and fragile and impossibly sweet.

"Like what?" I ask.

She chews her bottom lip. "I don't know. The marriages

I've seen up close—the only common thread is cohabitation."

"Exactly."

"Exactly what?"

"Who knows what marriage is?" For my parents, it was lying in the bed you made. "Could be anything. Could be two co-conspirators making a deal not to snitch on each other."

"I'm pretty sure there's supposed to be love involved."

I'm not. "And what's love? Exactly?"

She grins ear-to-ear. "I have no idea."

And I'm grinning back at her. "Me neither."

I've always subscribed to the Greek way of thinking, the idea of many loves—the love of God for man, affectionate love. I'm aware of eros; I've read Plato's *Symposium* a few times. It's always paled beside philia to me. The love of brothers—that I understand. Loyalty. Common purpose. Complete trust in another man's character.

"You don't have to carry me," she says, interrupting my thoughts.

"You don't weigh anything." She doesn't. Carrying her, my back is straight, my steps lighter than they've been in a long time.

"Yeah, I'm not heavy," she says, and emits a peel of laughter—a cackle of pure, odd delight—and I extend my neck, wanting, seeking, and she comes closer, black eyelashes fluttering to her cheeks, but I keep my eyes open and watch while she kisses me. Inexpert. Soft. Quick, off-center, and I groan, and she does it again.

And again.

Learning her way. Growing confident. Exploring.

My dick throbs.

I lengthen my stride, navigating the automatic doors, the

echoing casino lobby, the hall to the elevators, shoving down the impulse to reach out and punch the side of the drunk dude's head who gawks and sniggers. We're making a scene; it's only natural that people should stare.

Dina is a vine, fingers tangled in my hair, thighs squeezing impossibly tighter, pelvis pulsing. She's trying to get it, and I don't think she's even aware, or maybe she's past caring like I am, past everything but the need. Like when you see a lush field of trimmed grass and you gotta run, or when there's a stretch of empty road, and you have to open the throttle.

I jam the "up" button on the elevator until there's a ding and the shiny door slides open. Dina's making sounds now, beautiful sounds—needy whines and whimpers.

"We're almost there, baby," I pant into her mouth. She's experimenting with tongue now, slipping hers past my teeth, licking, tasting, darting away when mine gets demanding. I let her lead. I want to follow where she goes. I want to trip along behind her into this space I've never been before, a place where I don't give a shit about anything other than her sweet mouth and soft skin.

I've got the key card in my hand when we get to our suite. There's a beep, and I throw the door open and stride across the living area, into our room. I kick the door shut, peel her loose, and toss her onto the bed. Before she bounces twice, I've ripped my shirt off, and I've got my belt undone.

"Oh. Okay. This is happening," she mumbles, and she tears off my cut, tossing it off the side of the bed. Her dress follows, static spiking her hair. She wriggles backwards to the head of the bed, unhooking her bra and flinging it aside. It lands on the night table. Her eyes are glued to my cock, ruddy and veined and ready to go.

Shit. I dropped my jeans without takin' off my boots, and now I gotta bend over buck naked to untie the laces. With my bulk and abundance of hair, it ain't graceful nor quick.

She can't change her mind. If she does, I'll fuckin' lose it.

When I finally get my legs free, Dina's ditched her panties, and she's got her hand jammed between her legs, rubbing her clit, knees up, propped against the pile of pillows at the headboard. Her eyelids are half-mast like a drowsy cat, and she's panting fast.

"Oh, no. You don't come until my cock is in you." I lunge, grab her naughty hand and pin it to the mattress beside her hip. Her free fingers flutter up to kind of pet my chest. I'm wired. Taut. Vibrating with energy.

Alive.

"You don't get to make those decisions unilaterally," she says.

I bark a laugh. How could I not?

"Like hell I can't."

"This marriage is a partnership." She smirks and tickles those soft fingers down over my clenched abs, and wraps them experimentally around my aching cock. I hiss.

"So now we're married?" I grit from clenched teeth.

"I signed a paper," she sasses. "I said 'I do.'" She's cracking herself up, and then suddenly her smile fades.

No. Nothing is stopping this. I lean closer to take her mouth, turn off that clockwork brain of hers, but she's too quick. She takes her hand from my cock and shoves against my chest.

"We need to talk."

"We can talk after." I slide my palm over a smooth hip, softer than a kitten's belly, but she's got her thighs jammed together now, knees locked.

Guess we're talkin'.

"Okay. Go on."

"Do you have a condom?"

We're not using a condom. There's going to be nothing between her and me; I'm gonna feel that cherry burst and her channel flutter when she comes on her first cock.

"We talked about this. I'm clean."

"But how do you know?"

Jesus. I'd call it a mood killer, but apparently, there is nothing that can turn me off. She wants to talk STDs? I'm down. There's nothing about our bodies and our bodies together that I don't fuckin' dig.

"No symptoms. Last time I got tested, I was clean."

"When was that?"

"I don't know. A year or two back."

"You could have caught something since then."

"I haven't."

"But you don't *know*."

"I'm reasonably certain."

"Do you have a condom?"

"We're not using a condom."

"You sure as *hell* don't get to make that decision unilaterally," she says.

The corners of my lips twitch. I can't believe I'm having this conversation. I'm on top of her. I outweigh her by an easy buck seventy-five. She knows what I am capable of. And she does *not* care.

It ain't courage. Ain't ignorance either. It's something else. Something particular to Dina Wall. She knows her own strength, too. Just like I do.

I try persuasion. "I don't want to use a condom. I want to feel you." I brush a tender kiss across that pouty lower lip.

She narrows her eyes, flicking her gaze down to where

my thick cock is wedged against her hip. "I want to feel you, too."

And like that, I'm even harder. My cock jerks against her soft skin. I need the contact, need to reassure myself that I *will* get to feed this hunger so I can keep the need in check just a little longer.

"I wouldn't harm you," I vow.

And it's true. Deep in my marrow, independent of conscious thought, I already know my body won't let her be hurt. Never. In any way. It's not an epiphany; it's a revelation of what's somehow already existed—maybe since I first saw her. I don't know. It's all a mystery.

I am helpless against the power of a good mystery.

She clears her throat, all prim. "Your good intentions aren't a prophylactic."

I bust out laughing. "Aw, baby. You're gonna make me say it?"

"Say what?"

I lower myself closer until her small, pert tits brush my pecs and whisper in her ear. "Ain't been with no one for at least two years."

"Why not?"

Oh, this ain't goin' in the right direction. "I don't know. Tired, mostly."

She scrunches her head back into the pillow so she can give me a look. "But you're not tired now."

"No, baby."

"Not with me," she says.

I let her feel the weight of my hips. She sucks in a breath, and then she smiles. "You like me."

"I do." Why would I lie? I got her where I want her.

"You aren't afraid of your feelings."

"To the contrary. I'm fuckin' terrified," I murmur, and it's true. Somehow, I end up confessing everything to her. She's got some mythical Greek kind of magic. An Achilles heel. Icarus' wings. The reeds in the story of King Midas and the Ass's Ears.

I'm a sailor, and she's a siren, and I don't look, I leap.

Her blue eyes darken and her smile fades. "I'm scared, too. It's going to hurt."

Shit. I guess it will. Before—when this moment was theoretical—I shrugged it off, figuring it'd be uncomfortable for her, a little painful, but I'd make it up to her, and ultimately, it'll be nothing.

Now—I see it differently.

How can I hurt her? I can't. I just can't.

I push up to my knees. She stretches out to rest her hands on my bulky thighs, stroking my dark leg hair. Our bodies are so different. I'm big, tanned and weathered from the grime of the garage and construction sites, hairy as shit.

She's slender, and pale, and smooth as a moonstone.

And she rules me.

My body thrums for her. My mind contorts. I got a million things I need to worry about, and I can't remember a fuckin' one of them 'cause now she's kneeling on the bed with me, back arched, tits high and proud, bare ass resting on her delicate feet, kneading the same spot above my knee over and over with soft fingers, like a cat taken female form, confident in her own superiority.

Her head cocks. "Do you have lube?"

I swallow a cough, gaze dipping to her pussy. "Babe, I can see from here your thighs are slick. You don't need lube."

"Everyone says to use lube."

"That's if you're not wet enough. How wet are you for me?" My abs clench.

She kind of walks her knees apart and peers down at her herself, canting her hips up to see between.

Sweet lord. She parts her pussy with two fingers. She's slick and plump and pink, her little clit popped from its hood, shiny with her cream.

She slips a finger inside, and I suck in a breath. "Pretty wet," she says.

My throat is bone dry.

"I'll go find some lube if you want." The holy grail. The one ring to rule them all. The secrets of the universe. I'll get her whatever she wants.

She makes a noncommittal hum. "I'm wet. It should be fine." Her gaze rises to mine. "If it hurts, how long will it hurt?"

"If it hurts, I'll stop."

"I don't want you to stop until it's done." She settles herself back against the pillows again and lets her knees fall to the sides. "But if I say stop, stop."

"Okay." I go to her, my small autocratic queen, and I kiss her. I taste her, slow and thorough, until she's inhaling me like I've noticed her do. The tension in her frame eases. Her hips pulse in a rhythm. Her hands explore me, two skittish critters that can't stay put, stroking my wiry chest hair, testing the tautness of my ass, playing tentatively with my balls until my cock is tempered steel.

"Okay," she pants, her fingers curling around my length and drawing it to her tight, wet hole. "You can do it now."

I don't fuckin' know if I can. If she cries, what am I gonna do? I can't beat my own ass. Fuck.

I almost look around the room for help. I'm the man with the answers, but sweet lord, I want to pause time and read a how-to book. Drink a shot. Phone a fuckin' friend.

"Come on," she whines, notching me to her entrance.

"Gimme a second," I pant, grabbing her hands, twinging our fingers, pressing them to the mattress on either side of her bed-mussed head. Her eyes are bright. Trusting.

My wife. *Mine*. I don't have to share. I don't have to sacrifice for the greater good. She belongs to me.

Inside me, something shifts. Cracks. It's tectonic. And silent. The work of a moment, and the landscape of my soul is changed.

"I want it now," she demands, chasing me with her hips.

I focus. Quick and be done with it is my general philosophy, but not here and now. I cannot hurt her.

"Heavy," she whines, squeezing my hands, raising one knee to open herself even more.

She wants it. Oh, Lord, do not let me fuck this up.

I steel myself and push in. Only the tip. She's so tight. So hot. I freeze, every muscle aching from restraint. "How's this?"

Her chest is rising and falling rapidly, her eyes glued between us where my fat cock is nocked in her stretched pussy. There's a sheen of sweat on her forehead.

"I don't know. Do I really need to talk now?" Her thready voice is tinged with irritation. "Just keep going."

I kiss her while I push in more—inch by inch—because I'm a coward for her, and I don't want to see pain in her eyes. Except for her heavy breathing, she makes no noise.

"You're doing so good, baby," I mutter to her as I fight the urge to plunge deep in her wet heat. I force myself to work it in patiently, pausing for her to acclimate.

"Open up. Take my cock. A little more. Good girl."

Finally, hours later, I'm sunk in her to the hilt. She's taking all of me, and her ribs rise against my chest, her hip bones notched into the furrow of my Apollo's belt.

I keep kissing her, quick brushes, and somewhere along the line, I let go of her hands to cradle her face.

I don't notice how still she'd become until she starts to move. She begins by readjusting her knees, raising them higher and lower until she must find an angle she likes. Then she rests her heels on my ass.

She taps my shoulder. "You can move now."

I don't know if I can. I don't know if I can take the next level. It's so sweet now. I'm sunk in sugar, immersed in it, high as a kite on it.

It feels so good. Can you freebase magic? 'Cause that's what this is. Her feel, her sounds, her growing response to me.

She kicks me in the butt and rocks her hips. "Come on, Heavy. I want to keep going."

Okay, then. I thrust. Gently. Not my whole length, only a few inches. She bucks to meet me and grunts. It's a good grunt.

I pull out farther, almost to the ridge of my tip. She whimpers. A happy whimper. I slide back in, and her pussy grips me, hungry, and hot.

"It's good, isn't it? Your virgin pussy loves taking my hard cock, right baby?"

She doesn't answer. She's wriggled her hand between us, and she's working her clit, watching my cock plunge into her pink folds, panting heavier and heavier, raising her hips to meet me.

I want to lose myself, let myself go, but I won't. I keep the reins, speed up as she flicks herself harder, but I maintain control. I need to ingrain the moment she comes in my memory. I need to sear the image like a brand.

"You're gonna come for me now, baby." I cup a sweet tit, stroke the stiff nipple with my calloused thumb. She moans.

Her skin is slick with sweat, her abs tensing so I can make out individual ribs.

I tilt her head up. "I want you to look me in the eye when you come."

Her gaze flies everywhere. Back between her legs, the ceiling, my lips. I tighten my grip on her chin. "Try for me."

And then her blue eyes find mine and stay.

"Good girl."

Her pupils blow as her pussy clenches my shaft like a fist, and I come hard, in waves, filling her. She lets out an exultant grunt, and then she splays her arms and legs like a starfish, and I swear to God, she makes the exact same sound they make on soda pop commercials after they take a long swig on a hot day.

I laugh. "You liked that."

She grins like the Cheshire cat. "It sucked at first, but then I got used to it."

"And you liked it." I throw myself down beside her on my back. She's not freaking out about the cum like she did last time. Still, once I catch my breath, I'll go get her a warm washcloth.

"It felt *good*." She looks over to me, her expression approving and more than a little dopey. Prickles dance across my chest.

I grin. "I'm the best lover you ever had."

She snorts. "When you're the only guy in line, you're first and last," she says.

"Wasn't in line," I say, hauling my drained carcass up. "I was in your tight, wet pussy."

She snorts again. I trudge to the bathroom, flick on the light. I don't know why my body is so wrung out. All told, it wasn't a vigorous fuck. I'm feeling it, though. There's a burn in my biceps and thighs, and my abs are sore. From holding back?

I'm off center. My brain's dopey, too, and I don't like leaving her in the bed. I make quick work of wiping my dick. There are smears of blood on it. My stomach churns. Is Dina hurt?

I wet a washcloth and go back to her. She's still sprawled on her back. She doesn't seem to be in pain. She blinks at me when I kneel on the mattress. And she smiles.

My heartbeat trips.

"Knees up," I say, more gruffly than I intended. She complies, unbothered. I gently wipe the mess from her rosy folds while she watches me. My curious cat. There's not much red on the rag. She doesn't seem to be bleeding anymore.

"How are you feeling?" Again, my voice is deeper, rougher than I meant. She's oblivious.

"Thirsty."

I guess she's fine. I amble back to the bathroom, rinse out the cloth, and get her a glass of water. I'm halfway back to the bed when there's a ruckus in the main room. A door slams and raucous voices fill the room—women and men—and the radio begins to blare. Death metal. Dina curls in on herself. In an instant, she's on her side, hugging her knees to her chest, shoulders hunched.

Oh, hell no.

I stride to the door, throw it open, and bellow at the motley, drunken crew of my brothers and strippers—and one random bro in khakis and a button down. "Turn that fuckin' music off!"

Bush hops to, fumbling at the phone he's got hooked up to speakers. The room falls quiet.

"I ain't never seen his dick before," Bush mutters in hushed tones.

A stripper whistles.

I give her a chin dip and turn back to Dina, shutting the door behind me—less vigorously this time.

She's still curled in a ball, but she's peeking up, and her lips are curving.

And then the music starts again, a new song, more mellow but just as loud. I made myself clear. I square my shoulders, preparing to kick prospect ass.

Dina's smile broadens. "Oh, I love this song." She stretches, straightening as she rolls onto her back, pointing her toes.

I guess Bush can live.

Elvis sings "Can't Help Falling In Love," and Dina sings along, off-tune, kind of bopping her head. She climbs to her feet, unsteady on the mattress.

I stalk to stand at the foot of the bed, holding my arms out to her. She stumble-dances toward me, hips swaying in time with Elvis' crooning. She wobbles, straightens, and then darts forward.

I reach out, she tumbles, and then I've got her. I tuck her in my arms, my beard crushed against her tits. Her fingers trail through my tangled hair, combing idly through knots. She hums off-tune, happy, without an ounce of self-consciousness. My chest warms.

There's no way she's getting her hands bloody—no fucking way anything ugly is getting near her ever again. The truth of this slams through me—it rocks me to my core —and I force myself to breathe. Relax.

This isn't an emergency. I can control one weird little woman. The world rearranges itself for me. That's not arrogance; it's plain, observable fact.

Dina Ruth is mine, and I'm going to keep her. She'll fall in line, let me handle the ugly shit. Like everyone else. But for her, it doesn't feel like a burden. It feels like my right.

Beside us, the window shows the cityscape illuminated, a yellow glow rising from the horizon, the sky beyond lightening to an impossible, vivid blue.

The world is still. My ribs crack open. I ain't never felt this way before.

Dina's hair smells like my sweat. My scent clings to her clammy skin, too.

In the room beyond, there's a dull chatter punctuated by playful shrieks.

I hold this wisp of a woman, and for a moment in time, I owe nothing to any man. I'm not tethered to my brothers, my club, my business, my flesh and blood. I carry no weight at all. I'm free and easy.

There's far-off laughter and softness in my arms. My eyes drift shut.

I let it all go, and I dance with my wife.

9

DINA

The Beast, the President of the United States' limo, can withstand a biological attack because every inch is hermetically sealed. Except the driver's side window, which can roll down three inches. It can keep rolling on its steel rims if the Kevlar on the wheels is punctured. The metal plate running under the carriage can absorb the impact of a land mine.

My pussy's sore, and as I soak in the jacuzzi tub, lounging between Heavy's tree trunk thighs, it occurs to me that people talk about vaginas like the Beast.

Yes, a woman's vagina *can* stretch to pass an object the size of a watermelon, and sure, it's impressive, but it's not like *a good thing*. It's not a marvel of modern engineering. Like, I would enjoy seeing the Beast take a direct hit from a grenade and keep going. However, I am extremely ambivalent about whether I want to take Heavy's cock again.

It's poking me in the back right now. How can he be so hard again so soon? His giant noggin rests against the tile, and he's snoring. The bath was his idea, and he lasted five minutes.

I poke my swollen pussy lips. They feel raw. Inside, I ache. It's not unbearable by any means, but there's also a strange feeling low in my stomach. Not hunger—although I could eat. Not cramps even though I'm still spasming now and then. It's more like when a cool evening breeze runs over your skin when you're damp from the pool. It's a goose-bump feeling. A delicious chill.

The bath water is lukewarm, and Heavy's massive chest is hot against my back. He smells like hotel soap and muted colors—burnt orange, Air Force blue.

His faded tattoos blend into the dark hair matted to his arms and calves. A skull with hammers. A rifle above a dreamcatcher in green, yellow, and red, the word "Twitch" on a feather drifting loose below. A horned devil on a motorcycle encircled by the words: Fléctere si néqueo súperos, acheronta movebo.

If I cannot move heaven, I will raise hell.

My skin is a blank sheet of paper in comparison. I line up my forearm against his. The faint blue of my veins against his ink, the intricate barbed wire and thorns surrounding a coat of arms with a bare foot crushing a serpent, its fangs embedded in the heel.

I trace the snake. The image is from Poe. The story where a mad man walls up his enemy in the catacombs for revenge. The Cask of Amontillado?

This man is a book. It's in the ink on his skin.

What am I?

A snail crawled out of its shell.

I had a purpose when I went to him—I still do—but it's so complicated now. I'm so far out to sea. It's like his gravity supersedes my momentum.

It makes sense. He's the much larger mass.

Do I like him?

My "people I genuinely like" list is relatively short. Rory. Mia, my brother Kellum's long lost kid. She's me when I was little—all ears and eyes with nothing to say for herself. I don't mind my brother Jesse. He's quiet. Mia's mom Shay is good people.

I love my parents and Kellum and John, of course. And Cash—sometimes. But do I like them?

The people I like are still waters that run deep. Heavy's deep enough, but he's not still. He steams through life like the prow of a ship.

He's smart. He reads books. I like that.

He says what he means. And he doesn't do small talk. I *really* like that.

So, yeah, he goes in the "like" column. For now. We'll see how the quid pro quo unfolds.

I prop my feet up on the edge of the tub and curl my pruned toes. I don't usually stay in the tub after it cools to a certain temperature, but I'm a little obsessed with laying on Heavy's chest. It's like lounging on top of a bear's belly. Each time he inhales, my whole upper body rises.

Heavy is an experiential kind of dude. His bass voice rumbles, his grip feels like paws, and he smells so freakin' good.

He should be too much. Everything is too much unless I measure it out in the right doses, filter it through one of my many life cheats. Reflections, sunglasses, earbuds. Intellectualization, compartmentalization, conscious denial.

But with Heavy, I enjoy his muchness. It gives me a thrill. Like watching a lion prowl in real life, but from a safe distance.

What happens after he helps me kill Van?

We go our separate ways. We're co-conspirators. And

he's an MC president and CEO of Steel Bones Construction, and I'm a cybersecurity contractor who still lives at home.

Folks rely on him.

I am allergic to people.

He's the man in charge. I'm—

Frequently not in full control of myself.

The water is getting too cold. I raise myself, careful not to slosh too much. Heavy snuffles, but he doesn't wake up. I grab a fluffy towel on my way out of the bathroom and dab myself dry. It's almost noon. There's no sound from the living area except an occasional smoker's cough.

I pick out the softest outfit I can find, a white cotton raglan tee and black leggings. No bra. My boobs are still tender from Heavy's touch. I can hardly stand the whisper of fabric across my puffy nipples.

I'm unsettled. Drifty. So I text Rory. She texts me back emojis of a coffee cup and bacon. She's at her waitressing job. I knew she would be, but I guess I wanted to reach out. Touch an anchor.

What does Heavy think about me?

I have no idea.

He seemed to dig the sex. And we danced, which was weird, but nice.

He seemed concerned about my vagina afterwards. He kept asking if I felt okay "down there." I bet he read that novel where the woman won a guest editor gig at a fashion magazine in New York City and hemorrhaged the first time she had sex. That shit horrified me too when I read it in tenth grade.

I'm standing by the bed, staring at the bathroom door, lost in my head, when Heavy emerges, buck naked and dripping onto the carpet.

"There are towels," I point out. "They're on the shelves under the sink."

He grunts, cracks his neck, and stretches his long arms, throwing the lines of his massive biceps into relief.

I stare at him, arms folded.

He sniffs, wrings out his hair—again, right on the carpet —then casts me a glance. "Don't make it weird."

"I *am* weird."

"Then go make me a coffee." He rolls his shoulders and ambles toward the dresser.

Yeah. I want coffee. "I'm going to make myself a cup," I tell him, turning toward the door.

He ignores me, rooting through his duffle. He scratches his sculpted, muscular ass.

"I'll make you one too, I guess."

"Atta girl," he says. "I take it black."

That's so messed up. Do I get pissed?

I mean-mug him, and his lips curve, dark eyes sparkling. We're joking. That's what this is. He's teasing me, and I'm playing along.

I hike up my chin, straighten my spine, and sashay out the door. He chuckles behind me.

We're flirting. *I'm* flirting. I like it.

THE FLIGHT back to Pennsylvania is uneventful. I know what to expect from an airport now, so it's no big deal. I pop in my earbuds and follow Heavy. He navigates everything.

The guys don't travel with us. They're all passed out when we leave. Heavy says they plan to hang out for a few more days, take a helicopter ride to see the Hoover Dam. One of them is gonna fall out.

Rory and I meet up in *Elfin Quest* on the plane, but Heavy doesn't join us this time. He spends the whole time on his laptop and phone, barking orders and sighing like my dad used to when he was "disappointed" in Cash.

A prospect picks us up, but we don't go back to the clubhouse. Heavy tells the guy to drive us to the cabin.

As the miles pass and we head further and further into the country, my stomach starts to bother me. I'm not hungry. It's nervous energy. What happens now?

Heavy and I are married. The next step is for me to hand over the evidence against his enemies, and then he helps me kill Uncle Van.

I can do it. No doubt. But am I *ready* to do it?

I watch the corn and soybean fields go by and half-listen to Heavy conduct business on his phone. It sounds legit and boring. Lots of talk about material costs and permits.

I flick my thumb with my forefinger, rubbing the skin raw. If Mom was here, she'd nag. She was the best mother a kid like me could have, but she's never accepted that stimming isn't a bad habit.

If it's a bad habit, it's one I need at the moment. I don't *want* to kill anyone. I don't expect I'm going to feel *good* once Van is gone. It's not as if I'm fueled by vengeance, and I'll finally be able to rest once he's dead. I sleep fine now.

It's just fallen to me to pull the trigger, that's all. If I don't, Van Price will hurt more women. He could go after Rory again. He's never had to pay for a single thing he's done, so why would he stop now? I saw the video of what he did to Rory. It wasn't a crime of passion. He knew what he was doing.

They say I have tunnel vision, but my family has blinders of their own. Eventually, they'll let Van crawl back into their good graces, and then what will he do? Kellum won't let him near Shay or Mia ever again, but what about Cash? Cash thinks anyone who drives a truck is a decent guy by default.

My family can't conceive of a world where there are real villains, but I'm the one with a faulty theory of mind. They'd let him come around. Feed him at our table. Try to reconcile him with Kellum and Shay. And Mia.

My stomach clenches. I won't let that happen. Van goes nowhere near Mia. She doesn't have the words yet to tell if something bad happens.

As a human being, I have a lot of glitches, but if I have a strength, it's that I know myself. I'm introspective, and from what I saw at the regional program where I went to school, that's maybe not the norm for people like me. But I understand how *I* work. I know what I'm capable of.

I can kill Van Price, and I'll be able to live with it. I wish Kellum would have figured out some legal way to get justice for Rory and stop Van from hurting people, but he hasn't. Rory won't testify. She flat out refuses.

There's no other solution. No one else is going to do what needs to be done. I'm at peace with the decision I've made, but still, it won't be easy. I want to get it over with.

But instead of hashing out the logistics, we're heading into the countryside. We've turned off the single-lane highway onto a dirt road, and we're bouncing over ruts and winding up a gently sloped foothill. The trees are tall and old growth: oak, chestnut, and hickory with some pine and hemlock interspersed. It's different from the woods at home —thicker and darker. It's a fairy tale forest. It suits Heavy.

He's talking to someone new now. He's silent for long stretches, listening, firing off occasional questions, his face growing craggier with each drawn out reply.

After about a mile, we come to a log cabin in a clearing.

It's big, but it's not huge like my parent's lodge. There's a wraparound porch, a separate three-car garage, and what looks like a wood shop around the back. Unlike my parents' place—which is very much log cabin chic—this place is rough-hewn.

"Did you build it yourself?"

Heavy holds his phone away from his face. "Pardon?"

"Did you build the cabin yourself?"

"Yeah. With the club."

"It's nice."

He pauses a moment. "You like it?"

I said I did. The car rolls to a stop, and Heavy goes back to his conversation. I hop out and wander up the front walk, breathing deep. It smells like him here. Not the exact notes, but his palette, if that makes sense.

I trip up the wood steps to the front porch and turn to survey his kingdom. He's high enough on the hill that the woods and fields beyond spread before him, but the incline is steep behind his cabin, so the place feels nestled and private, not above it all.

Heavy has climbed from the car, but he's standing in the drive, staring up, his phone dangling at his side. Whoever he's on the line with is still talking, but his eyes are on me, his brow knit and his mouth turned down.

"I have to go into town," he says.

"Okay." I shrug and hop back down the steps. He shakes his head.

"It's club business. You gotta stay here."

He's leaving?

And he's leaving me here?

"No, I'll go with you." I like this place, but—my stomach is going to hurt if he goes. I'm not sure why, but it's already tightening.

"You can't. It's club business. I'll leave Wash here."

"Who's Wash?"

"The prospect." Heavy jerks his head at the guy who drove us.

"I don't know him."

Heavy's body tenses. "He won't go near you."

"Then why are you leaving him here?"

None of this makes sense, most of all why I'm arguing. Why do I care if Heavy goes? This place is fine. Peaceful. I'm not under a deadline. And I don't care if there's a skinny dude in saggy jeans hanging around or not. I'm good with my own company. I prefer it. Besides, I've been with people for days straight at this point. I should need alone time.

"He can keep an eye out." Heavy's almost bristling now, shoulders squaring, chin lifting. Is he mad?

"For what?"

Heavy doesn't answer. He glares. If it were anyone else, there's no way I could maintain eye contact. But since it's him, I stare right back.

I'm about to tell him where to get off when I register the roar of an approaching engine. It's loud, and it's coming fast.

Heavy slides his phone in his pocket as he moves to block the porch stairs, his hand tucked under his shirt and resting on the small of his back. There's a bulge. A gun.

What's going on?

Wash trots over. His hand's also behind his back.

Do I run?

Before I can decide, a massive chopper rounds the bend —extended front wheel, long body, twin tailpipes. Cherry red trim. It's my brother John.

He skids to a stop, and in one fluid movement, he releases the kickstand, dismounts, and strides over, halting mere inches from Heavy's face. John's shoulders are heaving. He's out of breath—like he's been running, not riding.

"Hi, John." I move to join them, but Heavy sidesteps, blocking me.

John doesn't answer me or glance my way. He's glaring at Heavy. Angry. Furious. It's crystal clear.

Shit.

I flick my thumb. Heavy's hand drops to his side, but Wash's is still hovering near his gun. My adrenaline spikes. I don't know how to defuse this situation. All my words are twenty feet deep.

"You have ten seconds to explain," my brother says. "And then I'm gonna kill you."

I can only see Heavy's wide back. It's straight, but not tense. "I married your sister."

John's entire bulk swells. He's a big guy. Until I met Heavy, he was the biggest guy I'd ever seen in real life. Watching the two of them confront each other is like the denouement of a superhero crossover—the Wall versus the Giant.

I'm fascinated, but I'm also terrified.

"Bullshit," John spits.

Heavy doesn't answer.

Time stretches. A blue jay calls from a nearby pine. Sounds like someone stepped on a squeak toy.

Finally, John coughs and breaks the staring contest to glance up at me. He holds out his hand. "Come on, Dina. I'll take you home." His lips peel back from his teeth as he turns back to Heavy. "I'll deal with you after."

"She ain't goin' nowhere." Heavy's voice is even, but then again, so is John's. Wash's hand hovers behind his back.

I'm stuck in my head. I don't want to go home, but I don't

want anyone to get shot. I should say something. Definitely. Words. I flick my thumbs faster. What do I say?

"Dina, come on." John snaps his fingers twice.

Like I'm a dog.

Oh, *bullshit*.

"No." I stop flicking and cross my arms.

"Dina." I know that tone. I've done something wrong.

I hike my chin.

John sighs. "Dina, what's going on? Are you scared? It'll be okay, I promise. Just come on. I'll take you home, and I'll sort it all out."

"I said you ain't takin' her nowhere." Heavy's voice is a touch less even.

"Fuckin' watch me," John says.

"I'm not going home," I blurt. Heavy's shoulders lower.

John lets his arm drop, but he doesn't step back. If anything, his chest puffs wider. "Explain it to me, Dina. What's going on?"

I'm not telling him about Van. I'd never make him complicit. He's a good guy. A dad. Ex-firefighter. He'd never go vigilante.

I have to lie.

I suck at lying. What else is there? I guess the truth. "Heavy and I got married."

"Why? Did he—are you—?" His face flushes bright red, and he chokes. "You're a dead man." He's frowning at Heavy again. More than frowning. *Aiming*.

I rush my words, and it all comes out in a jumble. "We went to Vegas. We got married. Then we went to a strip club. And now we're back." I shrug and force a smile.

John's forehead crinkles, and the muscles in his neck pop. His fingers twitch at his sides. "You took my sister to a fuckin' strip club? Did you touch her?"

He's asking Heavy, not me, but *I'm* the one talking to him. Talk about bullshit.

I hop down the stairs, ducking past Heavy. He's distracted, and he moves to block me a second too slow.

I'm now more than a foot shorter than them both, instead of being taller. They both bend their necks to look at me. Wash shuffles, uncertain.

I deal with him first. "You. Take your hand away from that gun. You're not shooting anyone."

Then I glare at John. "Yes, he touched me. We're married. I'm twenty-four. We had sex." I tilt my head. John's stance doesn't change. He bristles even more. What does he want to hear?

"It was good. Mostly." I consider. "Like—four out of five."

Wash wheezes.

John closes his eyes. "Four out of five?"

I swear I can hear Heavy's teeth grind.

"It kind of sucked at the beginning, but then it got good." I think for a second. "Like *Breaking Bad*."

John lets out a long exhale, and he looks at Heavy. "I came to you. Told you she was missing. You didn't say shit."

"She called home," Heavy says.

"What's going on, man?" John shakes his head. "You know she's—" He cuts himself off and compresses his lips.

My throat tightens. It always comes down to this, doesn't it? Dina is special. Dina has ASD. Dina is different.

Everyone knows better than Dina even though no one can understand her.

Bullshit.

I sidle closer to Heavy so that we're both facing John. "I'm what?"

I glare at my big brother. He shuffles in his boots and scrubs his thick neck.

"Dina, you know what I mean. Let's just go. We'll talk about it at home." He reaches for me.

A strange, indistinct sound comes from Heavy's chest, and his whole torso kind of inflates. Without thinking, I lay my hand on his forearm. John's gaze drops to where I'm plucking Heavy's shirt.

"I'm not going home. I'm where I want to be." I enunciate.

Heavy stills.

The crease between John's eyes deepens. "When did you meet him?"

"At the clubhouse." I didn't answer his question, but I'm betting he doesn't notice.

"What were you even doing there?"

"Can't I go out? Do I need your permission?" I'm on a roll now, spitting truth. "News flash. I'm a grown ass woman. I have a job. I have a fucking 401K. You're out of line."

John stares at where I'm grabbing Heavy. It seems to throw him.

"You're my little sister."

"She's my wife," Heavy interjects, and shivers race down my spine. He glares at John, intent, menacing.

I squeeze Heavy's forearm.

"I don't like this, Dina," John says.

"You don't have to." I make myself smile. I try for sweet and innocent.

"I'm gonna beat the shit out of you," John says to Heavy. "Later."

Heavy grunts.

"If you hurt her, I'll kill you." My brother and Heavy lock eyes, and there is a drawn-out silence. Then, John turns to me. "You have my number. Anytime. Day or night."

"I know."

John hesitates a few moments longer, and then he heads back to his bike. Before the engine roars, I hear him snort and say, "Four out of five."

And then he's gone, and Heavy shakes off my grip, all business. "Well, that's settled for now. I gotta go. Get inside," he says. "Eat something."

For a second, I consider arguing again, but now I'm well and truly done. I need quiet. I nod and head back up the stairs.

Heavy snaps and opens his palm.

Wash throws him the keys.

"Watch her," Heavy says, hoisting himself into the driver's seat. "But give her space. Don't touch her. Don't talk to her." He revs the engine. "But watch her."

He peels out, and he's gone in seconds.

Wash gawks at me, wide-eyed. "So do I watch you or not?"

"You heard him," I say and wave him away as I let myself into the house. I make it three steps before I fall back on my heels, my breath whooshing from my lungs.

Heavy lives in a *treehouse*.

It's the kind of treehouse I always imagined when I played in the very nice, but unambitious one my dad and brothers built for me as a kid. They wanted to stop me from climbing dangerously high in my favorite pine when I had freak outs. It worked. I couldn't climb my pine anymore. There was a treehouse in the way.

This house isn't a shed on stilts, though. It's magical.

There's a tree growing in the middle of the cabin—an elm based on the canopy visible through the skylight. From the outside, the tree must look like it grows behind the place, but the trunk is in the center of a great room, surrounded by a metal grate. Floating wood stairs lead to the second floor, a high-ceilinged loft, and everything is open and soaring and filled with light.

There is a stacked stone fireplace, and through a doorway, there's an office with floor-to-ceiling bookshelves. The kind with a rolling ladder on a rail.

A few mounted buck's heads hang on the walls. Two with twelve points, one with fourteen.

This place is nothing like Heavy's room at the clubhouse. It's polished and uncluttered and has a distinctly unlived in vibe.

I wander into the kitchen. It has everything. Professional gas range and hood. Butcher block countertops and farmhouse sink.

I open the fridge. Beer and condiments. I check the freezer. There's nothing but meat wrapped in butcher paper, labeled in black grease pencil. I grab the package that reads "Topside Sirloin." If I'm going to be here awhile, I might as well defrost lunch. I'm not making a meal out of horseradish and Worcestershire.

Since that's going to take a while, I keep exploring, noting the big screen hanging in the main room and the overstuffed leather sofas. This isn't a bachelor pad. It seems designed for company. There's a full bar, a pool table in a nook leading to a huge deck surrounded by towering trees, and—I peek out the French doors—an enormous hot tub and grill.

This is an amazing place. For a vacation rental.

I finally check out the office, saving the best for last. It's more like a library. Twelve-foot ceilings. Three walls of bookcases. A framed painting of a pin-up girl with her hair in a red handkerchief, propping her foot on the peg of a motorcycle, offering up her huge bare boobs. And a massive oak desk with nothing on it but a closed laptop and an old tin can filled with pens and pencils.

There's a modem on a shelf behind it.

I could work.

I finished all my open projects before I left, but it's weird not having an iron in the fire. I get a lot of work based on winning various hackathons and coding competitions, and there are some "impossible" challenges I like to work on when I have the time.

I have time now.

What's the other option?

Am I so pressed to murder my uncle?

With the high windows and the leaves fluttering outside and the quiet indoors, the whole endeavor seems a million miles away. A fever dream almost.

Am I really going to kill a man?

Emotion doesn't drive me. At least it never has. Is that what's driving me now?

Why did I appoint myself judge, jury, and executioner? That's never been my thing. It's the opposite of my thing. I don't worry about other people. I have enough on my plate with myself.

Have I gone nuts? How would I even know?

I miss the world making sense.

I miss Rory.

I miss texting her and meeting at the barn for a ride whenever. Six a.m. on a Tuesday. Five p.m. on a Sunday. If she was home, she'd meet me by Orange Blossom 'cause she won't ride any other horse. She wouldn't canter, and she'd never leave the trail, but she'd be there, happy to see me, content to listen or be silent.

And now she's gone. I rub my chest. It hurts.

Heavy has dozens of people. They call him constantly

and fly to Las Vegas for him and do what he tells them to do. I had one person, and she's gone, and she won't ever come back.

Despite the peacefulness, my brain is buzzy. Consternated. Work would help, but I can't bring myself to open the laptop. I could probably guess Heavy's password in less than three, and that'll just piss me off.

I wander the bookshelves. Here at last is something in this house that isn't in perfect condition. The scent hits me a foot away—paper and binding glue and whatever in the atmosphere that the pages absorbed wherever they were kept before this place.

Spines are broken, dust jackets long gone. I take down a dog-eared copy of Machiavelli's *The Prince*. There are passages underlined in pencil. *Everyone sees what you appear to be, few experience what you really are.*

I re-shelve the book, evening it up with its neighbors. There are thousands of them, and I can't make out the order. Not alphabetical. Not the Dewey Decimal system. A manual on motorcycle repair is shoved between *The Kama Sutra* and *The Thornbirds*.

And there, on a low shelf in the corner, is a worn box. It's a plain shoebox, but big, like it held work boots.

I know snooping is wrong, and to be honest, I don't think I've ever bothered poking into other people's stuff before. I never wanted to know what Cash kept in his drawers. Gross.

But I want to know what's in that box.

It's not right to invade other people's privacy, but that is a very convoluted principle. I don't care if people look at my stuff. I don't know why they'd want to, but how does it hurt me? It took me a long time to master the nuances. Mom had to make me a list—don't open closed bathroom doors, even after you knock, don't go looking for a pen in Pastor Don's drawers, but it's fine to look in Grandma and Grandpa's drawers, but only in the kitchen, not in their bedroom.

Shoeboxes on bookshelves weren't on the list.

I meander closer. "Photos" is scrawled on the top in block letters. Photos aren't private by definition, right? People share photos, and then they expect you to click "like." That's the whole point.

I sit down cross-legged and wince as my tender pussy hits the wood floor. I'd forgotten my little aches and pains. I readjust so my weight falls on my thighs and not my sit spot and ease the box onto the floor.

A delicious shiver runs down my spine. Invading Heavy's privacy is kind of a cheap thrill.

I take off the lid. There is a mess of loose photos, hundreds of them. Some are Polaroids; some are more recent, like the prints you buy online.

On the top, there's a faded color photo of a woman with a perm in a string bikini clinging to a big man in a cut. He has long, wild black hair and a bushy beard. He's shorter and thinner than Heavy, but the resemblance is unmistakable. He must be his dad.

The couple are at a picnic. There are other men in cuts and 80s-rific biker chicks hanging around in the background, smoking, laughing, frozen in time.

I carefully flip through the stack. There seems to be no order at all. So, of course, I systematize.

There are a handful of black and white pictures. A military portrait from World War II. The same man in a white T-shirt and jeans, straddling a motorcycle no bigger than my first dirt bike. There's a wedding photo. The woman is all smiles in a beehive and cat's eye glasses.

Then there are photos that look like my mom and dad's pictures from when they were kids. Christmases and backyard gardens and chubby toddlers in puffy snowsuits plopped in front of snowmen.

And then more pictures of Heavy's parents. They're always surrounded by people, but as the years pass, the pose changes. The dad's hairline recedes, and then he shaves his head. His mom goes from bikinis to tank tops and short shorts to collared T-shirts and mom jeans. It's about that era that she starts wearing a cross on a gold chain.

And as time passes, the space between them grows. They're holding hands, and then they're standing next to each other, and then the mom is holding a little girl on her hip, husband rigid at her side. Now she's got a chunky baby boy. Then she's clutching the boy and girl to her waist while she cradles a baby.

The dad's face is always stern and impassive. The mom's smile is wide and unchanging and not Duchenne.

The kids' expressions vary. The girl always has her hands propped on her hips, her eyes on the little one, but sometimes she manages a tight lip curve—*so* not Duchenne —and sometimes she just glowers at the photographer. The boy—Heavy—laughs or mean mugs or smiles gently. He's big, sometimes with a layer of puppy fat, sometimes stretched almost thin.

He touches the others. He slings an arm around his father's shoulder. Gives his sister a noogie. Carries the baby boy on his shoulders. Piles into a heap with his friends, a bunch of shaggy haired boys, almost always shirt and shoeless.

There's a picture where his mother's hair is shorn. He squeezes her hand as she barely manages to wrap her thin arms around his burly chest, peeking from behind him, a faint but real smile on her face.

It's strange, and it takes me a second to figure out why.

Heavy's not like that. He's not a toucher. He's not physical like my brother Cash who takes every opportunity to invade a person's personal space.

Heavy looms. He stands alone, above. He leads the way.

Except he touches me. He holds my hand. He's always picking me up.

He follows me.

Tingles skate across my skin, almost goosebumps, but not quite. I don't know what it means. I refocus on the photos.

I have to start a new pile. The mom and dad are gone. Most of the pictures are action shots now, badly framed, some blurred. Strips from photo booths.

I line them up, reconsider, flip a few. My legs are cramping, so I stretch them out, ignoring the increased pressure on my sore lady parts.

A teenaged Heavy posed in front of a motorcycle. Maybe fourteen or fifteen. Spine straight. Face sober. His hair dusts his shoulders, and he has a patchy beard and mustache. Off to the side, the girl—his sister—holds a little boy about four years old on her jutting hip. In the foreground, there's a handsome man grinning straight at the camera. He looks like the 1970s personified, although this has to be the early 'oos going by the girl's pink velour tracksuit tucked into furry boots.

The man has a full sleeve on his bare arm, a helmet resting on top of a rifle, a naked lady in an old-fashioned nurse's cap, the SBMC skull and hammers. There's a dream catcher in yellow, green, and red, like the one that Heavy has that reads "Twitch."

He's tucked a greasy rag into the pocket of his worn jeans. And the expression he's giving the camera—if he were in front of me, there's no way I could stand to look, but since this is a picture, I stare and stare, trying to figure it out. I've been leaning hard on my grade school lessons in "this is what feelings do to faces." At this point, I'm operating at my peak.

The man—he must be Twitch—gazes at the camera in pure delight with whoever is taking the picture. He's speaking with the sparkle in his eyes and the soft smirk at the corner of his lips, and even I can hear. Love. Joy.

It's clear the picture is meant to show off the bike— maybe it's new, or from the greasy rag, it could be a finished restoration. But Heavy and his siblings and the bike all fade into the background because of how the man looks at the photographer.

The tingles seep deeper until they're a swish and swirl in my core. Heavy looked at me like that. When we were dancing in the hotel room. Same sparkle. Same quirk of the lip nearly hidden in his beard.

The rest of the pics aren't posed. It's mostly Heavy and his band of brothers. A shot of them sitting on their bikes, everyone except for Heavy smooth-faced or with those smudged upper lip mustaches boys had in high school.

There are pics of parties. Concerts. Bonfires. Raised beer bottles, girls in belly shirts and coochie-cutter shorts hanging off the guys. Pictures of tattoos in progress. There's a rotating cast of secondary characters—including my older brother John and a man who's older than Heavy, but looks like his identical twin, albeit fifty pounds lighter—but the core four are always there.

There's a pretty guy with a man bun. A wiry dude with angry eyes. A tall guy. A muscular man with stiff posture. He disappears from the photos first. And then the tall guy goes.

And that's when the composition of the shots change. To

this point, the guys were all clustered together, no consistent order, but they were a group. A pack.

Then Heavy starts to stand out. He always did because of his size, but now, there's space between him and the others. No matter what the group is doing—laughing, smiling, glaring with hard faces—his expression is stone cold. Aloof. Disconnected and set apart.

Like me.

I sink back on my hands and shake my legs. They're going numb from sitting on the floor. How long has it been? The daylight is dimming. It must be early evening. I've been looking at pictures for hours.

I need to pee. And my butt cheeks have gone numb.

But I don't want to put the pictures back in the box quite yet. I want to stay with this sensation a little longer. I don't know the name for it, and I've never experienced it before. It's brisk. Rich. Expansive.

I know how Heavy *feels* in those pictures. I don't know why he's separate or what happened to make him other and apart. But I know the hollow echo, the sensation of floating off into outer space, of looking through a peephole at real life while you're inside, alone, with only yourself.

I *know* that.

And that means—even though he may not realize it—he could know me.

Not the autistic girl, the idea cobbled together from an 80s movie, a sitcom, and whatever he's read about Temple Grandin.

Me.

I forget to breathe for a second.

A car door slams at the front of the house.

I quickly, but carefully, gather up the pictures and return them to the box. In neat stacks. In chronological order.

Lucky for me, it takes a while for Heavy's boots to sound in the entrance way. Already, I know the weight of his step. It's like barbells dropped on a concrete floor.

I go to him. I rush.

He's standing in the middle of the great room, shoulders slumped. When I come out of the office, he straightens. His eyes find mine. A thrill zaps through my chest. He comes to me. I wait for him.

He lifts me up, takes my mouth, his tongue twining with mine, and it's not too fast. The transition isn't jarring. He's been gone too long, and now he's back, and that's as it should be. A bolt slides home. An arrow finds its target.

He walks me backwards, heading for the stairs, and I wind my legs around his waist, kissing him back, digging my fingers into his wiry, bushy hair. He smells faintly like sweat, and I like it. I like his roughness and how his lips are cold and taste like soda pop. I love how he holds me so tight to his chest it almost hurts.

"Were you good today?" he growls, kicking open the door to a bedroom.

"I looked at your pictures."

He drops me on a bed. A California King. "You snooped in my shit?"

"I organized them for you."

He chuckles as he peels his black T-shirt off. "Get naked, baby."

I'm not exactly aroused. My nipples are tightening, and there's a soft pulsing between my legs, but mostly I'm into this connection I've discovered, and how now he's here, and how thrilling it is—like Christmas Eve when you're a kid, like the moment in a magic show right after "Abra-cadabra."

I tug down my yoga pants.

He sits on the foot of the bed to untie his boots. "Is your pussy sore?"

"Yeah." Even more so after so many hours sitting on a hardwood floor.

He grunts, unbuckles his belt, and unzips his jeans. "Plan B, then," he says, and flops on his back, tucking a pillow behind his head. "Saddle up."

Huh?

He grins. Eyes shining. My lips rise to mimic his. It's automatic.

"Sit on my face."

Oh. Uh. I still have my shirt on. Do I take it off?

"Come on. Hop to." He clicks his cheek twice. Giddy up.

There's a twisting low in my belly, and the pulse becomes a throb. His face is going to be between my legs. His nose. His beard.

I huff out a breath.

"If I gotta put you on my face, I ain't gonna be pleased."

His cock is hard, and he's stroking it idly, thick root to ruddy tip. It draws me. I approach him from the side. Do I just swing my leg over his face?

I kneel beside his head and squat. He grabs my ass and holds me steady. It's like saddling up on a grizzly bear, all bristly on my thighs.

"Good girl."

The words make my pussy clutch on air. I like being called a good girl. Which is weird. In general, I'm not motivated by praise.

I am short, and his head is huge, so I don't have to lower myself very much before his tongue finds my folds. He reaches between us and holds my lips apart, and then he's licking, delving into my hole and lapping me up. It's a lot— it's too much—and then it's not enough.

I rock. He moans. His beard grazes my clit, and I grind. His nose nestles in the wet curls above my slit, and my skin heats every time he exhales. He's grabbing my ass, urging me on.

He's muttering something, but I'm riding his tongue, and it's too muffled to make out. Then his hands are gone, and he's moving underneath me like an earthquake.

I'm so close. My abs are spasming, the heat inside me is coiling, and it feels so good. His tongue is so *thick*. He fills me. Owns me. He sucks a lip into his hot mouth, and I explode, buck against him, squeeze my knees against his hard head.

He laughs, and the vibrations send waves of pleasure chasing the receding delicious ache of my orgasm. I have never come so hard alone as I have with Heavy. He's a different level.

I flop back, exhausted and pleased, and my back whacks his hard dick. He oofs.

"Oh, sorry." I flip and wriggle until I'm upside down and beside him on the bed.

He's grinning. "How about you return the favor?"

He's still working himself, but not furiously. I don't think he's close to coming. He's massive. And I have a gnarly gag reflex. I've never given a blow job before—obviously.

What does it even taste like?

I reach out and stroke him with my fingertips. The reddish purplish skin is soft, but what's underneath is harder than muscle. I climb over his calf to kneel between his legs, and he widens them to give me room. He shifts backward so he can prop himself up on a stack of pillows. To watch.

A thrum of excitement reignites in my chest.

He wants to see me take him in my mouth.

I like that. It makes me feel like he's under my spell. I'm not the Little Mermaid. I'm Circe.

I peel off my shirt, and his gaze drops to my breasts. He licks his lips.

"You gonna show me those pretty little baby apple tits while you suck my cock?"

I arch my back so they're on display. He groans.

"Please, baby. Stop teasing. I've been waiting all damn day." He grabs my forearm and gently draws me forward until my palms are braced on his massive thighs.

"I don't know what I'm doing."

"You can't fuck it up. I promise."

I lean down, and I dart out my tongue to taste him. It's earthy. Hint of salt. Not too bad.

I wrap my mouth around the head. He moans. I try to lick, but there's not much room to maneuver. Also, I'm kind of concerned about my teeth. I can't retract them, so there's no way to prevent a scratch here and there. I guess if it hurts, he'll pull out. He isn't. He slowly eases deeper.

My jaw is as wide open as it gets, and it's starting to ache. He's not even halfway in. I'm also slobbering a lot. When I back off to the tip, strings of spit cling to my lips. He groans.

I must suck, but his sounds don't sound unhappy. They come from deep in his chest. And he's muttering under his breath. I focus in on his words.

"Oh, yeah. That's it. You're fuckin' amazing. Your mouth is so sweet. You love to suck my cock, don't you, pretty girl? You want it, don't you?"

I do. Not the dick in my mouth. This is a C, C minus, experience at best. But I want him like this—barrel chest heaving, taut as a bowstring. Mind blown. By me. This giant is under my control. I'm the beast master.

"Yes," I mewl, and he kind of shouts. He takes my hand,

wrapping it around his base and guiding it, up and down, squeezing hard. I suck, and he moans. Loud. Unreserved.

"I'm gonna come in your mouth, baby," he pants. "You gotta back off if you don't wanna swallow."

I really don't. The cum leaking from him to this point has been salty and hot—which is *gross*. I hate pretty much all warm, wet foods.

But I bet he'd love it.

I want him to love it.

I want him to feel good.

Because I want to feel good.

And there's a link. A circuit. I can't understand it, but I know systems, and you don't need to know *why* if you know *how*.

He feels good, and I like that.

I ease off to say, "Do it in my mouth."

He shouts so loud it rings in the rafters, and he jerks, grazing my teeth, and spurts of hot, salty cum flood my mouth. I gag—hard—but I get it down. It tastes *awful*. I swallow several times, and he laughs, deep and warm. It's wonderful in my ears.

"Didn't like that, did you?"

"It's so nasty."

"Want to lick me clean?"

I kind of hack as if I have a hairball, and he laughs louder and drags me to his chest, cradling me there, smoothing my hair. I relax when I realize he was joking.

We lay there a while. He traces my spine and the tips of my ears. He likes to jiggle my ass, too, like he's testing the firmness. At some point, his dick stiffens, but not all the way. Just enough to poke me in the belly.

I sigh and let myself be lifted and lulled by the rise and fall of his chest.

I've almost drifted off when he whispers, "Did you miss me today?"

"I was looking at pictures. I lost track of time."

He's quiet. His body tenses. My shoulders hunch like they do when I know I got it wrong, but I don't know what I should have said.

"Did you miss me?" I ask him. Sometimes if you turn the question back around, people will tell you the right answer.

He coughs, and he's silent a moment. Then he says, "I need your help with something. Hacking a cell phone. Can you do it?"

"Yeah." That's pretty 101 if it's a civilian. "Whose phone?"

"A guy named Rab Daugherty."

"What'd he do to you?"

"Disappeared."

It's a few seconds before I figure out he's not going to elaborate.

I raise my eyebrows.

"That's it. Disappeared. Can you do it or not?"

I take a second to consider. "Not."

"You just said you could."

"Then why'd you ask again?"

He draws in a very deep breath. "This isn't a game, Dina."

"I don't think it is. The answer is not if you won't tell me what's going on."

"It's club business."

"Okay."

Again, there's a pause, like "club business" is some kind of explanation.

"We don't involve females in club business."

"A female does your books." I hacked Steel Bones' financials pretty early on. Deb has beautiful spreadsheets. She's gotta be high strung. "And females work at your strip club. And your lawyer is a female."

He huffs. "We don't involve *outsiders* in club business."

"Okay." I'm not going to point out that he just asked me to hack a guy's phone—which is club business. He must see the flaw in the logic.

He adjusts his pillow. Rubs his belly. Adjusts his dick. Then he says, "Rab's the VP of a rival club. He knows where to find a guy we wanna talk to."

"Who's that guy?"

He sighs. Very loud and long. "Knocker Johnson."

"The driver who got busted with the guns?"

"The driver's son."

"Do you want to kill him?"

"Why would I want to do that?"

I shrug. In the movies, that's what "talk to a guy" always means.

"You don't need to know this," Heavy says. His tone is curt.

"I don't want to help you kill anyone."

He barks a laugh. "You just want me to help you kill a guy."

I ignore his valid point. "I need his phone number. Billing address. Whatever personal information you can get me."

"Okay."

"And when you finish your business we'll get to mine?"

"I'll get the number," he says, sitting up and cracking his back. He swings his legs over the bed, lumbers to his feet, groans, and shuffles toward the bathroom.

All of a sudden, I'm cold. He didn't answer the question. I grab my shirt and tug it over my head, working over the conversation to see where it went sideways.

He asked if I missed him today.

What was I supposed to say? I didn't miss him. I was looking at pictures.

Should I have lied?

I don't like second guessing myself. I learned a long, long time ago that if I fall into that hole, that's all I'll ever do. You just have to accept that people are unknowable, communication is a crap shoot, and ultimately, people are going to do and think how they want regardless of what you'd prefer.

Heavy wants me to hack a cell phone for him.

I want him to help me conceal a murder.

It's a transactional relationship.

I should be comfortable with that.

Why does my stomach hurt?

Why am I lonelier now than I was all day by myself, sorting photos on the floor?

10

HEAVY

I don't want to be sittin' here watching Wash's pants sag below his ass crack as he hangs a framed bullet on the wall.

"Is it even, boss?" he asks over his shoulder, losing his footing on the step stool. Kid is high as a kite, but it's his complete lack of brain matter in a sober state that's impeding him earning his patch. He's actually less trouble stoned.

Tonight, we celebrate Roosevelt becoming a full-fledged brother. Wash—Wash might not make it.

"A little higher on the left." He adjusts it so the right corner is now higher.

Dude should have a level. We're a fucking construction company. How does he not have a level?

I check my phone. Dina hasn't texted. No doubt she's lost in her new project. A few days after I moved her in, she got bored and took a short-term contract with a firm she's worked for in the past. An idle Dina is the devil's plaything. She rummages in my shit, and she orders a lot of pizzas. The first week or two, I'd get home, she'd have a pepperoni food baby, and she'd need her belly rubbed before she'd wanna fuck.

It's better with her working. She tracked Rab's phone, and I began to see the possibilities. She's good. Based on Rab's intel, she found Knocker Johnson. He's holed up in a vacant hunter's cabin out by Lake Patonquin. The asshole probably watched our worksite burn the night he and the Raiders torched it, cackling to himself like the Joker. Dude has the style down. I bet he jerks it to Harley Quinn fan art.

We decided on our next step earlier at church. I don't like it, but it's our best move.

I want to go home to Dina.

Home is a strange, strange idea. I ain't had one in a long, long time.

The cabin never felt like home before, but there's something about a woman's shit lying around that makes it so. Dina's socks are in balls under the coffee table. She had an ergonomic keyboard and two extra monitors shipped to the house—on my dime. She's hacked all my accounts, set the thermostat to sixty-six degrees at night and blocked me from changing it. She's says I'm as hot as a furnace, and it's either set the temperature to freezing, or I sleep on the sofa.

She's made herself comfortable. It's been four whole days since she brought up her uncle. I tell her arranging a murder takes time. You can't afford to cut corners. I'm full of shit. Ain't sure if she believes me or not. I can never tell what she's thinking.

It's peaceful.

I can't make her do nothin' she don't want to do. My unparalleled powers of persuasion and intimidation are useless. It's an amazing feeling. Like nitrous.

I know it can't last forever. John and I have already had three heart-to-hearts about it. I've convinced him she showed up at the clubhouse looking for him, and we fell for each other. Now I know he doesn't believe me, but I let them chat on the phone, and he's keeping his peace for now. Dina told him she wants to wait and tell her parents in person after she knows whether or not she wants to stay with me. Fuckin' humbling having a woman say that dead serious, right in front of your face.

She's gonna leave.

I only got my house mouse until she wises up and forces my hand. Then I'll have to tell her I have no intention of letting her murder a man, and she'll have no reason to stay.

She doesn't feel like most people do. I didn't think I did, either, but damn if the world ain't full of surprises.

I feel.

I want.

I want Dina curled in my lap, playing with my chest hair while she watches horror movies from the 80s. I want the feeling when I walk through the door—be it at six p.m. or midnight or four in the morning—and her little feet pad across the hardwood floor as she comes to me, black hair stuck up at all angles, braless, eyes hungry.

She starts talkin' before we're in the same room, and it could be about anything—she saw a hare out the kitchen window, Rory called, the Worcestershire sauce in the fridge is expired, and expiration dates are a scam, but she threw it out anyway because it smells bad so it's in the trash, and the trashcan is out on the back deck because the bottle cracked when she tossed it, and then the whole kitchen reeked.

I know I can't keep her. I know she ain't a real wife. But I ain't giving her up, either. Not yet.

I like listenin' to her treatises on Worcestershire sauce. She says it wrong. It's adorable. Wor-ces-ter-shire, like it's a land of hobbits.

"How 'bout now?" Wash asks.

I lean back in my chair, exhale and steeple my fingers. "Little higher on the right."

There's a loud rap at the half-open door, and Wash startles, fumbling the wooden frame, makin' it even for a split second. Then Harper lets herself in. She's been to the salon. Her hair's shellacked to hell, and her face is painted on with a heavy hand. She's wearing a black top tied in front like a bow, showing her tits to the tops of her nips.

Anger simmers in my guts. It shouldn't have come to this.

She strides in, Hobs dogging her heels. He's wearing his usual goofy grin. He needs a haircut. He looks like a surfer. He comes straight to me, delight on his face, and clasps my hand. I slap his back.

"Hey, little brother. What you up to?"

He smiles, but he doesn't respond. After a few beats, he wanders over to watch Wash work, if it can be called that. Sometimes Hobs does that—zones out like he's put on pause or he's buffering or something. Head injuries are weird. He can still do Sudoku. Can't measure. He remembers the rules of baseball. Can't drive. It makes no freakin' sense.

Harper perches on the fancy boardroom table that drives Eighty Nowicki nuts. He's always grumbling that we're turning into yuppies. He's a dick, so I make sure the sweetbutts keep the marble polished to a high shine.

"We really doing this?" Harper says, nibbling at a manicured nail.

I slap the finger from her mouth. "Waste of money if you're gonna do that."

"My money to waste."

"So it is, so it is." Harper doesn't take a cut from the club businesses, though she's sure as shit entitled. She makes do with her lawyer billings, and she gouges us, so it's probably more than fair in the end.

"We really gonna welcome that cheating slut into this club with open arms?" Harper grimaces.

"Nevaeh Ellis is Forty's old lady. She took a bullet for him."

"A bullet from *her* ex."

"You got to get on board with this." I let a note of warning enter my voice.

"I don't have to do shit." Harper runs her tongue over her front teeth. It's a habit she has, but whatever brand of bright red lipstick she wears, it doesn't smear. "She's gonna mess him up again. She's a flake."

"Ain't your business."

"Like that wife you have tucked away at the cabin? When you gonna bring the missus around, little brother?"

"I'm not."

"So when are you gonna get our evidence off her?"

"I'm not."

She raises an eyebrow. "Come again?"

"I'm gonna find a different way."

And it's like someone pricked her with a pin. She deflates, setting her elbows on the table, resting her forehead on her fingertips. Without looking up, she says, "You. Leave."

Wash waves Hobs toward the door. Dumbass.

"She means you, dude."

Wash blinks, surprised, and he takes a damn long time to climb down the ladder and scuttle out. He doesn't shut the door behind him.

"Hobs, baby, get that, would you?"

Hobs does as she asks, and then he wanders back to the

wall, grabs the framed bullet the Dentist dug out of Nevaeh Ellis, and climbs the step ladder. Shit. I'm gonna end up hanging that myself, and probably patching the drywall to boot.

Harper raises her head. Her eyes are tired. "What do you mean 'a different way'?"

I shrug. "A different way." I ain't figured it out yet, but I will. I have to. I'm not letting Dina kill her uncle.

I'm expecting Harper to shriek and lose her shit, but instead, her shoulders slump, and she flashes a small, sad smile.

"You're a fuckin' goner."

"I don't know what you mean," I lie.

"Love is in the air," she sings, bitter as hell, shaking her head. "Never thought I'd see the day."

I don't bother to deny it. What else could this brand of stupidity be? "It don't affect nothin'."

"It doesn't?"

"We made a choice. We chose the club." Harper and I were so young that night at Twitch's wake. So wasted. But we both remember. We were sitting under a tree past the bonfire, polishing off the bottle of whiskey we'd snuck in to Twitch in hospice. Shirlene was passed out in my arms.

"Do you ever regret it?" I ask.

She laughs; the edge of the sound could cut rock. "Every damn time I fuck Des Wade."

The weight resettles on my shoulders—the guilt, the shame—and I see the echo in Harper's dull eyes.

Hobs sets the frame down, digs in his pocket, and takes out a pencil stub.

"Do you ever think about it?" I ask.

"No," Harper says, and then she exhales. "But I dream about it."

She knows what I'm talking about. Not the decision to stay in Petty's Mill, but the other decision. Our origin story. Our original sin.

We were so young, sitting on the front porch, sharing a joint. It was late summer. The sun was still setting. Dad was passed out in his easy chair. Mom had been gone a few months.

The laugh track of some old sitcom drifted through an open window. I was home for the summer from M.I.T. She'd just finished law school and had an internship lined up in Chicago for the fall.

We were talking about where we'd end up. Los Angeles. Paris. Shanghai. Dubai.

Somewhere far away. New. Busy. Alive.

No drunken father wasting away in front of the television. No loss haunting every room.

The world beckoned. The future.

A car pulled off at the top of our road, and Hobs jumped out. He was coming back from baseball practice. He was still wearing his uniform, his bat slung over his shoulder. He'd seen us. Grinned. Waved. Brushed his feathered hair out of his eyes.

He'd bent over. To tie his shoes?

There was a screech, a truck skidding to a stop out of nowhere, a shout.

Harper and I ran.

Hobs froze.

We screamed, "Run! Run!"

A figure in black with a burgundy pillowcase over his head, holes cut out for eyes, reached down, grabbed the bat —and as Hobs finally bolted—swung, connecting with a crack.

I ran, Harper at my heels, and I watched the bat make

contact again. And once again. And when we were a yard away, the man let the bat fly and leaped back into his truck, roaring off.

I kept running after the taillights, and when I turned, Harper was cradling Hobs in her lap, molding his bloody head, trying to hold the pieces in place.

At the hospital later that night, Dad heard that Stones Johnson had died earlier that day in prison. A heart attack.

And then it made sense. The black square on the man's wrist I'd seen when he'd thrown the bat.

It was an inked-out Steel Bones tattoo.

I was a different man then. I let months pass, doing the Hamlet thing. Thinking myself out of action.

Harper never went to Chicago. She stayed in Petty's Mill. She fed Hobs. Cleaned him. Taught him to speak again. Button his shirt. Zip his pants. And at night, she'd call me at college and tell me she'd seen Dutchy Johnson at the grocery store. The bar. The gas station.

We lost Dad. Then Twitch. I came home. And the little brother who I taught to ride years ago, I taught to climb on my bike behind me and hold on.

Then late one Saturday night, Harper talked me into coming with her to Sawdust on the Floor for a drink. It was almost closing time when Dutchy strolled in. The entire place was wasted. Harper was dancing. I was nursing a bottle alone at a corner table. I stood. Harper smiled and slightly shook her head.

She got Dutchy's attention in seconds. Took her less than fifteen minutes to lead him out the back door.

I followed.

I still don't know what she whispered in his ear. Was he cocky or stupid enough that he believed we didn't know what he'd done? Or did the prospect of revenge fucking a Steel Bones princess get the better of his common sense?

Harper got him all the way to the far end of the parking lot, right by her Jeep.

We hadn't talked about it, hadn't planned it. But I knew.

I knew about the switchblade she kept in her purse.

I knew if I didn't do it, she would.

So I slipped my blade from its ankle sheathe, and I crept up as she took off her top, tugged down her bra, and squeezed her tits, smiling, her eyes two black holes in the shadow cast by an old oak tree.

She kept smiling as I slit his throat, moving instantly to press her shirt to the wound so Dutchy's blood wouldn't spill on the ground.

I caught him against my chest. She grabbed his feet. We slung him into the back seat of the Jeep. He didn't stop breathing until we were a quarter mile down the road.

Later, she carried a bag of mulch and a sapling up Half Stack Mountain while I hauled a sack with Dutchy's remains, drained of fluids.

We took turns digging.

After I patted the earth firm around the sapling, I bowed my head, but I didn't pray.

I said, "I'm going to hell."

And Harper said, "Yeah. So am I."

I'm lost in the past, so when Harper's hand touches mine, I startle. "But I'd do it all again without hesitation." She squeezes. "Don't shrug off love like it's nothing, little brother. It's the strongest thing there is."

She groans, twists her chair, and the moment is gone. "I need a fuckin' drink," she says, slapping the table.

"We agreed you'd go in sober."

That was the first condition of me agreeing to her plan.

She goes in sober, armed, and with a tracker on her phone and sewn into her bra. A full contingent of men surround Knocker's cabin before she goes in—they're already in position—and if he makes a move toward her, she kills him. No hesitation.

We know Knocker has eyes on the club. He knows we're having a shindig. He won't be expecting a visitor tonight.

Harper first proposed this a few months ago after Knocker got out—before Dina, before the Raiders tried to kidnap Fay-Lee.

Harper figures she can trade on the fact that Knocker and her were kids around the clubhouse together, but if he gave a shit about that, he wouldn't have come after Steel Bones in the first place.

"I believed you when you said it'd be nothing." I hold her gaze even though the pain there strips me to the bone. "I'm sorry."

She sniffs and shrugs. A shutter drops, and her gray eyes are blank slates again. "I thought it'd be nothing. I wasn't lying when I said that. I like sex. Des Wade is hot. I figured it'd be fun."

"I shouldn't have let you do it."

She snorts. "How were you gonna stop me?"

"I'm bigger than you."

Something broke in her sometime this past year, and it cracked so quietly, I didn't notice. It was after she split from Charge, and he took up with Kayla. If I didn't know Harper like I do, I'd think it messed with her, seeing him happy with his new family, but she's never wanted that life. Georgie the Corgi is almost too much commitment for her.

Harper leans back and drums her red nails on the table. "Okay, brother-who-is-bigger-than-me. Tell me why we aren't going to use your hacker wife's evidence."

"You tell me. What happens when you take out your tablet and show Knocker Johnson an FBI file that says Des Wade and Anderson Watts put him and his old man away?"

Harper inclines her head. "He doesn't believe me."

"Knocker doesn't want the truth. He wants twenty years of his life back."

"What do you give the man who wants the impossible?" Harper muses.

"What did Cain want?" I ask.

"To kill Abel."

"And then?"

Harper shrugs.

"He wanted his wandering to be over. He wanted to build a city. To take a wife and fill her with his seed and found a dynasty."

Harper arches an eyebrow. "I'm not having Knocker Johnson's babies."

"You're a trial lawyer. Paint him a picture. Revenge is cold. Convince him he wants something warmer."

Harper leans back in her chair, a wicked smile playing at her lips. She's smarter than me. She's always seen through me. "Maybe Knocker Johnson isn't you. You've had a lot of time to get tired of revenge."

"Knocker's had nothing but time."

"And as soon as he was paroled, he set our shit on fire. I don't think he's done killing Abel just yet."

"Then he dies when you shank him in his hunting cabin."

Harper laughs. "You have such confidence in me."

"I know you." I know what fuels her. I know why she fights. I check out Hobs' progress. He's placing a nail. Harper is the most dangerous person in this club. She has a mother's love in her heart and a lawyer's conscience.

"I'm not going to shank Knocker. I'm going to wind him around my finger and bring him home on a leash."

There's no doubt in my mind that she can. If she chooses to.

"I can kill him," I offer.

"It would defeat the purpose. We're righting the wrongs of the past, aren't we? This is a story of reconciliation."

"Done," Hobs announces, folding the step stool and heading out. A man on his own mission.

"Good job, bud," I call to his back. He's already gone.

Harper and I both shift and admire his handiwork for a few moments in silence. The frame is perfectly even. It took me two weeks of work in the evenings to carve it how I wanted. It would've taken less time, but Dina is fascinated by my shop, and she wanted to know all about the machines. And then I needed to fuck her bent over the workbench. And the jointer. And the table saw.

The framed bullet looks good under the mount I made for Boots' amputated leg bones. I take another minute or two to scan the walls. They're the club's scrapbook, a testament to our survival.

Patches and medals from Korea and Vietnam, Iraq and Afghanistan. Old signage lifted from the Petty's Mill Steelworks before it shut its doors and was razed to the ground.

Danger: Gasoline. No smoking, hot work, or naked light.

Safety is the Eternal Vigilance for the Well Being of the Other Fellow.

The rows and rows of mug shots.

The sobriety chips. One day. One month. One year.

The memorial cards. The Shovelhead from Dad's first ride. The Fathead from Twitch's last.

So much history.

It bears down on me until my bones scrape.

"What happens after?" Harper asks, breaking the silence. "What happens when it's all over, one way or another?"

I'm the one who considers every angle. Every contingency. How come I've never imagined that far ahead?

I let the air slowly from my lungs. "We go for a long run. We tap a keg."

And afterward, I throw Dina over my shoulder, carry her to my bed, and lay back while she rides my cock, smiling, moaning from the back of her throat, her fingers clutching my chest hair.

"We'll live for ourselves," Harper says, her lips curved.

I grunt in agreement.

We both know it's a lie.

We decided a long time ago that these men and women we call family come first. Harper had her reasons. I have mine.

When your brothers look up to you, you have a choice. Lead or sit down. I choose to lead.

A leader doesn't get to lie on a soft mattress and ease his joints while a creamy-skinned nymph worships his cock. He doesn't get to neglect his duties to hang around a cabin in the woods, trying to carve a path into the perfect woman's stone heart through stubbornness and creative cunnilingus.

A leader carries weight.

Harper rests her thin, pale fingers on my hairy forearm again. "'Be happy for this moment. This moment is your life.'"

She stands and presses her forehead to mine, and then she squares her shoulders.

"The Dalai Lama?" I guess.

"Omar Khayyam." She rubs my brow with her thumb. Her makeup must have come off. "I love you, little brother.

Now I'm going to do some shots and raid Deb's desk drawer."

"You promised."

"I'll sober up before I leave." She tugs my beard. "You coming?"

"In a minute."

She stands, tugging her drooping top back up, and heads out to join the party. Once she's gone, I lean back and let my eyes drift shut, inhaling the familiar scent of stale cigarettes and beer.

One of my earliest memories is sitting in my dad's lap in this room before church, tracing the names and symbols carved into the old wood table that now hangs on the wall above the jukebox.

For just a moment, I let my mind wander. Far away. To Dina. To only her and I under a thin, white sheet. Her breath warm on my chest as she sleeps in my arms.

Nothing and no one else in the world.

It's a pretty dream.

So simple. So sweet.

So impossible.

11

DINA

I wake with a start, my heart slamming in my chest. My phone's going off. It's pitch black. Where am I?

Heavy's cabin. I suck down a ragged breath.

The phone vibrates to the edge of the nightstand. I snatch it just before it falls off and swipe without looking. There's only one person who calls me in the middle of the night.

"Dina?"

Rory's crying. What time is it? It's past midnight. I was sound asleep. Heavy's not home. Where is he?

Yeah, he had a thing at the clubhouse tonight. He said he'd be back late.

After I passed out, the wind kicked up, and there's an elm branch scraping across the roof. There's a whooshing of leaves through the window I left open a crack. The bedroom's chilly without Heavy. Eerie.

"Rory? What's going on?"

Rory does this every so often. She has nightmares.

"N-n-nothing," she stammers. She's hyperventilating.

"Are you okay?"

"Y-y-yes." She breaks into fresh tears.

"Did you have a bad dream?"

"It was *h-horrible*."

She won't ever tell me the details, and I don't push. "You should go get a glass of water." My mother always got me a glass of water when I woke up in the middle of the night.

"I don't want to get out of bed." Her voice is so small, like when we first met, and I had to lean close to hear her.

"There are no monsters under the bed who are going to grab your ankle."

She has a phobia about creatures under the bed and in closets. It's not serious, but then again, when we had sleepovers when we were both still in school, she refused to get out from under the covers until I turned the overhead lights on.

"Th-that reassurance is way too specific for c-comfort, D-Dina." She sniffles, and then there's a honk as she blows her nose.

"Do you want to get on *Elfin Quest*?"

"N-no." She doesn't say anything else, she just weeps. At least the hysterics have ebbed.

"Do you want to talk about it?"

"No."

I lay back, reach for Heavy's pillow, and tuck it to my chest. It smells like campfires in the early morning.

"Is everything okay? Like the job and stuff?"

"Yeah."

She cries softly, and I listen. I never know what to say to make it better. My Mom could do it. She can talk at you until you're not upset anymore. There's no rhyme or reason to what she says. It could be about the weather, but she has the words, and after a few minutes, whatever's wrong isn't solved, but you're calm and hiccupping. I've watched her do it a thousand times—with Grandma when she was alive, with Cash and Jesse when they were little kids, with Mrs. Lil and her other friends.

I don't have the words. All I can do is sit here and listen, digging my nails into this pillow.

Powerless.

I'm going to kill Van Price. I'm going to shoot him in the head, and then Rory won't have nightmares anymore.

Eventually, after a long time, Rory's sniffles grow further and further apart.

"Do you want to play *Elfin Quest* now?" Sometimes after she feels better, she does like to play until she falls asleep again.

"Not tonight," she sighs.

"I love you, Rory. You're my only friend." It's all I know to say.

"I love you, too, Dina. I miss you."

"I'll come see you soon."

"Oh, Dina. I'm so proud of you." There's a hint of the everyday Rory in her voice again.

"Why?" I suck. I'm lounging here in bed when I could have already made it so she doesn't have to be scared anymore.

"You finally left home."

That's nothing. I had to—to do what I plan to do.

"I know how hard it must have been."

"I took a rideshare. You just download an app."

She giggles, and the tension in my shoulders eases. She's feeling better.

"Don't go back, Dina."

"Why not?" All my stuff is there. It's where I live.

"Because you're happier now."

I am?

"You're happy now, period," she says.

"I wasn't before?"

"I don't know. You can't tell someone else what they feel."

"You just did."

She snickers again. "Well, you tell me. Are you happier now out in the big, wide world?"

I don't know. These days, I can't really understand what I feel. I don't even want to take the lid off the pot and see what's bubbling. I wouldn't be able to make sense of it—that I know for sure.

"I'll be happy when I see you again."

"Back at you, big sister."

A mellow warmth blossoms in my chest. I love it when she calls me that. I earned that.

"Sleep tight," I say.

"Stay on the phone until I fall asleep?"

"Of course." I settle in and listen until her breath becomes deep and even. There's still an occasional catch, but she's fading fast. I'm wide awake.

Why did I leave home?

To make Rory safe.

But what am I doing now?

I'm sidetracked. I'm letting her down. Again.

Am I a coward? Is that it? Am I so brave and badass when I'm home in front of a computer screen, but as soon as shit gets real, I flop and flounder around like anytime I try to go anywhere or do something new?

Am I playing a character in my own game?

Am I really going to kill a man?

I can't sit around anymore. I can't keep letting Heavy put me off with one excuse after another. I know that's what he's been doing, and I've been happy to let him.

Because I'm weak? Because I really can't do this?

I don't like how my insides feel. Sticky and sour. I throw my legs over the side of the bed. It's almost one in the morning, but I'm wired.

I tug on some black leggings and a soft white T-shirt.

I can't be in this cabin anymore. I have to talk to Heavy.

I slip on my pink ballet flats, trip down the stairs, and flick the porch lights several times. There's always a prospect around the place somewhere. Sometimes it's Bush. Sometimes a dude named Roosevelt who looks like he's recovering from a pretty bad car crash. And sometimes a red-headed kid named Hoover who asked me to please call him Tommy.

I wait a few seconds, and it's Tommy who comes bounding up from the garage. He's wide awake.

"Wassup?"

"I want to go to the clubhouse."

He runs his fingers through his shaggy red hair. He's a skinny dude, and his black cut hangs off his bony shoulders. "I don't know, Dina. Prez didn't say to take you to the clubhouse."

"Did he say not to?"

"No." He drags out the syllable.

"So you can. Do you have a car?"

"I have my bike."

"Okay. Let's go."

He seems to think a minute, but then he shrugs. "Boring as shit around here," he mutters. "Listenin' to fuckin' owls."

Tommy has a crotch rocket, and the pillion seat is almost nonexistent. It's good he's lean, and I have a narrow ass. He rides bent forward, so I get all the wind in my face. It's brisk and dewy, and it clears my mind.

He doesn't hold back, leaning into the curves, opening it

up full throttle on the straightaway. I get a bug in my teeth, and it's gross as hell, and I can taste it, but this is fun. It's dark, quiet except for the crickets and the engine, so the only sensation is speed.

I like speed.

We pull up at the clubhouse too soon. It's packed. Bikes and trucks overflow into the field across the street. Light blazes from the window.

"You good?" Tommy asks as I dismount.

I nod, and he skedaddles. Guess he doesn't want to be around to find out how the Prez feels about him bringing me to the clubhouse.

I haven't been back since I was here the first time. Heavy's been keeping me at the cabin. His choice, actually. Not mine. He says it's better if folks don't see us together. Because of the conspiracy. Which would make sense if I didn't have the distinct sense he's not committed.

My brain isn't frizzled by anxiety now, so I can take the clubhouse in. It's a renovated garage—a big one with an arched roof. There's a wing of more modern construction, but it's designed not to detract from the original structure. It's a cool building. Looks straight from the fifties.

The doors are on a rail, and they're open. I walk through into the huge main room.

I remember the pool tables and bar stretching the length of one wall, the jukebox and the dance floor, and seating scattered around. I also remember a bunch of people, but the joint is nowhere near as raucous as it was last time.

I scan the place. There's a bunch of women by the bar and no men anywhere.

Weird.

And then a loud voice hollers across the empty space. It's strong. And drunk.

"Ho-ly shit!" A woman wearing a big black bow as a shirt staggers toward me. "Is this the wifey?"

I recognize her from the pictures. It's Harper, Heavy's older sister. A few of the other women trail behind her like an entourage, but most stay at the bar and just turn to watch.

When she reaches me, she grabs my hands and holds my arms out to the side. "Let me look at you. Let me see the woman who brought down Heavy Ruth."

I didn't bring him down. I married him for convenience.

She smiles at me, and I don't even need to think. It's not Duchenne.

I don't like her. There's no way I can meet her eyes. Her entire face hurts to look at. There's too much going on. I yank my hands free.

She sniffs. "Touchy one, are you? That's not going to go over too well around here."

I'm not touchy. I'm the opposite. I'm anti-touchy.

There's an awkward silence. One of her entourage whispers, "Is she special?"

Another woman with magnificent eyebrows hushes her.

"Well, come on," Harper says. "You're here now. You should meet the other old ladies."

I hadn't anticipated this. I don't move to follow her when she turns back to the bar. "Where's Heavy?"

"Out back. Roosevelt's getting patched in. Brothers only."

I vaguely understand this. It's a ceremony. Roosevelt's being promoted from a prospect to a full member. Good for him. I like the guy. He's chill, and he shaves his beard close in ruler straight lines.

"Well, come on. They'll be done in a little." She stalks back to the bar, her drunken wobble almost imperceptible now. She's tall. "Built like a brick shithouse," as Cash would say. The bottoms of her black high heels are bright red.

As she approaches the gathered women, they move. She flops on a stool, and some women gather closer and others step away. She displaces people like a shark's fin displaces water. Like Heavy does when he walks through a crowd.

She pats the empty stool beside her.

I hop up. My legs dangle.

The women have sorted themselves into three clusters.

There's the group milling behind Harper, not venturing far, as if she's their gravitational center.

Then there are several older women sitting at a round table, playing spades—a lady with feathered bangs and a silver braid all the way to her butt, a chunky mom-type smoking a jay, and a woman in a tank top with teased, dyed blonde hair, her "wings" flapping as she talks with her hands. The fourth is a super-tanned woman with natural blonde hair and bangles up her forearms who Mom would have called "well kept."

Harper points to them. "Those are the *old,* old ladies. Don't fuck with them."

I had no intention to do so. The one with wings flips Harper off and keeps tellin' her story.

"These—" She gestures to the women in her orbit. "These are sweetbutts. Except Annie. She's Bullet's old lady."

"Divorced," the woman pipes up.

"You still let him in the backdoor after the kids are asleep," a sweetbutt cackles.

Annie shrugs. "Good dick is good dick."

"Amen," the chunky stoner lady says, raising her joint in a salute.

There's one group of women that Harper hasn't

mentioned yet. They're clustered at the other end of the bar with the bartender, a woman in a soft hoodie. Several are eyeing me, and a few of them are glaring at Harper.

"Those are the *new* old ladies." Harper spins to face them head on. As a group, they straighten and bristle. Unlike the sweetbutts, they're not intimidated, but they're clearly not amused, either.

"How 'bout you decide to not instigate for once and crawl back into that bottle of yours?" says a skinny, black-haired lady with a scar on her lip.

Harper lifts a wine glass, toasts the woman, drains it, and then leans over to whisper in my ear. Loudly. "That's Fay-Lee. Dizzy's old lady. Before she ended up here, she got locked in a shed. Everyone forgot about her. She almost died. You can see how it'd happen. Her voice is so annoying. Her folks were probably used to tuning her out."

The black-haired woman narrows her eyes. Is she gonna throw a punch? These women look like scrappers. Lots of big rings and hoop earrings.

"When you fuck Des Wade, do you wish you were locked in a shed instead?" Fay-Lee snarks back, unruffled.

"I'd rather bake to death in a shed than wake up to that smarmy motherfucker's face," Fay-Lee goes on, elbowing the blonde Barbie next to her. "Right?"

The Barbie smiles and shakes her head. "Be nice to Harper. She's obviously going through some shit."

Harper stiffens at that. "The blowup doll is Story. That's her actual name. Hey, Sunny—" Harper calls over to the older woman with the bangles. "Why did you name your kid Story?"

Sunny smiles, her white teeth blinding. "I dunno. I thought it was unique."

Harper takes a second to reply. She's refilling her glass

from a bottle of rum she snagged from behind the bar. "That's such a disappointing, uh, story."

"Lay off, Harper," the woman with the silver braid calls over.

Harper raises her hands. "No offense meant, Shirl."

Shirl snorts and shuffles a deck of cards.

Harper gives herself a little shake and points at Story. "She's Nickel's old lady. She's not that bright, but in a tight spot, she will shank your ass with a picture frame."

"Oh, come on, Harper," a woman with a purple streak in her hair says. "Drink your drink and leave the decent folks alone."

"That's Jo-Beth," Harper says. "I don't fuck with Jo-Beth."

The corner of Jo-Beth's lip quirks.

"And that's Kayla." Harper points to the plain woman in a ponytail beside Jo-Beth. "She's banging my sloppy seconds, so I don't fuck with her, either. Gotta keep the peace, you know?"

Kayla winces. Fay-Lee takes a step toward us. "Say, Harper? How does it feel letting the human equivalent of a used car salesman stick his poxy dick in your ass? Do you need lube with a dude that oily? Just curious."

"Poxy?" Harper lets out a cackle. "Where did you get *poxy*?"

"Her and Dizzy went to the Renaissance festival last week," the woman tending bar volunteers. She's drying glasses as if a cat fight is not about to erupt.

"That's Crista," Harper says.

"And you don't fuck with her either," the chunky woman playing spades calls over her shoulder.

"No, ma'am, Miss Deb, I don't," Harper agrees. "Crista is Scrap's old lady. She's—"

"Harper," Miss Deb interrupts, a warning in her tone.

Harper swallows whatever she was going to say. "Now, who did I forget? Don't want to leave anyone in a shed, so to speak." Fay-Lee flips her off. "Oh, yes. Nevaeh Ellis."

The women hanging behind us shuffle and titter.

"She's the one with the big hair at the end, the one trying to keep her head down, but frankly, that's a losing proposition with a rat's nest that size."

Nevaeh rolls her eyes.

"She's banging Forty at the moment," Harper says.

"She's Forty's old lady, and you know it, and you need to sober your ass up." Shirl, the old woman with the braid, lays her cards on the table.

Harper opens her mouth, but just then, a new song starts playing from the sound system.

Harper holds up a finger. "Hold on. I love this song!"

She hops off her stool and stumbles into the bar. Annie hauls her back to her feet.

"Turn it up, Crista!" Harper demands.

Crista fiddles with something and "Heart of Glass" blares from the speakers. The disco beat echoes off the vaulted garage ceiling. A sweetbutt whoops, and there's a change in the climate. Drinks clink on the bar. Heads bop.

"Don't you dance to this?" Fay-Lee asks Story. The blonde woman is fiddling with the jukebox. She must've picked the song.

"Oh, yeah." Story smiles wide, raising her arms and swinging her hips. Jo-Beth laughs, tripping over to join her, and somehow, their moves synchronize, as if it's a choreographed dance.

No, it *is* a dance. They've done it before.

More women are swaying now. A few of the sweetbutts seem to know the moves Story and Jo-Beth are doing, and they fall in beside them—happy, strutting, and weaving their arms through the air.

I recognize the moves. The women are dancing like Anise in Las Vegas, but also like my mom's jazzercise videos.

Chairs scrape and then the older ladies are out on the dance floor, too, shaking their stuff, singing along to the lyrics. Harper is standing alone in the middle of the gathering group, eyes closed, swaying side to side, wine glass raised in the air.

A minute ago, she pushed them all away, but now they're surrounding her, everything but the music forgotten.

"I don't get it." I don't mean to say it out loud.

"Don't have sisters, do you?" Crista, the woman working the bar, asks. She's come closer to see better.

"No."

"Well, you do now." She smiles. "They're a pain in the ass."

Before I can answer, a door slams in the back, and a stampede of boots and loud, deep voices flow toward us. A herd of men pile into the common room.

The women thrust their boobs and butts out a little further, and put some more shimmy into their hips, but they only have eyes for each other.

Fay-Lee climbs on top of the bar, kicking off her heels to dance in her bare feet. At the end of the next verse, she starts to peel off her shirt to a chorus of hoots.

Someone says, "Where's Dizzy? He ain't gonna like that."

"Better go get him, then," Fay-Lee says, twirling her top over her head and letting it soar.

Her bra follows. There's a great whooping and hollering. My hands cover my ears on instinct, but I can't stop watching.

"Little girl, you best get down now," a man who could be

Heavy's twin booms from across the room. "And put your damn shirt back on."

"Spoil sport," Fay-Lee hollers.

"Oh, let her be," an old timer shouts.

Over by the jukebox, Story and Jo-Beth put their heads together, and then their shirts and bras are coming off, flying through the air—they toss them at the man hassling Fay-Lee—and then the sweetbutts are stripping, too.

Story sashays over to her mother, teasingly tugging her blouse, and then Sunny's topless, too, laughing, shimmying her shoulders so her round and high breasts bobble side-to-side. They can't be real.

Sunny says something to the other older ladies—I can't hear over the music and my hands—and then they're tugging off their T-shirts, yanking hair free, tossing their tops to the floor, heads thrown back, laughing their asses off.

There are dozens of bare, bouncing boobs. Firm and perky. Full and high. Sagging and squishy with nipples the size of saucers. Tanned. Pale. Blue-veined. Puckered. Scarred. Flat.

There are so many smiles, so much laughter, and catcalls and deep rumbling chuckles as the men gather, grinning, watching, shaking their own awkward asses.

And there's Heavy. Taller than everyone. Broader. The gravitational center of it all. His lips are slightly softened; his eyes are dark as pitch.

He's watching me. Only me.

He crooks a finger. My insides burst into sparkles.

I go to him.

As soon as I'm at arm's length, he hauls me to his chest.

"Making friends?" he rumbles, lips wide now, the corners of his eyes creased. The sparkles flutter down my body like confetti. I'm electrified, all my senses wide awake, and it's not disorienting or disturbing, it's fucking *art*.

The beat pulsates in the air. Voices join and weave together like kites or ribbons in the wind, bright reds and greens and blues, and I don't know what anyone's saying, but it's okay. They're singing. The clubhouse smells like motor oil and beer and wood polish and leather. Like Heavy.

It's a symphony and everything melds.

There are no rules that I don't know. There are *no rules*.

I raise myself on my toes, grab Heavy's hair, and drag him down to my mouth. I kiss him, taste him, and he gathers me up in his arms until my feet don't touch the floor. Behind us, there's a roar. He makes my entire self come alive, and I get lost. I let go.

Then he sets me down gently, and his eyes light up brighter with an irrepressible twinkle.

I grab the hem of my T-shirt and cock an eyebrow.

He shakes his head. "Don't."

I inch the hem higher. "But I want to."

"Nobody sees my wife's tits."

"But everyone is having so much fun."

He seizes my wrists before I can pull my top over my boobs.

"Come on. Don't be such a square."

"A square?" Now he's grinning, and my lips widen, a mirrored reflection. This past week, his face has become the moon, and my expressions are the tide. I don't have to think about what to feel or show. If he smiles, I smile, as natural as gravity.

I lift a shoulder like coquette, let the neck slip down.

"Anyone looks at my wife—" he shouts above all the noise. "—I'll beat your ass."

"I'm Lady Godiva," I say as I toss my top into the heap. "Nobody better look." If anyone does peeks, Heavy wouldn't know. He only has eyes for me.

I'm not wearing a bra. Even though it's almost hot in the clubhouse, my nipples go hard. His fingers smooth down my back, and he curves his big hands around my hips. He shifts side-to-side to the music without budging his huge combat boots.

I can't dance. I let him sway me, and I wind my arms around his neck, stretching my spine so I'm as close to his craggy, smiling face as I can get. He leans over so his beard brushes my cheek.

"Beautiful wife," he murmurs.

My breath catches. My teeth ache from the sweetness. My heart bursts wide open.

Before I drown in the muchness, I collect myself, steady all the quivers, and peer around Heavy's side.

The other men have joined the fun, hauling women into their arms. Some ladies plaster themselves to bare male chests, and others playfully push the guys away.

The song comes to an end, and Harper calls, "Again!" The song replays.

We're surrounded by bodies—perfume and clammy skin and liquor fumes and the deep musk scent of wood smoke. The lights are low, and as Heavy holds me, I grow lighter and lighter. I'm filling with air. I'm floating. I'm dancing.

When the song ends again, a new one begins. Stevie Wonder sings "la, la, la, la, la."

There's a momentary grumbling from a few guys, and someone groans, "Story, Jesus Christ, what are you doin'?"

But the women shout the complainers down. The song keeps playing, and the dancing keeps going, slower now.

A portly old dude in a cut that reads *Pig Iron* plucks the chunky lady's joint from her mouth, sticks it in his own, and then squeezes her to his barrel chest. She shrieks and snatches it right back from his lips.

The girl Annie winds herself around a wiry bald guy —*Bullet*, going by his vest. Her tongue is in his mouth, and his fingertips are digging into her bare, dimpled ass. She's in a thong, her jeans in a growing pile by the bar.

A man who could be Heavy's twin, if not for the strands of gray in his long, black hair scoops a squealing Fay-Lee off the bar. She wraps her legs around his waist, and he swats her butt.

Over by the jukebox, a scary-looking dude hauls Story into his arms. She cups his jaw, swiping her thumb at the corner of his lips. They soften ever-so-slightly—not a smile, but an easing—and she winds her willowy arms around his neck.

The movie star handsome guy from Heavy's pictures —*Charge*—makes his way to where Kayla still sits on her stool. He stands behind her, enfolding her in his arms. She relaxes back against him, and he nuzzles her neck as they watch everyone dance. She smiles, and it's real. All the smiles are—wide, fleeting, or faint. They're all real.

Kayla still has her top on. So does the girl in the hoodie, Crista.

A lanky, muscular guy vaults over the bar to stand beside her. "*Scrap*" his patch reads. He plucks down her hood to whisper in her ear. She giggles and shakes her head. And then she points to someone on the makeshift dance floor. I follow Scrap's gaze.

There's Shirl, the older woman with the silver braid and feathered bangs. She's swaying in perfect time to the music. There are tears in the corners of her closed eyes. She wears two rings on a chain around her neck, a gold band and a small diamond. My gaze lowers to her hands. Her fingers are gnarled, her knuckles swollen. Looks like arthritis.

She's all by herself. The other older women have partners. The lady in the tank top is plastered against Grinder, and Sunny is shaking her butt in the face of a seriously blissed-out Boots.

Back behind the bar, Scrap asks Crista something, and she nods, her soft smile breaking wide. He brushes a kiss across her lips and hops back across the bar, making his way to Shirl. He takes her hand, and she startles until she sees it's him. Then she rolls her eyes, but he doesn't let go. He draws her into his arms and sways. Her screwed tight expression melts.

Heavy makes a sound. I can't tell what it means, but it comes from deep in his chest. I glance up. He's watching Shirl and Scrap, too. He squeezes me closer for a second, and then he whispers, "You'll wait here for me?"

I don't know where I'd go. I scan the room. Tommy's by a pool table, octopussing a sweetbutt with a bottle of Jägermeister dangling from his hand. Besides, the idea of being left by myself in a crowd of people for once doesn't break my mind. I've acclimated to all the sounds and smells. They're extensions of Heavy's. The people, too, somehow, seem like his.

And somehow, he seems like mine.

I nod.

Heavy presses a kiss to my forehead, his lips lingering, beard scratching, and for a second, I think he won't go, but then he drops his arms, crosses the room in two strides, and taps Scrap's shoulder. I feel strange standing by myself in the middle of the dancing couples, so I wander over to the bar.

Heavy takes Shirl in his arms as a new song begins. It starts slow with piano and voice, and then a guitar joins in.

"Who sings this?" someone asks.

"Supertramp," Crista says. She's leaning her elbows on the bar, watching. I hop up on a stool and sit with my back to her so I can see, too.

Heavy has to fold himself in half to dance with Shirl. After a few seconds, he gives up and lifts her. She hoots and slaps his forearm. He says something, his beard hiding his lips so I can't tell what. She cackles and collapses against his chest. He cradles her, spinning her with easy care.

I've learned that about him. He knows his own strength, and he's never unaware of the damage he could do. He's commanding as hell, and he doesn't ask permission, but he's never, ever rough.

Shirl's high enough now that she smiles down into his face. Her silver braid swings, brushing the pockets of her elastic-waisted jeans. In the dim light, through the haze of smoke, her wrinkles kind of fade, and if I squint, I can see what she must have looked like when she was my age.

She has a familiar face. Not like I know her, but like there's something in the cast of her features that I've seen in the mirror.

It's a niggling feeling, a "just outside the periphery of my vision" feeling. If I was like everyone else, I'd probably recognize it instinctually, but I can't read this language. I can only observe it, impress it in my memory, and maybe eventually, my system brain will collect enough data to make a leap.

That's what gratitude looks like.

That's grief.

That's longing.

What is that expression?

Is it love?

Could it be that simple?

I'm surrounded by people, and I'm lonely, but I'm also not—for maybe the first time in my life.

Crista taps my shoulder. "Look at Boots," she says.

He's ignoring Sunny's jiggling ass inches from his face, and he's scowling at Heavy. Sunny doesn't notice. She's waving at two men in suits who just came through the front doors. She winks at the older one. The other looks like Clark Kent. Not the 1940s Joe Shuster version. More like the muscled-out dude from the New 52 reboot.

"Plum, your ride's here," a sweetbutt hollers.

"I'd ride him home," another adds, just as loud. Jo-Beth slaps the woman on the back of the head with her clutch as she struts to join him.

Gus beats her there, and he's slapping Clark Kent on the back. Standing side-by-side, it's clear they're related. Father and son.

On the dance floor, Heavy gently lowers Shirl back to her feet. A stiff-backed dude with a military haircut is right there to take her from him, spinning her into a new step as another new song begins.

Heavy starts my way, but he's immediately intercepted. For the next several songs, I watch him try to reach me. He'll get a few feet, and then get pulled aside. I watch him listen to his people, face sober, or laughing at the right place. None of those smiles reach his eyes.

Everyone wants to speak to him. Everyone wants to touch him. The men slap his back. The women let their fingers wander over his vest or his arm.

All around him, men and women dance, and Shirl is passed from man to man until she's flushed pink and breathless from laughing and spinning, and there are no more tears in her eyes.

And then, finally, he makes it back to my side. He stands close, blocking my view, narrowing the barrage of sensation until my world is mostly him—his firewood scent, his size, his always audible breaths.

"Wanna go upstairs?"

I do, and I don't. I'm high on surfing this wave, but I also feel the end of my tolerance rushing at me.

And I want to take his clothes off. I want to scrub the places where those other women touched him, rub my skin against his until he's growling and wild and carried away. By me. By what I do to him. That thing I can't control or understand, but that I can somehow unleash just by being what I am.

"Dina?" he says.

"Yeah. Please."

He scoops me up, throws me over his shoulder, and he's halfway up the stairs before a guy blocks our path. It's Forty. Nevaeh's old man.

"You gotta come. Bucky and Lou are goin' at it. Hard. He's gonna kill the guy."

"And you can't—?" Heavy's already setting me down.

"Nah, I can't side against a brother, man," Forty says, scrubbing his neck.

"Go wait in my bed," Heavy says, smacking my ass with zero force. "I won't be long."

His bombastic voice is echoing from the rafters before I hit the top step. He's feigning anger. I know because he's never really angry. Pissed, sure. But he raises his voice for effect. I listen to him bawl people out on the phone all the time, and as soon as he disconnects, he'll use a perfectly normal tone to ask me if I want to order carry out for dinner.

I find his room easily enough. It's the last one in the original building before you hit the modern annex. I let myself in, flip on the overhead light, and dial down the dimmer until it's bathed in shadows. I kick off my shoes as I perch on the edge of the high mattress.

Even though I know for a fact that Heavy hasn't spent much time here lately, the place still feels lived in. There's an ashtray on a table with a single butt in it. I didn't know he smoked.

I prop myself back on my hands and look at his murder board. He's figured almost everything out. A bright red string runs from Des Wade to Anderson Watts. There are photos of all the key players—Steven Wayne "Stones" Johnson, Brian Lee "Knocker" Johnson, Robert "Slip" Ruth. There's even an index card now that reads "Boris Stasevich."

Part of me itches to rearrange the string, but most of me wants to get nowhere near that unholy mess. He pinned every piece of paper at an angle. Literally nothing is squared.

When the door opens, I start to smile. That didn't take long.

But it's not Heavy who stumbles into the room.

It's Harper.

"There you are," she says. "You and me. We need to have some words."

12

DINA

Harper still has her top on, but she lost the high heels with the red soles. Her toes are painted the same bright color. She has elegant feet, like the rest of her. Classy despite the drunken swagger. She pads over to me, swinging a wine bottle in a loose grip. She doesn't say anything. She sinks down beside me and stares at the wall.

"That's the unhealthiest thing in this goddamn clubhouse," she sighs after a while. "And I'm counting Gus' lungs and Creech's dick."

"It must have taken a long time to do it." I pieced the story together in a few weeks, but I have access to government databases he's never heard of.

"He's been at it for ten years. Maybe longer. I don't know what he did at M.I.T."

"Why didn't he become an architect?" I haven't thought to ask him, but I've wondered since I read those papers on sustainable design. He had his foot in the door. He was working with big names.

Again, she takes a long time to answer.

"There's something wrong with you, right?" she eventually says. "Asperger's?"

"PDD-NOS."

She raises a waxed eyebrow.

"Pervasive developmental disorder—not otherwise specified. That's what they called it when I was a kid, but then they got rid of that diagnosis, so now I have ASD. Autism spectrum disorder."

"So, what—you can't feel?"

"I feel."

"Good." She takes a last swig from her bottle, sets it on the nightstand, and repeats under her breath, "Good. So what's your problem?"

If she was one of Cash's asshole friends, I'd tell her to fuck off, but while Harper is a jerk, she's also blunt and honest. I like that, so I choose not to take offense.

"Alexithymia. I had a speech delay. I stim, but not much. I'm bad with people."

"I'm bad with people, too." She smirks.

"I noticed."

"It's a choice," she says.

"I noticed that, too." I flash a glance out of the corner of my eye.

She smiles. Duchenne.

Then she sighs and leans back on her hands so we're side-by-side, same position, both staring at the mess of newspaper clipping and photos and red string.

"You know, don't you?" she says.

I don't pretend not to understand her. "Yes."

"But you're not going to tell him?"

"He doesn't know?"

"No."

"I was pretty sure he didn't, but I wasn't a hundred

percent." I found out a few days into my research, but it was in the FBI documents and those are missing from Heavy's wall.

"Heavy was a little kid when it happened. It went over his head."

"But not yours?" I ask.

"I was older. I heard my parents talking in the kitchen after bedtime."

She pauses and gnaws on her lower lip. "The mill had just done its first round of layoffs. Dad, Eighty—that's Forty's dad—Big George, Ray. They all got pink slips. Mom was pregnant with Hobs and she was sick. The doctor was furious with her. Dad was furious at himself."

She exhales. "You've got to understand. The mill was everything then. You could hear the whistle for change of shift all the way at the elementary school."

"You aren't that old."

"Steel's not been gone that long. Not as long as they make it seem."

It's like she's talking about the distant past, but I guess the factories didn't all close at once. Some held on. There's still a parts plant in Stonecut County that hasn't gone overseas. Yet.

"Well, anyway, one day, that was gone. And what else were the men gonna do? Work at the Gas-and-Go? All of 'em?"

"They didn't move?"

"Some did, sure. But they owned their homes. And who was gonna buy property in a dying mill town?"

Her lips curve. "Des Wade saved this place when he redeveloped the waterfront, lured all those retirees here from Pyle." She squeezes her eyes shut for a moment, and then they fly open. "But Heavy saved these people."

She's taking her time, but I see she's answering my question.

"Heavy wanted to move to New York. Be the next Frank Gehry. But Twitch died."

"Twitch?" I've seen his name. It's on Heavy's tattoo.

"Shirlene's old man. Cancer."

"I'm sorry."

"He was—He was like a dad to all us kids. The most patient man I've ever met." She swallows, and for a second, her expression wobbles, but then she sniffs and hardens her eyes.

"I was interning in Pyle by then. We came back to a tragedy. The mill was closed. Pig Iron, Cue, Ray, Grinder—they'd all lost their pensions. Bullet had discovered pills and moved into the OTB. Creech and Bucky were making runs for the Italians, doing stupid shit. Pig Iron's house was in foreclosure. Everyone was hitting the bottle too hard. Riding like men do when they can't face going home anymore."

"But they didn't move?"

"To where? The other mill towns?" She takes a second. "Their homes are here. Their families. The loved ones they'd buried. The club. Everything worth anything is *here*."

I said it without thinking, but didn't it take me twenty-four years to venture away from home? I understand. It's more than a place. It's your bones. And people aren't the kind of animal made to leave their shells and find new ones.

"So it was after Twitch's wake. Heavy and I were sitting under a tree out back." She nods out the window. "And we decided whether to walk away or stay."

She exhales. "Heavy wanted to move to New York. Travel the world. Build things no one had ever seen before. He would have. He's fucking brilliant."

I know. It's a quiet brilliance, but it's so deep, I haven't figured out how far down it goes.

"It was his *dream*. He wanted more for himself than some nine-to-five in a hick town. He was doing it. It was going to happen for him."

She sniffs again, but she's not crying. "I was a mediocre law student, but he was on fire. Serious people wanted to meet him."

"But he gave it up."

"He gave it up," she repeats. "He came home, and we sold our parents' house and the acreage across the street from the clubhouse. And Heavy started a construction company. Put all the men to work. Sent Bullet to rehab. Bought Pig Iron's house at auction and signed it back over to him. Heavy's twenty-two, twenty-three, and he's hauling men twice, three times his age out of the dirt and riding their asses until they're standing like men again."

The pride and love in her voice shines through, perfectly clear, as if there's a label above the words. My chest warms.

"But western Pennsylvania didn't need another construction company. At least, not back then. But we had contacts. The Russians in New York. The Italians in Pyle. They could use a contractor who didn't ask questions about, shall we say, unusual requests? We filled a niche."

She stands and wanders to the murder board. "If this were a Hollywood movie, that'd be the end. Wide shot zooms out. Music swells. But the past is never dead, right? It's not even past."

"William Faulkner." I read *Requiem for a Nun* for an online literature course I took for my bachelor's. I hated it. I'm the type that needs reliable punctuation.

"Is it? It's something Heavy says all the time." She turns to stare at me. I look past her shoulder at the photo of a grinning policeman on the side of a highway with his foot propped on a wooden crate. "You suit him. I can see why he's in love with you."

"What?"

"You know he's in love with you, right?"

One time, Cash made me watch, like, ten minutes of homemade videos of guys getting slapped in the face by flying fish. That's how I feel. Like the faces. And kind of like the fish.

I have to blink through the dumbfoundedness to make meaning from the words. He's. In Love. You.

I shake my head. "He's not in love with me."

"How do you know?"

"I—" I don't.

She leans back against the wall and folds her arms. "He's head over heels. I'll admit, it's weird. He's not the type. I figured he didn't have it in him. Like me."

Or like me.

My pulse is rising. It feels like fear. But I'm also flushing. Hot. And there are squirmy, shimmery things in my belly. He. And love. And me—

"How do *you* know?"

"*I* can read people. Lawyer, right?" She flicks a pin on the murder board. "Besides, he doesn't dance with women. Or haul them to bed over his shoulder. Or disappear all the time when he's got shit he needs to do. It's obvious."

I had no idea. Is that love, though? Oh, shit. "Am *I* in love?"

Harper laughs.

Oh my god, I said it out loud.

"Couldn't tell you, chickadee. You don't exactly have an expressive face."

My lungs are tight. Something's tipping over inside me, and all sorts of things are sliding to the floor.

If I'm in love, what does that *mean*?

Harper shakes herself off. "Anyway, that's your business. Heavy is mine. So you're gonna listen to what I have to say. You get me?"

I nod. My brain's still whirling.

"He's not gonna let you kill that guy. Your uncle. Whoever. He's going to do it himself. Just like he's always done it himself when shit needs doing. And it probably won't be the one that breaks him." Her voice cracks. "But it might be. People like us—we believe we'll never break. And then we do. And he won't even be able to tell himself he's protecting the club."

An eclipse passes over her face. When it's gone, she's nothing but hard angles again.

"So you're going to send him your evidence against Wade and Anderson—and you're gonna make damn sure the name Robert Ruth isn't anywhere in any of it—and you're going to go back to wherever you came from." She stalks closer until she's less than a foot away. "Understood?"

I rise to my feet. We're chest to chest. She's several inches taller than me, but it's not such a distance that I can't meet her eye. Her gaze feels like a dentist's pick, but I hold it. She doesn't understand me.

"Or what?" I ask.

She broadens her chest, widening her eyes until the gray is ringed in white. "Do you need me to paint you a picture?"

"No. Save your breath. I wouldn't believe you."

Her jaw clenches, and her lips are parted, so I can see her teeth grind. "Do you know who the fuck you're talking to?"

"Yeah. The woman who lets him do shit himself. When it needs doing."

She hisses, and I wish I could parse the sound. Is it a threat, is it pain, surprise?

I want it to be pain. She's pissing me off. Heavy doesn't belong to her.

He's—

He belongs to himself.

But that's not true. I knew that well before Harper started her story. Everyone owns a piece of him.

"You're not as slow on the uptake as you act, are you, Dina Wall?" she says.

I shrug. "Are you as hard?"

This whole time, neither of us have moved. We're close enough to dance. To kiss. She's a miasma of coconut hair product, cake foundation, perfume, dryer sheets, and white wine.

She tilts forward and rests her forehead against mine. "I didn't used to be."

"What happened?"

I'm looking down at her satin skin and the mounds of her perfect boobs. Her throat bobs. Her breath is hot on my cheek. "The past is never dead. It's not even past."

"You love him."

"I love them all," she says.

We're quiet together for a moment. It's like this with the horses at night, the barn pitch black, nothing but soft snickers, shuffling hooves, and the warm smell of hay. Living things together in the dark. Mysteries to each other.

"You can't tell him about Dad," she says.

"I won't."

"He was protecting his family. Mom was bad off. There was no more insurance. He couldn't have known there were guns under the cigarettes. He wouldn't have done it if he'd known."

He knew. There's no way he was in on the plan deep enough to be sure he wasn't the one driving the truck that night, but that he didn't know what was really going on. A cigarette bust wouldn't have dominated the news cycle long enough to make Anderson Watts a household name across the state.

No, Slip Ruth knew about the guns. He set his friend up to take the fall. And the payoff would have been enough for his wife's treatment. And then for the in-home hospice. There would be enough to send his oldest child away to college after she'd spent years nursing her mother and raising her baby brother.

My mind is a murder board. I arrange the dates and times and documents and photos in my head, and I tack the strings. A mother who now wears a cross around her neck, growing thinner and thinner. A girl with a scowl and a little boy on her hip. A statement signed by Robert Ruth, attached to the bottom of a case that went nowhere because Robert Ruth died before the court date.

A statement that swears Steven Wayne Johnson acted in full and knowing cohort with Boris Stasevich, Anderson Watts, and Desmond Wade to run guns for the Renelli organization in Pyle.

Past that isn't past.

This isn't my family. Not my story. Not my tangled web.

But somehow it belongs to me all the same.

Somehow, it is mine.

"If you tell him, that'll be the weight that crushes him," Harper says, searching my eyes. I know what she sees. I see it, too, when I look in the mirror. Blankness.

"I won't tell him."

"How do I trust you?"

I shrug. She sags against me for a moment, straightening before I lose my footing, but she doesn't let me go. She clutches my biceps and squeezes.

"No one but me has ever looked out for him. Yeah, his brothers have his back, but no one watches out for his heart." She presses a hand to her chest. "I've got to go. I have a—" She closes her eyes for a second. "I have to go see an old friend."

Her shoulders grow rigid, and her chin raises almost imperceptibly. "I'm gonna be gone awhile. You need to go back home. Don't make him do this thing."

"*I'm* going to do it. He's helping. After."

"And he does what you tell him, eh?" She exhales a tired breath and pats my arm. "I'm late." She tilts her head to stare at the ceiling. "And I'm drunk."

She looks back down at me and smiles. It's real, but it's sad. She grabs my cheeks in her hands and smacks a kiss on my forehead. "Go with God, Dina Wall."

"I don't understand."

"Can't help you, babe. We're all just figuring it out as we go." She drops another wet kiss on my cheek, turns on her heel, and leaves, her laugh echoing down the hall.

HEAVY COMES up a few minutes later. Harper must have just missed him. He doesn't mention passing her.

The knuckles on his right hand are swollen and raw, but he doesn't waste time on the injury. He throws me onto the bed and barks, "Pants off."

And then in a blur, we're naked. He's hoisted my legs onto his shoulders, and I'm coming on his tongue. He circles my ankles with his rough palms and guides my legs wide, and he rises up, and now he's inside me, stretching me, covering me, his beard tickling the patch of my boobs that are always red now.

I don't come again quickly like I usually do, so he thrusts harder, contorting his back so he can suckle my nipples until they're puffed into peaks. I watch him. Eventually, he gives up on my breasts and focuses on nailing my G-spot. His eyes are screwed tight, his jaw tense, his lips slightly parted as he pants in concentration.

Does he love me?

If he does, why?

Do I love him?

Does love feel like your ribs are cracking open, but it's painless and also terrifying at the same time?

Can you fall in love this fast? Romeo and Juliet fell in love faster, but the teacher I had for English 9 made a point that Romeo was in love with Rosalind the day before he fell for Juliet, so men are fickle, and you should never agree to meet them in Mantua, which for some reason, she always said with air quotes.

Maybe this feeling is a biochemical reaction to having sex for the first time, but that's stupid because *all* feelings are biochemical reactions. *That's* ninth grade biology.

"You with me, baby?" Heavy grunts.

I don't want to lie, so I do a crunch and kiss him. And then I *am* with him. I'm swept away. My body clings to him. It dissolves into shivers as the orgasm tears through me, as if he's conjured it all on his own.

My body knows what it wants. But my mind—my mind's a broken clockwork stuck in a sliver of time.

He's in love with you.

Why does that change anything? If it's true, if it's not true, what does it matter?

It does. But I don't know *why* or *how* or what it means.

He finishes and passes out, but I can't sleep. I curl into his side and think. *He's in love with you. He's in love with you.* At daybreak, when Boom knocks at the door to tell him he's needed on a site upstate, I fake like his kiss wakes me up.

"Go back to sleep. When you get up, tell Wash to take you back to the cabin. And tell Hoover, if he's still around, he's in a fuck ton of trouble for bringing you here."

"I'm not doing that," I mumble and he tucks a tuft behind my ear, which is pointless, because my bed head does not comply. Then he clears his throat and stomps to the bathroom to take the world's longest leak. He leaves the door open as he hacks and grunts and makes all his grumpy morning noises. Eventually, I actually do fall asleep. When I wake up, I'm sweaty, my heart's pounding, and it's midday.

I dreamed about Rory. The video.

She didn't fight. She struggled for a few seconds, but Van overpowered her so quickly. He was so smug. He smiled the whole time. The footage was grainy, but his veneers shone.

He got her bent over the sofa, and then she froze. Her fingers dug into the back cushion, she cried, and when it was over, there was a huge wet stain on the suede. She didn't have a chance. Van outweighed her by a lot, and even though he's in his late fifties, he's a fit guy. He has a personal trainer.

And he's Van Price. Richest man in the county, best friends with the sheriff. She's the hired help, the daughter of the town's best known meth head. And who was her daddy? Did anyone ever find out? And didn't she go to that special program up in Anvil when she was in school?

Rory is the type of girl the good people of Stonecut

County get off on disbelieving. Why did it take me so long to leave?

I don't think I knew I was leaving when I did. Maybe not until this moment. But I can't go back. I don't want to.

My brain is a mash. My head hurts. My mouth is dry and sticky.

I swing my legs over the edge of the bed and scrub my eyes. The murder board screams at me, but I force myself not to look away. I flick my thumbs.

It was good to leave Stonecut County, but it wasn't right to come here.

It's not Harper's voice in my head now, telling the hard truths, it's my mother's. *You have to think about other people, Dina. Other people have feelings. You can't treat them like a means to an end.*

I didn't think. I did see Heavy as less than a person. A hired hand. He'd have no problem helping me dispose of a body. He's a biker, right? A criminal if you scratch the surface.

Now I hear Harper. *So, what—you can't feel?*

She's right. He's not going to let me kill Van Price. He's told me as much. He'll do it himself, and she's right, too, that it might not be the act that destroys him. He may be as indestructible as he seems.

But I'm not willing to run the risk.

He's mine.

I don't know much about love, but this is what I understand—it's a circle. Outside is the world. The circumference is people like Cash and Mom and Dad and Kellum and Shay and John and Mona and their kids—the folks who hold you in. And in the center are the ones you choose.

My brother Jesse. My niece Mia. Rory.

And Heavy.

Love's not a feeling. It's geography. It's where people belong.

Heavy belongs with me.

I have to leave.

Now. Before he comes back or sends someone for me.

I scrounge my black leggings from the floor and tug them on. I can't find my shirt. Shit. It's downstairs somewhere. I grab a T-shirt from Heavy's drawer, and even after I tie it in a knot in the back, it's ridiculous.

That's when I realize I had that entire conversation with Harper topless. And that's another fish-in-the- face feeling.

This is what I was afraid of—that I'd go after Van, and my brain would glitch. It's happening. My heart is pounding for no reason, and the light streaming in through the curtains is glaring. I don't have my purse. No sunglasses, no ear buds.

And the clock is ticking. There are steps in the hall, too soft to be Heavy's. They pass the door, and I let out the breath I was holding. I race to the shelf by the window, fall to my knees, pull out Plato and Dostoyevsky and the *Bhagavad Gita*. The gun is still taped to the wall.

I peel it loose, check the magazine. It's still loaded. I stole the gun from Van's safe after Kellum and Dad chased him out of Stonecut County. I bought the silencer off the dark web. I had it delivered to Van's vacant mansion on top of the hill, and I snagged it the same night I disconnected his CCTV to break in.

I need my phone. It's in my purse. Which is where? It has to be downstairs. Probably behind the bar. I remember setting it next to me when I was talking to Harper.

I tuck the gun in my waistband because there's nowhere else to put it. My dad would beat my ass for holstering a loaded weapon in elastic, but desperate times call for desperate measures.

I leave Heavy's room, walking with a purpose, but I don't see anyone until I get downstairs to the common room. The old lady with the dyed blonde hair—Ernestine—is collecting empties and discarded bras. Tommy has a mop, but he's standing in the middle of a wet floor watching bowling on the big screen TV mounted on the wall. The tattooed guy with the gauges—Creech—is sitting at the bar, scrolling through his phone.

I make a beeline for the bar.

"If you're looking for your personal effects, I made a pile over there," Ernestine calls, jerking her thumb toward the table where the ladies were playing spades last night. My purse is tangled in a red lace bra. It takes a second to unsnag the strap from the hooks.

I take out my phone. Thank goodness. I have almost eighty percent charge. The city's a couple hours' drive, but that's enough juice to do what needs to be done without wasting time to find or buy a charger. Now all I need is a ride. I glance over at Tommy. He's leaning hard on that mop. I don't think he's been to bed, and there's no way he's sober.

Would he lend me his bike?

Not without telling Heavy. Heavy will try to stop me. That won't matter, though, if I have enough of a head start.

I can drive. I have a license. I grew up riding dirt bikes and four-wheelers. But driving a car on a highway—I know my limitations. If I get overwhelmed, I could screw up and cause an accident. Back home, I catch a ride with Mom or Dad on the rare occasions I want to go into town.

I can't take a rideshare to a murder.

Shit.

"You look consternated, darling." The illustrated man,

Creech, beckons me over. "I got coffee. Come here and take a load off."

I'm at a loss, and coffee can't hurt, so I perch beside him. He bends himself over the bar to reach the coffee pot and pours me a mug.

"If you want cream and sugar, you gotta ask Ernestine."

She makes a harrumphing noise.

"Or maybe drink it black," Creech says, grinning.

"That's how I take it."

"All right, all right." Creech has a slight drawl, and despite the absolute cacophony of body mods and tattoos, I can see why he'd get enough action to earn him his reputation.

We sip our coffee together for a minute, and then Creech finishes a text and says, "Harper said you might need a ride?"

"She did?"

"Yeah, she mentioned it on her way out last night. Asked me to hang around in case you needed to go somewhere."

She must mean for him to take me back to Stonecut County. He doesn't seem to know that.

I can't make him an accomplice. But if I have him drop me off a few blocks from Van's building?

"Yes. I need a ride to the city."

"I don't take my bike up there. Folks drive like assholes."

Shit.

"We'll take a club Jeep," he says.

Okay. We're back in action.

"Can we go now?"

"Sure, darling. Don't want to finish your drink?"

I drain it in three gulps.

"A woman on a mission, all right." He slaps the bar and calls, "Later."

Tommy grunts and Ernestine waves.

We walk right out the front door to the garage, and in no time, we've left Petty's Mill, heading north on the highway.

A few miles down the road, I ask Creech if I can borrow his phone. I download a blocker app and block his contact list. Based on a quick scroll of his messages, there are at least three women who are going to be very pissed at him in a few hours. I had no idea people texted each other this much. Or how early in the day they send dick and pussy pics.

Creech keeps up a monologue all the way to Pyle, as my stomach knots tighter and tighter. He's considering buying into a friend's tattoo studio in Shady Gap, but he's not sure if the market is big enough because, "Shady Gap ain't nothin' but uptight milfs and old, paunchy dudes who drive hybrid SUVs."

He doesn't think the latest *Fast and Furious* was as good as the last one, but it's better than *Tokyo Drift*, which isn't that bad if you go back and watch it. He wants to do keto or paleo, but he drinks too much, but didn't fuckin' cavemen drink? Do I know if cavemen drank?

"Look that up, darling. Did—cavemen—drink."

All the while, my guts churn. My skin has broken out in a cold sweat. My sunglasses aren't dark enough to make the mid-afternoon light bearable, and I can't put my earbuds in because as long as Creech is talking, and he thinks I'm listening, he's not wondering why his phone isn't buzzing.

I keep swallowing because I can't breathe properly. It's like my ribs have frozen so my lungs can't fill. I flick my thumbs until Creech stares, and then I tuck my hands under my thighs and chew on the inside of my cheek.

I ducked into the bathroom before we left the clubhouse and shoved the gun in my purse. It hardly fit. The way the purse is sitting in the footwell, you can kind of make out the barrel pressed against the seam. It's not in Creech's line of sight, but it's there, round and obvious and pointing at me. My dad would lose his mind that I have a loaded weapon pointed at a person, even though the safety is on, even though I am going to aim it at my uncle and pull the trigger.

A wave of prickly heat crashes through me.

I am not going to turn around. I'm not going to change my mind. I am going to do this.

Before I had the idea to get Heavy to help dispose of the body, I had a plan. Shoot Van with his own gun. Leave it at the scene. Douse his corpse with every cleaner in the place. If my DNA is found in the condo, it's no biggie. I'm his niece. It just can't be found on his body.

It's a good plan. It wouldn't work if I had a motive, but I don't, do I? Van never hurt me. And no one would believe that I could murder a man to avenge my friend. Women like me aren't heroes, are we? Not in the caped and masked sense. Not in the *real* sense.

The closer we get to the city, the louder my thoughts are and the harder it is to make the responses that keep Creech talking. Eventually, he shuts up and starts flipping through radio stations, one after another after another.

My temples throb. My throat burns with acid indigestion.

Finally, he exits the highway onto River Street, the wide boulevard at the heart of the city that runs along the Lucka-hannock. There are tall buildings to the left and the prome-nade to the right. A fair number of people stroll along the water, but the sidewalks aren't crowded. It's a weekday. I'm counting on the people in Van's building being at work.

"Where to, darling?"

"Here is fine."

I'm a few blocks away from Van's condo.

"Here?" He frowns at me.

"The place I'm going is a few blocks up. I want to walk along the river. It's a nice day."

He looks out the window toward the tourists and benches and the kiosks selling hotdogs and souvenirs. Then he shrugs and pulls over onto a bus stop.

"If you're sure," he says.

I grab my bag.

"Yup." I open my door. "Thanks," I toss my purse over my shoulder, wave, and force a smile. His forehead's wrinkled, and he opens his mouth, but I'm already swinging the door shut and heading for the promenade.

I don't look back, but I catch him pulling off from the corner of my eye.

I'm alone. In the city. There's a gun in my purse.

It's bright out here. It smells like river water and exhaust. I'm stiff. As I walk, I feel like a skeleton puppet jerked on a string. All bones.

I pass a group of teenagers, shrieking at each other. I want my earbuds, but I can't get into my purse. There's a gun in there.

I'm going to kill a man. I'm going to do it because if I don't, no one will stop him. Except Heavy Ruth. He'll kill him for me. Because he loves me. Why?

So I keep walking. Past the intersection with Fourth Avenue. Then Third. Van's condo is at Second and River. His building is one of the last before the boulevard becomes lined with high rises with restaurants and high-end clothiers and spas on the ground floors.

Before I leave the promenade, I find a bench, and when there are no pedestrians approaching, I take out my phone. There are dozens of missed calls and texts from Heavy. I ignore them.

I pull up the program I wrote to disable the CCTV in Van's building, and I turn the whole place dark. Then I put my phone on airplane mode. If I had time, I'd have bought a burner, but I'm going to have to hope the police don't pull my records. If they start looking, they'll see I was at the Steel Bones clubhouse and Heavy's cabin. If they start unraveling the threads, they'll find the missing CCTV footage from Van's house in Stonecut and the package delivered the same day. If I get on their radar, eventually, unless I get lucky as hell, I'm fucked.

I can't get on their radar. I have a good chance. Nine out of ten people, if they know I'm on the spectrum, they speak slowly to me, enunciating very carefully. People see what they expect to see. And people are idiots.

I cross at the light and head toward the door leading from the garage under the building to street level. I walk at a slow pace, prepared to circle the block a few times, but my luck is holding. A guy leaves when I'm ten feet away, and he holds the door for me when I jog over. I flash him a smile, careful to meet his eyes.

That was the most hinky part of the plan. You need a pass card to get in from the outside. There's now one person who can place me at the scene of the crime.

I dash up the stairs and scurry through the VIP parking level. Van's Bugatti is parked in a space by the elevator. I don't see anyone else. My uncle is in the penthouse. There's a courtesy phone you can use to call up ahead. I debate surprising him, but if he's not home, I'd rather come back later instead of risk being seen for no good reason.

My hands shake as I press the number for his condo.

I can't lie. Or rather, I don't, and I'm no good at it. And my throat is swollen and dry.

"Hello." My uncle's voice is brisk and business-like.

"Hi, Uncle Van."

"Dina? Dina, what are you doing here?" I'm not sure if he's suspicious or confused or concerned or what.

"I wanted to see you."

"Okay, honey. Let me buzz you up. Is your mom with you?"

"No. She's back home."

"Okay. I'm buzzing now."

I hang up the phone and swipe the receiver and touchpad with a cleaning wipe from the travel pack in my purse. I use the wipe to press the button for the penthouse.

My heart is galloping. My palms are slick, and I'm trembling.

There's a ding, and the doors slide open, revealing a short corridor and a console table with a gold vase filled with fake peacock feathers. Van is opening his door as I walk down the hall.

"Dina, sweetie. Is everything okay?"

My uncle ushers me in, hand on the small of my back. He smells like aftershave and coffee. He's in a blue buttoned-down dress shirt and beige pleated slacks. He looks like he always does. Neatly trimmed and dyed brown hair. Clean shaven. Teeth too white for his age and skin too tan for the time of year.

"I'm okay."

He gestures to the sofa. "Do you want a drink, honey? I guess you heard your parents and I had a falling out."

He's already in the kitchen, rummaging. His condo was built before open concept hit big, and for whatever reason, he's never renovated. The living room where I'm sitting has a view of the river, and the place is huge—four bedrooms, five baths, a media room, a home office—but it doesn't feel that way. Everything is down a hall or through a doorway.

Van emerges with a glass of brandy and what looks like orange juice.

"You still like OJ, right, kid?"

"Sure."

He takes the armchair across from where I sit on the sofa and crosses his legs. He's wearing navy dress socks with taupe boat shoes.

"So what brings you to the big city?" He doesn't wait for an answer. "I'm happy to see you, kiddo. I've missed you."

I don't believe that. Uncle Van has been around since before I can remember, and he's always been generous on birthdays and at Christmas, and he always asks about school, but we've never had an actual conversation. I make him uncomfortable.

He's close to Kellum and Cash. He *was* close. They went on hunting trips, ski trips, boating down on Lake Patonquin, fishing out in Colorado. Dad, Kellum, and Cash. Uncle Van and my cousins Branch and West.

West is away at college now, and he doesn't see his dad anymore now that he has a choice. Branch is in Aspen with his mom. I follow them both on social media. West is like his dad. Branch is not unlike me. This will hurt them. Even if they hate the guy's guts—and there's no doubt they do—it'll hurt.

I'm going to do it anyway.

"So what's going on?" He doesn't wait for me to answer. "Let me guess. You've decided to move out. You want to tap into the trust. Get a place of your own."

I've made a mistake.

If I shoot him where he's sitting, the bullet could go through the window. If I aim for his chest, it would likely lodge in the upholstery, but I'm not that confident about my aim to take the risk.

I could stand up and pretend to go take in the view of the river, shoot him from behind, but then I'll be theoretically visible from the street. There might be CCTV cameras on neighboring buildings that I didn't account for. Also, I can't do things casually. I'd tip him off.

"Dina?"

Shit. He's talking. *Tap into the trust. Place of your own.*

"Yeah. That's what I want to do." There's truth in it. I don't want to go back to Stonecut. But I don't want a place of my own. I want to be with—

Focus.

"Oh, honey. Your hands are shaking." Van chuckles. "This is a big step for you. Did you talk to your folks about it?"

"No."

"They only want what's best for you."

I need to lure him to a second location.

"I know," I say. Could I ask to borrow something? A DVD from the media room? That would be weird. I'm weird. Maybe he wouldn't think anything of it.

"You shouldn't make a move like this without thinking it all the way through. There're the costs, but also, you have to think about how you're gonna handle the people."

"The people?" What is he talking about?

"The real world is not like living with your parents. You're gonna need to deal with people. All the time. Your folks run a lot of interference for you. You're not gonna have that. You'll need to build those skills. Communication. Interaction." He leans back and props his arms on the rests, watching me.

He's trying to fuck with my head. He doesn't want me to move out. Why not?

Money.

Same reason he tried to run off Shay. He has so much, but it kills him to have to share. He sees the trust my grandfather established as his. He administers it; he saved it from ruin back in the day. His.

I always wondered why feelings are so hard for me to understand when motivations are often crystal clear. It's my system brain. Uncle Van has an obvious pattern. Protect his hoard. Exploit the weak.

But he's not wrong. I'm going to need to work on my people skills.

But not now.

I sip my orange juice. Pulp. Gross. I force myself not to gag and keep going. When I'm done, I'll ask for more, and when he's in the kitchen, I'll shoot him when he opens the fridge.

"Can you talk me through it?" I ask. "How do I go about withdrawing my money from the trust?"

And I sit back and sip, watching his face as he plasters on a smile as he tells me how to withdraw my inheritance.

He hates the idea of handing over one red cent. It's killing him.

I'm almost done with my drink when he winds up a convoluted explanation of estate taxes. He clears his throat and stands. "We haven't even touched on capital gains taxes, but I need a quick break. You good? Want me to top you off?"

He nods at my glass. "I'm good."

He's going to the bathroom. Perfect. If he goes to the powder room, there are no windows. My heart rate kicks up a notch.

He smiles, sets his brandy on the coffee table, and heads down the hall.

I force myself to count. One. Two. Three. Four. Five. A door opens and clicks shut.

I put my glass on an end table and draw the gun from my purse. I twist the silencer to make sure it's tight and disengage the safety. Then I pad across the living room, following him.

I can hear Van pissing through the door. It's slightly ajar.

My chest is tight. My palms are sweaty.

I draw in a steadying breath, and I ease the door open, leveling the muzzle to the back of Van's head.

He doesn't notice. Not until he goes to wash his hands and catches sight of me in the mirror.

"Don't move."

His eyes grow huge. "Dina, what are you doing?"

"I'm going to shoot you."

"Put that down, honey." It's a command. He thinks he's still in control.

I line up my shot.

He raises his opened palms. "Whatever's wrong, we can fix it, okay, honey? Just put the gun down. You don't know what you're doing." Now his tone has changed. It's pitched higher.

"I'm going to kill you."

"Whatever you heard, it's not true."

"I saw it."

"Saw what? Honey, lower the gun. You never aim at a person, even if it's not loaded. Your dad and I taught you that."

They did. Many years ago at the targets behind Van's house on the hill. They told me to never aim a weapon at a man unless you intend to pull the trigger.

"It's loaded."

He turns, reaching for his pockets, eyes wild. Is he going for his phone? It's in the other room on the charger.

His hands fall limp at his sides. I guess he remembers. He has no way out of this.

"Dina, talk to me. Tell me what this is all about." His voice changes again. It's lower. Softer in an oily way. I focus on his chest. I can't meet his eyes. They're putrid and wrong. "What's got you so upset?"

"You raped Rory."

"I— What? Who?"

"My friend Rory. She cleaned your house. You raped her."

"Sweetheart, I don't know what she told you, but you *know* me. I'm your uncle, honey. I could never do something like that."

"I saw you do it."

"Honey—" His voice grows even more wheedling. I've never heard him like this. Even to my ears, he sounds like an actor reciting lines. "What you saw—you misunderstood. You know how you do that sometimes? It was a mistake. She came onto me and—"

I tighten my grip on the gun. He stops talking.

"I watched you rape her. And that's why I'm putting you down."

"You're confused—"

I interrupt. "It was the CCTV in the garage. It captures your living room through the bay window."

"Have you talked to Rory? 'Cause if you talk to her, she'll tell you. We—we got carried away. She'll tell you."

"I talk to Rory all the time."

He's quiet a moment, and the sound of his panicked breath fills the room.

"You're not going to do this, Dina," he finally says. "You

want to scare me straight? Fine. I'm scared straight. I'll leave your friends alone."

I raise my eyes to his face. I can't avoid it any longer.

My lips curve. His brow furrows. He's confused. Why? My mouth. It must look like a smile. It isn't. It's what my face does when I aim.

"Yes," I say and line up my shot. "You are."

I exhale and squeeze the trigger. There is a soft pop. Blood and chunks of brain splatter the wall like mud on a windshield.

He topples onto the tub ledge. There's a horrible smell. I don't want to name it.

I watch for a while to make sure he isn't breathing.

Then, I close the door and take small steps back to the living room. I stick the gun in my purse, and then I perch on the edge of the couch.

It's silent in the condo, and my brain is blank.

What do I do next?

I had a plan, but I can't remember.

I stare at the glass of juice, and I wait, and every so often, a voice in the furthest reaches of my mind screams, "For what? For what? For what?"

"Where's my goddamn wife?" I throw a table. It splinters against the bar. It's not enough. I need a bigger table.

Fuck.

Everyone's standing around, gawping, and they need to move. *I* need to move.

Ernestine said Creech took her home. That was hours ago, and Creech ain't answering his phone. She's not at the cabin. She's not at her parents—I had Wall call. Now he's pissed and glowering by the bar, working his phone, biding his time to beat me to death.

Which is fair since I can't kick my own ass.

I pace to the hallway and back. My lungs aren't right. They're caught in a vice.

She's so goddamn small. If the Raiders took her—my heart spasms. I can't have a heart attack now. God knows I been workin' on it all my life, but now, no—

I shake out my arms, roll my shoulders.

Raiders didn't take her. We got eyes on them. She's gone after her uncle. I know it. She ain't got any other irons in the fire. Forty's working on an address for the bastard. I can't ask Wall. If she's already—shit, shit, *fuck*.

If she killed the guy, I ain't implicating her to anyone.

My gut is a rock.

She did it.

Or she's gonna do it.

I put her off, and so she's gone to do it on her own. I rip at my hair. It's in my face. It's too fuckin' long.

I should have foreseen this. She ain't like other women. Other *people*. People put off the hard shit. They wrestle with themselves to avoid doin' anything. Dina—

Dina is unique in the world. Innocent, moral, and capable of murder, no doubt in my mind.

I fuckin' love her.

And she's clueless when it comes to half the shit in life. She's gonna get caught. Or she'll choke for a moment or stumble over a rug or something, and he'll kill her. Van Price is not a garden variety sleazeball. The Russians know his name. So do the Italians. I've made discreet inquiries. The man likes to hurt women, and he'll pay to indulge himself.

The roar comes out of me, bursts from my chest without warning, and I fling another table. It rolls, wobbles, and slows to a halt on its side. It don't even hit nothin'.

Wall wanders over and flips it back on its feet. Then he makes his way over to me, slow and deliberate. Shit.

He stops a foot away, crossing his meaty arms, staring me straight in the eye. Wall's the only brother close to my size.

"You want to tell me what the fuck is going on now?"

"No." I brace, figuring he'll swing on me. I'm gonna have to let him.

But his temper doesn't flare. Instead, he looks off to the

side, like he's thinking. "She's got herself in trouble, hasn't she?"

"Maybe."

He sighs. "How bad?"

I draw him further from the others. Lower my voice. "She's going after your uncle."

"Van? Why?"

"He hurt her friend Rory."

"What's she gonna do?"

"Kill him."

He shakes his head in disbelief. "Not Dina. She's a— she's basically a kid. She lives at home. Plays video games all the time."

"She came here to ask for my help to dispose of the body."

"What the fuck?" Wall can't seem to wrap his brain around it. "Why didn't you come to me?"

"She had collateral."

The veins in his arms are popping. His nostrils flare. "What collateral?"

"Evidence against Wade and Watts."

"How does she know about them?"

"She hacked us."

His jaw drops, and then he rubs his temple.

"She also knows where the bodies are buried. So, maybe the term "leverage" is more accurate." I can't help but smile. She's got more than a touch of evil genius in her.

"So you're telling me that my little sister had you by the balls?"

She still does.

Wall huffs. "Why didn't you come to me? Why'd you let her go off on her own? Shit. She's gonna get caught or killed."

"You don't think I know that?"

"If she gets hurt, I'll kill you," he says.

"Fair."

He glares at me. And then, out of nowhere, he slams a fist into my face. My head jerks back, and I rock on my feet, pain blossoming in my cheek, my brain ringing. I grunt and rub my jaw.

Everyone gasps.

"How the fuck is he still standing?" a prospect whispers.

"That's a down payment," Wall says, cradling his fists.

"All right." I glance around, and there's a half-dozen people tryin' to make themselves small. They should be doing something, not cowering slack-jawed, as if they can't believe their eyes. What do they think they've been intimidated by all this time? Did they think I was the friendly fuckin' giant? I don't go down easy.

"When do we go after her?" Wall asks.

"Now. I'll call Forty back. You can lead us there."

Only Nickel is unfazed. He's paring his nails with his penknife, waiting for orders.

We need to be in Pyle. Now.

But not on the bikes. We need a low profile.

My brain's sluggish. The fist in the face didn't help. There's a red tinge to the air, and I need—I need—

Jesus, why would Dina do something so *stupid*?

"Nickel. We need—" I can't find the words. I point to the garage and snap my fingers.

"The white van."

"Yes."

"I'll bring it out front. Gimme five." He strides off.

Where the fuck is Forty?

I take out my phone, but before I can dial, Scrap strolls

up. He's got a Sig Sauer. "Here." He racks the slide and hands it to me. "Loaded. One in the chamber."

He's got a black knit beanie and a rubber band tucked under his armpit. I take 'em, twist my hair into a bun, shove it into the hat.

"Got another hairband?"

Scrap hooks me up. I braid my beard, fingers fumbling. My heart stops trying to do an *Aliens* out of my chest. I'm doin' something. We're on our way. I'm gonna get that little idiot, and she ain't gonna sit comfortable for a week. A month.

There's a crunch of tires on the asphalt out front.

"Let's roll," Scrap says, heading for the door.

I grab his shoulder. He looks back, and I shake my head. "Me, Nickel, Forty."

"And Wall." Wall's trading his cut for a jean jacket. I incline my chin.

"But—" Scrap's face hardens.

"Parole," I interrupt.

His jaw ticks. I blow past him before he tries to argue. If I could do this alone, I would. If she's fucked this up, I don't want no one going down besides me.

And make no mistake—this ain't gonna touch her.

Nothing will.

She's—

Not expendable.

Footsteps stomp in from the back corridor. It's Forty. He's got the red cooler. "Let's go," he says.

I'm already heading out the front. Nickel pushes open the passenger door, and I hoist myself in as Forty hops in behind me.

"Where am I going?" Nickel asks.

"River Street and Second," Forty answers. He checks his

piece and returns it to the shoulder holster under his unbuttoned flannel. Then he tosses two pairs of black gloves up to the front seat.

"What's the plan?" Nickel eases onto Route 9, careful not to exceed the speed limit by over ten miles per hour. Once we cross the county line, he'll reduce that to five. This isn't our first rodeo. The van. The cooler. The gloves. We've done this before.

We've never been busted. Not since the blown job.

Or 'til today?

My fists itch to slam the dash, but the time for self-indulgence is over. I got to master myself. The red is fading from my vision, and my mind is sharpening again.

I should have done Van Price weeks ago. Presented it to Dina as a *fait accompli*. Why didn't I?

I don't hesitate. I sure as shit don't get taken by surprise. Until this moment. I shouldn't be so shocked. Dina ain't standard issue.

I've never met such an unpredictable creature of habit. I come home, wherever she is in the house, she comes padding to me, bare-footed, always in the same skin tight black leggings and tank. She starts talking as if we're mid-conversation, and it takes a second to catch up with her twisty mind, but when I do, I'm always delighted.

Because her brain is Amazonian. She wants to talk coding, geopolitics, Marvel versus DC, anthropology, philosophy, conspiracy theories, cloning, cryptocurrency, crypto-zoology, and whether you can teach yourself to fly an airplane with the Microsoft Flight Simulator.

She never talks about the same thing twice while she peels off her clothes, folds them the same way, puts them on the same chair in the same order, and waits patiently for me to get naked, too.

Sex and conversation, dinner, movie, shower, sex, sleep.

And the sex is never the same. She wants to try everything. She wants me to show her how, and then she wants to do it to me. I thought I was an open-minded man, but she's been fucking for a month, and I've learned I got hard limits I didn't think I had.

She trusts me. I underestimated her.

My knee jiggles. Hard. Nickel gives at an eye. "Want me to take it up to seventy?" he asks.

"Not 'til the interstate."

Everyone depends on me, but her faith is different. I earned my brothers' trust. I've put my life on the line for them, for their families. I've done what's needed doing. I've protected them. *Us.* They don't always approve of the hard line I take, but they know it's for the club.

All that means nothin' to Dina. I ain't done nothing for her. Obviously by the complete clusterfuck we're driving into.

Still, she trusts me.

Still, she clings to me. She comes to me.

I need to go back in time, try again, do this one thing right.

My window rolls down and the cool highway air hits my face.

I look over at Nickel. His finger is still on the button. "Looked like you needed to take a deep breath." He grins.

I drop my head back to the rest.

"I fucked up," I confess. The van is loud with the roar of passing cars, but Nickel hears me.

"We'll handle it."

"I should have handled it a month ago."

"The time is now, man," Nickel says. "The place is here."

"What kind of hippie shit is that?"

"The kind that's hanging on the wall of my therapist's waiting room. Dan Millman said that, by the way."

"Who's Dan Millman?"

"Fucked if I know. You want more? 'Failure is not a mistake. The real mistake is to stop trying.' That's some dude named Skinner. 'If you change the way you look at things, the things you look at change.' That's a guy named Wayne Dyer. That one's hanging up in the shitter."

"And this helps you?"

"The quotes? Nah, man. But if I gotta stare at them once a week so I don't lose my mind, I will. Small sacrifice." He grins again. His face is less gaunt these days. It's strange seeing him with meat on his bones. He's not soft by any means, but he's losing that skin-stretched-over-a-skull look.

"Story doin' good?" I know she is, but asking soothes me somehow.

"Yeah. She wants me to knock her up."

"Damn." It ain't been that long. "You ready for that?"

"Hell, no. I ain't been ready for none of this." He shrugs and smirks. "But you know. 'The time is now. The place is here.'"

We change lanes, and a few cars behind, a black Jeep signals to get over.

I can't believe I didn't notice until now. I need to focus. "Who's our backup besides Wall?"

"Charge. And Mikey," Forty says from the back.

"Mikey sees a lot of action for a dude without a road name."

"We should think about givin' him one," Forty agrees.

"How many times have we said that at this point?" Nickel snorts.

"Guess Mikey's Mikey." Forty sighs.

We lapse into silence, and I'm calmed, to the extent

possible. I stop trying Dina's phone. If she's in Van's apartment, I don't need her distracted.

As we enter Pyle, the calm slips away. Adrenaline hypes my mind and readies my body. I'm going to assume my little hacker took basic precautions. Scrambled the CCTV. Wore a goddamn hat.

Still, I can't walk in through the lobby. I am a memorable dude.

I make Nickel circle the block a few times. There's a side door.

"You got a crowbar?" I hold my hand open. Forty rummages a second and then lays iron in my palm. I inhale and tug my beanie down past my eyebrows. "I'm going in alone. I'll call when—"

I don't finish the thought, and my brothers don't argue. They know me.

As I reach for the handle, Forty claps a hand on my shoulder. "Be smart, my brother."

"When have you known me to be otherwise?" It tastes like irony as it comes out of my mouth.

And I'm out. I pop the lock in two seconds, pass the crowbar back to Forty, and I'm in. The stairwell is silent. I climb to the third floor and catch the elevator there to avoid the lobby traffic. I don't bother keeping my head down. If Dina left the CCTV up, it doesn't matter if my face is hidden, my stature will give me away.

I'm oddly chill. The elevator goes straight to the top, and I stroll down the short hallway to Van Price's front door as if I ain't got a care in the world. I knock friendly. And then Dina answers the door.

I force her backward, drawing my gun. The place is quiet.

She's pale, but she looks fine. No blood splatter on her

white tank. She ain't shaking. Is he not home? Has she been waiting for him?

"Where is he?"

She doesn't answer. She sinks to the edge of the couch and draws her purse onto her lap, her legs together, angled to the side. Her eyes are huge. She ain't blinking right.

"Dina, where is he?"

I stand in front of windows overlooking the river, raise my weapon and aim over her head. If he's in the back or the kitchen, I've got him covered. If he's not home, he'll be in my sights when he opens the front door.

"Dina?"

She just sits there, perfectly still.

"Dina!"

She startles, and then she flicks her thumbs. That's her only twitch that I've seen. She's got callouses from it.

"He's dead."

Jesus. It slams into me. Plows into my chest.

"Where?"

"I waited until he had to go to take a leak, and I shot him in the bathroom."

Acid scores my throat. Not Dina. Not my Dina.

"Stay," I snarl and tread carefully down the hall. The first door on the left is cracked. I see tile and a pool of blood. I edge the door open with my elbow, gun level and cupped in my palm.

A dude dressed like a stockbroker is slumped over the edge of the tub. His chest ain't movin'. His brains speckle the wall above the toilet, all over a framed painting of a sailboat. Impressionist. Even before the splatter.

He's dead. He doesn't have the top of his head anymore.

I check the floor. There are no footprints in the blood.

Jesus. She was at such close range. He could've wrestled the gun from her.

By some miracle, the spray didn't reach the door or the hallway. I wipe the knob with my gloved hand.

She killed him.

She did it.

My heart drops, whooshing in my ears. I tuck my gun into my waistband. There's too much viscera to clean. It's everywhere. You'd need to bleach the whole room, and a bleached ceiling is as good evidence as blood stains.

What the *fuck* was she thinking?

How long ago did she do it?

If the neighbors heard the shot, the cops are on the way. In this part of town, it'll be minutes.

I race back to the room. She's still sitting. Unperturbed. In shock? No. She's looking at something on her phone.

I grab her arm. The phone flies under the coffee table. I scoop it up as I drag her toward the door. "We need to go."

Now she struggles. Makes herself dead weight. "No. Not together. We can't be seen together. Why'd you even come here?"

"The police could be here any minute. We need to *go*."

"Why would the police come?"

"The shot."

"I used a silencer."

"You—" I stop a few steps from the door. She's glaring at me. Pissed.

White hot rage surges through my veins. *She's* pissed? I drag her back to the living room, throw her onto the sofa, dig my fingers into her arms.

How could she do this?

She's supposed to be innocent. She's supposed to be—

"Why?" I spit. "Why?"

She shrinks from me. There's fear in her eyes now. *Now.* Too damn late, she's scared.

"I told you. He hurt my friend."

I slice the air with my hand. That's not what I'm asking, and she knows it. She can't pretend—she knows what she's done.

"I said I'd do it."

"I never agreed to that."

I squeeze her chin, force her to meet my eyes. "I told you no."

She clutches my wrist, trying to loosen my grip.

"You don't have that power," she manages to mutter.

And the rage crests. I thrust her away, and she bounces off the back of the sofa. She scrambles to the corner, tucking her legs to her chest.

"*Now* you're scared?" I say it out loud. "Too late, Dina. Too fucking late."

"Wh-why are you a-angry?"

"This isn't 'explain feelings to Dina' time. Your DNA is all over this place. You have *motive*." My teeth hurt, my shoulders ache from the tension. "How could you be this stupid? Do you think this is a game?"

Her eyes fill with tears, stoking my fury. She can't play the manic pixie dream girl now. She blew a man's brains out in cold blood. We had an agreement, and she disregarded it when it didn't suit her anymore.

"I'm not playing a game, Heavy." She sniffs, and she grabs her purse, tucking it close to her hip. "I knew you were going to kill him if I didn't do it first. So I did it first."

"What?"

She hugs her knees. "I didn't want you to kill him."

"Why not?"

"I don't want you to carry weight for me."

"What?"

The rage hardens and cracks, morphing into confusion. And under it all, a whirling vortex stronger than a bad trip —terror.

She can't be taken from me. It would be—

It would be the end.

"It wouldn't be right," she says. As if that holds any water at all.

It wouldn't be right.

Losing her would break me, and she's operating on some kind of philosophical principle. My body has reverted to instinct, my mind is gone for her, and she's calculating her moves based on Kohlberg's Stages of Moral Development.

I've never been weaker than I am in this moment.

I can't.

I can't watch my bare heart huddled on a sofa, unrepentant, vulnerable. Unaffected.

I've never been small. I've never been scared.

I can't be. I can't afford it. There is too much riding on me. There always has been.

She's Delilah. My hair is shorn.

If I don't end this now, I will never be in control. Never again.

I step back. Take out my phone. Call Forty. "Send Charge up to get her. When he comes out, you and Nickel come up with the cooler."

"Done," he says and disconnects.

"Wh-what are you doing?"

"You don't need to know that, little girl." I turn away from her and stalk to the door to keep a lookout through the peephole.

"What's happening?"

"I'm fixing your fuck up. And you're going home."

"And you'll come home after?"

I grit my jaw. "You're going home to Stonecut County. You're gonna go back to your life, and I'm going to go back to mine." I glance toward her over my shoulder, but I can't meet her eyes. "Strangers on a train."

She makes an odd, strangled sound, and then she's silent. She doesn't argue.

This is what she wanted.

This is what she came for.

When Charge arrives, she doesn't even look at me. She clutches her purse to her chest and glides past me, chin up, face blank. No hesitation. No feeling.

I am the world's greatest fool.

I thought I couldn't fall in love, and then I did—and the woman with my heart can't love me back.

14

DINA

I thought Charge was going to take me back to my parents, but he opens the passenger door of a black Jeep, and John's in the driver's seat. Charge hands me in and shuts my door.

"Buckle up," John says. I can't read his tone of voice, but he's not yelling. His face is normal.

He's got to be mad. I'm—I'm not sure of the word.

My stomach hurts. Real bad. Like a horse kicked it. And my eyes burn. Jolts of adrenaline keep shooting through me out of nowhere, and I want to run, but I'm strapped into a moving car now, and I can't go anywhere.

I want to go back to Heavy.

He's furious. So angry he wants me gone. He thinks I'm stupid. That I see this as a game.

He sees me like everyone else—like there's something fundamentally wrong with me. I'm not right. Missing a piece. Not all there.

I thought—

I was wrong.

It's too loud in here. There's a gap somewhere in the soft

top—the Velcro strip isn't sealed all the way—and the wind is whistling through. The upholstery reeks of sweat. My skin crawls. I fold my elbows together and press them tight to my chest so the backs of my arms don't touch the seat. Also, the hurt in my chest needs pressure. It's not getting better; it's getting worse.

Hurts get better. Mom always pointed that out, and it's true. You stub your toe, and it feels a little better every second until you stop noticing a few minutes later. Same if you whack your funny bone or slam your finger in a drawer.

It's not true all the time. Fevers get worse until they break. Infections get worse until you get medicine. I've never broken a bone.

Is this how it feels? But nothing's broken. I'm fine.

I shot Uncle Van, and he dropped like a sack of potatoes. I'd worried my shot would go wide since my hands were shaking pretty badly at that point, but I was at such close range, I couldn't miss.

I want to tell Rory. I want her to know she doesn't have to be scared anymore. But I can't.

I flick my thumbs. I've torn up the skin around the nail bed. It's sore, but compared to my chest, it's not even pain. It's mere sensation.

It's so bright in here. I want my sunglasses, but the gun's in my purse, and I don't want John to see it. He'd flip out. He's a chill guy, but he keeps accelerating, and then cursing under his breath and easing back to the speed limit.

When Heavy said to go back to Stonecut County, I didn't want to, but now I wish I was there already. I want to be in my room with my things. I want to be left alone. I want to stop feeling this. It's too much.

"What did you do, Dina?" John says out of nowhere. We're on the highway now, heading north.

"I killed Uncle Van."

He curses. "I know. *Why*?"

"He attacked Rory."

He exhales, and his grip tightens on the steering wheel. "I understand that. Why didn't you wait for Heavy to help? He told me—too fuckin' late, but he told me—that you came to him? You asked him for help? Why didn't you come to me?"

He looks over, tries to meet my eyes. I stare out the windshield.

"You have Mona and the kids. I didn't want to make you an accessory."

"You can come to me with *anything*. Jesus, Dina. Don't you know that?" He's quiet for about a mile. "With Heavy— you don't understand who you're dealing with. He's not— he's a dangerous man."

I'm a dangerous woman.

It doesn't frustrate me that John can't understand that. He's my big brother. Ten years older. He changed my diapers when I was a baby. He built my treehouse with Dad and Kellum. I was only eight when he left home. I wasn't even speaking yet when he joined the Petty's Mill Fire Department.

"This could have gone real bad. You blackmailed him? Jesus." His Adam's apple bobs. John has the thickest neck of any man I know. It's even thicker than Heavy's, though not by much. "And since you went to him, why did you go after Van on your own?" He raises his eyes to the roof. "Fuckin' Christ, Dina, you're smart. I don't get it."

My temple throbs. The visor isn't blocking the sun at all. I shut my eyes.

"You can't just pretend this didn't happen. You need to

explain to me everything you did. You could get arrested for murder. You understand that, right?"

I sigh. Why does everyone revert to underestimating me? They get so close sometimes, but in the end, they can't take the leap. They can't fathom that I'm as capable as any of them. More so, in some ways.

"There is no evidence tying me to the scene. No CCTV. No eye witnesses. I have no motive. Rory never filed a complaint with the police."

"And if you went to Heavy, why do it without him? That's what I don't understand."

My head is too loud, and my stomach churns and churns.

I want to go home.

I want to go to the cabin.

I want the tires of Heavy's bike to crunch through the asphalt, and his boots to thump on the stairs. I want that feeling when he comes in the front door, ducking so he doesn't hit the molding. I don't know the name for it, but it's a lift and a slide. A tongue into a buckle. A deadbolt through a strike plate.

Click.

"I know you can talk, Dina." There's an edge to John's voice. He's losing patience with me. "Jesus. You killed Uncle Van."

"No one else was going to stop him."

He huffs. "So that means you had to? All by yourself? Is this some kind of superhero complex? From watching all those movies? Or is this a psychotic break? You gotta talk me through this 'cause it does not make any sense to me. None whatsoever."

His speed is creeping up again.

Every mile we drive feels like a greater depth, crushing

my lungs. How far up can a barreleye survive? And John demands to know why. Like I know, and if I do, like I have the words. I'm tired. My head is throbbing. The pain isn't fading. Not at all.

"Explain it to me, Dina."

"Why did you leave Stonecut County?" I ask him.

"What does that—?" He forces himself to exhale, and then he starts again. "I joined the fire department. You know that."

"Why not join the department in Stonecut?"

"They weren't hiring."

"But you could have come back. When there was an opening."

"I was with Mona by then."

"She kicked you out. You could have come home."

"I don't know, Dina." His voice raises. I'm not sure what happened between him and Mona, but they were split for years before they got back together. "I was in the club by then. And I never wanted to leave Mona." He scrubs his neck. "Why are you asking me this?"

"Because I always wondered if you left because of the job and Mona, or if you could see it, and you wanted to get away."

"See what?"

"And when Kellum told me you had yourself written out of the trust, I figured it was because you knew."

"Knew what, Dina? You're talking in riddles. I had myself written out of the trust because I don't care for the idea of any man besides me providing for my family. Simple as that."

I scratch my scalp. I want a hot shower. Steaming. Boiling.

"Van is—was—a bad man. He hurt people. Manipulated people. And no one was going to stop him."

"But why *you*, Dina?"

"Why not me, John? Why can't I be the hero?" My voice cracks. "Why can't *I* protect what's *mine*?"

I've had enough. John keeps talking, but the wind is whistling, and even though they're closed, the sun burns through my eyelids. I let the buzz in my brain swell to a shriek, losing myself in the pain that's not getting better, that's flowering in ever more acute blossoms, and want with all my heart to go home.

But we're not heading there. We're heading to Stonecut County.

15

HEAVY

There's a knock on my door, and whoever it is waits for me to say "come in" before they do. Forty marches in with Charge on his heels.

Brothers ain't never bothered to wait before. They're all treading lightly around me, like prospects who've done fucked up. I don't see why. I've been good-tempered. I even took those two tables back to my wood shop, and I've been fixin' 'em up at night. Maybe I threw the pieces in the bed of my truck with undue violence, but I was gonna have to do a good bit of sanding, anyway.

I ain't sleeping much, but that's not a problem. You get tired enough, you sleep. I guess I ain't tired.

"News?" I gesture for them to sit across from me. I've got my laptop open. I've been staring at a screensaver of a thatched roof hut on a beach in Fiji for—shit. Twenty? Thirty minutes?

"Pyle PD has put out an APB for Darren Elliot Sanderson," Forty says.

I exhale for what feels like the first time in a week.

"Chaos has been up to no good again." My lips twitch. It

ain't quite a smile, but there's a knot unraveling in my sternum.

"That bastard is a criminal mastermind," Charge drawls.

"Remind me. What did he do last?"

"Torched Rab Daugherty's tattoo parlor, I believe." Forty extends his legs, clasping his hands on his belly.

"It's amazing that the dude's fingers still have finger-prints after all these years." It's an almost biblical miracle. We've kept Chaos' hand refrigerated, but we've thawed it enough times that you'd think the meat would've fallen from the bone.

"The trick is letting it warm up to room temperature real gradually." Forty snickers. "You should've heard the noise it made when Nickel, like, dipped it in a pool of blood and kind of slapped it on the wall."

He accompanies the description with sound effects. I shake my head and let it hit me. Dina's in the clear. We're all in the clear.

Darren Elliot Sanderson—alias Chaos—has become a well-known figure in the east coast underground. Breaking and entering, arson, felony theft. We've never framed him for murder, but it fits the narrative. He's been committing his crimes with impunity, and now he's escalating.

"Van Price's valuables?" I ask.

"At the bottom of Lake Patonquin," Charge replies.

"She's in the clear?" I need to hear it.

"According to our guy, PPD was clueless until they swal-lowed their pride, reached out to the feds, and got a hit in CODIS." Forty looks like he can't believe the ineptitude, but Dina did her part by taking down the CCTV.

No one's come forward to say they saw her or us, so the locals had nothing to go on. Van Price himself was very careful to cover his own misdeeds. He made it easy. He was loved by all. No reason he'd be a murder victim except for a random robbery.

"I wish them great success in apprehending their suspect." I've been nursing a bottle of whiskey—well, several bottles of whiskey over the course of several days. I raise it and drain it. There wasn't much left.

"He's under an oak, isn't he?" Forty asks.

"If I recall correctly, it was a blue spruce."

"I must say, I do prefer the new way of doing things where I ain't the one takin' the heat all the time," Charge says, eyes twinkling.

He was our fall guy in the beginning when I was first finding my footing. For that, I'll be forever grateful. And for keeping Harper even all those years. They were always a mismatched pair, but he kept her from spinning out. Now— well, Harper and I are both alone, ain't we? It ain't a thing. Probably the natural state of affairs for people like us.

The three of us sit in silence for a moment.

"So you gonna go get your old lady, then?" Forty asks.

I don't let the impact show. It's easy not to. Second nature. "Don't got an old lady."

"Your wife, then."

"She ain't mine." Never was, right?

Forty narrows his eyes. "Sure." He draws out the syllable. "You're still mad 'cause she did the guy without tellin' you?"

"You wouldn't be?" I roll my eyes. He'd lose his damn mind.

"I wouldn't send my woman away over it."

"Dina Wall ain't my woman."

"You keep sayin' that." Forty lets the sentence trail off.

I know they've been talking. Gossipy bitches, pussy-footing around. I'm fine. I got my head stuck up my ass for a bit, but I'm good now.

Forty sniffs the air. "You haven't left this room in, what, two weeks?"

"You needed me?"

He shakes his head slowly. "You just might wanna get a sweetbutt in here. Freshen the place up."

"You grown a vagina and gone back in time to birth me, Forty?"

He snorts a laugh. "I grow a vagina, I'm gonna have plenty to do in the present, my brother." He fiddles with the queen on the chess set between us.

Charge takes advantage of the pause to pipe in. "Harper doin' okay?"

"You've heard what I've heard."

"Hope she knows what she's doing," Forty says, rearranging the board. He puts the knights in front of the rooks. "Angel says that Harper followed Dina up here. The night we patched Roosevelt in."

My spine straightens. "What?"

"Nevaeh still thinks Harper's the devil's spawn. So does Shirl. And Fay-Lee." Forty's ticking off on his fingers.

"The women have never liked her." Because she's a raging cunt. She's my sister, though, so I leave that part unsaid.

"Kayla likes her," Charge says.

"No shit?" That's hard to believe. Kayla's as sweet as they come. Low key, a little timid except when it comes to her son. The opposite of Harper.

"Yeah. Jimmy paints pictures in art class, and there's this fundraiser where you can buy magnets with the kid's doodles on it and stuff. Kayla always gives one to Harper."

"She does?" Will wonders never cease.

"And Harper puts 'em on her fridge," Forty volunteers.

"And you know that how?" I had no idea.

"We're neighbors. I drop by to borrow a cup of sugar on occasion." Forty winks.

"Nevaeh know that?"

"No, and you ain't gonna tell her. She doesn't know I've been on Harper to make nice with her."

"I bet she knows." Nevaeh Ellis is ditzy, but she can add two plus two.

"She ain't got confirmation, so she can't hold shit against me."

"A woman don't need proof to make you suffer," Charge opines, leaned back and grinnin' like an idiot.

"Kayla makes you suffer?" I roll my eyes. "What, dinner's sometimes a few minutes late?"

"She hear you say that, she'd make you suffer." Charge chuckles. "She'd do it real sweet and innocent like, but you'd be cryin' in your beer, man. Just like you are now."

"It's whiskey, not beer." And I ain't crying. I'm the same as I always am. Somewhat drunker and a touch more rank, but nothing has fundamentally changed in my life.

Except I've become a liar.

I can't breathe right.

Don't wanna eat.

I've gotta stay in this room so I don't pick fights and kill some mouthy hang-around by accident.

Can't go up to the cabin. Dina's toothbrush is in the bathroom. Her socks are under the table.

Can't read. My eyes won't stay on the page. I work, and I make careless mistakes. I need time to pass, but it crawls, especially at night.

Pain gets better with time. That's always been my experience. When we lost Mom and then Dad and then Twitch, so quick in succession—when I gave up everything I worked for, everything I'd dreamed, to come back here—at first, it seared. Gradually, though, the agony became mere grief, punctuated by more and more infrequent waves of fresh pain, until it receded almost entirely, throbbing only once in a while when shit gets too quiet.

But this is raw. Raw and salted.

I miss Dina.

I miss her more today than yesterday.

More this week than last.

On this trajectory, I'm fuckin' doomed by the end of the month.

"What's wrong with me?" I don't realize I said it out loud until both men bust out laughing.

"Same thing as always," Charge slaps my thigh between guffaws. "You know it all."

"In fairness, I generally do." This makes them laugh louder.

"All right, all right." Charge makes a show of wiping fake tears from his eyes. "I'm gonna put you out of your misery. I'll explain in small words so you can understand."

He exchanges a self-satisfied smirk with Forty.

"Your—woman—ain't—here. You—need—to—go—get —her."

I flip him a desultory bird. "I ain't pussy whipped like y'all."

"Can't say that no more," Charge says.

"Say what?"

"Pussy whipped."

"Says who?"

"Harper, for one."

"She says 'dickmitized' all the time." She's very critical of other women. Always has been.

"I don't make the rules." Charge shrugs, and then he

settles back in his chair, smiling, but he's lost the smartass smirk. "I ever tell you about when Kayla and I split?"

"No." I wasn't aware they had.

"It was early on. After that picnic when Harper, well, when Harper was Harper. Kayla didn't take none too kindly to it."

"You were an idiot for lettin' your ex anywhere near pussy you wanted to nail down," Forty says.

"Hold up." Charge's eyes gleam. "Ain't you the guy who lost hold of his woman for damn near a decade? You givin' me advice, flyboy?"

"Oh, that's low," I say and punch it in.

"Anyway—" Charge proceeds. "Kayla was mad. She said something. I took it wrong and ghosted her. If her parents didn't snatch her kid, maybe my pride wouldn't have let me pull my head out of my ass."

"This ain't like that."

"Yeah. I wasn't married to her at the time."

"Dina and I ain't really married." Grinder and Boots have told everyone about the wedding in Vegas, pretty much on a constant loop. Each time, the strippers get hornier, and I come out lookin' like an obsessed sap.

"Oh, bullshit," Forty interjects. Guess he's over the "flyboy" dig. "You've never done anything you don't want to do."

"It was for spousal immunity."

Forty snorts. "Charge? How long have we known Heavy Ruth?"

"Our whole lives."

"Our whole lives," Forty repeats. "How many times has he given a shit about legal liability?"

"That would be never," Charge answers.

I hate it when they do this schtick.

"And, Charge? How many times have we walked into this

room and seen our boy here staring at that psycho killer wall?"

"It's called a murder board," I mutter.

"Every damn time," Charge replies.

"But not today." Forty says, reaching over the table for my laptop and turning it to face him. "Today, we walk in and Heavy is staring at—is that a tiki hut?"

"How many women has he been with, anyway?" Charge pretends to count.

"Plenty. Back in the day." Forty skewers me. He's joking, but he's not. "But he's never shacked up with one in his cabin. Never spun one around the dance floor. Never lost his damn mind and destroyed club property over one."

"We all have our moments." There's not much I can say. I haven't been myself.

"What was it she did that made you send her away?" Forty asks, rhetorically.

"Homicide." I arch an eyebrow.

"'He who is without sin among you, let him throw the first stone.'" Charge smirks.

"She was reckless. Stupid. She knew I didn't want her to do it, and she did it anyway." And in the end, she didn't give a shit about me. I was useless to her. Not that it matters.

Strangers on a train. Emphasis on the strangers.

Both Forty and Charge are nodding solemnly, but it's crystal clear that inside, they're laughing at me.

They let the silence draw out before Forty speaks. "Why?"

"Why?" Because she can't. Because she doesn't. Because despite the world falling at my feet, telling me I'm different and special and a giant among men, it ain't true. I'm just a redneck greaser, and she ain't impressed.

"I don't know, Forty. You tell me."

"She did it so you wouldn't have to." Forty and Charge exchange looks.

My sluggish pulse picks up the pace. "Why do you think that?"

"It's pretty fuckin' obvious." Charge raises his eyebrows.

"Why wouldn't she want me to do it?" She didn't seem hot to pull the trigger. She was very businesslike about the whole endeavor.

Was it pride? Something about proving that she's badass? That just doesn't strike me as her.

Why can't I read her? I can read everyone.

"So you wouldn't take on her burden. She did it to save you from doin' it," Charge says, gently.

To save me from doing it. Is it that simple?

"Why would she want to do that? She came to me for help." There's a roaring in my ears, and my brain feels thick. Am I drunker than I thought?

Charge and Forty just stare at me.

"You need a ride," Forty says.

"A long ride," Charge concurs.

"This evening. After work." Forty's already on his phone. "That'll give you time to sober up."

"And shower," Charge adds.

"I don't need to shower to ride," I grumble.

A ride sounds good, though. Sweep the cobwebs out. I got an energy now I ain't had since I sent Dina away.

I guess I could stand to comb my hair. Eat something. Maybe a sandwich. Pit beef.

I stretch my arms and crack my neck, pushing back from the table.

"Well, our work here is done." Forty claps Charge's back and they both stand. "We ride at six."

"All right," I say, sniffing my collar. I smell sad. And musty.

The gears are turning again now.

Why would Dina save me from killing a man if she came to me for help to do it?

I ain't a stupid man, despite the evidence of the past two weeks.

I might not know what love is, and apparently, I cannot read a woman's mind, but when I'm in a hole, I quit digging. And I get ready to ride.

16

DINA

Cash came to dinner tonight on his motorcycle. My dumb insides went crazy when I heard the engine and the tires in the drive, and then I heard his loud voice, and I crashed.

I couldn't finish the code I was working on.

I don't like it here anymore.

It's quiet, and except for Mom and Dad, most of the time, there's no one around. And that's how I like it, right?

But my brain sucks. It's aimed an old-timey ear trumpet at every annoying sound in this place. The whippoorwill outside my window. The creak in the floorboards on the way to the bathroom. My old friends, the hum from the fluorescent lights in the kitchen and the whoosh in the vents when the air conditioning cuts on and off.

The smells are stale and gross. Lilac hand soap that clings to my skin for hours, no matter what other soap I use to scrub it off. Old bacon.

It's like I've tuned myself to loud and fast and new, and so I've over-sensitized myself to the niggling little shit. And it's all niggling little shit.

Cash's voice is the worst. He brays. He's bombastic. I'm a floor away behind a closed door, and I can hear him bragging about a buck he bagged last season. I can't handle it.

I jam my feet into my sneakers, trip down to the kitchen, and let myself out by the pool. The sun's lowering, and there's a cool breeze sweeping down from the mountain. Summer's not here quite yet.

I head to my treehouse, bounding up the stairs and plopping down on the balcony, sticking my legs through the slats so I can swing them in the air. They still fit. Barely.

The railing needs to be sanded and stained. Mia plays here a lot when she's over, and she's going to get a splinter. I don't think it's been power-washed since I grew out of it.

Of course, everyone knows I never have. No one bothers me when I'm out here. It's my private place. Noises don't bother me so much. There's more—birdsong and crickets and rustling leaves. But it's fine. Nice. I can be in my skin here.

I let the lengthening shadows and the forest sounds soothe my outsides, and slowly, the big hole inside me registers. It's terrible.

Yawning.

Thick as tar.

After Van did what he did, everything was scrambled. Misplaced. Wrong. Dealing with him would put it right. And it did. The police in Pyle have been keeping my parents updated. They called today. They've identified the DNA and fingerprints found at the scene. A man named Darren Elliot Sanderson. He's a suspect in a dozen crimes in five states over the past six years.

I ran a quick search on the guy. The last electronic transaction that I can confirm was enacted by him was at a liquor store ATM outside of Petty's Mill about six years ago.

I have no doubt he's buried under a tree on Half Stack Mountain.

I knew Heavy would find a way to cover my tracks. He's a genius. Not hyperbolically. In actual fact. He's smarter than I am. I bet he isn't sitting in a treehouse, picking at splinters, with missing insides.

I don't generally know exactly what's in there—I don't think about it, at least I didn't use to—but it's really fucking disorienting knowing that whatever was in there is gone.

It's like that cartoon, when the mouse fires a cannon at the cat, and the ball goes straight through, and the cat leans over and peers through the round hole in his middle, mystified.

But not funny. Awful.

Absence shouldn't hurt. It's not a thing. It's the opposite.

I want to call Heavy and talk to him about it, and I can't.

I want to ask him to explain what's going on inside me.

I want him to tell me what I did so wrong.

I don't want to be here, back where I started, alone, but knowing it now. Knowing it in every part of me. My arms. My mouth. Every sense is muffled, and it's ironic because I hate it. I want booming bass, but there's nothing but goddamn birds and fucking crickets.

A throat is cleared below. Softly.

I peer down. There's only one person who can sneak up on me, even now that I'm all messed up.

"Mia."

She grins. She has band aids on both elbows and a yellow plastic barrette in her hair that holds nothing back. She cocks her head.

"You can come up."

She bounds up the steps and plops down beside me, threading her skinny legs through the slats. She's got lots of room. She's only seven and maybe fifty pounds. They feed her, but it doesn't stick. Like me.

"I didn't hear your dad's truck."

"We walked up." Even her voice sounds like mine, like it did when I first started talking. Breathy and tentative.

"Here for dinner?"

She hums. We swing our legs together for a while. Her closeness soothes the ache a touch. Mia's her own person, but we were cut from the same cloth. Being with her is like being with an iteration of myself. We notice the same things. An ant crawling along the rail. The first firefly of the evening. When a light goes on in the garage. Dad must be showing Kellum and Cash his truck. He's having trouble with the clutch.

After a while, Mia drops her hand between us, searching for mine. She finds it and holds tight. "You're sad," she says.

"I am?" It feels bigger than that. Darker. Irreparable.

"You're frowning."

"Has grandma been making you read the books about the lost kittens?"

"The kitten should live with the firefighter. He wouldn't lose her."

"Agree."

Mia rests her head on my upper arm. "Don't be sad."

"I don't know what to do."

She thinks about this a second. "You should do something."

"I made a mistake. I don't think I can fix it."

Mia sighs. "I'm sorry."

We sit together, and the shadows grow longer, and my heart hurts. Cash's motorcycle is parked beside the house. It's not a *biker's* bike. It's a douchebag's bike. Still, it reminds me. And my heart hurts more.

I can't fix this. I can't make Heavy see. He's done with me, and that's that. I don't owe him. He doesn't owe me.

I'll stay here in my room and work and one day, I'll get divorce papers in the mail, and I'll sign them, and then it'll be the past.

I should do something.

Mia blinks at me. Did I say that aloud?

"I don't know what to do," I say.

"Fix it," she says, very somber and certain.

"Fix it," I repeat.

She nods.

"Okay," I say, rising to my feet. "Tell them I'm skipping dinner."

I don't know what to do, but whatever it is, I can't do it here. And now that I'm up, now that I've decided, the hole fades a little, shifts so it's not in the center of everything. So I can think again.

I don't want to wait for a rideshare.

And Cash's motorcycle is right there. How much different than a dirt bike can it be? It's not much bigger. There's not even room for anyone to ride pillion. He wouldn't want to send the message that he's willing to make any kind of commitment for any length of time.

I hope there's gas in the tank.

I smack a kiss on Mia's head, and she ducks.

"Tell your mama I said hi."

I trot back toward the house, sneaking in the backdoor to grab my purse from the hook and Cash's keys from the basket. Everyone's in the kitchen. Cash is still running his mouth. Dad laughs.

I was worried for the first few days after the police found Van's body. Mom cried a lot. Everyone sat around and stared out the windows. But each day, things edged back toward normal.

Van hadn't been a part of our daily lives since he tried to run Shay and Mia off the last time. There's been no real difference, only another layer, new silences that erupt unexpectedly, fleeting tears I don't see coming.

I wish Rory was better. She called late the other night. I guess the dreams won't stop on a dime. That's okay. She'll always have me, and during the day, things are looking good. She's on the schedule for full time now, and her tips are getting better.

She's making it work.

I'm going to do that, too.

I don't care what Heavy says when I see him. I'll make him understand. I don't know how, but I'll figure it out on the way.

I snag the keys and creep back out as quietly as I can, pulling up directions to Petty's Mill on my phone. I can get to the interstate, but after that, I'm not sure.

I sling my purse across my chest, take a deep breath, and start the engine. It echoes off the ridge where we're situated. I better go. There's no way they didn't hear that.

I peel off. Well, it's more like I ease down the drive, feeling it out, testing the gears. The bike is the same make as the dirt bikes we rode as kids. Everything's more or less where I expect.

I accelerate, and the wind rustles my hair and stings my cheeks. It feels good. It feels like forward momentum.

The sun is almost to the horizon, and to the east, the sky is turning purple-blue.

I'm sure this is a bad idea, but it's also the best one I've ever had.

I head down to Route 7 and turn south. My hands grow

numb from the vibration of the handles and the cooling breeze. I squeeze tight and butterflies go loose in the place where the hole has been since Heavy sent me away.

I'm gonna see him again. I don't care if he turns his back or sends me away again. I don't think that far ahead. I stop when I picture him. His wild hair and bushy beard. His brown, crinkling eyes.

The traffic is light—it always is out this way—and so I hear the engines well before I see them. I crest a hill, and there they are. At least a dozen bikes in formation. Big ones. The roar grows louder, and I recognize them before I make out a face or a patch.

I don't know what to do, so I keep going, and I pass them. The wind from the Bernoulli effect whips my shirt. Heavy. Nickel. Forty. Scrap. Charge. Creech. Pig Iron. Gus. Grinder. Bullet. Mikey. Roosevelt. John.

My brother raises his hand, waves, and grins. And bringing up the rear—Boom, Washington, and Bush. No Hoover.

I watch in my mirror as the line slows, swings onto the shoulder, and does a U-turn. There's a wide shoulder ahead, and I ease off, pulling around to face them.

I toe down the kickstand and dismount. My hands are chapped red; my skin is ice. I'm shaking.

What do I say? My heart skitters and leaps. A truck whooshes by, ruffling my hair. I try to smooth it down, but it's hopeless.

I wait, and Heavy pulls off onto the shoulder about twenty feet away. The others stop behind him, staggered left and right. The guys who wear half-shells take them off. A few peel off their gloves.

Heavy rises to his full height, swinging his massive leg over the bike in a smooth, practiced motion. He's wearing jeans with ripped knees, black boots, and his cut over a tight black T-shirt.

His jaw is tight. He's facing the setting sun, so his eyes are squinting. He's not smiling.

He takes a step, and another, and my legs move of their own volition, sweeping me forward, and then he's reaching, and I'm jogging, leaping, and he's gathering me up, and there's not a beat missed, not a moment wasted before I've got my fingers tangled in his hair and he's wrapped me in his arms.

"There you are," he mumbles against my neck, holding tight, swaying.

"Here I am," I agree.

"Where were you going?"

"To you."

He smiles. I trace his lips.

"I was coming for you, too, baby."

"And you brought everyone?"

"Package deal, right?" He chuckles.

"I'm sorry." I nestle closer, and he surrounds me, big, solid. Mine.

"You don't need to be, baby. I didn't understand."

"I'm not going to let anything hurt you," I tell him.

"You love me."

"I do." My eyes are wet, and my nose itches. "I want my insides back."

"Okay. I'll get 'em back for you." He's laughing at me, but I don't care. He's here.

"I love you, too," he says.

"I know. Harper told me."

And he laughs louder, so I tug his head back by his knotted hair, and then he kisses me.

Or do I kiss him?

It doesn't matter.

Click. We're back where we belong.

Heavy's brothers hoot and holler. The sun throws orange and purple and pink over the mountain, and after Heavy tosses Boom the keys to Cash's bike, I climb up behind him.

I'd thought it was the end, but it wasn't.

This is the part where we ride into the sunset. Together.

This is the beginning.

EPILOGUE
HEAVY, SIX MONTHS LATER

The Patonquin site is empty. It's Sunday, and we scheduled our guys, not Garvis, to be working security this afternoon. A concrete mixer is backed up to the annex footprint, ready to pour the foundation. Finally. Months after Knocker Johnson and the Rebel Raiders vandalized the project, we're almost finished. It's a good feeling.

I crack my knuckles and then my back, inhaling the crisp fall air. It's a glorious day in western Pennsylvania.

Des Wade is running late, but then again, he always is. Got to let everyone know that he's an important man. At first, he balked at meeting me here, but I told him there was a decision only he could make, and he's a self-important man, too. He wouldn't delegate. Especially not after I told him it involved the "special features" of his project.

He's coming. And he's coming alone.

If Harper and her new shadow don't show up soon, I might have to stall the motherfucker. Dina and I planned for every contingency except for what to say if I have to make small talk with his smarmy ass.

I could always pass the time beating him into the ground. Have him eat the printout of Boris Stasevich's testimony that I've got folded in the inside pocket of my cut.

That day in the clubhouse, when Dina propositioned me, she failed to mention there are whole passages of the documents that were redacted. But in the end, it makes no difference. The pages about how Wade paid for the guns and how he plotted with Anderson Watts to set up Steel Bones for arms trading—those parts are intact. And damning.

Well, they would be if Wade had a soul. He's a suit stuffed with ambition. Maybe something worse. Harper's still not the same. She's better, but—not the same.

A crow shrieks and takes off, ruffling the red leaves of a tall oak at the site's perimeter, and then I hear the purr of an expensive Italian engine.

Excitement shoots through my veins.

This is it.

This is the culmination of all I've worked for. That *we've* worked for. Making the past right—as much as that's possible in this tragic, sinful world.

I wish Dina were here. She fixed it so the cell phone in Wade's pocket and the GPS in his vehicle recovery system show him fifty miles away in Pyle. She's a criminal mastermind in the best possible way, but I don't put my wife in harm's way. Besides, she'd off him too quick. She's a very direct woman. No finesse.

A car door slams, and Wade's shoes thud in the dirt. He raises a hand in greeting and then scowls at the mud sucking at the soles of his thousand-dollar loafers.

He spins his key fob a few times before slipping it in the pocket of his linen slacks.

"Heavy. My man." We shake, and he slaps my back. He's

never hid his delight that he has Steel Bones dancing to his tune. One good thing, after today, I ain't gonna need to revise anymore estimates or refile any more revised blueprints for this dumbass.

He really peaked when he plotted the blown job. Or success has made him soft. And way too trusting.

Another engine, a deeper growl, approaches from the northern access road. There she is.

Wade squints, a hand shading his eyes as he looks at the bike roaring toward us. It is a strange sight.

Harper is on the back of the shiniest chopper I've ever seen—more chrome than steel—arms wrapped around a spectral figure. Knocker Johnson's T-shirt ripples in the wind, exposing the lean ropes of his biceps covered in faded prison tats and the black bars and squares that block out his Steel Bones ink.

He's bulked up since he torched the site, but his face is still gaunt, eyes sunken, nose angled all wrong. His black hair whips in the wind, and as he rolls to a dramatic stop, he smiles, baring his silver teeth.

If Wade was smart, now would be when he runs, but instead, a look of disdain crosses his face. He turns to me. "You invited my ex? Are you trying to get us back together, or do I need my lawyer, too?"

He must not recognize Knocker. He wouldn't unless he'd been keeping track of him for the past two decades. The badass rocker I remember from back in the day is gone. Only this charred, grim remnant remains.

"Relax," I say. "She ain't here to get you back."

Knocker's engine sputters into silence, and Harper dismounts. She picks her way between mud puddles to join us. Her look has changed. She's wearing painted on jeans, a skintight black tank top, and red stripper heels. And there's that leather choker around her neck with the metal O ring.

She says she's better. She's quit drinking. That haunted look in her eyes is gone. And she's been damn near pleasant with the old ladies. It's good, but—I don't understand it.

When I ask, she gets smart and tells me that when I get a wife my own size, I can poke my nose in her consensual relationships. I push, but all she does is pat my hand like a grandma and say not all mysteries are mine to solve.

Knocker stays on his bike. Harper did what she set out to do the night we patched Roosevelt in. She got us a truce. Knocker doesn't get too close, though.

Harper flashes a bright smile when she gets to us. Her gray eyes shine.

"Long time, no see." She opens her arms and goes in for a hug. Wade seems bemused, but he gives her a quick, impersonal squeeze.

"Almost didn't recognize you," he says.

"The outfit?" She smooths her hand down her hips.

"And the company."

She glances over her shoulder. "Oh, you mean Knocker?"

"That's his name?" He arches a wry eyebrow.

Harper winks at me. There's a twinkle in her eye now. The game is on.

"Oh, yeah," she says. "You might remember him as Brian Lee Johnson."

It doesn't seem to ring a bell. Wade shakes his head. "Afraid I don't know the man."

Harper takes a step toward Wade and smiles wider. "Yeah. You always were shit with details."

"Whoa." Wade turns to me, chuckling in an unamused

way. "You wanna control your sister? I'm here 'cause you said there was a problem with the project."

"There was. We got in bed with the wrong guy." Harper laughs, shrill and loud. She takes another step forward. Wade backs up. He's still a few feet from the orange plastic fencing around the foundation pit.

He draws himself up, every inch the offended master of the universe. "I didn't drive all the way out here to—"

"Turns out he was a criminal," Harper interrupts, taking another step. I move to block him between us, and Wade has to shift closer to the pit. "He set up my club, and Brian Lee Johnson, as arms traffickers. Can you believe it? Here in little ol' Petty's Mill?"

Now, *finally*, Wade catches on. His eyes dart to his tiny convertible. And then to the man on the bike.

Knocker has a silver pistol aimed at Wade's head.

"What the fuck, Harper?" Wade stumbles a step back.

"We have evidence," she says. "We could do to you what we're going to do to Anderson Watts. Did you know your old partner in crime has a thing for interns? Rigged some cameras up in the ladies' room in his office to keep an eye on them."

Harper rounds her eyes. Wade's pupils flicker wildly around the site, and he realizes there's no one here to help him. His tanning booth glow has blanched white.

"America is going to learn about all the senator's proclivities," Harper says. "There's nothing secret on the internet when you know the right people."

Harper grins. She loves having Dina at her beck and call. She has her doing cyber-sleuthing for some of her other clients. Dina won't charge even though I tell her she should. She says Harper is her other friend—besides Rory, she means. It's the strangest relationship I've ever seen—the killer shark and the weird fish from a thousand leagues under the sea.

Wade is sweating bullets now. I thought this would be more satisfying. I sure as shit didn't expect I'd be wishing it was over so I could get home to my wife. Life is strange. The most important things become inconsequential in the blink of an eye. The villain becomes a small, shaking man wearing ridiculous shoes.

"What do you want?" Wade spits. He's looking at me. Oh, that's a mistake.

Harper lunges forward, snatching his chin, digging those long red nails into his clean-shaven jowls, forcing him to look at her.

Wade raises his hand, and there's the click of a gun being cocked.

Knocker tuts. "Uh, uh, uh."

Wade freezes.

Harper bares her teeth. There's not even the pretense of a smile. "What do I want? I want a time machine. I want that Coldplay video where everything plays out in reverse. I want ten years of Scrap Allenbach's life back. I want my baby brother whole. I want the pieces of his skull back—the ones on Dutchy's baseball bat. Can you give me that?"

Tears are streaming from her gray eyes, and I hear the unspoken words, the ones she'll never, ever say.

She wants to be a girl again, no little brother to raise, to let down. She wants back the instant before she took up the mantle, like I did. The moment before she lifted her shirt and Dutchy leered as my knife sliced his throat, splattering her tits with blood.

She wants a choice.

She wants to make a different one, knowing better, knowing what we know now.

She wants it to have not cost so much.

When I look into Dina's eyes, I want the same damn thing. I want there to be more of me left for her. For the beautiful wondrousness of life.

But time moves in only one direction.

And Des Wade's wild eyes appeal to the part of us we sacrificed a long time ago.

"Do you want money? I-Is that what this is a-about?"

Wade stutters and begs as I lunge forward, forcing him back, and now he fights. Now he screams.

We grapple, and as I maneuver him to the plastic orange fencing, I catch Harper's eye. She nods.

I let Wade go. Step back. She drives her shoulder into his gut, and he loses his footing, slipping right through the slit I cut earlier with a razor blade. He falls, cursing us, and he's still alive when he hits the wet concrete with a muted thump.

I wave at the truck. It beeps, backing up.

"Get me out of here! Fuck! I get it. What do you want? People know I'm here. You're not getting away with this. Harper!"

He's still trying to bargain, still asking us to explain as he scrabbles at the concrete in a futile attempt to haul himself forward even an inch, when the mixer tilts and begins filling the hole. We dug this corner on a slant—Dina's idea—so we'd be able to cover his body with one load.

When the concrete is flowing steadily, Pig Iron hops out of the cab and walks over to watch beside us.

"Why ain't he trying harder to get out?" he asks over the screams.

"Looks like both legs broke on impact." I say.

Pig Iron spits over the side.

"Help me! You! You there!" Wade shouts, catching sight of him. The concrete rises. "I have money!"

"Fuck your money," Pig Iron calls down. "You got a time machine?"

"That's what I said." Harper winds an arm around Pig Iron's waist and rests her head on his shoulder. Wade's screams grow louder. He struggles, but all he does is sink quicker.

After a minute or so, there are steps behind us. Knocker comes to stand beside Harper. He stares into the pit, face as calm as if he's just taking in the scenery. He raises his gun and casually puts a bullet in Wade's head. The screams stop.

Knocker turns and heads back to his bike. "Come on," he says over his shoulder when he's almost there.

Harper shrugs, and without complaint, she follows him. I've never seen anything like it.

Knocker's bike roars, kicking up a cloud of dirt as he peels off, Harper waving from the back. Then there's only Pig Iron and I to stand vigil as we bury the past, and some wrongs are made right. For the most part, though, it's nothing more than two men who've seen too much, waiting impatiently to go home.

WHEN I GET HOME to the cabin, Dina's not there. I don't panic. It's part of the plan. I shower, eat a few sandwiches. Then I settle on the sofa and log onto *Elfin Quest*. Rory's online. We meet up and continue on through the Arcane Forest. Rory slays whatever attacks us, and I keep her amused with all the moves I've unlocked. The game costs more than my goddamn cable bill, but my fairy can do slow motion flips midair.

I'm kind of hoping Harper joins us—just to assure myself she's okay—but she doesn't log on. Dina invited her to play with us a few months back. Harper's avatar is a troll, and all she does is follow us around and shit talk the other players until they want to fight us. Rory and Dina find it endlessly hilarious, but we're never gonna get to Golden Mountain if we're stopping every few hours to brawl.

Around midnight, I hear tires in the drive. It's a prospect dropping her off. I sink back into the cushions, finally at ease.

She stomps up the stairs and across the porch, flinging the front door open too hard. Dina has the grace of a miniature drunk elephant. If she's on the move, I always know where she is in the house. I like knowing where she's at.

Today was hard. I know she was safe at the clubhouse, but that doesn't mean I liked it.

"Where are you?" she calls.

"In here."

She stalks in, sets a shoebox on the coffee table, and then marches over, straddling me and tucking her small bare feet under my thighs. At least she remembered to take her shoes off in the foyer. She snuggles up to my chest and exhales.

"What's in the box?" I set the controller down and stroke her back, pressing her closer. She wriggles. Her leggings are thin, and I'm already hard.

"Your murder board. I took it down. We'll have to burn it."

"Good lookin' out." It hadn't occurred to me, but yeah, dedicating a wall to my motive for murder is dumb as shit. "You have fun?"

"There were a lot of people, and the smoke from the

bonfire is all in my hair, and I had to sit next to Dizzy on a log all night long, and he smells like beef jerky."

"You like my beef jerky."

"Yeah. *Your* beef jerky." I feed my little environmental vegetarian so much locally sourced meat she's packed on a tiny belly. She's always squeezing it and jiggling it while she bitches me out for "stuffing her," as she calls it. I fuckin' love it.

"I still don't think anyone would believe Dizzy is me."

"In the dark, from the back, on grainy CCTV? You're twins." Dina insisted I have an alibi for today, so she took my cell phone with her to the clubhouse tonight and set up a party, patched-in brothers and old ladies only.

"Did anyone try to talk to you?"

"Deb and Ernestine."

That's not what I meant, but okay. "What'd they want?"

"They want me to tell you to call them back. They've got questions about the ride up to Spank the Devil."

Shit. I do owe them a call.

Dina goes on, "I told them to give me a list and leave it to me. Spank the Devil is in Stonecut County. I know the area."

"Baby, you did?"

She sighs and snuggles closer. "I can do all the booking and plan the route online. It's fine."

"You gonna come? The music's loud. So are the engines." We haven't talked much past the Wade business.

"I've got my earbuds."

"You're gonna need to shit in the woods if you come hunting beforehand."

She wriggles upright so she can peer into my face. She does this when she doesn't know if I'm serious. I glance up and to the side to make it extra hard for her to tell. I'm a dick.

"The campsites on Stonecut Mountain have facilities." She narrows her eyes. "Is this about how you don't want me shooting guns?"

"Just people, honey. I just want you to not shoot people."

"I'm not like you." She says this all the time. It's true.

"I know."

"Are you upset? About today?"

Yes, in my way, but it's an accustomed weight. Her slight heft on my lap more than counterbalances. I cup her ass and grind her against my hardening cock.

She arches an eyebrow.

I grin.

"Are you playing with Rory?"

"Not at the moment. I'm playing with you."

"It's rude to leave her hanging."

I slip my hands under her shirt, skimming the bumps of her spine, cradling her close to my chest.

"Gimme a sec—" She grabs the controller and taps off a message. *Off to fuck. Brb.*

I laugh as she drops it, peels off her leggings and top, and then digs her slender hands between us to unzip my pants.

"Be right back?" I say. "You planning to hit it and quit it?"

I stop laughing when she wraps her fingers around my dick, rises up, and angles me just so as she sinks down on my cock, already panting and sopping wet for me.

Her eyes are screwed shut, head thrown back, and she rides me, her knees braced on my thighs, her palms pressed to my pecs.

I sit, arms stretched on the back of the sofa, and I watch her use me, driving herself to the edge. Right before she comes, I flip us and lay her flat, braced over her as I stroke my dick into her sweet pussy, making her work her hips to get the friction she needs against her swollen clit.

"Who do you belong to, baby?" I growl into her ear.

She doesn't answer. Instead, she comes screaming, yanking at my hair. I follow her over the cliff, and it feels like the best high and the warmest welcome.

"You," she says when she catches her breath. "I don't know why you keep asking. The answer's always the same."

When I laugh, she frowns and wriggles to get free, but I hold her still, cradling her face.

"'Behold, you are beautiful, my love.'" I press kisses to her temples. "'Your eyes are doves behind your veil. Your hair is as a flock of goats, that descend from Mount Gilead.'"

She rolls her eyes. "Song of Solomon?"

I kiss her mouth. "'Your teeth are like a newly shorn flock, which have come up from the washing, where every one of them has twins. None is bereaved among them.'"

She giggles. "I do have all my teeth, you lucky bastard."

I grab her thigh and squeeze. "'Your rounded thighs are like jewels, the work of the hands of a skillful workman.'" I slide my palm up and cup her tits. "'Your two breasts are like two fawns that are twins of a roe, which feed among the lilies.'"

"Fawns?"

I elbow down until I can reach her belly button. I blow a kiss on her soft skin, and she screeches, whacking my shoulder. "Your beard itches!"

"'Your waist is like a heap of wheat, set about with lilies.'" I'm laughing now, too, as she squirms and shrieks.

Finally, she grabs a handful of my hair and yanks. "Knock it off!"

She smiles, and behold, it *is* beautiful.

"'My beloved is mine,'" she says. "'And I am his.'"

And I, a fallen man and an unredeemable sinner, praise the Lord.

～

NEW TO CATE C. Wells? The Wall family's story began in *Hitting the Wall*, and the Steel Bones Motorcycle Club saga began in *Charge*.

WANT A DELETED SCENE?

Sign up for the Cate C. Wells newsletter for a deleted scene
from Heavy and Dina's Vegas escapade.
You'll also get free novellas and updates and special offers!

ABOUT THE AUTHOR

Cate C. Wells indulges herself in everything from motor-cycle club to small town to mafia to paranormal romance. Whatever the subgenre, readers can expect character-driven stories that are raw, real, and emotionally satisfying. She's into messy love, flaws, long roads to redemption, grace, and happily ever after, in books and in life.

Along with stories, she's collected a husband and three children along the way. She lives in Baltimore when she's not exploring the world with the family.

She loves to chat with readers! Check out the The Cate C. Wells Reader Group on Facebook.

Facebook: @catecwells
Twitter: @CateCWells1
Bookbub: @catecwells
Instagram: @authorcatecwells

Printed in Great Britain
by Amazon

21532407R30199